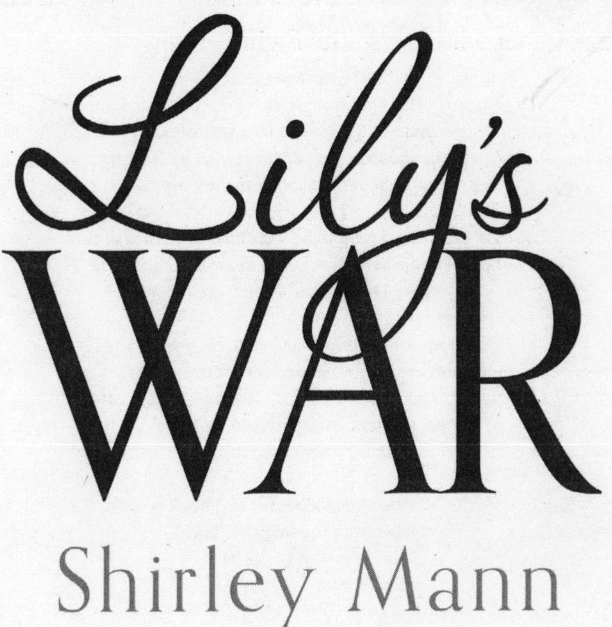

Lily's WAR

Shirley Mann

ZAFFRE

First published in paperback in Great Britain in 2020 by
ZAFFRE
80–81 Wimpole St, London W1G 9RE

A CIP catalogue record for this book is available from the British Library.

ISBN: 978–1–78576–937–5

Also available as an ebook

3 5 7 9 10 8 6 4 2

Typeset by IDSUK (Data Connection) Ltd
Printed and bound in Great Britain by Clays Ltd, Elcograf S.p.A.

Zaffre is an imprint of Bonnier Books UK
www.bonnierbooks.co.uk

To Eileen and David, my parents, who were the inspiration behind Lily's War

Chapter 1

Manchester, 1942

The knitting was the last straw. Lily cast off the end stitch, measured the uneven grey sock against its partner and made a decision. There had to be something better she could do towards the war effort than knitting irregular socks for soldiers.

She tried to pull them to the same length but gave up, throwing them in the knitting basket in disgust. 'I just hope that Tommy's got one leg shorter than the other,' she muttered to herself.

Lily looked around at the morning room of her parents' terraced house in Manchester. It was the only vaguely warm room in the house, with the black range struggling to keep an ember alive in a pathetic reminder of the blazing fires of pre-war days. She fingered the tassels on the dark green damask tablecloth next to the armchair she was curled up in. So often as children, she and her brother, Don, had peered through them from the other side, hiding from the haunting cry of the rag-and-bone man. She had been frightened then. That was before she knew real fear.

The room needed decorating. It looked as tired as the family did, she thought. The thermos was upright on a chair next to the table, standing to attention, waiting to be filled with tea at bedtime in case the sirens went off, forcing them to leave their warm beds to take refuge in the Anderson shelter in the garden. The pale cream blankets were on the chair next to it, neatly folded. The candles lay expectantly in their box, the matches on top. They were all becoming experts at this. Lily's shoulders drooped and she gave a heartfelt sigh. It was the same story every night, waiting for the drone of the planes, wondering whether that night would be their last.

'Mum,' she called into the back kitchen.

'Yes, dear' her mum replied, putting a tiny spoonful of valuable honey into the cake she was making. She had saved all her rations for this cake and she needed to concentrate.

'I'm going to sign up.'

'Yes, dear.'

Lily went into the tiny cold room at the back of the house, pushing past her thirteen-year-old brother, Don. Still in school uniform, he was hovering near the mixing bowl on the stone slab, dipping his finger in when his mother was not looking.

'No, really. I'm going to volunteer. I'm fed up with just doing fire watch duty. If I don't do this now, by next year it could all be over and I'll have missed my chance.'

'Missed your chance to get killed, you mean,' her dad appeared behind her, struggling, as usual, to light his pipe.

'Everyone's already gone,' Lily ignored him and held out her hand for the honey-smeared spoon.

Her mother automatically handed it over the head of her disappointed son and watched Lily lick the silver utensil free of every last vestige of honey. Lily's shoulder-length hair suddenly caught the late afternoon sun's rays, reflecting the golden shimmer from the liquid. Like many times recently, the tall, assured nineteen-year-old in front of Ginny took her breath away. She towered above her mother now and Ginny noticed with pride how Lily's casual shirt, tucked into the waistband of a navy skirt, showed off her neat figure. It was a shame they could not buy her a new shirt though, Ginny thought, the repeated darns and mends were becoming obvious.

'No, Lily, you're doing well at Liners. With everyone else gone, Mr Spencer is relying on you more and more and you've got a real chance to make something of yourself. You've still got another year before you'd be called up'

'I've already made something of myself,' Lily said with a grin. 'I was the back end of a horse in the Rusholme panto three years on the run, remember. No one can beat that for achievement.'

'War's ugly,' her dad butted in but didn't say any more. John Mullins was a Great War veteran whose memories of Gallipoli still gave him nightmares, details of which he had never shared before and he was not about to start now. John squeezed past the three members of his family and banged his pipe against the side of the Belfast sink to blot out the images that came unbidden. Meanwhile, Lily bounded out of the room, unwilling to brook any argument.

Ginny Mullins wiped her hands on the faded dishcloth and went over to her husband. She placed a tense hand on the darned elbow of his grey sweater.

'She's nineteen; a grown woman. She could be married by now,' John said, looking down at his diminutive wife. He gave her hand a reassuring squeeze, trying to convince himself as well as his wife. 'You won't stop her, you know you won't and it's not like she's been safe here.' He looked out meaningfully at the corrugated roofed shelter that had been their flimsy defence against German bombs during the Blitz when so many others had died.

Lily dropped down into the armchair in the morning room and blew out a noisy sigh. She was good at filing, typing and invoicing but when the ticker tapes came into the office sounding the death knell of another of Manchester Liners' ships, she experienced frustration and anger. She would run her finger over the names of the lost as they came in, trying to feel a connection with them, trying to send her strength to the injured and the families left behind. When she closed her eyes, she saw the heaving seas, grey pictures of listing ships, the spirals of smoke and the sight of flailing sailors in the water. She had failed to come to terms with a world that was no longer safe for her and for everyone she loved. All the security of a carefree childhood had been obliterated amidst air raids and streets that were reduced to unfamiliar rubble. Her journeys to work had made her a witness to the home guard, police and fire brigade frantically digging through flattened buildings while pale relatives stood by, chillingly silent in their fear and grief. She had too often heard the hushed tones in local shops as yet another family received the dreaded telegram. Lily tried to believe she was going to sign up for altruistic reasons, but she knew in her heart she was simply bored.

In 1939, she had just been allowed to go to dances, had started work and had a wage coming in. She had bought her first pair of kitten heels and was full of excitement about the future. But Hitler had other ideas. When she started at Liners, Lily had felt so important, bustling around the office holding a clipboard and dominating the filing cabinets. But then, once all the young women in the typing pool joined up, she was left with bespectacled, well-meaning colleagues who spent the whole day discussing how to make the most out of an ounce of sugar. And worst of all, most of the young men had gone too, leaving Lily to partner one of her schoolfriends, Ros or Hannah, at the occasional morale-boosting dances.

Then last week, when she was huddled with her family in the shelter, listening yet again to the ominous drone of the planes above her beloved city, she noticed that the habitual shivering had stopped. She was no longer afraid. She was ready.

Chapter 2

Ginny looked crossly at the envelope on the mat marked 'On His Majesty's Service.' It was all so quick, Lily was too young. She pushed her grey hair away from her horn-rimmed spectacles, fingered the letter for a moment but then reluctantly called up the stairs. 'I think it's here, Lily'.

Lily stopped brushing her hair and slowly placed the bevelled silver hairbrush on her walnut dressing table and rearranged the yellowing lace cloth under it.

She ran downstairs, almost slipping in her stockinged feet on the threadbare carpet.

'Careful love, you'll break your ankle', her mother said automatically.

'Well, I never have, have I?' Lily gave her mum a quick hug before taking the brown envelope from her.

Lily raced back up the stairs to her bedroom. It was a sanctuary that had comforted her all her life. She needed a moment's calm to erase the nagging guilt brought on by the wan expression on her mother's face at the bottom of the stairs. Lily had always been the organiser of the family;

the bossy one, her father would say. Sitting on the edge of the bed, she slid slightly on the silky pale lemon eiderdown and felt her knees give way. Raising her chin she sat down more firmly and slid her finger under the seal. The letter was very polite. It thanked her for her application, gave her a date for a medical and informed her that she would be interviewed about her education and schooling so she could choose the area that most suited her abilities.

Later, once the blackout curtains had been pulled shut and the black iron kettle had boiled, the family sat with their customary cup of Lyons tea and jug of condensed milk. The letter was on the table in front of them, speaking volumes with its black type. 'Well, the army's out,' Lily told her parents, prodding the poker into the three pieces of coal on the range fire. 'I just look terrible in khaki. I think you need a relative to get into either the air force or the navy,' she paused, dredging up information she had heard at the Red Cross centre, 'but do you think the fact that Paul is in the RAF would get me in there?'

She looked round for confirmation, but none came. Unsure, but wanting to fill the silence, she tentatively said, 'I think you can ask for the RAF if you have a relative in it. Is a cousin a near enough relative? So that's it then, air force here I come!'

Triumphant, she sat back to gauge the impact of her pronouncement.

'Anything but munitions,' her dad replied, reaching over to pick up a precious biscuit from the round tin on the table. The painting of the thatched cottage on the front reminded him of the England they were all fighting for. 'I'll not have you working in a factory. We didn't send you to a good school like Loreto for that.'

John Mullins was a printer at the *Manchester Guardian* in Cross Street. He had worked nights for as long as Lily could remember. Early mornings she would come down in her woolly dressing gown; he was always there carefully rolling up old newspapers for the range, his fingers black from the printing ink. The latest editions would be on the table. Lily loved knowing she was the first in the street to find out the latest news and felt her father's job gave her a superior, inside knowledge of world affairs. In the morning light, they would discuss the day's headlines over a cup of tea before he went up to bed in his upside down day.

She gave her dad an affectionate pat on his arm, leaving it there for a second. He smiled at her.

'I know, lass, but munitions *is* dirty work and you'd look awful in a boiler suit. It's a long way from an office job at Liners.'

'I'm a junior assistant,' Lily said, 'that must make me top brass material at least! That settles it, then,' she said, not pausing for breath. 'I will tell them I choose the air force. As I'm volunteering, they've said they'll consider any preferences I have, but they're not going to let me fly a plane and I'm no good at maps, so what else can I do?' She picked up the letter and scanned it for the umpteenth time.

'Mrs Cook's daughter's gone in the WAAFs,' her mother said, pouring out a drop more tea for herself and adding the sweet mixture from the small flowered, china jug. 'She looked very smart in her uniform when I saw her at the Co-op. And there's all them lovely pilots. You might meet one o' them and—'

'Nah' her dad interrupted. 'She'll marry Danny when he comes back. You mark my words. Any more of them biscuits, Ginny? The tin's empty.' He shook it and passed it to her.

Ginny headed towards the pantry, pausing in the doorway to smile at her daughter, who had sat upright in the chair at her father's words.

'What, that full-of-himself smarty-pants? I don't think so.' Lily cocked her head to one side. It was a struggle these days to recall Danny, the young sales rep who used to perch on the edge of her desk, pretending to need her wind-up pencil sharpener. She had been so surprised when, during her first week at Liners, he had walked through the door carrying his coat nonchalantly over his shoulder. She knew him immediately. Three years earlier, for an interminable six months, Lily had been subjected to her friend Ros's detailed description of his twinkling eyes and unruly black hair. He would often call round for Will, Ros's older brother, on the way to junior orchestra when Lily was there but with a two-year age difference, Ros and her friend were suitably ignored by the older and much more mature boys and Ros's crush went unreciprocated. But on that Monday morning at Liners, Danny had immediately recognised Lily and from then on he took it upon himself to help her settle in, giving her endless advice about how to deal with the erratic water boiler in the kitchen, how to use the teleprinter and how to avoid the miserable Miss Carne. She put up with his advice for about two weeks until she told him she was perfectly capable and would manage fine now, thank you very much, at which point he asked her out on a date.

Lily knew her parents had had high hopes for the well-dressed, polite young man who used to call to pick her up on a Friday night, even though he was Church of England and the Mullins family were Catholics. Lily's own father had been brought up a Baptist and had converted to marry Ginny, but they had both agreed they would not put their own children through the family arguments they had been forced to endure. This was a relaxed approach that prompted scandalised comments from their relations, but made them feel modern and enlightened. They would whisper in the kitchen about what a 'nice sort' he seemed, and her mother had already checked which hats she had on the top of the wardrobe in case an announcement was made. Even Hannah and Ros had started talking about their bridesmaids' outfits.

But their dates were abruptly curtailed when he was called up in '40. Now he was no longer a young salesman whose mum made his packed lunch, but a Tommy in khaki. For a while, Lily missed his cheerful personality but not his irritating assumption that they would become a couple. Their first date had been a surprise – not the usual cinema trip, but a tour of Manchester's historical sites. She remembered with a blush that she had made him laugh when she tried to impress him with her knowledge of history and made a mess of pronouncing the city's original name, Mamucium. Lily was proud of the fact that she had stayed on at school to take her Highers and usually she felt a superiority over lads like him who had left school at fourteen, but Danny was different. He had read books that she had never heard of, kept abreast of current affairs, and actually understood what had happened in the build-up to the Great War. He was also very cultured from his schooling at Manchester Cathedral School and she knew, from his rendition of carols that last Christmas, that he had a beautiful voice. She tried so hard to be sophisticated, but he always seemed to see through her. Their last date was only a picnic in Heaton Park when he had proudly presented her with an egg sandwich the size of a brick. His jokes were terrible but, somehow, they always ended up rolling around in hysterical laughter. It was only at the end of the date as he gently kissed her, and his hands tightened around her shoulders, that she had suddenly suspected he really cared for her.

Once he had left, however, she decided she had no intention of pining away, and despite her parents' constant enquiries about how Danny was doing, she started to date other boys who were not yet conscripted, and she consigned Danny Jackson to a pleasant memory of a first romance. His long and chatty letters came on a regular basis and always made her feel guilty when she forgot to reply. His recent ones told her how he had become a tank transporter driver, she suspected somewhere in Africa, and they always gave a picture of adventure, fun and camaraderie. She knew this was likely far from the truth, but he always made her smile and for a moment, Lily remembered him grinning at her from across the post room. She shook her head to get rid of the vision of a good-looking young man teasing her.

'Nope', she told her parents, tossing her golden hair back, 'it's a high-flyer for me. And a good looking 'un to boot.'

Chapter 3

The next few weeks flew by for Lily, with an interview and a trip to Preston to have her medical and pick up her uniform. The train journey was the first one she had ever taken on her own and felt like the beginning of a new independent life. She watched the ruins of Manchester fade into green fields where animals were grazing. The late autumn colours were a complete contrast to the grey of the devastated city she was leaving behind. The war seemed to move further and further away with the clickety-click of the wheels on the track, and as she dozed, Lily thought about the last three years. It was amazing how quickly everyone had adapted to the war, accepting without question that what started as just shortages of bacon, butter and sugar would soon become two hours of queues at the shops to get anything at all, that their houses were freezing cold in winter because of a lack of coal, and that normal life was turned upside down as its citizens left to fight in countries they had only learned about in Geography lessons at school. But the hail of bombs from the air during the Blitz had threatened the Mancunian spirit like no other catastrophe in its history. Wave after wave of bombers dropped their devastating payload on streets Lily had walked along all her life, obliterating any trace of the ordered existence that had moulded her idyllic childhood. Lily smiled to herself, thinking of her petite mother standing in her nightie in the garden shaking her fist at the dark planes above. It had not taken long for the people of Manchester to rally and refuse to be beaten, in spirit if not in fact. Sometimes, Lily felt so cheated of a young, carefree life that she longed to rail against the fates that had placed her and the whole world in this situation. Only last week, when she had had the temerity to complain in a butcher's queue, she was greeted with a look of disdain from the woman next to her. The look was followed by the comment that Lily had come to loathe so much: 'Stop moaning, don't you know there's a war on.'

But as Lily arrived in Preston on that cold November day, she shivered with excitement as it suddenly occurred to her that war could offer her the challenge of a lifetime and open up opportunities that she could never have envisaged.

The panel of RAF interviewers had been impressed with the fact Lily had taken her Highers and she watched with excitement as the admin officer stamped her application with the word 'Approved.' She could not believe it, she was going to be a WAAF, a member of the Women's Auxiliary Airforce, Aircraftwoman Mullins, ACW Mullins for short.

Once she got home, she carefully laid out her uniform on her bed, proudly showing her mother the neat piles of shirts, ties, tunics, skirts and thick, grey, ugly Lisle stockings. Ginny perched on the bed, fingering the blue-grey woollen cloth of the straight skirt.

While Lily paraded up and down in her navy blue bloomers, Ginny Mullins tried to look enthusiastic, until she got up to look out of the window to disguise brushing a tear from her cheek. Lily was too busy fiddling with the buttons on the wrong side to notice.

'They've put them on this side so I've got space for all my medals,' she explained proudly.

Ginny looked down and busied herself with the duffel canvas bag that was to hold her daughter's worldly goods.

'No, Mum, they all have to be put in in a certain order. There's a list somewhere.' Lily started to ferret underneath the neat pile, upsetting things she had taken off onto the floor. Ginny tutted and leaned down to pick up her daughter's discarded civvy clothes.

'They'll have to be put away until the end of the war,' Lily told her. 'We wear uniform all the time now.'

Ginny gathered up the familiar skirt and pretty top and stroked them. She had a sudden premonition that these would be the last memories of her little girl, and she looked sadly around the room. It was going to be horribly tidy.

The uniform was quite scratchy material, Lily discovered, and the shoes were certainly going to hurt. She spent hours in front of the mirror, pretending to salute, giggling to herself as she peered up from the cap peak in what she hoped was a superior manner. Patch, the Jack Russell, sat to attention at the bottom of the bed and looked suitably impressed.

Lily had been told to report to her first training post at Innsworth in Gloucestershire, and the last few hours before she left were surreal. She raced around at home, bumping into her mother, who was constantly behind her, trying to sneak a hot water bottle or a writing pad into Lily's bag. Then the whole family rushed for the bus to London Road. Her dad ceremoniously handed over some plasters for marching practice but then made sure the farewells were brief and perfunctory, which Lily appreciated. She looked back over her shoulder as she moved along the crowded platform. Looking smaller by the minute, her mum was clutching her dad's arm and her brother was trying to grin. Lily had an urge to turn around and run home. But all around her, other young people were leaving to go to their posts. She was just one more.

In a gesture of defiance that she was sure would frighten the Germans, she had purposefully put on the tiny residue of bright red lipstick she had pinched from her mother's drawer, working on the principle that her mother was already married and did not need any help. All around her there were people with kit bags, greatcoats and pieces of paper clutched in their hands. The scene was grey. The skies, the uniforms and the hastily gathered bags – even people's faces.

The red lipstick had been a good decision.

As usual, Lily looked for something to take her mind off the current situation. There were four young soldiers with kit bags standing to one side as she swept in an unconvincing swagger towards carriage C of the Birmingham train on the first stage of her journey. One caught her eye, making her pull up the collar of her new unwieldy greatcoat. He called out, 'Pucker up love, gi' us a kiss to send us off.'

She hurriedly turned towards the train door and stepped up onto the train, but her bag got stuck in the doorway, leaving her tugging and pulling while the boys laughed.

Finally, one of them stepped forward and said, ''Ere, let me 'elp. It's all them nylons you got in there, in't it?'

Lily was torn between gratitude and rebuke, but he was good-looking and she ended up giving him a lop-sided grimace.

She swung gracelessly into the carriage, narrowly missing a woman with a cat in a basket. The cat hissed at her and Lily snarled back, baring her teeth. She caught sight of the rest of the group of squaddies on the platform grinning at her.

'If that's the best we've got to lead this country to victory, we're in serious trouble,' Lily thought, aware they were probably thinking the same thing.

Lily put her bag on the rack above and fell back onto a torn, upholstered seat, squashing in between a snoring soldier and an elderly man in a faded tweed jacket.

She looked round at the crowded carriage. Everywhere there were sleeping servicemen – in corridors, on seats, on floors. There was a mêlée of kitbags and the air hung heavy with the persistent fog of cigarettes. Lily was lucky to get a seat. She adjusted her collar and sat up a bit straighter. She caught sight of one soldier with a bandage over his eye and another with a sling. For the first time, Lily felt a moment of panic. What had she done? She could be going into work with her tin of sandwiches instead of heading off to fight a war. But then she shook herself and inwardly repeated the same speech she had given her mother – that Manchester had been hell during the Blitz and it was not over yet; that she would be more worried about her family than herself and also that she would be safer on a camouflaged airfield with planes that could fight back, than she would be at home.

Lily suddenly felt very important and got out her Hemingway novel bought from the station newsagent. Her English teacher had always mithered her to read it and the man in a pin-striped suit next to her had looked impressed when she picked it up so she had bought it. Its title, *For Whom the Bell Tolls*, suddenly seemed a harbinger of doom.

'I wish I'd got a mag instead,' she thought ruefully, but she lifted her head back, looked down her nose at the dull cover and opened the first page.

When the train started to slow down for Birmingham, Lily opened her eyes. She peered out of the window with interest. The city was very different from Manchester or even Chester, which she had passed through on her way to North Wales for childhood holidays. Lily wondered how the girls who were being sent abroad were coping. She picked up her book from where it had fallen onto the carriage floor and stood up to get off to make her connection to Gloucester. In the WVS canteen, she pushed her way past all the other service people who were looking for their metal mugs. Lily rooted her mug from the top of her bag. In a moment of shamefaced admission, she said a quiet 'thank you' to Mrs Cook. The Mullins's neighbour had been relentless in regaling them with advice from her superior position as the mother of an established WAAF, but it did mean Lily was prepared and she took her mug to the front of the queue for a lukewarm tea. There was only just enough time to drink it though before her train to Gloucester pulled into the platform. The guard checked her rail warrant and she was on her way again. She looked round, trying to see whether anyone else looked like a new WAAF, but there were not many women, except for factory workers in boiler suits with turbaned scarves over their hair. Two of them smiled at the young recruit and leaned across the carriage to offer her a sugar sandwich. She munched on it gratefully, realising she had forgotten to have breakfast. The countryside blurred past her, places she had never been. Her heart suddenly fluttered at the enormity of the adventure before her. This train, too, was packed and a crowd of experienced troops were chattering in easy camaraderie. Lily felt self-conscious and very much the new girl.

She had to concentrate from Birmingham to count the now-unsigned stations, aimed at confusing any invading enemy, and smiled to see other passengers doing the same. A navy lad, who had been sitting on the floor near Lily, suddenly jumped up as the train slowed once more. He asked the elderly man opposite where they were and swore loudly when he was told 'Gloucester', prompting a sharp look from the man who glanced meaningfully at the women in the carriage. The naval cadet muttered an apology, grabbed his kit bag and climbed over the sleeping service people who were crammed in every corner of the compartment. Lily stood up, flustered.

'Want me to get your bag down, Miss?' her elderly fellow passenger asked.

'Oh yes please,' said Lily, glancing in the mirror to see her hair was messed up and there was no sign of the rebellious lipstick.

While he wrestled with her bag, Lily straightened her hair and quickly put on another layer of Rosy Red.

'This could be my first offence,' she suddenly thought, pursing her lips. 'I'm not sure whether I'm allowed to look like a human being or not, but hell's bells, I need this.'

This was it. She had arrived at Gloucester. It was November 1942, and, as far as Lily Mullins was concerned, the war was waiting to be won by a young woman from the north of England.

Chapter 4

Danny leaned back against the huge tyre of his transporter, then quickly sat forward again. The metal and rubber were too hot, and burned through his uniform.

'Damn, one day I'll remember I'm in the desert and that it's nearly 100 degrees,' he said out loud, to no one in particular.

Danny sighed, leaned back slowly this time and drew a long breath on the strong African cigarette he had bartered for in the small village they had just passed through. It had cost him two garibaldi biscuits, but it was worth it. He took a sip from his tin mug of the liquid they jokingly called tea and put the cooler metal against his brow, rolling it from side to side. He swilled the liquid round his mouth to eradicate the taste of sand. Like a man dying of thirst who tortures himself with an image of a glass of water, Danny closed his eyes to recall a cold winter's day in Manchester. The painful jolt in his stomach was worth it if it took him back for just one second to Lyons Corner House where he had tasted a better tea . . . when he had had the nerve to imagine a future for himself and the beautiful girl with the deep golden hair opposite him. She had no idea she was so funny, sat there, so prim and proper in her new red velour hat. He had to be disciplined with these thoughts; they were like barbed wire. It was strange, he only allowed himself to think of home . . . and Lily . . . when he needed a moment's escape.

The week had been a bad one. They had lost two tanks and a transporter just like his in air strikes, and several men had been killed or injured. He had watched the medics running down the convoy, stretchers folded and knew that, once again, he had been lucky and that the planes had attacked the start of the convoy not the middle.

At the beginning of 8th Army's trek through the desert, he had scrabbled for cover in the sand whenever the air strikes began, but then one day, as he looked up at the swarm of enemy aircraft, he decided that if one of the bullets had his name on it, then there was little he could do and he may as well go quietly. Once he had decided that his fate was not in his own hands, it had all become remarkably easy.

Danny looked up at the pure blue sky and scanned it for aircraft. Nothing. He could enjoy his smoke in peace. They had been told they had an hour to rest before having to move on but being stationary in the open desert was always a risk, so he reasoned there must be a problem up ahead with some of the machinery. The sand was proving to be a dangerous enemy with grains constantly clogging up working parts of engines, even in the new American Grant tanks.

None of them had any idea where they were any more and the endless dunes gave them no clues. Danny felt he was a pawn in a big game of chess that someone else was controlling. While thousands of men fought fiercely just hours in front of him, Danny's convoy followed behind, with the tracks of the huge tanks rattling backwards and forwards, never allowing him to forget there were tons of metal just inches from the back of his neck. He carefully shifted through the twenty-one gears of the monster he was driving and thundered through the desert, moving when the truck in front moved and eating and sleeping when they were allowed. He had been called up two years earlier and had enjoyed the early part when he was training, taking advantage of the opportunities to learn new skills and become a competent mechanic. He had even learned to cook. But since he had been shipped out to Africa, the fighting had been intense, the progress slow and communications chaotic, and the enormous beasts of tank transporters were easy targets. Since the dreadful defeat at Tobruk, morale had been low and Danny had almost lost faith in the commanders. But as a lowly Tommy he had learned to keep his mouth shut and his thoughts to himself.

The hot sun and a fly gently buzzing around his head lulled Danny into a doze. This would never do, he needed to be alert, ready to move, but when he peered round the front of his vehicle he saw a long line of trucks standing still and shimmering in the sunlight. Time for a letter to Lily, he decided, and pulled out his pencil and thin writing paper.

28th November 1942

Dear Lily,

I thought I would write to you while I have a quiet moment. I suspect you're shivering in the cold but believe me, a bit of cold during the day would go down very well with me. The days are so hot and then the temperatures at night really plummet and it's hard to keep a cool head when you're sweating like a pig, but the lads are all trying to make the best of it and as the sergeant keeps telling us there's no point moaning and as long as you still have a ciggie and match, life can't be that bad.

Thanks for your letter. I'm really pleased you've joined the WAAFs, although as a Tommy, obviously I feel hurt for the army that they won't benefit from your varied talents! Remembering our trip out to Alderley Edge when you swore it was a right turn back into town when actually that path led over the Edge, I am sure the RAF will value your ability to read maps. Please don't tell the pilots whether to turn left or right! They could end up in Scandinavia.

Time's flown for me, it's been so busy, and I tend to think of you still sat at your desk in Liners. Manchester seems a million miles away. I'd tell you how many miles, but they would blank it out . . . I always smile when I think of your arched eyebrows and disdainful looks when I tried to perch on your desk. I tell myself you were really pleased to see me; please don't tell me if you weren't. It would ruin my day.

I don't suppose you know where you're going and you wouldn't be able to tell me anyway, but you'll have to train first and that involves a ridiculous amount of marching up and down. Don't forget the plasters! I hope you meet some nice girls. The lads here are a good bunch, although the sarge can be a bit of a pain in the neck. He worries about stupid little details like smart uniforms and shiny boots, when we're covered in sand, sweat and sand-flies. Actually, perhaps I'd better not say too much about that, he's probably the one who reads these letters before we send them. (Sorry, Sarge, only joking about the uniform. I will obviously get the butler to launder and press it before tomorrow, I promise!)

We've just eaten. At least I think it was a meal. They can be pretty sparse at times but there are a lot of us to feed and the field kitchens aren't exactly state of the art. We all fill up on potatoes as much as we can and Mum occasionally gets a parcel of goodies over to me, which is so welcome, I can't tell you. She sent corned beef the other day and I broke the stupid little key that opens it. I was so mad, I had to use a screwdriver to break it open. It was quite an operation, but worth it. I never knew I would feel so strongly about corned beef. But you know the tins are the German's secret weapons, don't you? So many Tommies bleed to death from trying to open the damned tin, it saves them a fortune in bombs!

There has been one bit of good cheer though. We got some beer! It was flown over to us to boost morale. Someone said it had been flown strapped to the wings of fighters. No wonder it spurted out of the bottles! It tasted great, even though it was a bit warm. We were given it by some ENSA glamour girls. They even gave us some cigs. I'm not sure which was more popular, the beer and cigs or the sight of some very pretty girls in floral dresses and straw hats!

I get letters from the girls – both Pam and Maureen are fine. They're in the navy, as you know, but seem to be home port based at the moment, so that's good. I think Mum and Dad are fed up with rattling round that drafty house, but at least they've got Mutt for company. His constant demand for titbits keeps them occupied.

Anyway, I'd better go, it's an early start and a long day tomorrow. I think of you often. Your smiling face keeps me going when I get fed up.

I know you think you're sophisticated and a woman of the world, but it's a dangerous war out there, so do keep your head down.

Don't run off with any 'fly' boys!

Love,

Danny

He folded the letter into his top pocket, next to one he had written to his mother last night. He had started to tell his family less and less about the war, concentrating on complaining passionately about the food, a subject he knew would give his mother's concerns a focus. It was hard to say something yet reveal nothing. Each soldier's letter was carefully scrutinised to make sure no information could be gleaned that might be of advantage to the enemy. Danny's initial sense of adventure had been quickly suppressed by the relentless grind of misery, discomfort and hunger had epitomised life on the move but the worst was the reality of the seemingly endless numbers of supine bodies that were laid out along the route, testament to the fierce fighting that he and his tank transporter had missed the day before. Buzzing with flies and beginning to stink in the heat, it was a smell that Danny, and every other survivor of the desert would never forget. The units were constantly on the move, bivouacking in makeshift tents. He hoped the newsreels were being judicious in what they showed back home of the war in Africa. He knew his parents often went to the pictures and he could imagine them sitting in the cinema, bolt upright, eyes staring at the black and white version of the carnage he had witnessed. Surely Pathé would not be that honest to a nation longing for good news? Danny had almost stopped worrying about himself but he worried constantly about how the death of their only son would devastate his parents. It was simply luck that had kept him safe this long. He did not dare think about how the odds of survival were decreasing.

One thing Danny had learned to do was to switch off images that disturbed him, so he went back to the girl in the red velour hat. He loved imagining her standing opposite him again. He pictured her laughing and he felt a jolt of pure delight.

Instead of the miles and miles of sand glistening in the relentless sun, he saw Lily on one of their first dates up to Higher Swineshaw Reservoir. Manchester, with its chimneys and elegant buildings, was stretched below them in testament to a history of growth, elegance and prosperity. There was no hint of what the fates had in store for it. It was a beautiful day and the bilberries had just come out. He remembered Lily was trying to keep up with him as he tackled the steep path in front of them. Eventually, she had stopped, saying indignantly, 'Danny Jackson, if you have any hopes of ever kissing me, you have to stop marching off up this hill and let me get my breath.'

With that, he had run back to where she was and swept her up into his arms. She had tossed her head back and laughed as he tried to run with her up to the top. She knew how to flirt, he reluctantly acknowledged. He also knew how innocent she was and how predatory servicemen could be.

'Take care, Lily' he pleaded as he buried his cigarette in the sand and prepared to climb back into his cab.

Chapter 5

It was six a.m. and Lily hugged her coarse, grey blanket, hanging on to the last remnants of sleep and warmth. The barracks at Innsworth were freezing, hardly warmed by the antique boiler in the middle of the room. She glanced up at the small window above her iron bedpost, pushed back the blackout blind an inch and saw the panes were imprinted with beautiful snowflake patterns. It had been a baptism of fire for Lily since she had arrived at Gloucester station just one week ago for a month's initial training.

In the bed next to her, a brown woolly hat poked out, dislodging the sanitary towel that was looped over the huddled figure's ears as an eye mask.

Lily scanned the now-familiar room. Behind each bed, the blue-grey WAAF uniforms were hanging up like regimented puppets. Brand new when they were given out, they had been pushed, pummelled and re-positioned in a vain attempt to give each girl individuality.

Now every single one of those girls was part of an enormous war machine.

Alice, the girl next to Lily, groaned and turned over, leaving her ineffective face mask on the rough pillow. Alice had established herself as a force to be reckoned with from the very first day when she swept into the hut, clomping down the wooden floor in her heavy, black lace-up shoes, making straight for the bed next to Lily.

'Lordy, these beds are awful,' she had exclaimed in strong Lancashire tones to the whole room. She pushed the three separate mattresses together and frowned. 'My backside'll soon disappear between these. No wonder they call them 'biscuits', they're as hard as my Auntie Mavis's shortbread. I wouldn't give the cows this bedding,' she added, prodding the straw pillow.

Alice had been brought up on a farm on the Pennines and was a product of harsh conditions with a healthy respect for nature and absolutely none for would-be invaders. Lily, a cosmopolitan girl, was quick to realise that her own city nous was completely outdone by a girl who could move a herd of cows with just a stick.

Alice immediately decided she and Lily were going to be best friends and with a mixture of calm control and a great deal of giggling, she gained Lily's undying love.

Lily looked round enviously at the curled-up figures in the beds. They did not seem to find the endless rules here difficult. She traced the icy patterns on the window above her, catching sight of the piece of paper the girls had stuck behind the cardboard that formed the blackout. It was a

'Naughty Chart' and Lily could just see her name at the top of the list. She was getting into trouble for everything: inadequate kit inspections, reporting for duty a couple of minutes late and, most of all, forgetting to salute an officer.

The door opened with a bang and an impossibly cheerful hut corporal charged in, yelling instructions and threats in equal measure at the same time as the loudspeaker went off. Up and in uniform an hour earlier, she had no sympathy for lay-a-beds and she banged on the end of each bunk with a baton as she marched through the line of beds like a steam train. Every girl had quickly learned to tuck her feet underneath her to avoid the thwack of the wood.

The groans in the room were universal but all twenty girls tumbled out of their beds and started to scrabble for their tin hats holding their wash kits.

Lily hopped from foot to foot on the freezing floorboards and then poked her toes under the bed, trying to find her shoes.

'Hell, I forgot to polish my buttons,' she realised, remembering looking with pride the night before at her gleaming shoes, her hat which was buffed, and her gloves which were neatly folded, but she had forgotten the damned buttons, which were decidedly dull. Pulling her pyjama sleeves down over her hands, she grabbed her jacket and started to rub furiously at the brass domes, but it was too late, everyone else was heading across the freezing cold parade yard for the ablutions block.

Alice was in front of her and Lily had to push her way through the throng of girls.

'Alice, Alice,' she hissed. 'I've forgotten to polish my buttons. What am I going to do?'

'Do the crime, do the time,' her friend retorted over her shoulder.

'Can't you stand in front of me? Maybe he won't see.'

'That man could see through a brick wall.'

'I'm doomed,' Lily said.

'Yep, it's no dancing for you this weekend,' Alice muttered through her teeth as she swilled her face in the freezing water.

Lily's shoulders drooped.

'I've got cabin fever and I've been looking forward to being allowed out – and there's a dance this week.'

'You'll have a much better time on duty here, stamping up and down in the cold or cleaning pans,' Alice said, then relented. 'He might not notice; you might get away with it.'

The two girls looked at each other. Their grimaces said it all.

Amy, a thin, wan girl from Coventry came up behind them. She was the quietest in the group. The close quarters had encouraged all of them to chat openly about their homes, boyfriends and their experiences of the war so far, but Amy was a closed book. She always managed to appear without a sound somehow and Lily jumped as she almost stepped back into her. 'Sorry,' Amy said, apologising as usual. She smiled across at them both. 'I could stay and keep you company if you like, Lily. I'm not fussed about going out.'

'Don't be daft, Amy,' Lily replied. 'I'll be doing jankers somewhere and even you're not noble enough to want to clean kitchens or peel spuds. No, you go out and have a good time. It'll do you good. Besides, look at this hair of yours! We've got to get it to curl for your big night out.'

'Well, that won't happen,' Amy fingered her completely straight brown hair. 'Maybe you'll just get a warning. He's not that mean.' She emptied her faded pink hot water bottle into the sink.

'You never think anyone can be horrid,' Lily said.

She looked enviously at Amy's sink of warm water. In her early morning panic, Lily had forgotten her hot water bottle with its residue of warm water.

'That's so typical of me,' Lily grumbled inwardly as the familiar pang of homesickness waved over her. 'Oh Mum, how am I ever going to survive without you to look after me?'

Putting her penny in the plughole to hold the cold water, Lily started to rinse her face quickly to get the torture over with. She rubbed the mouse-gnawn soap against her flannel as if it were a tarnished button. The rules were being stringently imposed on all of them. One hair out of place, one item of kit in the wrong order and there were penalties. One thing she was learning in this war was that there was no sympathy for anything except the precipice between life and death.

Washing and getting ready for the dreaded morning fitness session was a very brief affair on these cold mornings. There was no comfort in the ablutions block and no one wanted to dawdle. They all dressed in their vests, the 'blackout' navy blue knickers and plimsolls and headed out into the early morning light. The air was painfully cold and the only thing to do was to embrace the exercises with gusto to prevent frostbite setting in. Some of the larger girls struggled with jumping up and down and the panting got louder and louder, but they all had to admit, reluctantly, that they were getting fitter and the WAAF skirts were starting to be a little looser around their waists.

From being a group of individuals from different backgrounds, Lily's unit had merged into one entity, marching up and down the parade ground, eating together, getting dressed together and sleeping next to each other. They helped each other with their ties, unused to such male accessories, and they measured each other's skirts to check they were exactly sixteen inches from the ground. Lily had been surprised to see how quickly they had started to think of themselves as part of a whole rather than individuals or as someone's daughter or sister or sweetheart. They moved as that entity now, dressed in their uniforms, towards the cabbage-smelling cookhouse for breakfast, chattering about the two abiding subjects of conversation – hunger and cold.

'Oh for an egg from a real chicken!' Marion said, for once voicing the thoughts of many. Reconstituted egg was like eating rubber and if the girls had not been facing two hours of marching up and down in the freezing winter temperatures, they might have pushed the congealed omelette to the side of the plate. But gnawing pangs of hunger and a rumbling stomach did not help one's posture on parade and a slouching torso was soon picked up by the sergeant.

'Susie, don't eat off your knife.' Marion peered in disgust at the offending girl next to her.

Susie, a no-nonsense blonde from Wolverhampton, made a face once Marion had turned back to her meal, and continued eating off her knife, to the stifled laughter of the group.

Marion was from Chelsea in London and was looked on as a more sophisticated being. She was nineteen, like most of them, but her knowledge of glamorous places such as Bond Street and Westminster gave her an edge on the girls from the provinces. Marion never lost an opportunity to remind her fellow WAAFs that she was not used to roughing it and that she came from a family of titles and insignia. Her uniform was handmade, and she made a point of stroking it as she laid it out for morning inspection, while the others suffered from scratching and chafing from the rough, standard-issue WAAF woollen cloth. Marion revelled in their envy, making the most of flaunting the tempting array of face creams, dried fruit and magazines that were regularly delivered to her pigeon hole.

'I can do without,' Alice muttered to Lily, 'but I don't need reminding all the time that I'm suffering.'

Lily looked around at the group at breakfast and cupped her hands around her mug of tea to savour the last dregs of warmth from the weak liquid. These women were becoming her family and could be just as irritating. She said a quick mental 'good morning' to her own family and filed out of the hut, swishing her egg-smeared irons through the soapy water in the tank by the door, readying them for the next meal. She joined the throng and went into the corridor to get her jacket, hat and gloves to go onto the parade ground for the endless marching up and down that was square-bashing.

Chapter 6

'MULLINS!'

Lily closed her eyes in capitulation.

'ACW Mullins, your buttons aren't polished.'

Well, what difference is that going to make to the war, Lily thought. *Is Hitler going to be blinded by the brightness of my buttons and wave the white flag?*

'I'm sorry, Sir, I did try but . . . '

'See me in my office at 0900 hours tomorrow and I want to see my face in those buttons and shoes.'

The waiting row of girls craned their heads towards Lily in a united gesture of sympathy as she mentally put her hair rollers back in the drawer for another week.

By teatime, Lily's feet were aching, her neck hurt and she was feeling particularly sorry for herself. She had caught up with her writing and folded each letter into its envelope – one to her parents, one to Hannah and Ros, and another to Danny. Now she finally got on with the task she had been putting off all day – polishing those darned buttons. Lily sat on her bed with resignation and started rubbing them with Duraglit, using the ingenious button stick to keep the uniform away from the pad. She heard the door close quietly and Amy came in, looking pale and shrunken. Amy reminded Lily of the puppy her neighbours had bought just before war broke out. Those doleful eyes had the same look; scared, but hoping for affection. The group's concerted effort to bring Amy out of herself was slow progress and Lily, taking in the drooped shoulders, doubted whether today was a day for girly banter. Even so, she tried.

'Hi Amy. You'd think it was the end of the world that my buttons are a bit dull. Don't tell me you've been caught as well.'

Amy sat on her bed three down from Lily and slumped. Tears began to fall.

Lily, with her jacket still in her hands, got up and went over to her, putting her arm around the sobbing girl.

'What is it?'

There was no reply, just shudders from the girl's tiny frame.

'Come on, tell me.'

Amy pushed over a telegram she was clutching in her right hand.

> Mother died at 5 a.m STOP Dad with her STOP A relief after all she has suffered STOP Funeral Thursday if you can get leave STOP Alf

Lily held Amy until the sobs subsided.

'It was the Blitz,' Amy finally said. She was on Red Cross Duty on 14th November two years ago. Her legs were shot off and she's been in hospital ever since.'

Lily thought back to the *Manchester Evening News* headlines about the Coventry bombings and remembered how everyone had been shaken by the reports. The calculated attack was aimed at destroying the factories and infrastructure, concentrating on causing maximum damage to roofs to allow bombs to fall through more easily. It had seemed such a vicious, calculated raid, even to the point that water mains were targeted so that the fires couldn't be put out. She remembered her dad's pale face as he had put the kettle on the range that day, throwing down the first editions on the table in disgust.

'This is the nastiest war we've ever had,' he had said to his wife and family as they huddled around the fire having their cup of tea. No one has ever targeted civilians like this before. This isn't war, it's annihilation.'

Amy's grief suddenly gave way to a bitter anger that seemed out of place in this timid girl.

'She was helping people. Out there in the dark, being bombed but still helping people. She was such a lovely mum, always at the door waiting for us to come in from school, wanting to know how our day had been. The last two years, she's just been lying in that hospital, unable to move, but even so, she's tried to be cheerful, telling Dad what to do and giving me advice on how to cook shin beef. It must have been an infection. They always said that would be the danger. But it's not that that's killed her, it's the Germans . . . it's . . . that man.'

Lily hugged her tighter, letting the distraught girl's tears fall on the newly-polished buttons of her jacket. They sat like that for ages until the rest of the group bustled in and Amy slunk away towards the ablutions block. Lily stared uselessly at the retreating figure.

Saturday night was a cold one, but the group had been given a pass for a rare night out – all except for Lily, who had been put on gate duty. Amy sat huddled up on her bunk. She had hardly spoken since she had received the telegram. Proffered mugs of hot chocolate from the stove in the corner were taken by a pale hand that shook slightly with only a wan smile. Even Marion tried to interest her in a new magazine she had received.

Shaking their heads, the girls turned back to the task in hand – a welcome night out. They all spent an hour getting ready, Lily sitting cross-legged with her skirt hitched up, watching on enviously as she waited to go on duty. It reminded her of days with Hannah and Ros, as they got ready for the Boys' Brigade dances. The chatter was the same, she thought, taking in the sisterly banter, swapping of hairspray and turning the unattractive Lisle stockings inside out to make them smoother. Ros was working in a munitions factory now and Hannah had joined the land army. Lily wondered what they were doing tonight. She hoped they were going to a dance.

The group walked to the entrance where the girls were cadging a lift in the supplies truck and Lily waved them off as they walked away, arm in arm, trying not to sound excited as they passed her. Alice paused to give her a quick hug.

Lily could see her breath as she stood in the tiny office by the camp gates and banged her hands together to try to get some feeling into them. Life was so precarious, she thought, as she marched up and down on the spot to keep warm. This war was tearing families apart, making people like Amy face tragedy and hardship at an age when they should have been having the best times of their lives. Lily's father rarely talked about the Great War, but her Uncle Joe was always going on about it. She felt guilty remembering how she and her brother had made faces behind his back as he talked about 'going over the top'. She made a mental note to show more of an interest and ask him more about it when this was all over, and she resignedly got on with checking her list to see which vehicles were expected in.

The following night, the atmosphere in the Waafery was subdued. Word had soon got around the whole camp about Amy's mum and the normal chatter and banter was suppressed as the girls searched for something to talk about.

Amy sat in the corner at a desk, pen in hand, but she was staring at the wall more than she was writing.

'She's got leave for the funeral at least,' Alice whispered to a small group of them who were half-heartedly playing whist. 'That's something. It'll be hard though; her older brother's in the navy and in the Far East somewhere so he won't be there,' she added, claiming her trick. 'Apparently, her dad's gone to pieces and her other brother's only young.'

'That's Alf isn't it?' Susie put in. 'I heard Amy talking to Ma'am earlier. She said he was trying to be the man of the house by sending the telegrams out. It broke me up, I had to flee to the bog.'

'Yes, I think he's only about fifteen,' Alice replied, looking over towards Amy, who was wiping tears from her notepaper. 'My mother told me our neighbour's just heard that her son's been killed in Tunisia. I used to play 'Catch a girl, kiss a girl' with him,' she faltered and then shook her head to bring herself back to the present. 'They say there's been heavy fighting there. How long is this bloody war going to go on?'

'Let's start to think about Christmas to cheer ourselves up,' Susie said, sitting up and taking a deep breath. She needed to dispel the panic that threatened to engulf her about her two brothers on ships in the Mediterranean. 'Let's make some decorations to leave for the next intake, that'll make us feel more festive."'

The group all murmured their approval and put their heads together to assign each other jobs. They were trying to keep as quiet as possible, whilst constantly glancing up at Amy in the corner, who had finally started to write.

The barracks were quiet on Thursday morning but once Amy had left on the bus, there was a lifting of the mood and during square-bashing the girls guiltily found themselves giggling at nothing in particular. The Corporal was getting crosser and crosser at the wobbly lines the girls were forming and eventually started to use his baton to push them into position. He knew that the points that his baton kept striking were the exact spots where the medical officer had inserted a needle two hours before with their smallpox vaccinations. To distract him, Susie kept insisting on turning left instead of right.

The tall, grim-faced Corporal was not impressed and put Susie on a charge. She pulled a face which he spotted and put her on another one. He then kept them parading up and down for an extra half hour meaning they had to run straight into dinner.

'Well, that wasn't worth the rush,' said Susie in her strong Midlands accent, as she sized up her plate of spam fritters, lumpy mash and baked beans.

'Be grateful,' said Alice crossly, rubbing her sore arm.

'. . . there are people starving in the Far East,' three of the girls finished for her.

'I'm fed up with being so bloody grateful,' Susie replied, pushing her fork reluctantly into the greasy fritter. 'Especially now I won't get off base on Friday.'

'Well, normally on a Friday night, I go to the Dorchester,' Marion interjected.

'I go to the bloody Royal Oak for half a pint if I'm lucky,' Alice muttered under her breath. 'Come on, you lot,' she added. 'There's another dance in town on Saturday, let's see if we can get passes and get down there to check out the talent before we leave here.'

In a pact of tactfulness, they had all claimed last week's dance was not very good and that there was no one of any interest there, just a group of local farm lads, in seventh heaven at the sudden influx of glamorous WAAFs. Marion had been indignant and extremely snobby all evening, looking down on all the farmhands as if they were an inferior species. The rest of the group had spent the whole night making apologies for her.

With a full turn-out likely for this week's outing, the fritters were instantly forgotten and they started to fantasise about who might be there.

'I heard there's a few sailors passing through,' said Lily.

'Don't be ridiculous,' Marion interjected. 'I'm not going out with anyone of a low rank. My family would be horrified if there weren't enough tapes on their shoulders.'

'Oh, not the navy,' groaned Susie, completely ignoring Marion, 'you know what they're like. A girl in every port.

Give me a man whose plane is firmly planted in Blighty. Not going anywhere. Well, not for a while anyway. Hey, there's all those Spitfire pilots to look forward to.'

'Don't fall in love with one of those,' Lily warned. 'I've been told about them. They really think they're something, and they've hardly had much training. You'd think they were bomber pilots in those fantastic new Lancasters.'

Over the past few weeks, she had become more and more fascinated with those wings on the chests of pilots, not because of their appeal as men, although there was a glamour attached to their dashing uniform, but because they were able to disappear into the clouds and head towards the sun, away from the gloom of a December Gloucestershire day. Poor Danny, in his khaki uniform in a large ugly tank transporter, could not compete, she ruefully admitted. Lily found the lessons on the range of RAF planes fascinating. Sitting up straight, she drank in the information about the different types of pilots, what planes they flew and what they had to learn in training. She envied them their little world of a quiet cockpit, the silence only broken by the halting intercom from their Squadron Leader. She didn't think about the gunfire or the burning balls of flames she'd seen on the newsreels. At night, before she went to sleep, she found herself imagining herself as an Amy Johnson or an Amelia Earhart, pioneering flying for women.

Maybe by the end of this war, I could learn to fly a plane, she thought, opening her eyes wide at the possibility of a different future from the one that had been mapped out for her before the war.

Lily the pilot, was mentally striding through the airport in a victorious post-war Britain with a confident smile, as passengers parted like the Red Sea to let her pass.

'Do you want those beans?' Marion said, bursting into her reverie.

Chapter 7

The dance was the little group's swansong before they were moved off to their next training posts, and it was a lively affair. They all drank too much cider, danced their feet off, flirted outrageously with the local farmers' sons, and when they arrived back at the barracks, they hugged, swore eternal affection and promised that they would meet up after the war. All the irritations of the past few weeks were forgotten and even an unyielding Marion got enthusiastic hugs.

The following morning, with sore feet and sore heads, there was no time for sentiment. The sergeant drilled them up and down with relentless determination on their last square-bashing at Innsworth before they looked at the noticeboard to find out their postings for their specialist training.

The girls gathered in the hallway, waiting for the admin staff to pin up the lists on the wood-edged board. Finally, two secretaries marched importantly down the corridor and the girls parted to let them in, crowding round as soon as the last pin was in place and craning their necks to see where they were being sent. Lily searched down the alphabet to M. Next to her name was the word 'Blackpool' and in the adjoining column, the words 'wireless operator'. She scanned down to find Alice's name, her heart racing, but Alice beat her to it.

'Blackpool!' Alice pronounced triumphantly and then more doubtfully, 'Hmm, wireless operator.'

'Phew, that means we're together,' said Lily, reaching over to give her a hug.

Marion called from the other side of the crowd of girls, 'Me too.'

'Bloody hell,' Alice mouthed at Lily. 'You might know we'd get the princess.'

Amy came over to them both and said gently, 'I'm for Blackpool too.'

Lily grabbed her hand and smiled. 'I'm so glad, Amy. It'll be nice to be with friends.'

Amy nodded, but she had become detached and even quieter since her mother had died. The girls had tried to include her but she sat apart, hugging her knees in the armchair in the corner, hardly saying a word. They were all worried about her but between lectures, marching and exams and the endless Freedom from Infection tests and kit inspections, there was little time for sympathy.

Travel warrants were issued for their next posting but first, some of those who had volunteered, including Lily, were allowed a three-day pass to go home for Christmas.

In the run up to her leave, Lily was so excited she could hardly eat. It had only been a few short weeks, but she already felt she was inhabiting another world. Alone at night, under the bedclothes, the early homesickness tears had dried quite quickly and Lily had found it easier than some to adjust to being away from home, but the regular letters from her mum always brought a pang. Now, when she closed her eyes at night, hugging the rough blanket to herself, she allowed herself to imagine luxuriating in the prospect of her cosy eiderdown. Home was always the same, the same china cups on the morning room table, the same clock ticking, Patch snoring under her dad's chair. But was she the same girl, she wondered?

'Lily, stand still for a minute and come and talk to us,' Ginny shouted up the stairs, but Lily was too busy racing from room to room to check that everything was exactly where she had left it in her Manchester home. The bus journey home from the station had been a sharp reminder that the war was not only affecting those in uniform. She had felt a sickening lurch of her stomach spotting rubble where the Boys' Brigade hut used to be and suddenly needed reassurance that her home was still untouched by the war. The continued destruction came as a shock to her. Despite the early years of the war when Manchester was pummelled from the air with relentless destruction, she had naïvely believed that once she joined up, she would take the war with her, leaving Manchester in peace. Her stomach turned with relief when she first spotted the solid bricks of her home and her mum racing out of the front door to greet her. From that moment, Lily had felt her shoulders relax. Now, pausing by her own bedroom window, she glanced again at the corrugated sheeting shelter in the garden and shivered. She pleaded with it to carry on keeping her family safe while she was away.

'Mum, the house looks great,' she said, hurtling down the stairs at her customary speed. 'You've found the decorations,' she added approvingly, looking up at the ceiling strewn with red and yellow paper chains. 'Although, they look newer. Are they? And the branches make a lovely tree.' Her mum had done everything she could to make the room look jolly. Despite the worn cushions and faded wallpaper, the Christmas scene was familiar and comforting. Determined to eradicate the misery of war, Ginny had spent hours re-making the paper chains, using bits of old wrapping paper from the back of the dining room cupboard. Lily smiled when she noticed the little Father Christmas she had made out of felt when she was in primary school in pride of place on the mantlepiece. Government warnings that Christmas had to be a parsimonious affair had been carefully manipulated in the Mullins household to allow Ginny to make it look reassuringly cosy and welcoming. Lily breathed a sigh of relief.

'Well, it's not what we're used to', her dad said, coming in from the hallway, 'but I cut the branches down from the garden and they'll do. We can use them for firewood afterwards and the tree will grow again after the war. And despite the Government saying only presents for children, we've done what we can,' he added with a small amount of pride.

'It's all wonderful,' Lily said, grabbing her mum's arm and twirling her round in front of the tiny pretend tree in a bucket trimmed with brown paper.

'Eh, it's good to see you, lass,' her dad said. 'The house has been so quiet, hasn't it, Ginny?'

'Well, I'm back for three whole days, so I'll try to make as much noise as I can,' Lily laughed, ruffling her brother's hair as she waltzed past.

'I haven't missed you a bit,' Don replied, ducking out of her way out of habit. 'It's been blissfully quiet. And anyway, I'll be joining up soon'

'You're thirteen,' his mother said, 'the war'll be over by the time you're old enough.'

'That just wouldn't be fair, it'd be typical of Lily to get all the fun.'

'I know, such a shame, after all, the war would have been over by now if the Germans had had two members of the Mullins family to deal with.' Lily told him with a grin.

'There's a letter for you from Danny,' her mum interrupted, looking slyly at Lily to gauge her reaction.

''Bout time he wrote,' Lily said, busily rearranging the paper to get at the presents under the tree and pushing an inquisitive Patch out of the way. Danny seemed a long way away, but she was always surprised how pleased she was to get a letter. She felt a certain satisfaction that he wrote so regularly even though she barely had time to reply. He had always been so certain that they were a couple but she wanted him to know she was now a woman of the world with little time for childhood sweethearts.

'Move over, Patch, there's nothing here for you.'

John and Ginny shared a glance and John winked at his wife.

After the trail of unsuitable boyfriends that had called for Lily over the years, Danny, the young salesman, was one they both hoped would lead to something more permanent. Lily always seemed frustratingly impervious to his charms, but John Mullins had seen through Danny's apparent insouciance and registered the gentle care that he took when he was helping Lily with her coat. They were both pleased when Lily agreed to write to the 8th Army soldier and cursed the war for interrupting such a promising romance.

Lily was rummaging through the small pile of presents under the tree, searching for a tag with her name on, when she had an unbidden memory of Danny. The last Christmas before he left for the army, he had brought some biscuits he had made for her mother, presenting them to her nervously. They were as hard as rock but Ginny had been very touched and Lily saw again his anxious face as the expert biscuit-maker took the first bite. He was easy to like but Lily had plans – and now she was in the WAAFs, a young salesman from her home city was not a part of those plans. She shrugged her shoulders and carried on sorting out the presents.

Christmas was an upbeat affair compared with previous years as they celebrated the victory over the Germans at El Alamein, along with the rest of the country, and the Mullins family made the most of it. Don, in particular, took the opportunity to bolt down huge slices of sponge cake. He could hardly remember the feasts his mother used to prepare before the war, but when the sweet, crumbly mixture hit his tongue, his taste buds burst into life again. He put his arms around his mum, unable to speak. At thirteen, Don was growing fast and Ginny struggled to put enough food on the plate for this gangly youth. She constantly gave up her rations when Don was not looking, but this Christmas, with Lily's two shillings a week pay, she had been able to buy a few little extras on the black market. She scanned the heaped plates on the table in front of them all and nodded in satisfaction. It was a small moment of triumph for a housewife after three years of war.

Chapter 8

12th February, 1943

Dear Lily,

I'm sorry I haven't written for a while, I'd just settle down to write to you and some bright spark would have a better idea how I should be spending my time! Honestly, these boffins don't have any respect for a chap's private life! Hope you managed to get some leave and had a good Christmas. I thought of you with your paper hat on, pulling a cracker . . . if you made some. If I remember, your arts and craft capabilities were limited to paper aeroplanes in the office, so I hope you've improved your skills.

It's been unbelievably busy here, but I think we've made some headway. Last week, we had a bit of a break and stopped in a local village. So now we've got some camp followers! The locals follow us around and brew tea for us. It's quite a brew! They soak the tea first and then add boiling water and serve it to us very proudly in our tins. Don't think your dad would be too overwhelmed with the strength of it but it does taste OK and it gives them a bit of cash too. It's hard for them to earn a living when their land is in the middle of a war zone. You'd be impressed with me. I can now say, 'Ana-mashkeen ma-feesh valoose,' which means, 'I am a poor man, I have no money,' which is true on army pay. They don't look as if they believe us though. They are so poor, and we must seem rich in comparison.

Someone had the nerve to suggest that we drivers burst our tyres deliberately every time we get hungry, which is a terrible thing to say! But we've perfected the art of mixing sand with petrol in a can to make a fire. It can be a bit dangerous at times if we don't get the proportions right and, of course, we have to do it all from under a tarpaulin, so the enemy can't see the smoke, but it works fine – as long as you're not the one having to do it. I did it the other day and had to grab for the flap in a coughing fit from being in a confined space.

If I am careful, I can sometimes get a sneaky fag at night – you do have to make sure the red glow of the tip doesn't show, though – and last night I looked up at the stars and thought how beautiful the sky was and how messy the world below is. I'd love to bring you back here when the war's over. It is a fascinating country and the people are so warm and friendly. You'd love the children. They have the biggest, brownest eyes you've ever seen.

So, a belated happy Christmas! Give my regards to your mum and dad and think of me looking up into the clear blue sky wishing for snow . . . fat chance!

Anyway, Lily, I'd better go, looks like we're on the move. Remember the one rule of this war: never volunteer!

Love,

Danny

Danny looked at the letter he had just finished and smiled. It always cheered him up when he wrote to Lily. She appeared, disturbingly, in too many of his dreams. From the first moment he had seen her with her nose in the air at the office, he had fallen for her. She had tried to be so grown up and sophisticated but then she gave that delicious giggle and he knew there was only ever going to be one girl for him. 'Bring back Liners,' he thought, thinking back to those innocent days. He'd never expected to say that. He had wanted to be a doctor, but as the youngest of three children, there was just not enough money to put him through training. However, life as a salesman at the shipping company had come quite easily to him. He could organise his own time, he really liked the customers and found that his easy manner gained their trust and, therefore, their custom. He prided himself on giving them the best deals to get their goods around the world and he loved to think he was making a difference to British exports. He was ambitious too and had already told his father he was going to be a company director by the time he was forty. The war was just delaying his plans.

It had been the strangest Christmas Danny had ever spent as they fought their way across to the ultimate goal of Tripoli. He was part of the 7th Armoured Division that had become known as the 'Desert Rats', a nickname that had come to exemplify the last three years when they had scrabbled their way up and down the desert in victory and defeat. Travelling between eighteen and thirty miles a day, it was just after Christmas when they finally reached Tripoli and their dusty tanks and armoured cars rolled into the city, proud and triumphant to be witnessed by the guest of honour, Winston Churchill. Danny had felt tears welling up as the pipers of the 51st Highland Division led the parade past the old Roman amphitheatre, and glanced at his fellow soldiers, who were all blinking with emotion. He heard Churchill's words as he addressed the troops that February morning: 'When this war is over, it will be enough for a man to say, "I marched, and fought, with the Desert Army."' All Danny could think of were the thousands of men who would remain forever in the silent war cemeteries of the Western Desert.

He tucked the letter into the envelope, knowing it would be opened and checked by his commanding officer before being sent.

His last memory of Lily was when he had called in at the office to say goodbye to everyone before being conscripted. A busy filing clerk in her first job, full of self-importance, she had barely looked up and any hope he had had of her rushing into his arms in tears at his parting were dashed by her casual, 'Oh, bye then, good luck,' as she pecked him on the cheek and headed towards the filing cabinet.

He had done everything, he constantly told himself. He had taken her out on as many fun dates as she would agree to. He had tried to think of things that were not just a boring and predictable drink at the pub, but bike rides, walks into the hills with picnics. He had got to know her parents quite well and knew that her mum liked him – she always gave him an extra piece of cake. He wasn't sure about her dad. Danny knew he was very protective of his daughter and had caught Mr Mullins giving the young suitor a sideways glance when Danny was trying too hard to be the perfect date.

He had spent the last two years telling himself that if he just bided his time and kept writing to Lily, she would eventually have no choice but to fall in love with him and his plan A – the one before the Plan B of becoming a company director – would come to fruition and she would marry him.

Chapter 9

Blackpool was even colder than Gloucestershire had been and on leaving the station the girls were greeted by seagulls, heralding their arrival with disdainful squawks. Alice stuck her tongue out to taste the salty air while the rest scanned the horizon, which was tinted with that rose-pink light that only seaside towns have. Walking along the front towards their digs, the girls breathed deeply, with the guilty feeling of being on holiday.

Number 110, Palatine Road was a terraced three-storey house with a white front door and matching bay windows. There were red flagstones on the short path from the wooden gate but to one side the tiles had been lifted and there were neat rows of cabbages echoing many of the other houses in the street. They were keen to make a show of their solidarity with Dig for Victory, as well as wanting to put fresh vegetables on their tables.

Marion strode up the steps to the front door and knocked firmly. The door opened to reveal a formidable figure. With her arms folded over her checked pinny, her tightly rolled hair, and a huge pair of cloth slippers, Mrs Porter fitted the Lancashire landlady description to a T. She herded the girls upstairs, reciting a terrifyingly long list of rules and regulations. There were five other WAAFs in the house, she told them, as she marched them past a room full of chatter on the first floor next to a tiny bathroom and up two flights of stairs to the attic. The once-whitewashed room had five beds crammed against the eaves. There was hardly room to put their bags down.

'Hello, you lot,' a girl with a cockney accent and bleached hair greeted them from the end of the best bed in the room. Tucked in the corner, it had space at the side for a small bedside table.

'I'm Viv,' the girl announced. 'Sorry, but as I got here first, I bagsied this bed. Hope you don't mind.' Viv carried on unpacking her bag and placed a picture of her family on the Formica table next to her. It was a family group in front of a block of tenement flats with the gaunt face of a woman in a turban and pinny, a man in blue overalls and three small boys with scuffed knees. A younger Viv was standing between them. In front of them all was an elderly lady in black, sitting on an upright chair, with one gnarled hand clutching a wooden stick in front of her.

Marion sniffed and put her bag down on the bed under the window and Amy hung back until Alice and Lily had chosen their beds. Mrs Porter warned that they were only allowed to fill the bathroom wash basin with cold water to the red line as they would be taken to Derby Baths for their weekly ablutions. Then she prodded her watch as she told them tea was at six sharp and left the girls to sort themselves out. The experienced WAAFs automatically all laid out their clothes in the same order, pushing their gas masks and tin hats under the beds. Alice, Lily and Viv kept up a constant chatter, swapping stories about their training so far. Viv had been at Morecambe so knew the best Blackpool haunts, she told them with pride. Amy sat, listening with a vague expression on her face and Marion unceremoniously moved Viv's dressing gown from the peg on the back of the door to make room for her own handmade uniform.

'Is she always like that?' Viv whispered to Lily on their way down the thin, red floral carpeted stairs to tea.

'Yes,' Lily replied with a sigh. 'She seems to think she's above us and so superior because her family's got money. If I hear once more that her uncle is a Wing Commander, I'll scream.'

Alice butted in from the stair behind, 'I can't believe she's ended up in Blackpool with us. On the way here, she asked for a porter at the station! I could have died. There were service people all over the place struggling with kit bags and Princess Marion demanded help with her bag . . . and what's worse, a porter came and helped her! She made a great show of giving him a shilling. A whole shilling! I'd have moved her bag for that.'

'It just shows, if you behave like royalty, you'll get treated like it,' Lily said.

'Well, she isn't bloomin' royalty here,' Alice replied, pushing the door open into the dining room.

The room sported an alarming display of swirling wallpaper that was so old it had probably been put up before the Great War. The fireplace was blocked up with newspaper and the nicotine-stained yellow curtains were hanging off the pelmet on one side. The faded carpet had been trodden by guests for decades and in the middle was a long wooden table with small, red plastic salt and pepper holders at each end. The other WAAFs were already tucking into their Woolton pie, vegetable pie recommended to all rationed households by the Minister of Food, Lord Woolton. Marion was sitting at the long table, helping herself to the limited amount of reconstituted dried milk for her tea. The other five WAAFs smiled, nodded hello to the new group and passed the remaining food down to the new arrivals.

'Well, I can forgive Mrs P anything,' Viv said, sitting down next to Marion and giving her a meaningful glance as she quickly took the milk jug from her, 'as long as she keeps finding enough veg to make a boring pie taste like this.' At home, in the east end of London, she explained, there were hardly any shops left where they could buy food and they had been close to starvation. Her dad was in the Far East and her mum worked long shifts at the local factory. Viv would do night shifts so that between them, they could look after her three young brothers as well as her elderly nan, who was quite a taskmaster and constantly complained about the paltry food available. Viv had had to travel miles across the city and queue for hours just to get a stale loaf of bread. Alice and Lily caught each other's eye, realising the deprivations they had experienced so far were nothing compared to what Viv and her family had suffered.

There was not much time to enjoy the delights of the seaside town. Their days were filled with lectures about the King's Regulations and how to conduct themselves off camp, the RAF, information about the different ranks and Morse lessons in the huge hall of Olympia. They were slowly learning to make sense of the noises that came out of the wireless sets, ignoring the marching that was going on outside their window. The girls had giggled at first, as the troops outside had broken step and tiptoed past to try to avoid disturbing them, but gradually Lily managed to sift out all outside noise and concentrate. She was surprised to find the Morse made complete sense to her and she soon mastered the alphabet. The Morse signals got quicker and quicker and sometimes gradually reduced in volume, but Lily found a peace in the reassuring noises coming out of her headphones. It was as if the war was blocked out by the rhythmic tones.

Unlike many of her schoolmates, Lily had not left school at fourteen but had continued her education until she was seventeen, though she had struggled with lessons that did not interest her. History, French and English were her favourite subjects, but Mother Philomena despaired of her Geography and science. She muddled along, envious of those who found lessons and exams easy. Her personality had grown as her academic application dwindled and she had found it easier to entertain people by making them laugh rather than getting an A grade. It had become a bit of a mask to be the class clown rather than compete with the brainier girls, but finding she was good at Morse was a bit of a shock and she still wasn't sure how to deal with it.

Alice, with her farming background, seemed to be unphased by it all and took every day in a calm, matter of fact manner. She just shrugged her shoulders and dealt with the crisis of the day in her down to earth Lancashire tones.

One evening, when the bedroom was a seething mass of premenstrual tension, Alice took charge.

'I have three squabbling brothers,' she told Lily and Viv, who were rebelling against Marion's insistence that her range of expensive cosmetics merited Viv's bedside table, 'and even they're not as bad as you lot.' She turned to Marion.'That table is Viv's, Marion. She was here first. Deal with it.'

Marion knew she was beaten and, with a pout, put her treasured bits of makeup under the bed.

Each item of their kit was identical and in the confined space of the top floor room, there were constant arguments about who owned what. Marion was particularly pernickety about her worldly goods and she would attack the whole room if she thought one of the girls had been using her things.

One day, when Alice and Lily were off duty, the two of them spent a very pleasant couple of hours at the funfair on the front. In a gaudy gift shop, they found some children's stickers that proclaimed 'This belongs to . . .' with a space for a name. They inserted Marion's name and when she was out of the room, they placed one on each and every one of her things, including her pillow, her shoes and even her hair clips. The following morning, she was furious, but her anger was undermined by the fact that a stray sticker had come off her pillow and stuck to her forehead. It wrinkled as she berated the group of girls who were holding onto each other in fits of giggles, completely unabashed. Marion stormed out of the room, determined to take her revenge by getting to the jampot on the breakfast table first, unaware she still had the sticker on her head. She had no idea why the other WAAFs in the dining room were laughing at her and even Mrs Porter slyly passed her the toast with a knowing grin. In a fury, she made sure she took nearly all the milk that was in the small jug next to the teapot.

They were all having to learn lessons about how to cope with deprivation and compromise, and that included Marion, but Lily's years of dealing with conflict using a smile and a joke failed dismally when confronted with the impassive face of Sergeant Horrocks. The sergeant was a woman in her late twenties, her once-pretty face soured by a scowl she wore most of the time. Small in stature, with endless clips to hold back her greasy brown hair, she seemed to revel in any discomfort that the girls were facing and her mouth would twist into a smile when she saw their misery at the cold, the food or the conditions. Lily, in particular, could do nothing right and any infraction was jumped upon, leading to a charge or a penalty. As soon as Lily had arrived, the sergeant's eyes fixed on the young WAAF, making Lily squirm in discomfort. It was almost as if she recognised her. Being the victim of a vendetta was a new experience for Lily, who needed to be popular, and she was struggling to know how to deal with being so disliked. Unable to break through the icy barrier with the sergeant, she concentrated on making the other girls laugh, often at the expense of her superiors, and Sergeant Horrocks was perfect material for a merciless mimic.

One day, coming out of the Winter Gardens, Lily was at her wits' end. The sergeant, in a bid to humiliate her, had picked her out for a particularly gruelling inspection and had measured her hemline, her sleeve line and the distance between her collar and her hair. Lily re-enacted the scene for her friends.

'This is me,' she pronounced to them all, pointing at a lamp-post outside the entrance to Olympia. 'Notice how slim I am? Now guess who this is.' Warming to her audience, Lily clicked her heels into place, held back her hair with one hand and 'inspected' every aspect of the lamp-post, prodding it with her finger as she tutted and snarled. The girls had to hold onto each other as they succumbed to the giggles. Lily strutted through the middle of them. She was very good and so absorbed in her role-play that she failed to see her victim emerge from the doorway. Sergeant Horrocks was on her way to her own billet in the next street to the girls but when she spotted the little group, she doubled back around the corner so she could spy on them from a distance. Her eyes narrowed as she watched the little scene being played out in front of her. Lily carried on in blissful ignorance, prodding the lamp-post with renewed enthusiasm and flicking off imaginary strands of hair from its 'collar'. Sergeant Horrocks slowly reversed back down the street behind her, nodding to herself. Alice looked up and frowned, unsure who the disappearing figure was but, in any case, elbowed Lily and motioned with her head that they needed to move off the pavement. The sergeant strode away with small, angry steps. Her stomach was in a whirl. From the first moment she had spotted the golden-haired girl, the sergeant had experienced a fury she thought she had left behind a few years before when her brittle heart had been broken. How dare that slip of a girl have this effect on her? She had tried to reason with herself that it was only Lily Mullins's appearance that recalled such painful memories, but now she had a reason to hate the girl herself. It felt good.

Lily Mullins thought she could get the better of her, Agatha Horrocks, did she?

'Well, we'll see about that,' the sergeant muttered, twisting her mouth sideways.

There was also one other person in their group who was impervious to Lily's mischievous sense of humour and that was Amy.

Amy was speaking less and less, barely noticing what was going on around her. She went around like an automaton, hardly saying a word and staring into space as the girls chattered and giggled whilst getting ready for bed.

'We have to do something,' Alice confided to Lily and Viv in the hallway one tea-time. 'I've asked to see the welfare officer and she said she will come over tomorrow.'

'I think we have to give Amy warning,' Lily said.

'OK, let's confess and see what she says,' Alice agreed.

The confrontation did not go well. Alice and Lily sat on either side of Amy with Viv opposite in their room after blackout that night. Marion lay on her bed, pretending to read a magazine. Amy sat in silence as they gently tried to tell her how worried they were about her. Her eyes were blank as they gradually introduced her to the idea that they had been so concerned, they had asked for help from the welfare officer.

Amy shrugged and her hand lay limp in Alice's.

'OK,' she said finally.

There was nothing else the girls could do. Alice patted her hand and they stood up to get their pyjamas on.

The next morning, the gong was sounded from downstairs as usual.

Lily moaned and covered her head with her blanket. 'It's still dark.'

'That's because of the blackout,' Viv muttered from under her pillow.

'No, it's because it's February and it's ridiculous o'clock.' Alice chimed in.

Lily peered out from the blanket and her eyes gradually adjusted to the dark. She looked over at Amy's bed and sat upright in horror.

'She's gone,' she started.

'Who?'

'Amy' Lily told Viv, who by now was grabbing at the light switch.

'She can't have done, I didn't hear a thing,' Viv said.

'You wouldn't hear if a bomb dropped on the house,' Marion retorted from her bed, glaring at the others who had stood up and were staring at the discarded pyjamas and abandoned bed.

'What do we do now?' Lily asked them both.

'We have to tell someone – and now,' Viv replied, taking control. 'Where can she have gone, at night and in the blackout?'

The day became a nightmare. The three girls were taken to be interviewed by the welfare officer and the military police. They were marched along by Sergeant Horrocks, who glared at Lily as if it were her fault. But the truth was they were all wracked with guilt, convinced that they had pushed Amy to take drastic action and felt directly responsible for the young girl's disappearance.

'They've got the lifeboat out,' a girl called Fran told them with a frown at dinner-time.

Lily grabbed Alice's hand and squeezed her fingers in an attempt at reassurance.

Neither of the girls could eat much of the macaroni cheese and they struggled to concentrate throughout the afternoon. Marion had been too busy eating everyone's leftovers to be overly concerned.

'She'll turn up when she gets hungry,' she said confidently. 'Either that or the police will find her. She can't have gone far; she didn't take her purse with her.'

But the day dragged on and there was no news. At bedtime, the bedroom seemed empty and colder than usual and Lily wrapped her blanket around her to try and stop the shivering.

'It's such a cold night,' she said. 'Where the hell is she?'

'I'm sure they'll have found her by the morning,' said Viv, 'so get some sleep.'

But they tossed and turned and eventually Lily sat up.

'It's no good, I can't sleep while poor Amy is out there, freezing and starving to death. I'm going to see if I can find her.'

'You can't go out, the police will get you if you are out without a pass,' Viv warned, but Lily was already putting her greatcoat on over her pyjamas.

'OK, we'll all go,' Alice said, pushing back her crumpled covers. 'All for one and all that. But if we get caught out at this time of night we'll be in trouble.'

Marion turned over and plumped her pillow.

'I'll just stay here in case she comes back'

The other three glared at her and sneaked down the stairs, avoiding the fourth step that creaked, turned the key and slipped out of the front door, putting it on the latch so they could get in again.

'I hope the Jerries don't choose tonight to bomb Blackpool,' Viv hissed.

They all stood and waited for their eyes to get used to the pitch black, clinging onto each other in fright. They were risking so much being out this late without a pass.

It was Alice who took a step forward. 'Come on, if we're going to do this, we may as well make it worthwhile,' she whispered.

Alice started off down the street with determination. Lily and Viv looked at each other, shrugged and raced to catch up. There could be no going back.

Chapter 10

4th March, 1943

Dear Lily,

I hope this letter finds you. I don't know where you are now, but I hope you are keeping safe, warm and well-fed. I can't remember the last time I had a beer but I'm sure you're finding regular supplies of cider. I envy you. It's amazing how important food becomes in wartime, isn't it? Do you remember bananas? I have dreams about them, with ice cream and a chocolate topping! We're eating some pretty strange combinations, but I do draw the line at sheep's eyes, which I know some of the lads have been offered by the locals!

I'm fine. It's been a bit hairy here, but I've made two really good mates. We're known as the 3Js: Jackson (me, but you knew that!), Eddie Jenkins and Frank Jones. They are both doing the same job as me and we have a lot of laughs in the middle of this mad world. Eddie's from Bideford. Sounds a nice place – lovely beach. He had just qualified as a geography teacher – your favourite subject! Frank's a city boy like me. He's a bus driver from Bristol and has got a great accent that really confuses the old man. You know we call our captain the old man, but actually, he's only twenty-seven!

Yesterday, I split my trousers! I had to clamber up the transporter in a hurry and in the process managed to rip my backside. Frank and Eddie were in a pleat watching me try to walk backwards so as not to embarrass myself but then someone mentioned that the locals are amazing at sewing, so when we came to a village, I changed and took them to someone in a little hut to be repaired. They were done within an hour and they were sewn brilliantly! There wasn't a mark to show they'd been torn at all. Even Pam, with her embroidery skills would have been impressed. You once said you had trouble sewing on a button, so perhaps I should bring one of the tailors here home for you!

I'm meeting all sorts here. Last week I met a Ghurkha. They look fierce fellows but are amazing fighters. They have huge knives but will only draw them to fight. If you ask a Ghurkha to show you his knife, he has to cut himself, so I've learned to stop doing that, but the knives do look like something out of Arabian Nights*! Eddie was making his way back into camp on Tuesday* *and he suddenly felt a knife at his throat. It was the Ghurkha on duty – they move so silently, Eddie hadn't heard him. He was very grateful they don't fight for the enemy, I can tell you.*

I wish I could tell you about what's going on here, but I'm not sure I know. We are just moved on, sometimes at a moment's notice, so we're always at the ready.

I hope you're OK. I know we're all coming across things that we haven't dealt with before and it can be hard, but we're tough Mancunians . . . remember that!

Take care,

Love,

Danny

Danny looked again at Lily's last letter. It was only short but it did tell him about one of the girls whose mother had died and how it had affected all the WAAFs in Lily's little group. He breathed deeply, trying to send waves of support across the continents. He was developing a deep need to protect Lily and it was a new experience for him. He was the youngest in the family and had been indulged as only the last born can be. His sisters bossed him, and his mother just smiled and patted his arm when he had tried to suggest he should take more responsibility. In a war where he was just a foot soldier, he often felt out of control and he found it calming to close his eyes and concentrate on how he could be the strong, capable one. Life was going to be so different when he got back . . . if he got back.

He looked over from his tent to his transporter. He had come to love it as a safe haven, despite the fact that it was so huge it should have been impossible to miss from the enemy aircraft who regularly sprayed the convoys with rapid fire, but so far it had survived unscathed. The drivers had all become increasingly concerned about the Americans, who flew so high to avoid being shot down, that there had been instances when they had mistaken the allies for the enemy.

'Danny, stop dreaming, we need to get these vehicles cleaned up and ready for moving.' Frank's voice shook him out of his thoughts. Frank was a welcome hand under the bonnet of a transporter. He had started out as a mechanic and just before the war began, had started to drive buses as well as fix them. They were all learning a great deal from this young man who was two years older than most of them, but he was also like an older brother and kept them all in line. Danny immediately sprang into action, jumping up from the makeshift hammock he had erected to keep him off the relentless sand. The two men worked in partnership, carefully dusting off the engine parts and adding oil where necessary.

'I heard that the pub I used to go to near Old Trafford was bombed,' Danny said in a muffled voice from the depths of the engine. 'Jerry did us a favour there. It really was a dive, but I hope the Albion still stands. I'd miss that old place and I want to show you it when this is all over. You'd like it. Lots of atmosphere.'

Frank looked up in surprise at him. It wasn't often that the men talked about after the war, it was seen as bad luck. Danny caught sight of his expression and grinned ruefully. 'You're right, I shouldn't plan that far ahead, but I was just thinking about home and normality.'

'Normality is an engine that clogs and planes that bomb us, that's all the normality we need to deal with right now.'

Danny nodded and they worked on in silence for a bit.

'Still thinking about that girl, what's her name? Lily?' Frank asked eventually.

'Nah, there are loads of them just waiting for Danny Jackson to come home. I won't know which one to kiss first.'

Frank laughed and looked sceptical. 'Yeah, sure. I believe you.'

At that moment, the familiar drone of a plane came out of the desert sky.

'Move it!' Frank was already half way to the makeshift bunker. Danny looked up for just a fraction of a second too long and then he gauged the distance between the transporter and the dugout and realised he would not make it. He had to make a decision – to dive under the transporter and hope the pilot missed his aim, or head out into the open and risk being in the target area.

'He who hesitates is lost' he angrily repeated his father's words as he hurled himself under the fuselage and waited to see if the gunfire strafing out of the sky towards the convoy had his name on it.

Chapter 11

'Where do we start?' Alice whispered.

'The pier,' Lily said with conviction.

'Why the pier?' Alice said.

'I don't know, it's just Amy seemed to like walking down to it.'

'OK, the pier it is,' Viv agreed and they set off, walking on their tip toes to avoid making a noise past all the boarding houses on the front.

The moon suddenly came out from behind the clouds and the girls were able to see where they were walking.

'It's bloody freezing,' Lily said through gritted teeth.

'It's colder for Amy,' Viv retorted, doubling her pace.

They silently sped along the pavement towards the pier, which looked sad and forlorn without the bright lights of the amusement arcades. The waves were lapping at its pillars, making a rhythmic sound which was almost reassuring in its normality.

When they got to the pier entrance, the gates were locked. All three of them laced their fingers against the cold iron and stared through to the wooden structure beyond.

'Now what, Lily?' Viv said.

'Let's look underneath.'

They all scrambled down to the beach and Lily called softly, 'Amy, Amy, are you there?'

There was no reply and they eventually gave up and clambered back up onto the prom.

'The Tower.' Lily said decidedly.

In silence, they made their way towards the Tower, which loomed like a dark metal monster over Blackpool Promenade.

'What time is it?' Alice asked.

'Two o'clock,' Lily replied, tilting her watch towards the moonlight. As she did so, she looked down the road and suddenly hissed, 'Police! Run!'

They turned and fled back down the prom towards the digs. The two military police officers started to run behind them.

'Split up!' Viv gasped. 'I'll turn next right, you carry on. I'll see you back at Mrs P's.'

The other two didn't have time to argue and ran as fast as they could. Fortunately, the police were quite a way behind and the girls had a head start.

Alice and Lily fell into the doorway of Mrs P's and pushed the door closed as quietly as they could. They were gasping for breath but stuffed their fists in their mouths, waiting to hear whether their pursuers ran past or not. There was a reassuring patter of one set of feet that gradually faded into the distance and they breathed a little easier.

They stayed as still as statues in the lobby waiting to see if Viv would appear. It was a good ten minutes before the door was slowly opened and a bedraggled Viv collapsed into Alice's arms.

'Can't speak . . . had to run miles . . . think he's gone . . .' she gasped.

'Oh I *am* glad to hear that,' a voice came from the stairs.

They turned in horror to see Mrs Porter, complete with pink curlers and a clashing red dressing gown standing on the stairs, fuming.

'Close that door and pull the curtain before we're all in trouble for breaking the blackout,' she said, her face stern.

'We . . .' Lily began.

'I don't want to hear it, but your officer will in the morning. Go to bed.'

'But . . .'

'Bed. NOW.'

They crept upstairs, veering to the right to avoid the statuesque figure that towered over them, arms folded, breathing heavily.

They did not dare speak when they got to their room, instead just gave each other a quick hug and got into their freezing cold beds, shivering from terror and exhaustion.

Lily glanced over at Marion, tucked down in her bed, seemingly oblivious.

The next morning, all the girls slept through the alarm until Marion woke them up.

'It's seven thirty, I've had breakfast, you've missed yours. I gather you didn't find Amy. I might have known it would be a wild goose chase.'

'Don't you care about anyone but yourself?' Alice yelled at her.

Marion considered this for a moment then shook her head.

'Well, certainly not some stupid girl who wanders off in the middle of the night and expects everyone else to traipse after her. And if I'd known you were going to be like this, I'd have left you sleeping and then you'd all have been on a charge.' She stood defiantly in the doorway, challenging them to argue with her. They were all so furious, they could not speak, let alone argue. They pushed past her down the stairs.

Mrs Porter was waiting for them in the hallway.

'Well?' she said, threateningly, clutching a tea towel like an instrument of torture.

The other five girls in the house were all sitting at the table with their plates in front of them. They were keen to watch the excitement and peered around the door frame to catch a sight of the guilty parties.

'We . . . we . . .' started Lily.

'We what?' Mrs Porter spat back.

'We went to see if we could find Amy.'

They all hung their heads while Mrs P absorbed this information.

'And where exactly did you think you might find the poor girl? In a bar or a dance hall maybe?'

'NO!' Lily looked up in horror. 'We just couldn't bear to think of her out in the cold. We just had to do something.'

'And those men following you, I suppose you're going to tell me they weren't boyfriends then?'

'Mrs Porter,' Viv interjected, calmly. 'They were police officers and we had to run to escape getting caught.'

Mrs P was silent for a moment, looking from one girl to the other, trying to weigh up whether they were telling the truth. 'Hmm. Well, we'll see about that. Get yourselves a cup of tea. You've missed breakfast and I'm not doing any more. You'll just have to be hungry; it's more than you deserve.'

Marion went past them with a smug smile on her face. She stopped at the mirror next to the hat stand and patted her hair before sweeping through the front door.

The Morse code did not make any sense to Lily that morning. At twelve o'clock, she could not stand it any longer. Marion, Viv and Alice watched her take off her headset and stride to the front of the room. They looked at each other and did the same.

'Yes?' Sergeant Horrocks barked.

'I'm sorry, Sarge, but our friend is missing and I can't concentrate until I know what has happened to her.'

'I am aware of ACW Hodgkins' situation. And what exactly do you think you can do about it? The authorities are out looking for her.'

'I think I know where she is,' Lily told her. 'I would like to be given leave to go and look.'

'You should tell the authorities. Leave it to them,' the sergeant replied, putting her head down to carry on with her paperwork.

'Please, Sergeant,' Lily begged, looking at Viv and Alice for support. She felt tears threatening to fall and blinked them back. A professional attitude was what was needed here.

The sergeant looked from one to the other of the four girls with intense dislike. At that moment, a commanding voice came from behind them.

'It's like this, Sarge . . .' Marion suddenly said, drawing herself up to tower above the little group.

The other girls swirled round in surprise to face her.

'. . . Amy is in a very vulnerable situation and has problems dealing with strangers. She won't show herself to anyone she doesn't know and I believe that we, her friends, can coax her to give herself up.'

Lily took one look at Marion's calm, superior face and for once was stunned into silence.

The sergeant stood up.

'Wait here,' she said, walking towards the door, leaving the four girls standing at the front of the room, watched by the rows of WAAFs who had adjusted their headsets to be able to listen to what was going on.

'Where do you think she is?' Alice whispered to Lily, watching the heels of Sergeant Horrocks click out purposefully into the corridor.

'The Italian Gardens . . . she told me her mother always wanted to go to Italy and never got there. I've only just remembered her talking about it and how her mum would have loved the gardens here because they would have given her a taste of Italy.'

'Well, we'd better go and find her there, then,' Marion said.

Alice took a sharp breath in and turned to say something cutting to Marion, but Lily dug her in the ribs.

'Leave it. Let's see what they say and whether they'll let us. It's been more than twenty-four hours; she'll be in a terrible state.'

The door opened and the commanding officer strode in, trailed by the welfare officer and the sergeant. The CO was a tall, thin man with a moustache. He was rarely seen and all pretence of listening to Morse was abandoned as everyone jumped to their feet to salute.

Those at the back craned their necks forward to hear.

'So, ACW Mullins, you think you know where Hodgkins is?' the CO said.

'Yes, Sir. I think she might be in the Italian Gardens. She explained how she wished she'd taken her mum there.'

'Very well, you can take two hours to see if you can find her. Take this WAAF here, Hill, is it?' He looked away from Marion and turned to the sergeant for confirmation. 'Here are your passes. The other two can go back to their desks.'

Alice was dumbfounded. She could not move, she was in such a fury.

'Yes?' the tall, commanding CO peered down at her.

'Nothing, Sir, it's just that ACW Hill doesn't know Amy like I do.'

The CO shrugged with complete disdain at her outburst, gave her a stern warning look and walked out of the room. Sergeant Horrocks sat back down at her desk, glaring at the rest of the girls in the room, who had suddenly become absorbed in their wireless sets.

Alice grabbed hold of Lily's arm and hissed, 'You find her and keep Marion out of the way. I couldn't bear it if she found her. You know how she would lord it over us and never let us forget.'

The welfare officer beckoned Marion and Lily into the corridor, leaving Viv and Alice with no choice but to go back to their seats.

'Now, listen you girls. We're letting you go because what ACW Hill said makes sense. We know Hodgkins is hiding somewhere and the sight of police wouldn't encourage her to show herself. So, we're prepared to give you time to look for her, but you must report back at the first sign of her. Do not, and I repeat do not, try to deal with any medical emergency yourselves. One of you stays with her and the other comes straight back here. Do you hear me?'

'Yes, Ma'am,' both girls nodded.

'And take a blanket and some water with you.'

As they set off Lily's mind raced, trying to remember where she had gone with Amy on their last weekend off. It had been a cold, sunny Sunday afternoon and they had wandered among the flowerbeds, full of winter foliage and an odd promise of spring with early snowdrops. Amy had commented that the flowers had not realised there was a war going on and it was strange that they were coming up as if nothing had happened. Lily hurried along the front towards the gardens with Marion just behind her. Her heart was thumping. It had been such a cold night and without food or drink, Amy could be in a really bad way.

Marion, for once, did not speak, for which Lily was grateful. She pulled up her collar against the biting wind and prayed silently.

When they got to the entrance to the gardens, Lily stood for a moment, deciding which way to go.

'Let's try the shelters.'

The first two were empty apart from some pigeons pecking at the ground. As they approached the third one, tucked out of sight, they spotted a huddled figure, almost hidden in the corner. Lily, the sense of relief threatening to engulf her, signalled to Marion to stay where she was and crept up to the still figure.

'Amy,' she said gently. 'Amy, wake up. It's me, Lily.'

There was no movement and Lily felt her heart lurch in panic.

'Amy,' she said, more urgently, putting out her hand to touch the girl's arm. 'Amy, please wake up'.

There was a slight murmur from Amy and Lily let out a long breath.

'Go back to Olympia and get help!' she shouted to Marion. 'NOW!,' she shouted again, realising that Marion was rooted to the spot.

Lily watched Marion finally run off back down the path and sat down next to Amy. She carefully wrapped the blanket around her friend, cuddling her to get her warm.

'You've given us all such a fright,' she said quietly, not knowing whether Amy could hear her or not. 'This war is bad enough without you going off and putting yourself at risk. We've been so worried about you.'

There was no response, so Lily kept on talking, tenderly stroking Amy's arms.

'You know, we get strength to deal with all this from somewhere and you've been amazing. But running off doesn't help anyone. Think of your brother, how would he manage if anything happened to you? And your dad? They all need you, now more than ever. You need to be strong, Amy. Your mum would want you to be strong. We're going to get through this war together and we're here to help you. Even Marion!'

There was a flicker of movement from Amy and Lily ploughed on. 'Yes, Marion. It was her who managed to get us a pass to come and find you. She's a force to be reckoned with, that's for sure. I'm sure even the CO was cowed by her.'

I've got to keep talking, thought Lily, *otherwise she might drift out of consciousness again.*

She went on, 'We came to look for you last night, nearly got nabbed by the MPs. I don't think Alice has ever run so fast. And we got back to find Mrs P in full battle dress on the stairs. We really thought we were in for it, but she was really quite sweet actually when she found out where we'd been.'

I'm rabbiting on now Lily thought, *I hope they come soon. I don't know whether to give her any water or not. Oh, I don't know what to do. Hurry up, Marion.*

'Do you know, I've got a nice cousin, Paul, who'd like you. He's in the RAF. Training to fly Lancasters. You'd like him too. He's a bit of all right. Nice blond quiff and lovely blue eyes. I'll save him for you. Wait till we get to our next posting, it'll be all dances and glam pilots. You'll come out of your shell then, won't you?'

The little body had slumped again, and Lily looked anxiously at the path. It was horribly empty.

Lily was getting desperate. She started to nervously hum 'You Must Have Been a Beautiful Baby,' rocking Amy backwards and forwards.

'You've got to be kidding, Mullins,' she muttered after two verses. 'You'll finish her off. Oh come on, pleaaaaase,' she begged the heavens.

It seemed an age, but finally the welfare officer, two medics with a stretcher and Marion came running towards them.

The medics immediately took charge, put Amy on a stretcher and wrapped her tightly in blankets. The welfare officer just nodded in approval at Lily before turning to join the rescue party, which was half running down the path towards the ambulance.

Marion turned to Lily and said: 'Now let's allow the experts to do their job and we can get back to a cup of tea.'

But Lily was shaking and her teeth were chattering. Her feet didn't seem able to move.

'Oh, for God's sake, pull yourself together,' Marion snapped. 'We've got one hospital case; we don't need another. My feet are freezing, my hair is messy enough to scare the Luftwaffe and I want to get back in the warm.'

That made Lily move. Her anger permeated the shock that had engulfed her and she haltingly began to walk back towards Olympia.

All the way back, Marion kept up a tirade about how she had had to run all the way back while Lily just sat in the shelter. She saw herself as the heroine of the hour and was obviously rehearsing her story for the mess that night. Lily, absorbed in the trauma of the morning, was too relieved that Amy had been found, and was still alive, to bother arguing.

'It's a cider for you,' Alice said that night, pushing through the throng at the bar in the Carleton. 'Sometimes, nothing but alcohol will do the trick.'

For once, Lily had been quiet all day. She still felt cold and shivered from time to time.

She grasped the glass gratefully, sipping at the amber-coloured cider. She felt its power reaching down into her stomach and she sighed deeply.

Alice elbowed her way through the crowd of locals and servicemen and women, steering her friend towards a small table in the corner.

'Now, you can tell me all about it. I've heard Marion's version of how she saved the day, but I want the story from you.

'Alice, it was horrible. I felt so helpless,' Lily blurted. 'I thought she was dead. I didn't know what to do.'

'You did exactly the right thing. Kept her warm, kept talking to her. What else could you have done?'

'I don't know, first aid, something . . . anything.'

The feeling of complete uselessness had overwhelmed Lily all day. She had gone over and over the scene, trying to work out how she could have helped more, but no matter how hard she tried, there was no answer.

'I want to do something with my life,' she said finally. 'I want to know how to deal with disasters, I want to do something apart from making people laugh.'

'OK,' said her friend slowly. 'And I want to be Prime Minister. So, let's start on the "improve Lily and Alice campaign" and by the end of this war, we'll rule the world. In the meantime, we'll have another cider, which will hit the spot and mean we'll at least think we already do!'

Chapter 12

Amy's health improved slowly in the hospital. Her dehydration and hypothermia were rapidly treated and physically she picked up within a few days, but her mental state was still fragile, and it was decided she should be sent to a psychiatric hospital near her home in Coventry for a while. Alice, Lily, Viv and Marion all went to visit her in the Infirmary, taking valuable chocolate they had cajoled out of a surprisingly compliant Mrs P. They were shocked at Amy's pale, thin face and despite perching on her bed and regaling her with tales of unfathomable Morse tests, Sergeant Horrocks's dreadful new haircut and Fran's attempt at flirtation with a tall, attractive warrant officer, her responses were sparse and disinterested.

'We'll just have to hope she improves when she gets home,' Alice said despondently as they left the hospital.'

Marion pulled her coat around her. 'I've done all I can; it's up to Amy now.'

Alice frowned at her. She hated to admit it, but Marion was probably right, albeit in a callous way. They had exams the next week and the pressure had been mounting on them to improve their Morse speeds. Amy was in the hands of the experts now.

A few days later, the girls were taken into a large room above Burton the Tailors and given headsets to wear. They were all nervous and there had been several torches under the bedclothes the night before as they each crammed for the test. Lily listened carefully to the dah dits and transcribed them with a furrowed brow.

'How do you think you did?' Alice asked her afterwards as they left the room. 'I couldn't hear for that bloody band.'

'What band?' Lily replied.

'The brass band in the background. Didn't you hear it?'

'No,' Lily replied, then thought a moment. 'Oh, yes, now you mention it, I heard it at the beginning, but then it disappeared.'

'No, it didn't. It went on all the way through. I found myself humming along to "When You Wish Upon a Star" instead of listening to the Morse. It was a nightmare.'

'Well, I didn't hear it once the Morse started,' said Lily.

Later in the afternoon, she went to get her marks for the test. She clutched them to her breast as she skipped along the corridor.

'At last, I've done something right' she said out loud.

'Well, that will be a first,' she heard from behind her. Sergeant Horrocks had come out of a door on her left.

'Did well in the test, did you, Aircraftwoman Mullins? There's more to being a WAAF than hearing a bit of Morse.'

'Yes, Sarge,' Lily replied, trying to keep the triumphant tone out of her voice.

'We'll see tomorrow when you have to take your set to pieces and put it back together again.'

'Yes, Sergeant.'

Lily's shoulders drooped. She knew the sergeant was right. She was technically hopeless and all the cramming in the world with a torch under the bedclothes was not going to help her.

Alice was an expert at the buttons and whistles as the girls called them. She could wire plugs, fix kettles and change fuses as easily as the others could light up a cigarette. Alice was sympathetic to Lily, but pragmatic.

'You probably won't ever be posted to the desert and have to mend your set, so I wouldn't worry. I only just scraped through the Morse and you did really well in that.'

'Yes, but I have to pass the test or else I'll be shipped out of here back to munitions.'

'Nah. You have to stay to keep Sergeant Horrible in line.'

'What is it about that woman?' Lily wondered out loud. 'What have I ever done to her? Why does she hate me?'

'I don't know,' Alice said, suddenly recalling the scene with the lamp-post outside Olympia, but then shook her head.

Maybe that person I saw was Horrocks. But surely, it couldn't have been that. It was only a bit of fun, she reasoned, deciding to keep her suspicions to herself.

'Anyway,' she said out loud, 'she's a bitter, twisted woman, so you'd better watch out for her.'

The following day was like a bad dream for Lily. Her mind went blank when she was faced with a broken set. She twiddled with a few wires, tried to push them back into the set and then hopefully tried pressing the Morse key. Nothing. She was nearly in tears with the frustration and looked around at all the other bent heads, calmly getting on with the task at hand.

The male officer who was overseeing the test came over to her. 'Having trouble?' he said gently.

'Yes, I can't seem to make it work.'

'Well, it won't unless you switch it on,' he bent down and whispered. She was a good pupil and obviously suffering from exam nerves.

Lily smiled gratefully at him and flicked the switch, but felt her face going bright crimson. A reassuring clicking noise came from the Morse key and she breathed a huge sigh of relief.

Lily gave herself a talking to. *How am I ever going to be a pilot if I can't even get a small radio set to work? I'd probably forget to turn the engines on and then wonder why the plane wasn't moving. This terror of technology is getting beyond a joke. I have to deal with it.*

She sat in gloom in the mess later that evening. Alice tackled the problem head on.

'We're actually the perfect WAAF between us,' Alice reasoned, 'I have the technical skills and you have the practical ones.'

'Oh, that's just great, we'll tell the air force we have to go everywhere together so we can do one job between us,' Lily replied despondently.

'Well, yes, we could do that or . . .'

'Or what?'

'You can help me to be better at Morse and I'll help you to become more technical.'

'Sounds simple, but you have no idea how thick I am,' Lily replied.

'Don't be silly, you've got a brain, you just need to key into the bit that will help you understand it all.'

'Have to be a bloody big key!'

'But first, we get an evening pass for tomorrow from that lovely Officer Hales and we go out. Alcohol will help,' Alice added, pushing Lily towards the warrant officer's room.

'Enter,' Sergeant Horrocks's terse tones called from behind the door.

Alice groaned. 'What's she doing in there?'

'Waiting to turn us down for an evening pass,' Lily replied resignedly.

Sergeant Horrocks was seated behind the desk, almost masked by the huge pile of paperwork in front of her.

'We were looking for the warrant officer, Sergeant,' Lily ventured.

'Stand up straight and straighten your tie. Uniform infraction. On a charge, ACW Mullins.'

Lily slumped, mentally counting up this week's offences, which now came to three.

'Stand up straight or there'll be another charge,' Sergeant Horrocks barked at her. 'Warrant Officer Hales has been called away, what was it you wanted?'

Alice glanced at Lily. This was going to be harder than they thought.

'We wanted to ask for a pass for tomorrow night, Sarge.'

Sergeant Horrocks looked up from one to the other, resting her stern gaze on Lily.

'I somehow think ACW Mullins is going to be otherwise occupied once she's been up before the Duty Office in the morning. I suspect it will be extra cleaning duty in the kitchens, they've got a busy night tomorrow,' she added gleefully.

Lily closed the door behind them and sighed deeply. 'What is it with that woman?'

'I don't know, but it's ruining our social life,' Alice put her arm around her friend's shoulders.

'Bloody marvellous, everyone else is drinking and dancing their way through this war and I'll be doing jankers in the kitchen at the mercy of a five-foot tyrant who hates me.'

The following night, the girls flopped on their beds back at Mrs Porter's. Lily had just half an hour spare before she had to report to the kitchens. Alice decided desperate measures were called for and went downstairs to negotiate with Marion to buy some gin from her at twice its cost. Marion had just lost a shilling at cards with one of the other girls and was not feeling generous but after some hard bargaining by Alice, gave in and went to her locker in the hall to unearth a bottle. Alice took it triumphantly into the bedroom, balancing two enamel cups as she closed the door.

'You'll have to imagine the lemon and ice . . . oh and the cut-glass goblets, but at least it will have you set up for kitchen duty.'

'I can't,' Lily smiled ruefully. 'You know the penalty for drinking on duty.'

'OK, but I'll save some for when you finish and then the memory of bits of congealed bacon fat from behind the sink will fade.'

'Thanks a lot, I hadn't thought about that,' Lily grimaced, looking longingly at the tin mug. She glanced at her watch.

'Hell, I've got to go, don't drink it all without me.'

Alice grinned and pretended to take a large swig. Lily threw her pillow at her and then put her coat on to leave.

The congealed fat was only one of Lily's problems that night. The cooks had been preparing a buffet for the CO and visiting brass and there was a mess everywhere, with flour splattered across the work surfaces. It took two hours for Lily to scour them with boiling water and caustic soda and then she still had the floors to do. Lily stood up, stretching her aching back and looked in despair at the floor. It was filthy, covered in grease and dirt. She resignedly reached for the squeegee and got down on her hands and knees, putting a rag under her, but nearly gagged when she got to the drain at the top end of the server. It was full of muck and Lily had to look away as she scooped it up to dispose of it. Any illusions that the RAF was going to be glamorous were completely dispelled.

Finally, she was able to leave the spotlessly clean kitchen and head back to the billet in the dark, dragging her tired feet. She came around a corner near the Medical Centre but faltered as she saw a figure coming out. It was Sergeant Horrocks firmly shutting the door behind her and hurrying down the steps. Lily was in no mood for an altercation so pressed herself back against the wall, and the sergeant went straight past her as if she did not exist and scurried off into the dark, clutching her handbag. Lily stood and watched her for a minute, puzzled.

She reached Mrs Porter's and found Alice sat up in bed, with the two mugs of gin next to her in readiness. Marion and Viv had gone to the pub with the RAF men from down the road.

'You are an angel,' Lily said to her friend, reaching out for the proffered cup. 'My hands are red raw, I am now officially an expert in filthy drains and may have found my future career as a cleaner. But Alice, listen, you'll never believe what I've just seen.'

She tucked her feet under her on her bed, drank hungrily at the gin and told Alice what had just happened.

'You mean she didn't even notice you?'

'No, not a flicker of recognition. It was really weird. It was as if she didn't even see me.'

'Do you think she's in trouble? That would be divine justice, if she had got into trouble while she's doling out punishments to everyone else.'

'I don't know and, quite frankly, I don't care tonight, I'm so tired. I just know this gin is like nectar and I want another cup.'

Chapter 13

The following night, Alice and Lily tracked down Warrant Officer Hales and got a pass each. Viv and Marion already had theirs so the four of them decided to go to a dance at the Palace.

It seemed an age since they had gone to a dance and they could not contain their excitement as they got ready. Viv yelped after she burnt herself on the poker that they used to spread boot polish on their shoes. 'Dammit, will anyone really think these shoes are patent and not standard issue? I do this every time.' She sucked her fingers to ease the pain.

'It's such a shame we only have our uniforms to wear,' Marion complained, patting her blouse into her skirt, 'I have the most adorable little Dior number that would be perfect for tonight.'

'Such perfection might be wasted on the *hoi polloi* of Blackpool,' Alice said, rubbing her scalp with some liquid out of a bottle. 'I'm not sure this Eau de Cologne works. Oh, for a real bath to be able to wash my hair properly.'

At last they were ready, uniforms neat, hair in place and in high spirits. Even Marion was struggling to find things to moan about.

A night out was a rare treat and they were all equally determined to forget the war and have some fun.

The dance hall was full of couples in uniform who were whirling around the dance floor to a band playing Glenn Miller. The four girls stood in the doorway, having given their greatcoats to the cloakroom assistant who carefully marked them with individual raffle tickets and hung them up next to 100 other identical coats.

They looked quickly around them, eyeing up the talent and the possibilities of the night. There was a glittery ball hanging from the ceiling and it cast a rainbow of colours across the dance floor making the sea of dull uniforms below appear sparkly and gay.

'Come on, we've only got passes until nine thirty so we'd better get a move on,' Alice said, pushing the others towards the bar.

Armed with gin and Italian vermouth, they stood for a moment while the last strains of 'Chattanooga Choo Choo' finished playing. A handsome soldier came up to Alice and whisked her away for a dance. She grinned back over his shoulder as she allowed him to put his arm around her waist and draw her to him. The strains of 'My Baby Just Cares for Me' rang out and Alice concentrated on her feet, moving them purposefully across the floor.

Lily was tapped on the shoulder by a tall, serious looking young man in a naval uniform. 'Would you like to dance?'

'Yes, please,' she said and took his arm. He was a good height as a dance partner but his hand around her waist was too tight and Lily pulled back a little as they joined the dance floor. Immediately two of his friends approached Marion and Viv and they disappeared into the throng.

'What's your name?'

'Lily. What's yours?'

'Doug, we're training here, what about you?'

'Yes, wireless operators,' she mouthed as they got nearer the band.

'It's just begun for us, hasn't it? Funny to think some people have been in it for years already.'

'Yes, there's a big war out there,' she said thoughtfully, a dark-haired Tommy's face emerging from her memory. A similar scene from three years before came back to her, when it was Danny who was leading her around the dance floor at the Boys' Brigade in Manchester. It made her smile to think of it; his dancing was not up to Doug's, although he did have a great deal of enthusiasm, she recalled.

Two quicksteps and one waltz later, Doug steered Lily towards the bar and ordered her another gin and It. Lily twirled the glass in her fingers and looked sideways at her dance partner. He was quite good-looking, she decided, and he had been quite a nifty dancer, but his conversation had been a bit stilted and she wondered whether he was nervous.

'Where are you from?' she asked him, trying to draw him out.

'Portsmouth. That's why I joined the navy. All my family are in it. Said it would be a way for me to see the world, but so far I've only got to Blackpool. You?'

'Manchester.'

'Both places have seen a bit too much of this war already,' he said, avoiding looking at her.

Lily wondered what had happened to make him so pensive and decided it was going to be her job for the evening to cheer him up.

'Come on, let's really let our hair down and have some fun.'

He gave a rueful grin and took her hand. They gave themselves up to the strains of Duke Ellington songs and found they really were in step together. After a couple of dances, Alice came over and grabbed her arm from behind, pressing it hard. Lily immediately recognised the universal female message that it was time for a trip to the ladies' room.

Lily excused herself, agreeing to another drink as she sent Doug off to the bar.

'What's the matter?' she asked Alice when they were in the sanctity of the ladies' room. Her head was spinning a little with the dancing and the alcohol.

'It's my feet.'

'What's wrong with them?'

'They're too big,' Alice bemoaned, looking down at them and curling her toes upwards.

Lily burst out laughing.

'It's all right for you, you've got size five, mine are size seven. They're always getting in the way and he's really nice. I keep treading on his feet, it's a disaster!'

'Tell all,' Lily said, smiling as she turned with a wobble to adjust her hair in the mirror. She did not need another drink.

The young soldier was from Edinburgh and had, according to Alice, the most gorgeous Scottish accent. He was naturally known as Scottie and had a wonderful sense of humour that had kept Alice in giggles all evening, but the dancing had been fraught with danger and she was worried she had broken his toe.

'He was hobbling off to the bar. I don't think he'll come back.'

'Yes he will. I saw the way he looked at you; he likes you. Anyway, there's only one way to find out. Off you go,' Lily said as she propelled her friend back into the fray.

Doug was waiting with two glasses in his hands where she had left him, and Scottie was hovering nearby. Lily did not say anything but just pushed Alice forward.

Lily grinned as she watched Alice stick her bottom out so that her feet were pushed slightly backwards. She looked very ungainly, but Scottie seemed not to notice. Viv passed by with her partner and looked at Alice and then quizzically at Lily, who just smiled and shook her head in mock despair.

There was not much time for conversation, so Lily just threw herself into the joy of dancing with a tall, handsome man who knew how to lead her effortlessly around the hall. The gin had definitely gone to her head and by the time he reached down to kiss her, she was happy to lift up her face and close her eyes.

'Can I see you back to your digs?' he asked.

'What time is it?' Lily said, propelled into reality.

'Ten past nine.'

'Oh hell, I've got to go. Where are the others?'

Viv, Marion and Alice were all by the cloakroom, ready in their coats. Marion looked cross.

'Where have you been? We've been waiting for ages. If you make us late, we'll be in such trouble.'

Lily quickly found her cloakroom ticket and pushed it towards the girl behind the desk. She was still putting her coat on as she ran towards the door. Doug was waiting for her.

'Sorry, got to go,' she panted. 'Going to be in trouble. Maybe next time . . .?'

She trailed off, shrugged apologetically and raced off into the dark. The other three were already ahead of her.

'That's a promising romance nipped in the bud,' Lily thought. 'I'm like blooming Cinderella and my Prince

Charming is back there, abandoned and bewildered. Oh, will I ever get it right?'

The four girls ran full pelt back to Mrs Porter's house, giggling as Alice pounded her feet determinedly on the pavement.

'Look at them,' she gasped. 'I could march to Africa and back with these feet, but they can't find their way across a dance floor without causing death and destruction.'

They burst open the front door to find Mrs Porter purposefully coming out of the kitchen into the hall, a huge fob of keys in hand. She stopped when she saw them bunched together in the hall and pursed her lips.

'Just made it, I see. Shut that blackout, quick.' She manoeuvred Lily out of the way to turn the key in the lock. 'Honestly, you lot are more trouble than a pile of Germans. I just thank God my Polly is married with three young 'uns and not out there chasing men.'

Chapter 14

Danny's convoy was now in open desert and a prime target for enemy aircraft. A rumour was going round that tank transporter operatives were being killed faster than infantry because they were almost impossible to miss. Since he had dived under the fuselage, the convoy had been attacked on a regular basis. Only two days ago, a bomb had dropped on the transporter in front of Danny. The debris had scattered for 100 yards in all directions and he had had to cower behind the huge wheels to avoid being hit by shrapnel and bits of metal. The driver had fortunately been in the latrines at the time, so emerged from the roughly erected tarpaulin to see his machine being blown to smithereens. Despite his usual reasoning that fate had once more decided to let him live, Danny was having nightmares and now when he wanted to write to Lily, he struggled to even hold a pen. He laid his left hand on top of his shaking right and tried to reason with himself. Maybe he was feeling more weak than usual because he was suffering from soldier's blight, he decided. He was certainly spending far too much time in the latrines. He took hold of the pen more firmly.

'I will beat this,' the soldier told the desert around him. Danny settled into the uncomfortable position against the wheel arch and started to write.

20th March, 1943

Dear Lily,

How is life in good old Blighty? I do hope you're finding time to have some fun. Not too much, mind you! You must be trained by now. I often wonder whether I'll see you popping up out here. Some WAAFs have been posted nearby so I keep my eye out for you. It would be good to see your smiling face; it's not been much fun here recently. I bet you look really important in your uniform. The 3Js are still in one piece, I'm glad to say, but I'll be pleased when we're on the move again. We don't seem to be getting very far. The heat's unbearable and there's very little shade. This is my third year at this game. I can't believe it. The time flies when we are in action and drags really slowly when we're sat about, but we keep each other going with stories, some of them, I suspect, aren't true, but they make us laugh. I'm thinking of making up stories about some glamorous life back home but, truth be told, I'd just be glad to have my life as a salesman back. I find the skills come in useful though. I'm becoming an expert at haggling! I now have it off to a fine art and can wangle three ciggies for a small amount of tea. We're allowed to talk to the men, but we don't see many women out here and those we do see scurry past us like we're the devil . . . you wait till they meet the Americans! You'll be getting them there soon, I suspect, now they've finally decided to join the party. Then I will worry about you! All those Yanks strutting around, bribing you girls with nylons. You just watch them and don't believe a word they say!

So, time for a brew, I think. Look after yourself.

Love,

Danny

He breathed deeply; that was better. It always helped to write letters to Lily, not only because it brought a war-free time into focus but also because he felt he could share some of his everyday life with her. She was living a completely different war, but a war in the services nonetheless. His letters to his mum had to be so studiously casual and vague so as not to worry her, whereas with Lily, he knew they were both going through extraordinary experiences and it helped to write a little about what was going on, even if the truth was hidden behind platitudes and banter. To dole out advice made him feel as if he was a man in control of something, although in reality, he grinned to himself, he had never been in control with that self-assured young lady.

The grin turned into a grimace as he was suddenly doubled up in pain. He was going to have to go back to the medical tent. The hot sun and unclean water were wreaking havoc on his constitution and he was losing weight at an alarming rate.

He made a request to the orderly for yet another supply of diarrhoea tablets, but all he got was an order to go immediately to the medical officer.

'Got the runs?' the MO asked him.

'Yessir'

'How long have you had them?'

'Three weeks, Sir.'

'Eating?'

'Not really, Sir.'

'Hmm. Sick bay for you, I think.'

Danny's heart sank. Sick bay was a boiling hot tent with nothing to do all day but read the same magazines that had been passed around for three years.

'I feel fine, Sir'

'Seven days in sick bay,' came the unsympathetic reply as he dismissed Danny with a wave of his hand.

In fact, once Danny was offered no choice, his body gave in to the weakness that had been threatening to engulf him for nearly a month. He slept for hours on end and struggled with the stomach aches that doubled him up in the latrines for hours.

Fed on weak tea, mashed potato and eggs, he finally stopped losing weight and the symptoms subsided, but his boredom did not.

Jenkins and Jones visited him after five days but the tales they had to tell did not make Danny feel any better. He had missed some fierce fighting and his two friends, while making jokes and minimising the drama, had obviously been shaken by the experiences. Eddie, in particular, looked a little pale. It was a challenging transition going from teaching in a grammar school in Bideford to being just behind the front lines.

Danny threw off his covers in exasperation.

'And I'm lying around here, being useless while all of you lot are taking on the Hun. It's ridiculous. Orderly,' he shouted across the ward.

'Where do you think you're going?' the man in the white coat said, bustling towards him and putting a restraining hand on his arm. At that exact moment, Danny swayed and the orderly reached forward to grab him.

'You're not going anywhere just yet, Jackson.' Frank said. 'You'd be a liability. We don't need you. We can manage on our own you know.'

Danny sank back, overcome by weakness.

'No you can't. You'll get into trouble without me to keep you in order,' he muttered.

'Stop being so bloody heroic. You're hardly going to frighten the enemy in this state, are you?'

Danny watched his two friends leave the tent laughing and joking. He felt like an outsider. While he recuperated, he should have been able to enjoy the rest, after all he had been involved in a flat-out war for more than two years now, but he couldn't. He just felt isolated from his mates and as if he was missing out on the action. To occupy himself he wrote to Lily again.

26th March, 1943

Dear Lily,

I'm stuck in sick bay with a stomach bug and am feeling very sorry for myself. As you know, I hate being ill. Remember the pneumonia I had last winter that you called a head cold. I knew I was dying but you were very unsympathetic, as I recall. Well, I would like to worry you with tales of anguish and torment, but apparently I am expected to survive, which is a shame since I had hoped you would be wracked with remorse and would spend the rest of your life in widow's weeds in recompense for the dreadful way you treated this poor, ailing soldier. But, the fact is, I actually ate some meat today and I may, possibly, make it through. I've had a week of sitting around on my backside, chatting up the nurses and being generally demanding, but now they are all bored with me and have moved on to chaps who really deserve a bit more attention. This is obviously a blow to my pride and means I will have to skulk out of here within the next 24 hours back to the holiday camp that is my everyday life.

So, how are you? Have you had any leave recently? We are allowed a few days off here and there but in reality there is nowhere to go. There is very little chance of any relaxation, but we can occasionally find a little bar and take some time for ourselves. I am beginning to hope there may be an end to all this mayhem and I want to plan our first date when I get back. I thought we might go fishing near Reddish Vale and take a picnic. Imagine lying out in the sun on the bank while our supper attaches itself to our lines. I seem to remember there's some good chub and roach there and maybe even some brown trout. I'm sure you'll be really impressed with my fishing abilities. It's the hunter-gatherer in me! You do realise I am the original Tarzan, don't you? So, none of those city boys or, Heaven forbid, one of those Yanks for you, young lady! It's a real man you need. Have I convinced you yet? You can't blame a man for trying. You don't realise, it's either you, Lily Mullins, or the broad nurse who can carry one patient under each arm! You have to take pity on me and save me from this fate, Lily!

Love,

Danny

Chapter 15

The Americans had landed. Since Pearl Harbour, there had been little doubt that they would finally join the allies, and a frisson of excitement went around women all over the country as money-spending, glamorous Yanks arrived on British soil. The Blackpool WAAFs were no different. They had heard the moans from British servicemen who were not quite so impressed, finding it hard to compete with the endless supplies of cigarettes, a fizzy drink called Coca Cola, and chewing gum that the Americans could offer the British girls. And then there were those nylons.

'Oh, for warm, smooth legs instead of having to turn these horrible Lisle ones inside out,' Viv said with deep feeling, throwing her cap onto the bed and flopping down beside it. 'Just the thought of it's enough to lure me into the arms of a Yank.

'Viv Lockett!' Alice exclaimed. 'You be careful, you know what they say, "One Yank and they're off!"'

'Oh, keep yours on,' Viv retorted, 'I'm only joking.'

Lily and Alice caught each other's eye. They'd already seen Viv go through an alarmingly large number of servicemen and her flirting was becoming legendary. Viv's young life in the East End had been nothing but a succession of constant demands by her three brothers, her exhausted mother and her bad-tempered grandmother but WAAF life had opened up a new and exciting world for her and she was making the most of every minute. She had already regaled the girls with stories of boys whispering suggestions to her and while Alice and Lily had been shocked, Viv had welcomed the attention, proclaiming proudly that she would have a man by the end of the war.

Every week, rumours circulated that the Americans were heading north, but then they arrived at Bamber Bridge, just down the road from Blackpool. The girls caught their first sight of them at the mess. They were impossibly glamorous, and looked like film stars, complete with sunglasses that they called 'shades', even though Blackpool saw very little sun. They spoke in an appealing drawl and it was Marion, surprisingly, who was completely bowled over, forsaking the British military men for the more exciting stories of New York or California. For once, lineage didn't seem to matter.

At the pub that evening, Marion was the first through the door, deserting her roommates and making a beeline for Archie, Harry and Les, boys from 215 Squadron. Her voice rose above everyone else's and she revelled in every moment of attention, giggling and laughing loudly at their jokes. Alice was not impressed.

'You wait,' she told Lily and Viv. 'They'll flirt like mad and then get straight back on those planes home, leaving Marion in the lurch. She's asking for trouble,' she added, looking over as Marion gave an affected shriek of laughter.

It seemed to Lily that the war was going to all their heads. It was a necessity of life to have a boyfriend and every male was pounced on. There was a giddy atmosphere in the mess, the pub and on the dance floors as the men determinedly lived for the moment. Blackpool rarely saw any bombing raids and they had become used to living in a bubble where the war was a far and distant threat. It had started to feel unreal.

Lily sat in their room one night, reading Danny's letter over and over again. She had just finished her reply to him, but it had been a difficult letter to write. He had been a long way from her thoughts during the past few weeks, but the last letter worried her. His casual words did not fool her for a moment and she realised he had been really ill. She closed her eyes. Recently, she had been having problems remembering what he looked like but as soon as she read his letter, the picture of his chirpy face came back to her, only on this occasion, the face was pale and wan and he looked a great deal thinner. She suddenly sat up straight. It had never occurred to her that he might not come back. No, she told herself, he was indestructible. She pushed all the terrifying scenarios that were racing through her brain to the back of her mind. Danny was like a solid rock in her life and he was going to survive this war in one piece. She refused to have it any other way.

Lily picked up her pen to write to her parents. They were next on the list and she guiltily acknowledged that they, too, had been pushed to the back of her mind while she got on with her busy life. This new world she found herself in was exciting, her Morse test results were excellent and she was beginning to feel that she was becoming ACW Mullins, not just Silly Lily, the nickname Don had given her when he was a toddler. The uniform gave her a status and an importance she had never felt before. She walked taller, clicking her heels along wooden corridors. She was commanding respect from the officers who were training them because she was learning fast about the different types of aircraft, she had a passion for the world of the RAF, and for the first time in her life she knew what she was talking about. It was a novel experience and she was loving it.

Then there were the men. Lily's experience was very limited before Danny, apart from a few bungled kisses after the Boys' Brigade dances, and she knew she was naïve. She had known Danny since she was thirteen and, to be honest, he had always seemed more like a big brother to her, but now she was a grown woman of nineteen and romance was a more serious proposition.

She had been watching Viv and Marion out of the corner of her eye and while she did not approve of the overt flirting, she did have a sneaky practice at looking up through her eyelashes in front of the mirror.

'Stupid bat!' she told her reflection and leaned down to swill her face with freezing water.

'You just watch it, Mullins. This is a false world and none of it is real. You just remember who you are and don't get caught up in this merry-go-round. Knowing you, you'd be the one to fall off.'

With this warning to herself in mind, she felt superior to those girls like Viv and Marion who were being caught up in the maelstrom. However, she was enjoying her new-found freedom and was making the most of being a WAAF with an important job to do.

For that reason, she decided she would give Doug another chance and she urged Alice and Viv to fly the flag for the United Kingdom and spurn the Americans for home-grown men. They left Marion with her Yank entourage in the mess and went off to meet Doug, Scottie and a Welshman, inevitably called Taff, to go to the cinema.

'There aren't nearly as many air raids here as there were in Manchester,' Lily said to Doug as they walked in the balmy evening to the second showing at the Imperial, 'and with these long summer nights, you could almost forget we are at war.'

'Too risky to come over this far west,' Doug said, 'and besides which, what industry is there here? They're not interested in the Pleasure Beach.'

'I don't care what the reason is, I'm just enjoying not having my sleep disturbed four times a night,' Lily replied.

Doug smiled vaguely at her and moved towards the ticket kiosk. He was a pleasant companion but amidst the polite chatter, Lily felt he was holding back. They settled into their seats as Pathé News came on. She glanced across at him and watched his face become an impassive mask, almost as if he didn't hear the rousing music or see the black and white images of Italian towns being bombed by the RAF. She put her hand on his arm, but he didn't respond and she decided she would leave any questions until he was ready to talk.

The film was *The First of the Few* and the handsome face of David Niven kept Lily entranced as she followed the suspense of the story. It struck a chord with her as it triumphed the Spitfire and she felt a shiver of excitement at being part of the RAF. At the end of the film, they all stood for the National Anthem but Lily was thinking about her future. Once the training in Blackpool was over, she would be sent to an airfield where she would be helping pilots to communicate. It was a thrilling prospect and she felt she was ready for it.

The little group came out into the rain and scurried along the pavement, dodging the puddles and racing ahead. Lily got the giggles and Doug's face finally broke into a grin.

'It's good to see you smile,' she said, twirling round in front of him.

'I know, I'm sorry, it's not been easy.'

Lily waited. She didn't want to push him but Doug slowed down, letting the rain dribble down his face. He haltingly started to speak, telling her that his family had been at a matinee at the Princes Theatre in Portsmouth when there had been an air raid two years before. His two little nieces had been killed and his brother had been badly wounded. He told her in a matter-of-fact voice and in a way, that made it worse.

Lily put her arm around him and gave him a hug. She didn't know what to say but was learning that sometimes words aren't necessary.

They walked on to Mrs Porter's in the dark and this time it was Lily who gently reached up to kiss him. He was impassive for a moment and then fiercely kissed her back. He didn't seem able to stop. He was trembling but grabbing at her clothes in a desperate fumble. She recoiled at his passion and pushed him away in panic but he kept thrusting himself onto her. He was too strong for her and she felt his hand go under her skirt. 'No, Doug, no, get off me,' she gasped. He didn't respond and pushed his hand up her leg. At the same time, he was reaching for his trouser belt. She was becoming really frightened and used all her strength to push him from her, using her knee to bang into his groin. He lurched back in pain and finally Lily extricated herself from his arms and stood back. He was panting but lowered his head.

'I'm sorry,' he said. 'I must go. I'm sorry.'

Lily watched Doug in shock. He was stumbling, shaking his head from side to side in embarrassment and shame. She slowly got her key out, her hand shaking. She shook her head at her stupidity. She had taken Doug – and everyone else for that matter – at face value, and because they were all in the services, she had trusted everyone she had come across. It was a shocking awakening that a war did not erase people's problems, it just exacerbated them.

Chapter 16

Lily did not tell anyone about her experience, not even Alice. She decided Doug's behaviour was a reflection of the strain he was under from his nieces' deaths rather than an inherent flaw in his character and that he had enough to deal with without her making him a pariah, but she avoided him in the mess and at dances and he equally avoided catching her eye. Alice asked her what had happened between them and Lily replied casually, 'Oh, I'm not sticking to one man. I'm keeping my independence. Remember, I am going to pioneer women's flying and after all, David Niven may come along and then where would I be if I was stuck with some lame man?'

The incident had more effect on Lily than she was prepared to admit, but she decided she was going to try to push it to the back of her mind and concentrate on her career as a wireless operator. She reminded Alice of her promise to help her with the technical side of the course and got out all the books and instructions. Alice took her in hand in the same way she had helped her brothers when they were struggling with their times tables and they both concentrated on improving their weaknesses.

As always when she was trying to ignore something, Lily became obsessed with her latest goal and instead of going to the mess or the pub in her spare time, she would badger Alice to watch her take her set to pieces and put it together again. Every night that week, Lily got her manual out to stare at the diagrams. She tried turning the diagram the other way up but still it made no sense. At the weekend, after three hours of trying to explain to Lily what all the wires were, Alice's patience was beginning to wear thin and she was missing a night out with Scottie.

'Why have I always got two bits left over?' Lily said one night as she looked down at two screws that were left on her pillow.

'I don't know, but does it matter if it works?' Alice said in desperation, looking at the clock. 'If we don't get a move on, the pub will be closed. Come on, Lily, let's call it a day. You know we haven't got long.'

'You go, I'm going to start again.'

'Oh, for heaven's sake,' said Alice, with exasperation. She looked over at Lily, who was concentrating hard on a screwdriver, shrugged and got her coat.

The girls, unaware of Lily's attempts to blot out her experience with Doug, decided that their friend was becoming nothing short of boring and began to lose patience with her. But, with no other distractions, Lily started to put effort into her work for the first time ever and as her marks improved she became even more determined to succeed.

One night, when they were getting ready to go out and Lily was still at Olympia with her head in an instruction book, the girls gossiped about how different she was.

'She's even beginning to walk like Sergeant Horrocks,' Viv said, 'have you noticed, she clicks along the corridors?'

Alice nodded glumly.

'Frankly, I think she's becoming a pain in the neck,' Marion said, 'but then again, she always was. I personally think she's an empty-headed girl with little substance, but now she thinks she's God's gift to aviation. I've no time for her.'

Alice and Viv wanted to argue with Marion but, used to her outrageous outbursts, they just nodded. They had no ammunition to fight back with. Lily certainly had changed and even Alice could not work out why or how to bring back the friend she knew.

Marion, in the meantime, was concentrating on getting her hair to wave perfectly. She had crimped it with her fingers for an hour but it was still flopping into her eyes.

She started to ferret in Lily's things.

'What are you doing?' Alice demanded.

'She's got some wax somewhere. She had a candle she melted, I know she did.' Marion was rifling through Lily's tin hat, which held all her valuable bits and pieces.

'You'd go mad if she did that to your stuff,' Viv remonstrated.

'Ooh, look, she's got a tiny bit of Max Factor lipstick. That's too brash a colour for her.' Marion carefully put some on her own lips, pursing them up to make a pout.

Alice lost her temper and grabbed the lipstick as she pushed Marion out of the way.

'Get lost, Marion. Get your own lipstick, you know how valuable that is to Lily.'

'Oh well, I'm expecting my new consignment from Elizabeth Arden next week, they've developed new colours specifically to go with our uniforms. I won't need any of Lily Mullins's dregs then.'

She started to put on a sort of skin coloured liquid under her eyes. Viv, who suffered from terrible spots, really wanted to ignore her but then gave in.

'What's that?

'It's what they use on wounded soldiers, a sort of camouflage paint. It's going to be all the rage. It's just perfect for any slight puffiness under my eyes.'

Viv knew she was on a hiding to nowhere but asked anyway if she could borrow some.

'No,' came the stark reply.

They all carried on getting ready in silence with none of the cheerful banter that usually accompanied their preparations for a night out. The atmosphere was always so dull without Lily. She used to be the life and soul of the group but she was so focussed on work these days and seemed to have lost her sparkle and as a result, the group felt duller too.

An hour later, Lily came back, smiled wanly at them all and gave a distracted wave of her hand when they announced they were off. She did not even register the colour of Marion's lips. She had not bothered with makeup for weeks.

Viv and Alice went off arm-in-arm behind Marion who strutted in front of them. They were making the most of their final weeks in Blackpool and had gathered a fan club of men, both American and British. They giggled to see how the men vied with each other to get the girls' attention. Doug was still part of the crowd and he had started to flirt seriously with Viv.

'What about Lily?' Alice asked Viv, when they were on the way home after she had witnessed a particularly passionate embrace between Viv and Doug. 'Shouldn't you ask her whether she minds?'

'No, it's her loss. And you know what they say, all's fair in love and war,' Viv retorted, flicking her hair back.

Alice shrugged and let the subject drop but she decided to mention it to Lily that night.

'Lily, Viv's getting very close to Doug. How do you feel about that?' Alice whispered while they did their teeth in the bathroom.

'So?'

'Well, I thought you might mind, you were going out with him after all.'

Lily wondered for a moment whether she should say something – warn Viv, perhaps? But then she looked up to see Alice scrutinising her face and flicked back her hair carelessly. She still felt somehow, that Doug's behaviour was her fault and she was not ready to confess her own gullibility.

'No, I wasn't, I just dated him a few times. If Viv wants him that's fine. I'm concentrating on getting good marks in my exams, I haven't got time for men. I told you, I'm going to use this war to really get somewhere in life.'

Alice peered to see if Lily was telling the truth but Lily wasn't giving anything away. Alice frowned and took down her pyjamas from behind the door. This wasn't the Lily she knew, she had become hard and her determination to be top of the class was resulting in a rift between them. Alice was still struggling with Morse and Lily, despite her promises, seemed caught up in her own world and never seemed to have time to help her. The Lily who had been so caring and worried about Amy was a long way away.

By the time two more weeks had passed, Alice had almost given up trying to get through to Lily. The close friendship between them had dwindled to one of polite roommates. Alice realised how lonely she was without her friend but did not know how to get through to the Lily she had once known.

Chapter 17

It was the morning of the final exam, the WAAFs had gathered in the lobby to Olympia and were chatting nervously. Lily stood with her head held high but Alice felt sick. She had tried, really tried to concentrate on the ridiculous little noises that came out of the set but she was still making basic mistakes.

'Good luck, Lily', she said gently.

'Oh, yes, and you,' Lily replied in an offhand manner.

Alice sighed and started to move up the line towards the rows of desks waiting for them, headsets neatly placed.

Marion whispered from behind, 'Where's Viv?'

They looked round and scanned the line of girls but there was no sign of her. They all sat down but there was one desk empty that morning and from time to time Marion and Alice glanced over at the vacant space. The examiner then announced they would have until noon to finish their papers and counted them down to start, leaving them little time to worry about anything except the Morse that had started to come faster and faster in their earphones.

Alice felt panic rising in her stomach and tried to concentrate on the signals coming through. The expected speed was six words a minute and by the time the clock struck twelve, there were quite a few gaps in her transcribing. She looked back over her work.

'I think I've just about done it, but I hope the RAF doesn't rely on me to get its planes home.'

Lily was already standing up, looking, Alice thought grimly, ridiculously confident.

They went straight towards the mess for dinner. Alice was suddenly ravenous. It was cauliflower cheese and she tucked in. The chatter was all about the test and Alice announced she didn't care anymore. She had done her best and if the war effort didn't like it, then it could lump it. Her cows were missing her and she could always go home.

There was going to be a party that night and even Lily had promised to join them to celebrate the approaching end of their course. Their heads were bent as they talked about their plans for going out so none of them heard Warrant Officer Hales approaching.

'Attention!'

There was a scramble as they all got to their feet and saluted. Even Lily was getting quicker at it.

'I need Mullins, Hill and Colville. Follow me.'

With a puzzled glance at each other, Lily, Marion and Alice obeyed, following her into the foyer where Viv, looking pale and tired, was standing next to Doug. They were both in their uniforms but each had a small pansy attached to their lapel. Viv was also holding a small bunch of them in front of her.

'We're getting married,' she chirped in a high-pitched tone. 'And we want you to be witnesses.'

Lily looked sharply at Doug who caught her eye for a second and then looked down at the floor.

'Well, that's a bit sudden,' Marion said. 'What brought this on?'

'We just want to be together that's all,' Viv said, grabbing Doug's arm. 'Come on, we're due at the register office at one, we'll have to hurry.' And she started off towards the front door, leaving them all to follow in her wake.

The little group of girls turned to WO Hales who nodded, dug in her pocket for passes, and handed them out without saying a word.

They ran to catch up with Viv, who was heading down the street at a fast pace. Lily reached out to catch Doug's arm and pulled him back, looking at him quizzically.

'It's your fault,' he whispered bitterly, glancing to Viv, who was skipping along ahead. 'If you hadn't split up with me, I'd never have been in this position.'

'Is she pregnant?' Lily demanded in a whisper.

'Yes, of course she's bloody pregnant, you don't think I'd be doing this if she wasn't, do you?'

'Well, it's not my fault. You idiot.'

'Come on, we'll be late,' Viv called over her shoulder.

Lily dropped back, letting her hand fall from his shoulder and Alice almost ran into her.

'Lily, what the hell's going on?'

'I'll tell you later' Lily said, but her face had gone pale.

The wedding was a rushed affair, almost as if Viv was worried that Doug would run off if she gave him any time to think. He muttered 'I do' and then they retired to the Clifton Arms to have sausage rolls and cider. Viv made a great show of throwing her little bouquet of pansies over her shoulder towards Lily, Alice and Marion. Lily didn't even try to catch them, but Marion lurched forward and grabbed them.

The happy couple were allowed to go back to married quarters, so it was a subdued trio who curled up on their beds in their pyjamas at Mrs Porter's that night. The discarded bouquet was in a jug on the table next to Viv's empty bed.

It took Marion to speak first.

'Well, that was a turn up for the book. I suppose that's her out of the WAAFs now.'

'Yes, well, it will be when the baby arrives,' Lily said.

The other two nodded. They had worked that one out. Alice and Marion started to talk about the past few weeks, pin-pointing events that now took on a new significance. The times Doug and Viv had disappeared on the way home, under the cover of the blackout, the proprietary way Viv had treated Doug when they were in a crowd and how recently she had spent far too much time in the toilet first thing in the morning. The future of the pair was dissected and debated and it was agreed that the fact that Doug would have to move on shortly to take up his position on a ship was decidedly not a good start to married life.

It was later in the evening when Marion was snoring contentedly on the other side of the room that Alice tackled Lily.

'OK, Lily Mullins, tell all.'

There was a short silence before Lily started to fill Alice in on the events of the past couple of months. Alice kept quiet until she had finished, hearing the catch in Lily's voice as she described what had happened in the dark doorway. She crept out of bed and moved across to Lily's bed, pushing back the blanket to sit next to her friend. She put her arm around her just as Lily started to sob.

'It's my fault, I should have said something. I knew how he was and I could have warned her. He was holding in so much anger and passion, he wasn't thinking straight.'

'Well she knew exactly what she was doing,' Alice said, in her matter of fact tones. 'She wanted to get out of this war and this was her exit pass. She's got what she wants – a man, a baby and an escape route from Morse.'

This made Lily smile reluctantly in the dark.

'I'm sorry, Alice, I've been horrible. I just had to shut off from everything. I couldn't believe how shaken I was. I've never had a man touch me like that before and it frightened me.'

The two girls talked well into the night. Under the cover of darkness, they talked openly, revealing their sheltered upbringings and how the WAAFs had opened up a strange, new world for them. It was bringing them into contact with people they had never come across before and they were both re-evaluating.

'I have so much to do, Alice,' Lily finished, 'until I came here, I was happy to just work at Liners until I married and had children but now, I'm not so sure.'

'I know, I was destined for a life on the hills, wearing wellies, but I've found I'm really good at technical things and I'm beginning to think there must be more I can do – preferably indoors and out of the rain!'

They gave each other a hug and as Alice tiptoed back to her own bed, she added quietly, 'I'm glad you're back, Mullins, I've missed you!'

Chapter 18

4th April, 1943

Dear Lily,

You'll be glad to know I am out of hospital and back on duty. Perhaps I shouldn't have rushed to get back! We're moving on so quickly at the moment, there never seems to be a minute to take in where we are and certainly not much time to write. The towns where we stay just start to become familiar and hey presto, we're on the move again. It's unsettling and sometimes I can't remember which country we're in. At least we stay together as a group, which helps. I can't imagine what it must be like if you have to keep leaving friends behind – because you do make real friends in these circumstances, don't you? I hope you've found some nice friends, to say you're naturally chatty would be a polite way of putting it, so I am quite confident you are finding people you can get on with. You certainly need people to have a good laugh with and to keep this war in proportion.

Jones and Jenkins are saving my life. Not sure about my sanity, but their ridiculous sense of humour is certainly keeping me going! Last week, ENSA put on a show and we three volunteered to be the three witches from Macbeth *in a comedy version – well it was never going to be a serious one, was it? It was hysterical and I can honestly say we went down a storm. My 'toad' ingredient was a dead rat we had put a green beret on and it became the star of the show! I've discovered I have a secret side to me . . . I love dressing up and playing a part. I was always in the school plays, you know, usually as a shepherd with a checked tea towel on my head, but making people laugh was a great tonic for me, blow the audience! I may have to join Sale Operatic when I get back. I'll book you in for the opening night!*

I finally caught up with some mail from home this week and I got your letter as well, so thanks for that. It was really good to get all your news, and news from Mum too. Manchester has been a bit quieter than usual, so that's a relief and Mum's found a good supply of bruised fruit, so she's thrilled and has been busy making purée puds, but Dad's just been moaning that there isn't any pastry around it. Mum says she's banned him from mentioning apple pie more than once a day! He's really busy with his warden role but is feeling frustrated he can't join up. He did his bit last time, but I think he does envy me sometimes. He can have it! I'll sell it to the lowest bidder!

Time to go, I've got to go on the stage in this ridiculous comedy we're all in. Write soon. I do look forward to hearing all about those spam fritters.

Love,

Danny

It was hard to remain so positive at times, Danny thought, folding the letter into the envelope. The *Macbeth* show had been a desperate attempt by ENSA to cheer the men up. The fighting in Tunisia had been relentless and, in reality, the show had been a hurried, almost frantic evening, thrown together while they were preparing for the invasion of Sicily. He had heard of the plight of thousands of Italian troops who had been captured and knew that the British captives did not get such humane treatment. Since his close call in the desert, Danny had felt his odds of surviving the war were becoming more and more limited and he was having to fight against a feeling of hopelessness. Acting the fool in the *Macbeth* show had been a useful mask against reality. He sighed and tried to remember the words his father had uttered as he saw him off at the station that first morning. 'Remember you're a Jackson and we stand tall no matter what life throws at us. You will survive, God willing, but make sure your spirit survives too. The first is out of your hands, the second isn't.

Danny got back into his tank transporter, started up the familiar throaty engine, and thrust the unwilling gear stick into first gear. There was only one way forward.

It was a couple of weeks before he had time to write again.

18th April, 1943

Dear Lily,

I hope you're well and enjoying some nice late summer weather. I'm fine. Still managing to keep my head down. It's either full-on action or we're hanging round for hours, which is what's happening at the moment, but at least it gives me time to write to you. We've been in the same place for about a month now and we're ready to get back on the road. It's stupid really, we should be appreciating the lull, but to be honest, we feel that if we sit around here for much longer, then we're not helping the war to finish. I've been quite bored really, there's only so many times you can strip an engine down and put it back together but it has given me time to dare to think beyond this war and I keep dreaming of being back in Manchester – that is if the Jerries have left us a bit of it to enjoy! It would be nice to walk in Heaton Park. We could take Patch and Mutt, they'd love it! I bet you're fully trained now and strutting round in that uniform. I hope you're taking care of yourself.

Jenkins and Jones are in good form, but another guy had to get married, a Polish girl he met here is pregnant. It's a scandal, as you can imagine, and certainly gave everyone something to talk about. Apparently, he only met her once and they can hardly communicate, but now they are having a baby together. He's having to do the honourable thing and marry her and they'll have to spend their lives together, probably in her country once the war is over. He doesn't speak the language and the culture is certainly different. Believe me, her dad's letters indicated he wasn't having it any other way! So they'll have to make a go of it. Talking of babies, there was a woman the other day who stopped us en route and begged us to give her some dried milk for her baby. Needless to say, we've had black tea all week! You could give all your food away, they're so desperate, but we get into real trouble if we do and there are regular inspections to make sure we have supplies. An army marches on its stomach, we keep getting told. Well, mine's empty most of the time, so it's a good job I'm driving a tank transporter, I wouldn't get very far walking!

Take care, keep your head down when you're strutting around!

Love,

Danny

Danny, Frank and Eddie had sat round the night after the wedding, quieter than usual and more pensive. Frank spoke first.

'So lads, how are we going to cope with another God knows how many years without sex?'

They all looked at each other. It was a valid point.

All in their early twenties, being celibate was not a state any of them would have chosen, and there had been raucous comments about the lack of complaints about cold showers that were rigged up behind the latrines. But, like their fathers before them, sex was something that belonged in marriage and any fumblings before that had to be with a certain type of girl.

Eddie looked pathetically into the gloom of the warm autumn evening.

'It's no wonder I am happy to fly at those Jerries, I've got so much aggression building up in me.'

They all nodded in agreement, hand-to-hand combat had been a strange way of relieving their frustration, but in a way it had given them a temporary respite from those pent up sexual urges.

'It's bloody tempting to give in to those girls,' Eddie went on. 'They're certainly good looking and up for it. Some of them will do anything for food.'

Danny agreed but quickly reminded his friends of the rising number of soldiers who were hauled out of line during the regular sexual disease checks.

'You're all right, you've got that nice girl you keep writing to, what's her name, Lily?' Eddie said to Danny. 'At least you've got a reason to behave.'

Danny smiled mysteriously at them all. He never discussed Lily with them, not wanting her to become a topic of soldier gossip. She was more special than that.

'The rest of us just can't win,' Eddie added glumly.

'No, we'd better just win this war and then we can go and find ourselves wives,' Frank laughed, getting up to get yet another cup of black tea.

Chapter 19

The girls' time at Blackpool was over all too soon. They had completed their three-hour tests to match them with an area that would suit their abilities. The test had consisted of a section on maths, general knowledge and an aptitude test. Lily had scraped through the maths questions.

Lily packed her bag once more but this time she was going to be on her own and she was very nervous. She proudly fingered her new badge that denoted her as Aircraftwoman, Second Class and looked round at the empty room. The others had all had to catch the early transport and the stripped beds seemed to make the room echo as Lily moved quietly around sorting out her bag. The goodbyes had been rushed, and all too soon Lily had been left alone in the room. She picked up her duffel bag, slung her gas mask strap over her shoulder and paused momentarily to look back before she closed the door, imagining for the last time the five of them all jostling while they got dressed or bickering about who had the curlers.

Walking slowly down the stairs, Lily edged to one side out of habit to avoid the creaky step and made her way to the hallway. Mrs Porter was coming into the back kitchen from the outhouse with the washing, undoubtedly getting ready for the next intake. She barely glanced up and just nodded a cursory goodbye, too occupied with sorting the sheets and pillowcases on the kitchen table. Lily walked out of the front door and closed it quietly behind her. Her footsteps resounded on the pavement in the stillness of the morning air and the only other sound was the mocking squawk of Blackpool's seagulls from above. She stood at the bus stop feeling tears prickling the back of her eyes and blinked. The rail warrant in her hand was first for Cranwell and then onto East Kirkby, a Bomber Command station. She should have been excited but all she felt now was sadness – sadness that she was leaving a group of girls who had become like family to her and also that she now had to grow up and stand on her own feet.

The platform was a mass of service people, which helped Lily merge with the sea of khaki, blue and brown crowding onto the train. On one side of the carriage were four naval men who made the usual jokes about how she could sit on their lap. She ignored them and found a few square inches next to the window on the opposite side, next to some other WAAFS who were all chatting excitedly. They too were bound for Cranwell but were then, they told her, going on to Metheringham, a station further down the road. Claiming a splitting headache, she gave only brief answers to their questions and stared out of the window. The countryside seemed to fly by. It was late summer 1943 and the fields were looking slightly parched. She tried to recognise towns and villages as the train sped through but they were all new to her. The land gradually became flatter and the skies looked enormous. As ever, there was a constant buzz of chatter in the crowded compartment but for once Lily did not join in, needing her own thoughts to be clear and uninterrupted to gradually assimilate the move from Blackpool. The intensity of being with the same people for several months had made the move to East Kirkby feel like being turfed out of a door into a freezing cold day without a coat.

Cranwell in Lincolnshire was a real airfield and Lily felt nervous as the train stopped at the camp's own station. As the doors opened to disgorge the new batch of WAAFs, Lily paused for a minute to take it all in before being told to 'Step lively!' by an impatient warrant officer. Lily peered around her to see the airstrips and was gratified to find she could identify Oxfords, Masters, Tiger Moths, Blenheims and Spitfires, even through the camouflage. She watched the blue-uniformed figures bustling about importantly and felt very alone.

Lily followed the other girls towards the impressive college building where the orders were given out. Cranwell was currently closed as an operational station to provide a major training centre for pilots and there were cadets everywhere. Lily looked up to see a damaged roof above her. The girl in front was whispering to a group of newcomers that a Whitley plane had hit it in fog, killing three crew members.

The queue of girls huddled through the back door of the college and were marched through the long corridors past impressive pictures of men with moustaches and insignia into the dome in the centre, with scaffolding and tarpaulin covering where the plane had hit. Lily marvelled for a moment at the history and pomp and ceremony of the organisation she had now joined. She felt overawed by the grandeur and thought back to the simple life she had lived before in the suburbs of Manchester. Without the war, she would have gone on working at Liners until she married and then lived the same life as her mum, cooking, cleaning and looking after the menfolk and children. She might even have been married by now she realised with a jolt. She took a deep breath and encouraged herself to feel privileged that she had been given the chance to explore a bigger world. It was just a question of how she was going to get through it all. How she was supposed to cope with all these changes, losing track of friends who had become like sisters to her, and how she was going to make her mark on the world? It was all too overwhelming. It was such a big war and she was only a tiny part of it.

Administration took ages as usual, so it was late when Lily and her truckload of fellow WAAFs were finally taken to East Kirkby, a newly-opened station that was to supplement Scampton. Scampton was famous for 'Operation Chastise' a raid on dams in Möhne, Sorpe and Eder earlier that year. Lily, like everyone else, had heard about the bombs that destroyed the dams, causing huge damage to industrial buildings down in the valleys below. She had joined in as they all pored over the old atlas in the mess, searching for the areas that had been hit. Listening to the chatter on the truck, Lily heard whispers that Scampton had also recently sent Lancasters to North Africa from there. She suddenly remembered Danny and made a mental note to add him to her list of letters she had to write.

It was about seven o'clock at night when the new batch of WAAFs were assigned their huts at East Kirkby. She walked slowly down the aisle, noting the familiar round-bellied stove at one end, the black card stuck to the windows and the little piles of nightclothes on each of the mattresses on the bunks to denote they were occupied. She breathed deeply and dismissed the vision of her little bedroom at home, with flowered curtains and all her teddies from childhood propped up on the shelf above her dressing table. Even the tiny, cramped bedroom in Blackpool had seemed more welcoming than this.

'This one's yous,' a dark-haired girl with a strong Glaswegian accent on the next bed said pointing at the bed on the left. Lily looked at her and her prepared smile froze. The girl had matted hair and filthy fingernails and was clutching the dog end of a cigarette.

'I'm Gladys, everyone calls me Glad. Who's you?'

'Um, Lily'

'Stow yer kit. There might be a wee bit of Ovaltine left. You've missed tea, if you can call that fucking shite tea. I wouldna feed it to the bleeding rats myself.'

Lily couldn't think of a suitable reply, so she forced a smile and turned to unpack her kit bag.

Chapter 20

12th August, 1943

Dear Lily,

I am writing this perched on the tailgate of my transporter. I've got my cuppa so all's right with the world. The summer went fast didn't it? It's already August and I haven't done any fishing! We've moved on but, as you know, I can't tell you where to, but we have moved across a sea! The heat isn't as bad here but now we've got rain, by the bucket load. I'm trying to think of a summer in England with its gentle breezes and drizzle. I won't complain about the British weather ever again. The terrain here is very different from where we've been before and we're struggling to get to grips with it, but I'm finding the language simpler and, the women here are certainly easy on the eye! I got a newspaper yesterday, that was a real red-letter day. I found it on the side of the road. I guess one of the top brass had dropped it, but we all pored over it to see what was happening. It was several weeks old but it was still great to read about what's been happening. We read that Churchill had spoken in the House of Commons saying we had to face the Germans in a stand-off fight somewhere. I hope that doesn't mean here!

So, are you running the RAF yet? Some of the higher up brass here are getting a bit full of themselves and it seems a uniform can make you power-crazed. I hope you're looking out for those kind of people . . . and avoiding them!

We keep coming across donkeys. They're more at home on these tracks than we are with our great big vehicles but they look so out of place amidst all this huge artillery and give us a superior look as we trundle past them as if to say,' this is our road, get out of our way'. They don't half make a noise at night too. Still, it's better than hearing planes I suppose! The powers that be are all getting their knickers in a twist about malaria and are making us take tablets every day and keep our arms and legs covered. They keep giving us mosquito-repellent, but that seems to have the opposite effect and attracts them in swarms.

Time to sign off, so TTFN

Keep safe,

Danny

Danny looked round at the landscape. Sicily was certainly prettier than the desert, despite the scars of the weeks of fighting that they had experienced. The trip across had been a struggle, with choppy seas and Danny had been glad of a strong stomach, although it had meant he was aware of the shelling from above, whereas Frank was oblivious and having retched into the sea for the whole journey, no longer cared whether he lived or died.

They had all been relieved that the fighting had not been as severe as they had expected but they had had a hard job finding their way round demolished bridges, road blocks and mines, thoughtfully left behind by the Germans. He had fallen in love with Sicily, its olive groves and its people who ran out into the streets to offer the soldiers wilting flowers, drinks and love as they followed their leaders in surrender. That was one of the problems, he and the other two Js admitted. The girls, too, were only too anxious to surrender and were happy to offer themselves as trophies of war to the good-looking young men who arrived on their shores ready to joke and remind them they were young – and hopefully give them some longed-for food.

Danny looked around the small town where they were billeted for the week while they carried on clearing the way forward. The houses were bombed-out but some had remnants of pink or white plaster and railings from front balconies. The street was speckled with an occasional faded red geranium, determinedly blasting through the dust that pervaded every street he travelled through. As a tank transporter driver, Danny's convoy was always a day or two behind the action and he was becoming immune to the devastation that he had to drive through, but there were tiny specks of beauty in Sicily that shouted out at the convoy in belligerent defiance.

He scanned the empty streets. He was getting worried about his friend Pete, who had a sweetheart at home called Daisy. He had been lured into a local bar by a girl two hours earlier and had not been seen since. He knew how easy it was to be comforted by a comely girl who was willing. He had made a promise to himself at the beginning of the war that he was going to avoid the clinches that lasted one night, the romances that blossomed and faded faster than those geraniums on the street but it was hard and, sometimes, particularly in the early days after the harsh deserts of Africa, he had had several close shaves. Danny groaned and toyed with the idea of denouncing his life as a monk.

Chapter 21

Lily had never met a prostitute before and Glad was a revelation. There were no secrets in the Gorbals and her hair-raising tales of her colourful life took Lily's mind off her loneliness. Glad worked in the Domestic Group as an orderly and was regularly summonsed for VD and lice checks, far more than the other girls, but she was philosophical about it.

'Good to keep a check on it and it's better than having to queue at the bleedin' doc's. Hope they keep the lads' peckers as clean,' she winked at Lily, who had managed to perfect an interested but bland expression at these outrageous statements.

The work had proved to be more taxing than Lily could ever have imagined and the shifts were split into three every twenty-four hours, meaning that the WAAFs never seemed to be in the same place for long – or awake together to enjoy themselves as a group. Her crews flew Lancasters, great beasts of planes that cast huge shadows across the runway and roared like lions when fired up. The seven crewmen on each plane were young, fresh-faced and full of a false confidence. She recognised her brother's tendency to swagger when under pressure and decided to treat them all like younger brothers.

'Ooh, proper egg and bacon,' Len, one of the rear gunners, sighed, signalling Lily to join them one morning. 'I knew there was a reason why I signed up for the RAF.'

As a ground wireless operator, Lily was allowed to join the crews for breakfast, but rarely got away with sneaking a plate of the coveted bacon. She joined the table next to Len, tucked into her toast and tried not to seem envious. She looked around carefully at the young men before her, studying their faces. She had met them two days ago and was struggling to remember their names. The tall, blonde, thin one was called Freddie, she remembered. He was the wireless operator. His right temple was pounding and he seemed on edge. Next to him, the slightly balding Pete stretched out his hand for more bread. It was shaking but they all kept up a constant flow of banter, disguising their fears behind bravado. Lily smiled at them with a newly-found affection. She sat quietly, content to listen while they told unlikely tales of heroism. The truth was this crew had only been on local ops so far, on the look-out for interlopers, but today, judging by their nervousness, the briefing had probably revealed a longer flight which meant they were heading into enemy territory. Lily was learning fast how important secrecy was and the girls had talked about how the crews received their orders on flimsies – made of rice paper – so they could eat them if they had to ditch in enemy territory.

'We'll have that drink tonight, Lily, see you in The Bluebell,' the captain, Dave, said his tea in hand. 'I've left the coin so you can all have a drink on us.' He did not need to explain that the tradition at The Bluebell was to leave a coin in the split in the ceiling beams to be used to buy a round if the crew did not return. Lily shivered but smiled back, nodding, trying to look as if his 'generosity' was as normal as buying a round at the Crown in Manchester.

An hour later, she shielded her eyes before the dawn sun and heard the roar of the engines – four per aircraft. The Lancasters made more noise than any of the other planes and it still gave her a mix of terror and excitement to see them start up. She watched them taxi down the runway, tensing as she imagined the seven young men cramped inside and went to take her station in the control tower. As a ground wireless operator, she was responsible for transmitting weather information, any diversion signals and recalls. She had to take notes on any communications from the planes, making sure they were immediately sent to Group for action. She was constantly passing messages and had to send information on 'found wind' so that they could all fly on the same course using the natural air currents to help them. She knew that experienced navigators ignored this information, preferring to make their own judgements up in the sky, but it was her job to make sure it was sent. The Morse could travel so much further than the radio signals or voice calls, so she took over from the telephone operators as soon as they were out of audio range. Imagining them across the Channel, she said a quick prayer for them all. She thought particularly of the crew she had had breakfast with that morning. The pilot, Dave, was older than her at twenty-two. He had a wife, Pat, and two children, John and Flo, and he had shown her photographs of them with pride.

Lily's stomach turned over. This was real, not the pretend war she had been playing at in Blackpool. It was time to put the training to good use. She adjusted her headset, put her head down and concentrated. The noises of the Morse suddenly made even more sense when she knew it was Freddie's hand on the other end of it. After an hour, she found she was beginning to recognise his touch. It was her and Freddie's private world, at least she hoped it was. The possibility that her coded messages were being intercepted somehow made her more determined not to make any mistakes. She blocked out the constant chatter and signals that were being sent by the enemy to confuse them and thought for a moment about the band playing in her earphones at Blackpool. Now she understood how important it was to be able to home in on a crew's frequency.

When it went quiet, Lily knew all the planes were in enemy territory. She had heard the expression 'deafening silence' but had not understood it until now. She could hear the ticking of the clock, or was it the beating of her heart? It seemed as if she was suspended in time and although she registered the hustle and bustle around her of other personnel dealing with aircraft, her own call sign 5FP was all she was focused on. Once that was tapped in by the crews, she had to hurriedly write down the information and pass it on. After a while, the WAAFs in the room were told to stand down and she knew the planes were all getting on with their jobs. Lily couldn't think about what that meant for the people on the ground in the German towns, she just had to block that out and do her own job. Leaving her receiver on so she could hear any changes, she took off her headset at the same time as the WAAF next to her. They smiled at each other and Lily stood up and stretched.

'That's my first one out. I couldn't believe how nervous I was.'

It was true, her shoulders ached and she realised how tense she had been.

'That's OK,' the redhead told her, 'you'll soon get the hang of it. I'm Freda by the way. Freda from Stoke. That's in the Midlands,' she added unnecessarily. 'Welcome to East Kirkby.'

Lily smiled the same automatic smile she had been using since she arrived. Blackpool had been her world for nine months. Alice, Viv, Marion even, had become her life, and to swap to being a new Lily overnight was too much for her to cope with. She felt bereft without Alice, in particular, and could not even think back to their last hug at Mrs Porter's without filling up with tears. Alice, who by now was on her way to Scotland. Alice, who had cuffed her across the head affectionately when Lily had sobbed uncontrollably, saying, 'You big ninny, you'll survive and you know what that new song says . . . "We'll meet again . . ." Now go and win that war. I'm off to Scotland where I'm going to meet lots of lovely pilots and teach all those Sassenachs how to speak with a lilt just like that gorgeous laddie, Scottie, taught me so that the locals can understand them.'

Alice had paused for a minute and then had shaken her head.

'Shame I have to leave him behind but these dainty feet of mine can't just dance to the tune of one man!'

Lily tried to ignore Freda's chatter and like her neighbour, Mary, a quieter girl with short brown hair, only answered where necessary, giving some essential information about herself. Freda had been at Blackpool a year before Lily and seemed to have spent time in all the old haunts that Lily knew so well. She felt a pain in her stomach at the memory. While Freda wittered on, telling Lily all about her conquests both in Blackpool and East Kirkby, they all kept alert, listening for their station's call sign. They spent the day knitting and writing letters and there was a quiet hum from the endless chatter.

'Did you hear about the great fun we had with a pigeon last week?' Freda, who talked so fast that her words merged, had a captive audience. 'You know the pigeons are sent with the planes, ready to be released with up-to-date coordinates if the crew have to crash land?' She looked at Lily to make sure, as a newcomer, that she understood the significance of the pigeons.

Lily nodded distractedly.

Freda warmed to her subject.

'Well, one turned up in the fireplace in the mess, poor thing. It was exhausted. It must have flown miles. Good job the fire wasn't lit. About four of us managed to catch it but it was me that got the paper off its foot, even though I got covered in soot.'

She looked to make sure the girls were all impressed.

'They sent out the rescue and found the crew just off the coast thanks to me . . . and the pigeon. We had to clean it up and then we sneakily released it so it wouldn't have to spend any more time being cooped up in a Lanc. We had to pretend it had died so that no one suspected anything. So, we had a very good funeral for it, complete with a shoe box. It's 'buried' just under the control tower windows. Just think, in years to come, some archaeologist could find the empty box and wonder why on earth it was buried. It's so funny!'

Triumphant, she finally drew breath and sat back waiting to make sure she had everyone's attention but just then her Morse started to buzz and she had to turn away.

'Here we go, let's pray they're all in one piece.'

Lily glanced down at the runway where the emergency tenders were lined up, hoping not to be needed. She tried to concentrate on her own headphones.

There was no chat in the room for ages as Freda and some of the other girls responded to crews who were approaching the other side of the Channel. All that could be heard was the relentless tap, tap, tap. Lily looked at her finger poised over the Morse key, twitching, waiting to be used, waiting for the right call sign.

Annie, a girl from Swansea, was listening intently. Her dark hair fell over her eyes and her shoulders were tense. She was on 'Darky' watch. Her job was to deal with lost pilots who needed an emergency landing place. It was often the most boring shift, but tonight, tension was in the air. Everyone sensed the op had been a major one. She had to give vital life-saving information to men who had never landed at East Kirkby before and had no knowledge of the sort of country they were in. The machine cranked into life and Annie whirled round to tune in. The crew she was communicating with would be in desperate need of help. Her shift was nearly over but she was too absorbed in what she was doing to glance at the clock above them. Her shoulders were hunched over in despair as she tapped and tapped with determination. Freda nudged Lily. For the first time, she recognised the body language of a wireless operator who knew the situation was beyond hope. Lily imagined someone's son, brother or husband frantically trying to stop their plane from crashing. She gulped. Annie's finger was white as she tried to get a response but, defeated, she sent off her report in the hope a plane would be sent to look for the crew at the last co-ordinates. She sat back and stared into space waiting for the next call.

The rest of the girls put their heads down, in unison, suddenly mesmerised by their frequencies. Lily's headset remained deafeningly quiet. She felt alone, despite knowing that there was a full team around the building trying to bring the planes in safely. Then the messages started coming in thick and fast and Lily had to respond to several planes searching for that familiar runway. As the planes approached, the radio operators were giving instructions to circle above at 500 feet until the runway was clear of the previous plane. One by one, the ones that had made it back landed. Some, she knew would be damaged and the crew injured. Her heart was thumping and she was sure Mary could hear it above the tapping of the Morse. She looked up and caught Mary's eye and they tried to smile at each other.

'First time?'

Lily nodded.

'Keep calm, we just do our job.'

Then Mary suddenly turned towards her Morse set, concentrating to hear a faint buzz. Her face was tense and she was sending Morse at a slow, steady rate. A little while later, they all heard the sickening thump of a fuselage pancaking onto the runway. The girls looked up in horror to see a badly-damaged Lancaster burst into flames at the perimeter of the airfield. Trying desperately to ignore the commotion that broke out below, they went back to their jobs.

The blackboard on the other side of the glass between them and the telephone operators was filling up. Some had 'landed' next to them, some had a line through them. Then there was only one gap left on the board. F for Foxtrot.

Their shift had ended and all the girls except Lily moved towards the 'out' door. The 'in' door would remain closed until the new shift came in so that they did not meet and breach security, but Lily did not move. She looked through the glass at the officer in charge for permission to stay and received a curt nod in response. The next shift came in, silently, and took their places. The girl who was due to take over from Lily sat at the spare set in the corner.

'Come on Freddie,' Lily inwardly urged.

The control room on the other side of the glass was a hive of activity with people hurriedly doing their jobs. They were busy organising the ambulances and fire crews as well as the maintenance staff to the array of planes below. The flames of the crashed plane lit up the evening sky and the fire brigade had moved onto other aircraft, leaving it to burn like a funeral pyre. She looked at the blackboard with the alphabetical list of planes and code letters for crews. The blank column next to Dave's flight's codename somehow looked bigger than all the others.

Lily's mouth was dry. She felt sick. She watched the ambulances screech off the runway to take the injured to the hospital and prayed harder than she had ever prayed in her life. Dave's children's happy faces photographed at the seaside flashed before her eyes and she blinked to send them back to the beach and those innocent days before all this began.

She pressed her headset to her ears, straining to hear every sign but all she could hear was the thumping of her heart.

'Not my first one,' she pleaded with God.

Chapter 22

Lily became mesmerised by the ticking of the red second hand on the clock and she started to synchronise it with the drumming of her redundant fingers on the desk. She tried to concentrate on something else and thought back to a walk on the hills behind Manchester she'd taken just before the war broke out. The person by her side had been Danny, carefree and laughing at her as she had struggled to keep her hair out of her eyes. She smiled wanly to herself. It had seemed such an innocent time and she longed with every fibre of her taut body for those times to come back. But it seemed an age ago and like another life. Where was he now, she wondered? Her hand was hovering above the dial, urging it to buzz, and she jumped with fright when she suddenly heard a slight noise. Was it a signal? She frowned and hunched over her set, tensing her whole body. Stop, listen, ignore the crackle, ignore the noise below, concentrate, she urged herself. Then she heard it – through the slush, her call sign followed by F for Foxtrot. She almost cried with relief. They weren't mangled in a crash, ditched in the ocean or burnt to a cinder, they were on their way back, but they communicated they were in trouble and their instruments were down, leaving them navigationally blind. She turned to give the information to the WAAF behind her who rushed it through to Control but then looked in bewilderment at the set in front of her. 'What now?' her mind went blank.

'Pull yourself together, Mullins,' she muttered fiercely. 'Just do your job, get them back to the coast, then let the others worry about the rest.'

She tried to remember the training she had been given in a warm room in Blackpool and started to respond, slowly and deliberately. The signal came stronger now and she was able to get a fix on it. She repeatedly communicated the station's call sign to the Lancaster, watching the empty skies out of the window in between staring determinedly at the set. She imagined Pete searching wildly for Lincoln Cathedral and thanked God there was no fog. She scanned the skies.

At last she saw it! The Lancaster was in one piece, apart from some charring on the left wing. She willed it to land safely as it veered from left to right out of the clouds. It certainly was not a text book landing and the huge plane bumped its way along the runway, finally shuddering to a halt in front of the control tower just as the blinds were pulled down for the blackout. The emergency services sprang into action. Lily signed off and grabbed her bag to race out of the door, leaving the next shift to deal with the aftermath.

Lily wasn't allowed onto the runway but had to stand helplessly in the corridor, trying to peer through the crack in the door to watch the action outside. She saw stretcher bearers running towards the plane and her stomach leapt.

'Please don't let them be badly injured,' she urged the heavens.

Finally, she gave up and headed towards the debriefing room. There were admin people scurrying backwards and forwards and she grabbed one of their arms as they hurried past.

'Can you tell me about the final Lancaster crew that's just come in, please?'

He looked at her panic-stricken face but questions were a scandalous breach of security. He went to move off down the corridor but then paused and turned back to smile at her reassuringly.

Lily had no option but to go to The Bluebell and wait.

There were quite a few WAAFs already there, including Freda. For once she was quiet and alone, gulping at the cider in front of her, but she spotted Lily and called her over. Mary had gone straight to the hut, she whispered conspiratorially, and Annie, who was a devout Welsh Methodist, had been seen going to the chapel to say a prayer for the crew from the 'Darky' call who had been lost in the sea. Freda, with more experience, seemed less affected than

Lily by the day of drama and filled her in on the other girls. Annie was married to an army sergeant who was in France and Mary was too shy to enjoy herself much, she told Lily. Looking carefully at her, she added, 'I'm hoping some of your new intake will be a bit more lively.'

Lily felt anything but lively and gave a very weak smile. Freda carried on, delighted to have a new audience. She told Lily how just a few nights before, Mary had been dancing with one rear gunner whose body had been prised out of the freezing compartment at the rear of one of the damaged Lancasters. Another, who had bought Freda a drink, was badly burned and had been taken to hospital for a seven-day saline bath. Freda recounted these tales like a shopping list. Lily gulped and went up to the bar to ask for a half of cider. She felt chilled and knew she was shaking. The two girls sat huddled together on the hard sofas but Lily found it difficult to show a great deal of interest in the constant stream of gossip that Freda was regaling her with. She looked down at her glass and thought of her brother, Don. Somewhere there would be a mother and father, sisters and brothers dreading that knock on the door that would come only too soon. Don was only fourteen but if the war went on another four years, he would be called up. She shivered.

After an hour or so, when Lily was really struggling to show any interest in Freda's inconsequential chatter, a fellow WAAF came in and whispered quietly to them so the rest of the bar could not hear, 'They're out of debrief.'

They both looked towards the door. Two airmen came in. They belonged to the crew that Freda had had breakfast with that morning. She rushed up to greet them, giving them both a relieved hug. Lily realised Freda's need to talk was a mask to disguise her anxiety. The barman had lined up some pints on the bar and silently handed two of them over to the airmen. The ritual in The Bluebell was alarmingly practised.

No one wanted to ask questions and the air crew didn't volunteer any information. They just sat quietly nursing their drinks.

One by one, the crews came in, all of them subdued and not very talkative. Then Lily saw Freddie.

'Freddie,' she called. He nodded at her and touched her arm, grasping it slightly as she ran up to him. She took hold of it and guided him to the bar, getting him a pint. They went and sat down in a corner of the room. She didn't speak, but knew he would talk when he was ready.

'We got lost coming back,' he said eventually, whispering so the others couldn't hear. 'We'd been hit by flak and our instruments were out. Pete's in hospital. I think he's going to be OK but his war's over. Without the navigation equipment, we had to wing it back. We had to veer off the coast and come in from the north. We were worried we were going to run out of fuel, but Dave was amazing. God, that man can fly. He cut back on the throttle and managed to steer us in. We thought we were going to have to ditch near the coast but we made it. There are others who didn't.'

Lily just pressed his arm and nodded. There was nothing she could say. They would be going out time and time again, facing fear and death. They would all deal with it in their own way. Some would become quieter, some louder.

Len came and joined them. He had a bandage on his head and looked grey. Then Paul, Bob and Arthur arrived, all looking grey and worn out, followed by Dave. He smiled at the little group and sat down.

'You did well, Lily. You found us and saw us back. I can't tell you how relieved we were to hear your messages. Thank you.'

Lily's throat constricted and she looked down to hide the tears.

'So, lads, a quiet night and then hopefully a twenty-four-hour pass tomorrow. Where shall we go? I've got some money to claim back from this beam.' He reached up and triumphantly reclaimed his coin.

Plans towards normality helped them all to take a deep breath and they all started to chatter, putting the last twenty-four hours behind them, knowing this was just the beginning.

Lily took herself off after a while, leaving the men to recover. She was absolutely exhausted so undressed hurriedly, falling onto her bed. She glanced across and saw Mary huddled under her blanket. She started to toss and turn but then worried she would wake Mary so tried to keep still, blanking out the visions of burning metal that were in her head until she finally fell asleep.

With the next morning off duty, it was well into the day when Lily woke. She sat up with a start wondering what had woken her. She heard laughter and peered through the window to see two WAAFS perched on the fronts of bikes ridden by airmen, hanging on for dear life as they raced around the corner. She heard cheers and quickly dressed to go and watch. There was a large crowd who had gathered at the end of the huts and they were all shouting and yelling encouragement. Glad was there, in uniform, but with fag in hand, leaning against the hut casually.

'They're all letting off a bi' o steam and quite right too. That was fuckin' tough shite.'

Lily felt her shoulders drop and some of the tension of the last day or so started to drain away. She smiled at Glad.

'I'm glad you're here, Glad.'

Glad lived up to her name and despite her colourful background was proving to be a positive force in the hut. Her matter-of-fact attitude never seemed to fail her and she dealt with every situation with a calm pragmatism.

Both girls started to giggle and loudly cheered on the girl from their barracks who was on the bike in the lead.

The following day, Lily and Freda decided they had had enough of the aroma emanating from Glad's bed and they plotted to grab her before she got dressed and deal out some good old-fashioned washing. East Kirkby was lucky to have a reasonable supply of water, so they got hold of some buckets of water from the showers and left them outside the hut. Then they went in as nonchalantly as they could and called to Glad, 'Come on, Glad, come and see these new airmen who've just arrived.'

'Show me the way,' she said, her eyes brightening.

They took her outside and then Lily grabbed the first bucket and doused her in water. Freda grabbed the soap and started to scrub. Glad screamed and lashed out with her long fingernails. Lily stood in front of her, with her hands on her hips.

'You're a lovely wee Scottish lassie and I believe you're an excellent orderly, but you are not going to survive this war if you don't clean up a bit.'

'Get your fuckin' hands off me. I'll see you in hell before I give in to yous all.'

The three of them got covered in soapsuds as she lashed out at them and suddenly, they all started to laugh. Glad fell onto the floor, giggling louder than the rest and rolled about clutching her sides with tears pouring down her cheeks.

Two girls called Phyllis and Marie ran up with fresh supplies of water and threw it over the girls.

'There now,' Lily said, with a satisfied nod of her head, 'you look a lot better and certainly you smell better.' She sat back on her heels and grinned at the soaked Gladys in front of her. The water was dripping down her face and she spat it sideways out of her mouth.

'That's a shockin' waste o' water. You'll be in terrible trouble for that, you know.'

There was a sound behind them. A corporal standing behind them with her arms folded. They all stood up quickly.

'What exactly is going on?'

'Um, we thought ACW Perkins could do with a bit of sprucing up,' Lily said defiantly.

'You're risking a charge, ACW Mullins'

I'll have that on my gravestone, Lily thought, resignedly.

'But we're under the protection of the flag,' Phyllis said, pointing upwards to the Union Jack fluttering in the breeze.

The corporal frowned.

'We'll see about that' and turned on her heels to walk away.

They all clustered around Phyllis.

'Can we really get away with it because of the flag?' Helen asked.

'I don't know, it just occurred to me. I saw somewhere that if something happens under the protection of the British flag then it is like a sanctuary.'

'You may be safe from her but you're not safe from me,' Glad countered, grabbing the last of the water in the bucket and chucking it at Lily, who gasped as the cold liquid hit her face.

She started towards Glad but then stopped. 'OK, that's fair,' she laughed. 'But, now we've found out about the flag, it'll be a weekly wash for you unless you do it yourself and next time, we'll get Doris Billings to help us.'

Doris Billings was five foot ten and wrestled in her spare time. For once, Glad looked intimidated. 'OK, OK, it just seem'd a fuckin' shame to waste water on me, that's all, when I'm bleedin' gorgeous as I am.'

'Not gorgeous when I have to sleep next to you,' Lily retorted, and linking the dripping-wet girl's arm, they headed back to the hut.

Chapter 23

Lily couldn't believe that a prostitute from Glasgow had propelled her out of her depression. Glad was a breath of fresh air in a world of deaths, long shifts and rules and regulations and her unquestioning attitude to life was exactly what Lily needed. She was really struggling with the increasing number of airmen who swaggered around the camp one day and were gone the next. The others around Lily seemed to cope with it better than she did but she had never come across death before. Her grandparents had died before she was born and all her other relatives were in sterling good health. The Lily who had swirled around the Christmas tree at home just a year earlier seemed from another dimension and while other WAAFs seemed to be making the most of this war, Lily had been feeling very down and vulnerable and had not been able to snap out of it. She realised that Alice had provided her with a crutch that she had come to rely on but now she was on her own.

One Sunday morning, Lily was off duty and decided to take herself off to church. Born and brought up in a liberal

Catholic household, she had never taken her religion very seriously and had breezed through the Catechism with what she believed to be a healthy scepticism. Her father was a Baptist who converted when he married Ginny, and her mum had a very Irish attitude to deity and saints that as long as they were all up there doing their job, there was no need to worry.

The nuns at Loreto had despaired of Lily, failing to make her see the disastrous path her frivolity was leading her along. She had been told off for reading a light-hearted novel hidden inside a philosophical work by Teilhard de Chardin during a retreat and had recklessly discussed whether confession had any value in the modern world with a visiting priest, prompting scandalised glances from Mother Philomena. Getting on the bus to Lincoln, she smiled as she remembered putting a towel around her head to see whether she would look pretty in a nun's habit.

Not quite the right attitude, she conceded to herself, paying the conductor her 1/3d for the fare.

But this morning, she needed the quiet of a church; the sense of something that had endured two thousand years and the reassuring words that were second nature to her.

Lily stepped off the bus and looked up at the impressive frontage of Lincoln Cathedral. She realised why the pilots scanned the ground for the distinctive landmark towers, indicating they had made it home.

It was raining so she marched on quickly to St Hugh's where mass was due to be held. Making the sign of the cross with the holy water by the door, Lily felt engulfed by a familiar feeling of peace. She queued for the confessional box and recounted the same sins she had told since she was seven before making her way down the aisle to kneel and make her penance, just finishing in time before mass started. The Latin washed over her as usual, but Lily used the time to assess the last ten months. She knew she had grown up enormously but suspected she still had a long way to go. She looked up at the statue of Mary, smiling beatifically on the assembled congregation and grimaced.

'It's all right for you, you had an angel telling you what to do. I'm down here all on my own, trying to deal with potential rapists and vindictive sergeants,' she silently told the statue. Thinking about an angel made her glance round, then shifting along the pew in an action reminiscent of Form 3a, she 'made a space' for her guardian angel. She apologised to the invisible figure for forgetting his/her constant vigilance over her chaotic life and unaccountably started to feel better. She had never really questioned her religion but seeing superstitious young men praying or kissing the side of their Lancaster before they took off on raids, clutching the same parachute like a security blanket and then not returning had shaken her belief that there was anyone at all out there looking after any of them.

She looked along the row at the faces of the servicemen and women who had crowded into St Hugh's that morning. Their expressions were so intent, there was some serious praying going on. Lily suddenly thought of all the churches all over Europe, both in enemy and allied countries, where mothers, wives, sisters and other service people were sending up similar prayers.

'It must be like the Tower of Babel up there. I do hope the English pray louder than the Germans.'

It was time for communion and Lily edged out of the pew with everyone else, standing with her hands clasped, waiting to put out her tongue for communion. The choir was singing 'Sweet Sacrament Divine' and Lily hummed along in her mind, remembering the Whit processions at school through the gardens to the grotto, hands held in prayer, her white veil flapping across her face.

She noticed as she took communion that the priest looked grey and tired. He was obviously being stretched to the limit supporting his flock. In fact, when she looked around, everyone looked tired. She could have done with a bit of red lipstick to brighten things up.

When Lily came out of the church after mass, the sun was shining, and the early morning rain was twinkling on the pavement. She checked her watch – plenty of time for a cup of tea. She went into the nearest Lyons and gave her order to the girl behind the counter, adding a request for a carrot biscuit from the plate in the glass-topped cabinet in front of her. She smiled as she thought of her dad's favourite biscuits and then had a pang of homesickness. Her mum would have gone to mass this morning and would undoubtedly have said a prayer for Lily.

I'll write to them this afternoon, she determined, sitting at a table in the window, and maybe I should catch up on a letter for Danny. I've been a bit lazy with him too.

The door opened and a young woman walked in. It was Amy!

Lily started to her feet.

'Amy!'

The girl turned and froze as she spotted Lily. She was wearing a bright red dress and had on far too much makeup, which stood out against her bleached blonde hair. She was painfully thin and looked ill. She was tottering in heels that Lily hadn't seen since before the war. Her red fingernails completed the transformation from the mousy haired girl from Mrs Porter's.

She frantically looked towards the door to see if there was any escape, but Lily was too quick for her and blocked her exit.

'Amy,' she said quietly, 'come and sit down. It's so lovely to see you. Please.'

Amy reluctantly sat opposite Lily, perching on the chair as if it were covered with nails. She twiddled her fingers around her thumbs, looking around nervously.

'What are you doing here?' Lily asked, nodding to the passing waitress, indicating another cup was needed.

'I . . . I . . .'

Lily took a deep breath and assessed her former friend. She was slightly grubby and there were ladders in her stockings, but worst of all her face was pallid and her eyes darted nervously. It was going to take all Lily's patience and newfound experience to deal with this situation.

'Amy, please tell me what's happened.'

Amy raised her head in defiance and looked challengingly at Lily, but still didn't speak.

'I'm still your friend,' Lily said in a reassuring voice, 'and I'm not going to judge you.'

There was still no response.

'Look, Amy, I sleep next to Gladys from Glasgow who has had, shall we say, a chequered career and I'm not the one to condemn anyone for the way they're dealing with this stupid war. We've already been through a lot together; remember I *am* your friend.'

Amy looked at her suspiciously and took the cup from the disapproving waitress, who was handing it to her as if she might be infected.

After several minutes of twiddling her teaspoon around the cup, Amy started to speak.

'I'm still on sick leave, honest. I haven't gone AWOL. The doctors have said I've got mental problems. They wanted to give me electric treatment, but I ran away.'

She looked up to gauge how Lily was reacting. When she saw there was no change in her expression, she carried on.

'I found some girls who took me in but there was no money.'

Again she stopped and looking searchingly into Lily's eyes.

Lily put her hand over Amy's and gave it a squeeze.

'They showed me a way to make some.'

The silence was palpable.

Bit by bit, the truth came out and two cups of tea later, Lily had the whole story.

Amy had been taken in by girls who worked in the local factory but made extra money on the side by 'entertaining' the troops. For a couple of weeks, Amy had resisted, but by then she was drinking more and the girls' behaviour started to feel less shocking. She went out with a sailor and he bought her nylons and gin. She found she could bargain certain actions for food and drink.

'I'm only doing this for now,' she said, looking down at her feet. 'I'll go back to Coventry soon and see my dad, but right now this is all I can deal with.'

She looked up, almost inviting Lily to argue with her, but Lily kept quiet, just nodding gently.

'I can't feel anything, Lily, there's nothing there.'

Lily had a sudden longing to see Alice's solid frame at her side but gave herself a little shake.

'OK, Amy, this is what we're going to do. We're going to go back to where you are staying and get you changed into something more suitable and then you're coming to camp with me. We've got a lovely welfare officer who will help you.'

Amy stood up, pushing the chair back with a scraping noise.

'No, I can't . . . I can't.'

'Yes, you can.' Lily took her arm, put some coins on the table and pushed her towards the door. 'You can't go on like this. This isn't you. You're not well. Your family must be frantic with worry. We're going to sort this together.'

Amy's strength seemed to ebb out of her and she let herself be walked up the main street and even muttered directions to Lily.

Lily's mind was racing. How much trouble was Amy in? Her dad must be worried sick and the police would be looking for her. They arrived at a squalid flat above a chemists and Lily watched as Amy gathered a few measly belongings and crammed them into a bag. The four beds were unmade, there were empty baked bean tins on the floor and the dark green curtains were still drawn. There was an overriding smell of cigarettes and Lily was dying to open the window to let some fresh air in but made do with just opening the curtains a little so that Amy could see to change into a blue skirt and a blouse with stains on the front. She put the high shoes upside down on one of the beds and then delved underneath for some flat brogues. Lily noticed a picture of Amy's mum, dad and two brothers on a table next to some blankets on the floor, which

Amy stuffed into the bag as well. Amy quickly scrawled a message to the three girls who lived there to explain her sudden departure but her body language had changed. She was back to being pliant, mouse-like Amy, content to be shepherded and guided by Lily.

The guards on the entrance to the camp looked very suspiciously at the blonde-streaked Amy when Lily reported back. She asked to see the welfare officer and was not surprised when they said they weren't prepared to let either girl through the barrier until the officer came to meet them. Lily explained the situation to the tall, kindly woman, taking her slightly to one side so she could whisper. The welfare officer looked over at Amy who was standing with her head down in the guard-room. All the bravado had gone out of her and she looked very young.

The welfare officer took charge.

'Come with me, dear. We need to make some telephone calls.'

Amy followed meekly, glancing at Lily fearfully.

'It will be OK, Amy,' Lily smiled. 'They're here to help you and won't let you be hurt. I will check up later and see how you are doing, I promise. I'm here, Amy, I'm not going to abandon you.'

Amy nodded resignedly and went out of the door. Lily stared after her.

Chapter 24

Lily's shifts were relentless as the bombing raids on Germany increased in frequency, but in between the frantic schedules she managed to visit Amy at the East Kirkby Medical Centre. Lily began to see the colour come back into the girl's pale cheeks and the blonde hair was beginning to grow out. On the day Lily finally made Amy laugh, she came out hugging herself in glee. The welfare officer had had intense conversations with Lily about Amy, bridling with indignation when she heard about the electric shock threat. Pulling strings, the officer arranged for Amy to see a gentle psychiatrist who had gradually gained her trust. They were starting her on some new medication used for traumatised service people and she was, bit by bit, starting to lose her haunted look. After a couple of weeks, Amy was finally sent back to Coventry, accompanied by the sympathetic welfare officer, who used her own forty-eight-hour pass to go with her. On the day she left East Kirkby, Lily went to see her off and gave her a hug.

'I really don't know what I'd have done if you hadn't been in that café that day,' Amy said shyly. 'Thank you . . . you're my guardian angel. That's twice you've saved my life.'

Lily watched the truck pull out and waved towards the back of it. She smiled to herself. That'll teach you to go to church, Mullins.

The following week, Lily had a particularly harrowing night duty. The last few weeks had drained her emotionally and physically and she couldn't remember the last time she had relaxed and let her hair down. The raids were more regular and she was having repetitive nightmares about planes going down in flames. The empty chairs at breakfast were constantly being replenished with young, fresh faces. They seemed to be getting younger and younger.

There had been heavy losses and the WAAFs were becoming partially inured to the tragedies that were unfolding around them. But they were also aware they were simply storing up their reactions for after the war. Now was not the time.

Lily was off duty and was moping around the hut. Freda took matters in hand, recognising that Lily was suffering from what they all called 'the blues'. She insisted Lily should go out and when she asked around on her behalf, she found that two other girls were free as well. Lily had been so involved with Amy's rehabilitation and endless night duties that she was almost surprised when Mary and another girl, Beryl, told Freda they would love to join her and Lily at a showing of *The Talk of the Town*.

Before she went, she just had time to write a letter to Alice, keeping her up to date with Amy. The common-sense replies from Alice, who was still in Montrose, had kept her going and although neither of them mentioned any losses, she knew she too was going through similar tragedies. When the bleakness of it threatened to engulf Lily, she pictured Alice with her size seven feet, striding towards her Morse set. It helped. She toyed with the idea of a letter to Danny, she had received two from him and he definitely needed a reply, but she decided to curl her hair instead.

There was a queue for the flicks that night and the three girls stood in line, chattering about the comparative charms of Clark Gable versus Cary Grant. For the first time in ages, Lily felt the tension start to seep out of her hunched shoulders. There were three airforcemen behind them and they were mucking about, pretending to be Clark Gable in *Boom Town*. Their American accents were appalling, and the girls couldn't help but laugh. By the time they went in, the boys had very firmly positioned themselves next to the three WAAFs. One was called Ted and he had freckles that crinkled on his nose when he smiled. He leaned in towards Lily as the plot thickened in the film and finally put his arm behind her, dropping it onto her shoulders. She gave him a warning look and he took it away but after the film there was an hour left before the girls' passes ran out so they went to the pub for a drink. Lily started to relax as the banter increased and she found she was enjoying herself. The three boys walked them back to the bus and Ted gave Lily a peck on the cheek as she turned to him to say goodbye.

'I could take you for a little spin in my plane if you like,' he said tantalisingly over his shoulder as he walked away.

Going up in an operational aircraft for a joyride was strictly forbidden but Lily had heard of it happening. She stared after Ted and felt a shiver of excitement edge up from her toes to her head. She had forgotten her dreams to fly, and the thought of soaring above Lincolnshire was a heady prospect.

Ted was definitely going up in her estimation.

It was three days before Lily could see Ted again. He had arranged to meet her in the NAAFI at dinner time and whispered to her that she needed to 'be prepared.' It was a day when the top brass were all in a meeting and everyone was slightly more relaxed as there had been no flying the day before due to ground fog.

'Meet me at two at number four hangar and don't tell anyone,' he said quietly. She nodded, too excited to speak.

'We're doing a low-level formation exercise, I can taxi round and pick you up there with the rest of the crew. Keep it quiet though.'

At five to two, Lily cycled to the hangar. The rest of the crew were already there and she approached them carefully, not knowing whether Ted had told them she was coming, but she need not have worried.

'Here she comes – Miss Earhart,' one of them said, a short, stocky ginger haired chap.

Another, taller young man with a moustache handed her a helmet and a parachute. 'Put the helmet on and tuck your hair up,' he said.'

The crew surrounded Lily as they walked across the runway and she climbed into the Lanc, cursing the straight WAAF skirt. Aircraft were not designed for women and especially not women in skirts. As she tried to climb sideways into the plane, she was aware that the young navigator was behind her and was getting a full view of her backside as he rushed forward to propel her up.

She tumbled into the fuselage, marvelling that there was so little space – or comfort – and positioned herself against the side of the plane, trying to perch on a tiny ledge just as she felt the fuselage begin to throb. She caught a glimpse of the four Merlin engines out of the window by the navigator as they revved up and Lily wasn't sure whether it was the engines making her shake or the thrill of finally being in an aeroplane. She glanced across at the navigator, a boy called Bill, who looked as if he had hardly begun to shave. He had his maps and compass spread in front of him. He smiled at her. The runway was speeding underneath them and then the huge machine lifted into the air, leaving Lily's stomach behind on the ground. The roar of the engines was so loud, she could hardly hear, but bit by bit, her ears got used to the sound and she found she could hear the voice of the navigator telling her to look out at the other two planes that were flanking them. The enormous wings seemed only inches away from Ted's plane and as the three Lancs flew in line abreast, Lily held her breath. The airmanship was so impressive. Bill told her they were going towards the Wash and Lily glanced down, seeing flat fields and cattle scattering in alarm. She smiled as she saw two farm workers hurl themselves against a barn, unsure whether the low planes were friendly or not.

In a matter of minutes, they reached the coast. The sea was blue on this warm early October afternoon and the sky above merged with it as they sped out over the waves. Lily wistfully remembered days out to North Wales with her mum and dad, making sandcastles and eating ice creams. Maybe she and Danny might take a trip one day, she suddenly thought, and then drew herself up with a frown. Danny? Why was she thinking of him? She shrugged, dismissed the thought and concentrated on the ground below. A few minutes later, they swept around towards land again and Lily lurched forwards. She felt her stomach tighten and realised she was going to be sick. In a panic, she turned away from Bill and looked for something to be sick into, but there was nothing in the confined space of a war plane.

As she hurled her dinner against the side of the plane, she heard Bill chuckle.

'It happens to the best of us,' he said, handing her his handkerchief and smiling back at her when she had finished, but Lily was too mortified to smile back. By the time they landed, Lily could not look Ted in the eye, but he knew nothing about her throwing up all over the side of the plane, so he was just grinning at her in triumph.

'See that? Perfect flying,' he crowed.

She nodded and clutching Bill's handkerchief to her mouth, muttered her thanks and scuttled off to her hut.

That night, she went into the pub to meet Ted as arranged. He was with his crew, who all smiled knowingly at her. She cringed and touched him on the arm, signalling she needed to talk. They drew to one side and Lily started to speak, spluttering her apologies out, but he interrupted her.

'Don't worry, we've all done it. Bill does it regularly. Anyway, forget it, I want to know what you thought of your first flight.'

Reassured by his casual attitude, she enthused.

'It was the most amazing thing I've ever done. It was spectacular and the flying was so amazing. It was amazing to see the land below and I was amazed at how little everything was.'

'So I gather it was amazing, then?' he grinned.

'Yes, sorry, but I just got so carried away. It was the most amaz— incredible thing I've ever experienced.'

'Flying is my life, the war's given me that chance at least. I just wish the Germans would leave us in peace to get on with it. But I am going to be a commercial pilot after the war . . . if I get through it that is.'

Lily was horrified. 'Oh, please don't say that. You're such a brilliant pilot, you'll get through it fine.' But even as she was saying it, she knew that her voice was faltering and that she was as uncertain as he.

The evening was a happy one, spent with the whole crew in the pub and as Lily returned Bill's hankie, she felt part of a team in a way that she hadn't since Blackpool. This was potentially very dangerous, though, as the day before, one of the telephone operators had been completely traumatised at hearing over the airwaves a dog fight of a crew she had become very friendly with. Unable to have a two-way conversation, she had been forced to listen to the boy she had danced the foxtrot with the night before screaming in agony as his plane burst into flames – and then nothing. Lily could only hear Morse, but her imagination was vivid and her dreams were already a morass of burning metal, gunfire and mangled bodies. She didn't need to hear the pilots' voices to feel a close link with them. To become friendly with young men who were facing those sorts of dangers every day was a risk she had tried to avoid.

But that night, the pub was so relaxed, she attempted to forget about everything else and, realising she was starving after being sick, went through three packets of crisps. However, this wasn't quite enough to soak up the two glasses of cider she had drunk. Fiddling with the little blue pack of salt at the bottom of the third packet of crisps, she noticed that Ted's arm was around her shoulders.

Oh well, maybe it's time I let go a bit, she thought and smiled up at him. He had nice eyes, she decided.

Ted kissed her gently at the end of the evening and she decided to respond, feeling his lips press against hers. He finally drew back.

'I think you are a lovely girl, Lily, but you need to know, I don't intend to get involved with anyone until this war is over. There are too many war widows out there already.'

'I think that is a very sensible attitude and I agree completely. I've watched people rush into relationships that are doomed to failure and when I marry, it's for life,' she said, slurring her words slightly as she determinedly nodded her head.

'So now we've established that, does that mean I can kiss you again?' he laughed.

Chapter 25

Getting mail was the highlight of the day and Lily was a good correspondent. She wrote regularly to her family and to Alice and Amy, and their letters back were eagerly anticipated. Her letters to Danny were briefer. He always seemed to go to the bottom of the 'to do' list. Lily was having more and more trouble remembering what he looked like. That was until she received a letter from him. Then, she could just picture Danny talking and hear his voice in the way he wrote, and his letters always made her smile. They were comforting, somehow. A reminder of a less complicated time. But he was on the other side of Europe and good-looking pilots, like Ted, were right here with her.

Lily's mum, who was much better at writing than her dad, regaled her with titbits of information about how she was trying all the recipes out of the National Food Campaign booklet. She was apparently becoming quite an expert at cooking everything on one unit of heat and now it wasn't quite so warm, the coolness of the larder meant she was able to store a few days' food at a time. She told Lily she had discovered curry powder and was using it to spice up potato pie, but her dad, a stickler for meat and two veg, was accusing his wife of 'going all foreign' on him. Her letters were often accompanied by a raisin cake, which made Lily extremely popular in the hut. Glad, in particular, had a sweet tooth and would bribe Lily with cigarettes in exchange for a large slab of the cake.

Glad was a mine of late-night stories, most of which made Lily blush vivid red under the cover of darkness as she whispered her tales. Lily tried to close her ears as Glad openly discussed her colourful life on the streets of Glasgow but found she was fascinated and, she hated to admit it, a little bit excited by the freedom of such an open attitude to an act she had been brought up to believe was a duty, and a sacred one at that. Glad missed out some of the details so Lily's knowledge was extremely sketchy and the thought of a man and woman in bed was something she didn't want to dwell on. Her mum and dad shared a bed for heaven's sake!

Glad had been brought up in the Gorbals, a rough area where survival relied on quick wittedness, resourcefulness and sheer guts. She was the third in a family of five brothers and three sisters and her mother had struggled to make ends meet. Glad's dad worked at John Brown's shipyard, but he drank far too much and sometimes came home violent, lashing out at Glad, her mum and her sisters. Glad explained how he had worsened since 260 German bombers attacked the site in 1941, killing more than 500 civilians. The family had lost their home and had had to move in with a neighbour, cramming an extra ten people into an already crowded tenement. The murky window onto a very different sort of life was a shock for Lily and some of the other girls, but Mary nodded in a way that led the rest to realise she understood what Glad was talking about.

'I left home,' Glad said. 'I couldn'a stand it no more. I had to find somewhere to live and a way to make my living. I tried, I really did, but there wasn't much work in Glasgow at that time and, oh, I don't know . . .' she shrugged. 'I found an easier way to get by an' I was doin' all right at it until this war came along. War and conscription's not good f' business so I volunteered before they made me join up. I thought I'd find myself a new career.'

Her voice was almost proud as she described her fall into hell and she didn't court any approval, disapproval or condemnation. She just didn't care. She was who she was and was making no apologies to anyone.

Lily finally turned over after Glad's life story had come to a chapter's end and thought about the strange places that war takes people to. She would never have come across a prostitute and she certainly would never have learned to like one. Her prejudices were based on ignorance and a blissfully ignorant upbringing. She couldn't help but smile when she thought what her dad would say if he knew she was sleeping next to a prostitute.

Better than sleeping next to a German, she mused as she drifted off.

The next morning, Lily got some post – a letter from Alice, who was apparently dancing her way through the war. The only problem she was having was understanding the Scottish accent. Lily sympathised with this, knowing that sometimes when Glad got excited, there ensued an incomprehensible torrent of Scottish slang, swearwords and jargon. Alice also told of the worries about the coming winter on the Lancashire hill farm. With intense pressure by the Government to produce more food, her parents were struggling to buy the feed for the animals, so Alice was sending much of her RAF pay home. This apparently meant that she had to flirt outrageously so that men would buy her drinks. The thought of the solid Lancashire woman batting her eyelashes like Viv made Lily giggle.

Oh, I miss that girl, she thought.

The second letter was from Amy, who was finally back at home and beginning to take control of her life. She told Lily that the psychiatrist had been wonderful and had made her see how important it was that she should be strong for her dad and brother. They had been struggling to keep going after the funeral and had been so worried about Amy that her dad had stopped eating. Seeing him dwindle into an emaciated shadow had made Amy snap out of her depression and she had eventually marched into the house, straight through to the kitchen and started to make an onion and cheese pudding. She told Lily that standing at the kitchen table, preparing food, she was sure she had heard her mum saying 'Thank you, Amy' and from that moment on, she had taken on her mum's role, bossing and organising the two men in the house. The RAF had given her a combination of medical and compassionate leave and she had been left free for the next six months to support her family.

Lily sat back on her bed and frowned for a minute as she fingered the letters in her hands.

Hmm. Nothing from Danny. Strange. Normally she couldn't shut him up.

Chapter 26

Danny peered warily out of the copse. He could not feel his left leg. He did not dare stand up but he tried to extend the muscle to make sure it was still there. Frank had fallen asleep, uncomfortably perched against some tree roots. Alan and Charlie were leaning against each other and Charlie's mouth was open. Danny had spent the last hour straining his ears to hear whether Charlie was about to start snoring.

If I look that pale and wan, then we're in trouble, Danny thought, taking in Frank's grey, exhausted face in the dim moonlight. He glanced at his watch. Half past five in the morning. They had been there for fourteen hours now, four of them, hiding like moles in the Sicilian countryside. He looked through the bushes and could see the enemy vehicles just a couple of hundred yards away. He could just about make out the uniforms of the Germans as they tried to sleep on the bench seats of the trucks.

Danny was cross. It had been such a stupid mistake. The four of them had been diverted because of a mine that had exploded, blocking the route. Their huge vehicles had been left behind while the smaller trucks moved forward round the debris but then the transporter drivers were told there was another route they could take. It was an old farm track but it was just about wide enough to allow them to pass. Danny drove warily down the unchartered Sicilian road, bumping the sides and hoping the Germans had deemed it too insignificant to place mines. As night fell, they stopped to bivouac and he, Frank and the two others were dispatched to look for water. To avoid detection by the enemy, they had dodged this way and that, in and out of trees. Leading the little group, Danny looked up and realised they were lost.

'I'll go and look over the ridge,' Frank said, zig-zagging across the vegetation.

When he got to the top, he suddenly stopped and then started to walk, very slowly, backwards, signalling to his comrades to hide. He hissed that he had come across a German soldier having a leak but that he did not think he had been seen.

The four of them went on their bellies into the side of the hill, trying desperately not to crunch any leaves.

'Here,' Frank hissed. 'There's some sort of den. Some kids must have made it or maybe someone's been hiding out in it.' He parted the foliage and inside they found a circle with the remnants of bits of food, some scrappy rags in the corner and a homemade bow and arrow.

'I'm not sure this will save us from the Hun,' Danny whispered, moving the bow so he could make himself as comfortable as possible.

They had been there all night, unable to move or speak, listening to the patrol that was just over the hill above them.

Frank woke and moaned gently. Danny reached over and put his hand over his mouth, signalling to the wide-eyed private to keep quiet. They were all desperate for some water and food but had not dared to open their packs where they knew there were life-saving supplies. They had all wet their pants, unable to move to relieve themselves and there was a rising stench.

Danny settled back in his perch, working out they had at least another hour before the October morning dawned and the German patrol would move on. He was worried that, back at camp, Eddie would have sounded the alarm and his company would walk straight into the Germans in a bid to find them.

He mentally had a conversation with his father, who always seemed to know the right thing to do at a time like this. It was strange, he had never talked to him about the previous war. His dad had been a foot soldier just like him and had seen action in the fields of Flanders. He occasionally saw his dad's hands shake when someone mentioned it, but he really did not know what had happened there. It helped Danny to think that his dad had been through something similar and had survived to bring up a family. He smiled to himself. At least his dad had managed not to be a monk then.

There was a noise outside the copse. Danny froze and they looked at each other with the intensity of four men who didn't know whether the next moment would be their last.

Chapter 27

Ted took Lily's mind off everything. His solid, attractive presence was there in Lincolnshire, whereas Danny was thousands of miles away – just a vague memory from a distant life. Cycling along a back road in the autumn sunshine, she took a moment to delight in the flatness of the Lincolnshire countryside. The hills above Manchester had always put her off cycling and her only memory was of a day out with Danny when she opened her mouth to say something on their way to Hyde and nearly choked with a mouth full of gnats. To shut out the piercingly disturbing memory and any Lincolnshire gnats, she kept her mouth firmly shut and pedalled furiously behind Ted to keep up.

Ted had brought a picnic and they stopped at a little village shop to buy some Corona. At their chosen picnic spot, the fizz spurted out of the bottle covering the pair of them in the orange coloured liquid.

'Darn it, that will take some getting out,' Lily complained. 'I'm already having trouble getting my blouses clean. Last domestic night, I had three shirts I couldn't send to laundry because they were torn or stained.'

'I'm becoming an expert at ironing,' Ted replied ruefully. 'My grandmother would be horrified.'

The services demanded high standards from its servicemen and women and the daily inspections held them all to ransom as they begged and borrowed bits of equipment to provide a full kit. Freda, in particular, was an expert at discovering the order in which the huts were being done and she had taught Lily to race off to the one above theirs on the list to borrow shiny or ironed items that had already been checked, placing the booty triumphantly on their own biscuit mattresses in the nick of time.

'I'm really struggling with the mending though,' said Ted, slyly glancing up at Lily, putting his thumb through a hole in his shirt and waggling it at her.

Lily was torn between being helpful and knowing that her stitching would make a seamstress weep. But, aware that he had a series of ops coming up, she took pity on him.

'OK, give it to me when we get back and I'll see what I can do. I'm not promising haute couture though.'

'That's why I love you,' he laughed, pulling her to the ground.

Lily froze. She didn't want to be loved, at least not by an airman who was going out on a week of ops.

'Sorry, I shouldn't have said that and you're right,' Ted said, sitting up again. 'I could love you, Lily, but we both know that would be a mistake.'

Lily gathered up the picnic thoughtfully. Could she love Ted? She looked across at him as he packed up the bikes, his floppy blonde hair dropping into his eyes. He was good looking and she certainly enjoyed his company, but love?

He was obviously embarrassed at his slip and they cycled back in silence. When they arrived at the camp, she put her hand on his arm.

'We're having a lovely time, Ted, and I really enjoyed today but I agree, let's just live for the moment and we'll see what happens.'

He nodded, gave her a peck on the lips and turned his bike towards the sheds.

Two weeks later, Ted, wearing a freshly mended shirt, was dead.

Chapter 28

Lily woke up, got dressed, saluted every officer that passed and got through the next few weeks. She did her job, watched fresh-faced young men tuck into their egg and bacon breakfasts and tapped relentlessly on her Morse key in renewed determination, as if her concentration could bring her crews home safely. It was accepted that no one ever asked what had happened to those that failed to come back but Lily had to know about Ted. She gleaned bits of information from colleagues who looked at her oddly as she questioned them as casually as she could. Piecing together their reluctant comments, she worked out that Ted's crew had dropped their bombs but had then been hit by fighters, causing a fuel fire. He had tried to throw the aircraft into a corkscrew to avoid the pursuing enemy, but they were lit up like a flaming comet and the Messerschmitts had honed in on them relentlessly, bringing them down just as they reached the Dutch coast. The whole crew had been lost. The drinks that night had been put on the lost crew's tabs in the knowledge that the toast would be passed without question by the officer in charge, his mind preoccupied with writing seven letters to seven families.

A welcome letter arrived for Lily. It was from Alice. She was being transferred to Metheringham, just down the road from East Kirkby, and had a forty-eight-hour pass before she had to report for duty, so offered to meet Lily in Lincoln. It was exactly what Lily needed. For the first time since Ted had gone down, she felt a spark of life and raised her head a little higher. Lily was due a day off and almost ran to the bus early the next morning to meet her friend.

Lily hopped up and down outside the station, more excited than she had been in weeks. At the sight of the unruly red hair and the solid frame of Alice coming out from the platform, she rushed forward, gulping in air.

'Hold on, Mullins, you'll squash me!' Alice laughed as she tried to extricate herself from a clinging embrace.

Lily could hardly speak.

'I am . . . so . . . ridiculously pleased to see you,' she said finally, grinning from ear-to-ear.

'Good, glad to hear it. Now where's the best place for tea in Lincoln? We have some serious catching up to do.'

They headed towards the Bishop's Pal, a Women's Voluntary Service canteen in the hallowed surroundings of the Bishop's Palace. Its chintzy armchairs, polished tables and vases of flowers were complimented by home baked cakes and tea. Alice ordered a scone and settled back luxuriously into the armchair, taking in the November frost on the lawn that sloped down outside the window, showing the rooftops of Lincoln way below. Lily tucked into one of the famous jam tarts and as she wiped away the last crumbs, opened her mouth to speak.

The WVS woman smiled as she brought them their tea, having to wait while the two heads separated for a moment and drew breath. They smiled up at her absent-mindedly, paused for a brief second and then carried on talking.

'Sounds like this war is getting too much like hard work,' Alice said, taking in Lily's pale face and tense expression as she finished her story about Ted, lost crews and Amy.

'Listen, Lily, no one said this was going to be easy, but we have no choice. I'm not learning to speak German, and I hate sauerkraut, so fighting for our country is what we all have to do. And you, young lady, are going to have to deal with everything it throws at you. There are people all over the place facing much more than you've come across so far.'

Lily sat back and nodded slowly. She knew Alice was right and she also knew that the no-nonsense words were exactly what she needed to hear.

'Now, ACW Mullins, I want to hear all the gossip. I want to hear about the dances, the flirting and the number of times you've been put on a charge for not saluting since I let you out of my sight.'

The afternoon passed quickly and the tea cups were constantly replenished as Lily told Alice more about Amy and then made her laugh with stories of Gladys's antics. In return, Alice told her about Scotland and how she had tried to learn Scottish dancing, causing havoc on the dance floor. Lily started to giggle and then neither of them could stop. The waitress grinned over at them and the elderly couple on the next table smiled indulgently. It was as if laughter in a war-torn world had become a precious commodity.

Lily made her way back to the camp with a lighter heart. Metheringham was not far away from East Kirkby so the girls had plotted regular meetings.

The following morning, Lily was summoned to the Admin Office. A stern looking warrant officer handed her a piece of paper. Lily gasped as she read the words 'Transfer approved.'

Her hand shook as she looked up at the officer who was staring impatiently back at her.

'A transfer, sir? Where to?'

For a moment, she had forgotten the cardinal rule. No questions.

The officer looked at her with raised eyebrows and Lily started to stutter.

'I'm sorry, sir, but I just . . .' She trailed off, gradually accepting the inevitable.

'When do I go?' she said flatly.

'Get your things and meet the transport at the gate at 1100 hours.'

Lily tried to focus on the piece of paper but the rising panic meant her eyes darted meaninglessly across the black type. She focused. Upper Heyford, Oxfordshire.

She looked at her watch and broke into a run, realising she only had one hour to spare.

As she raced across the compound, she had an imaginary conversation with Alice, bemoaning the fates that were conspiring to deliver yet another blow to their friendship. She could have wept with frustration and muttered up to the sky in angry protest. 'How could you? Just as I was beginning to feel I belonged. Just as Alice had come back on the scene.' The clouds continued to float by with casual abandon, uncaring and unconcerned.

'Damn,' she said as she threw open the door to the hut. Gladys was curled up on her bunk reading a magazine but looked up as the November air wafted into the room. Lily grabbed her kit bag and tried to remember the order everything had to go in.

First shoes, then underclothes, all her toiletries, books, letters, then her RAF shirt and on top the tin hat.

She had almost finished packing when she realised she had forgotten the shoes that were under her bed and had to start from scratch. All the time, Gladys was plying her with questions that she did not know the answer to.

As the clock ticked on towards the hour, she ran out of time and patience. 'Darn it, where's my gas mask?' She scrabbled under the bed. Everyone kept their makeup and hair rollers in their gas mask container so she hurriedly had to unpack the top half of her bag to squash them in the middle.

'Glad, I haven't got time to say goodbye to everyone. Will you tell them for me? I'll write and let you know how I'm doing.'

Glad sighed. 'And I was just about gettin' used to yous. Now, I'll have some snotty-nosed rookie next to me.'

'Yes, and they'll have to get used to you,' Lily smiled. 'Good job we've got you civilised, ready for her.'

'Hah! It'll take more than a lassie from Manchester to civilise me. I only let you think you've tamed me so's I can pinch your mam's fruit cake.'

'This darned war, it just gets in the way of everything! And just as my best friend's been posted down the road.'

Lily stood for a moment, bag in hand, almost on the verge of tears. Gladys got up and strode over to her. She took her by the shoulders and looked steadily into her eyes.

'So, you're off. Well, all I can say is, you'll be fed, you'll have a bed to lie in and you'll not be facing a German soldier at the end of a bayonet, so I'm nay exactly sure what it is you're fussing about. Now take care of yourself and come and see me when you get up to Glasgow when this is all over.'

With that pronouncement, she plonked back on her bed, stuffed a biscuit in her mouth and carried on reading her magazine.

Lily smiled weakly, nodded and walked out of the hut.

Chapter 29

The four men had almost stopped breathing. The tiny crack of a twig outside their hidey-hole had put them on full alert. A grubby face peered in through the bushes – it was a child. A boy of about eight years of age, dressed in rags and very thin. He stared in disbelief at the four soldiers who were cowering in his hideaway.

They beckoned him in and Frank put his finger to his lips to warn him to be quiet. Danny signalled that the Germans were just over the hill by imitating a moustache above his mouth and pointing. The boy nodded and crouched down beside Frank and the other private, Charlie. They stayed like that until they finally heard the engines of the jeeps start up as the sun started to pierce the foliage. The purr of the motors faded into the distance. Alan used sign language to tell the rest to stay where they were, bayoneted his gun and edged on his stomach out of the copse. Nobody moved until they heard Alan's voice calling to give them the 'All Clear.'

They moved slowly and gingerly, their muscles contracted in pain from being immobile and Danny steered the young boy out of the den. As they stretched and stamped their feet, they delved into their packs to find the welcome water and rations, offering them to the boy, who took them greedily.

Danny tried to communicate, '*Come ti chiami*?'

'Georgio.'

'*Cosa . . . stai . . . fare qui*?' Danny was struggling now. His grammar and vocabulary were not up to this. How did the Italians say 'doing here'?

A torrent of Italian came out of the boy's mouth as he looked from one to the other of the men.

'*Lentamente*,' Danny urged, trying to slow him down.

Piecing together a few words here and there, he gathered that the boy's whole family had been killed in a bombing raid by the allies and that he had been living alone in the woods for the last four months. To realise that the 'good guys' had caused the obliteration of this boy's family was a shock to the British Tommies and Alan handed over some valuable chocolate that he had hidden in the bottom of his pack.

They tried to persuade Georgio to come with them back to camp but he vehemently shook his head. He pointed north, explaining he was going to find his aunt and uncle. When Frank tried to take his arm, he pushed it roughly away and sped off up the hill. When he got to the top, he turned, saluted, grinned and then disappeared over the top.

Chapter 30

'Come on, Gorgeous,' the driver said, helping her to swing her bag under the tarpaulin covering the back of the truck. 'You're the only one. I've got to get these supplies there PDQ.'

'Pretty Damned Quick' turned out to be a ride on a rollercoaster and Lily was bounced unceremoniously around in the back of the truck as it swung around corners on its way to Oxfordshire. Lily closed her eyes to hold onto her last sight of East Kirkby and had to concentrate hard so as not to be sick over the boxes of food supplies.

'Just as Alice had come almost within cycling distance, wouldn't you know it?' she challenged the box of cornflour next to her.

Upper Heyford was a very different camp and, as a peacetime base, was established with trees and mature hedges. Lily could see it was bigger than East Kirkby. An OTU – Operational Training Unit – she hoped it might be calmer, but she also suspected it would be more boring. She was told to report for equipment at 1500 hours which gave her time for a quick bite to eat in the cookhouse and its clean, pastel walls with paintings of fruit, vegetables and flowers made her feel quite cheerful. After a passable macaroni cheese, Lily was marched towards the WAAF guard-room where they allocated her a billet and gave her some bedding. She was then marched to her hut by a squat corporal who swung her arms stiffly by her sides and Lily almost had to run to keep up with her. In the entrance to the hut, she spotted some notices about dances, cinema, theatre performances and events in the mess. Thinking that Upper Heyford might not be as bad as she had thought, she was shown her bed and started to put out her things in the regimental order that was finally becoming second nature to her.

At just before three o'clock, Lily went to the Watch Office and then up to Flying Control. She saluted and introduced herself to the corporal who was in charge. Her name was Barbara and she showed Lily round the now familiar equipment that she would be using. She also told Lily about Upper Heyford's gruesome nickname – the Rhodesian Graveyard – which came from one course of trainee pilots who had suffered such heavy losses during training that they were almost wiped out.

Lily's shift began immediately and she realised that the base's status as a training unit meant that there was not the camaraderie of an operational station. It was a busy but mundane night as she helped new navigators find their way to pre-established coordinates and back to the base.

The hesitant Morse from the other end made her aware just how new to the job these young men were, but there was no adrenaline, no cheering groups as the planes flew off or landed safely, but, she hoped, no deaths either.

The following morning, she woke with a bad neck and back. She had not had time to rearrange the three biscuit mattresses and they had parted underneath her so that parts of her were hitting the cold, wiry springs underneath. She groaned.

The girl in the next bed turned to her and whispered, 'Hi, I'm Hilda. Welcome to Upper Heyford.'

'I'm Lily,' she replied, 'been transferred from East Kirkby. I have no idea why or what for but that's normal these days, isn't it?'

They both grinned just as the loudspeaker announced reveille to get them up.

Following the crowd of girls to the ablutions, Lily heard a familiar voice.

'I really can't abide this cold water any more. My maid would die rather than expect me to wash in cold water.'

'Marion!' Lily exclaimed to herself, edging her way around the group in front of her to where the voice had come from. She was almost pleased to see such a familiar face.

'Well, if it isn't Lily Mullins,' Marion said. 'Who'd have thought you would still be in this war? I thought they'd have sent you home by now.'

The initial pleasure at seeing Marion was replaced by memories of that vicious tongue and catty comments and Lily stopped in her step forward to give Marion a hug.

'Hello Marion,' she said, looking at the soft, white dressing gown and pink fluffy slippers that made Marion stand out from the crowd like a white swan amidst brown mallard ducks. The rest of the girls had stopped too and crowded round to see the newcomer who seemed to know the most unpopular girl in the camp.

'I thought all your insurrections would have guaranteed you a place in the munitions factory by now,' Marion said haughtily.

'Strangely, no. I seem to have survived the RAF's efforts to suppress my spirit,' Lily replied with more confidence than she had shown against this imperious being when they were both in Blackpool.

'Well, you'll love it here. It's right up your street. It's very frivolous and full of people who drink too much.'

Lily gasped. 'It's good to see you too, Marion.' She turned away and started to brush her teeth furiously. Hilda looked at her curiously but didn't say anything until they got back into the hut to get dressed.

'Know her, do you? The princess? '

Lily smiled. 'Yes, and we used to call her that too. I was at Blackpool with her – billeted in the same room.'

'Poor you. Must have been a nightmare.'

'Yes, it was, but she seems to have got worse,' Lily said as she pushed her hair under her cap to try to keep the odd strands from touching her collar.

'Oh yes, she keeps us all on our toes' Hilda said. 'I've met her type before. I used to work in a haberdashery shop on the Wirral and the women from the posh houses in West Kirby would come in, lording it over us but I soon learned to ignore them. So, I've loads of practice dealing with the Marions of this world but for some strange reason my vast experience with ribbons and bows doesn't help nearly as much in this stupid war!' Both girls started to laugh and by the time they had got to the NAAFI, Hilda and Lily had become good friends. A tall, athletic girl with brown hair, who strode everywhere, Hilda towered over Lily. She seemed to have the knack of getting to the front of the canteen queue which Lily decided was a definite advantage in a friend. Hilda had been sports captain at school and was constantly cajoling the girls to join her in a jog before breakfast. She had a brother who was a footballer for Tranmere Rovers. He was in the Middle East and Hilda was constantly worrying whether he was getting any food.

'Things seem to be hotting up,' she confided in Lily when they manoeuvred their trays through the tables to find an empty space. 'We're on the edge of it all here, but they are training more and more pilots. Something is definitely happening.'

Lily frowned, trying to remember something her dad had said in his last letter. Always hearing titbits of news that may or may not find their way into the papers, he had hinted that 1944 was likely to bring some major push into Europe. For a moment, Lily had a pang that she was on a training base and not in the thick of the action.

'We had so many courses last month that the whole airfield felt as if it was in a plane on circuits and bumps,' Hilda said. 'The noise every night was deafening; it was impossible to sleep.'

Circuits and bumps were the endless takings off and landings that every pilot had to do before qualifying and many of them were noisy and messy affairs. Hilda told Lily tales of how rookie pilots made mistakes, including one who had managed to select 'undercarriage up' instead of 'flaps down' as he came into land, gracefully sinking to the floor. He blocked the intersection of the runways, effectively bringing the airfield to a standstill and had to suffer endless ribbing in the mess as a result. Hilda did not add that such mistakes also cost lives.

The shifts were relentless but quite boring. Fortunately, the social life was making up for it. Hilda had taken Lily in hand and helped her to organise her shifts so she could attend the dances at Oxford Town Hall on a Saturday night. In preparation, she gave an enthusiastic lesson on how to jitterbug in the hut beforehand, causing hilarity and mayhem amongst the bunks as the floor vibrated with the girls' heavy shoes leaping backwards and forwards.

It was difficult for the ground staff at Upper Heyford to get to know the crews because of the quick turnover of courses, but Hilda's easy manner with men had gained her a pivotal role as one of the gang and she had already got to know some of the American crews from nearby stations. On the night of the first dance, she led the way into the Town Hall and immediately muscled her way into one group by the door, introducing Lily to a crowd of good-looking Yanks who were obviously part of a regular crowd.

One was standing in the middle of the group but kept looking at Lily. She tilted her head back disdainfully, which made him smile. He was blonde with impossibly high cheekbones and piercing blue eyes. Lily ignored him as the obvious Adonis of the group who would expect – and receive – all the attention. This Saturday night, she decided, as the newcomer, it was obviously destined to be her turn. Unimpressed, she sat on a chair and talked animatedly to a small, slightly older American called Johnny, but after a few minutes, the Adonis walked towards her.

'Excuse me, Johnny, but as you're married and are wasting this lovely lady's time, I am going to cut in on you.'

'I was talking to Johnny,' Lily said witheringly, but Johnny, accepting defeat, moved away, leaving his chair free for his friend to sit on.

The Adonis's name was Kit and he used every trick in the book to appeal to Lily but they all failed dismally. No matter how much he flattered her, tried to make her laugh or regaled her with tales of heroism, he saw no softening of her features.

Hmmm, this is going to be a challenge, Kit thought delightedly. The English girls had been a pushover so far and he was getting bored. Used to attention and instant success, he had been finding he had been going through the motions but without any real interest. This young lady was a different proposition though.

Lily was not impressed. Kit reminded her of Davey Butler at the Boys' Brigade. The unrivalled king of the Rusholme empire, he had taken on the challenge of getting the aloof Lily Mullins to dance with him, but she had refused, instead choosing the boys with a good sense of humour who made her giggle. Kit's good looks and put-on charm left her feeling cold and she glanced around the room to see if Hilda could help her escape, but Hilda just smiled knowingly as she floated past on the arm of a Canadian airman, with raised eyebrows expressing approval of Lily's 'conquest.'

After half an hour, even Kit's ingenuity was beginning to fail him, and he was beginning to think he should retire gracefully while he worked out his next strategy, but then another girl approached.

'Lily, my dear, how are you? How lovely to see you and how gorgeous you look tonight.'

'Hello, Marion,' Lily said dully, looking down sceptically at the same uniform she had worn now for two years.

'I've been meaning to track you down, but it's just been so busy, I haven't had a minute. Oh, hello,' she said, pretending to only just have noticed Kit.

'Kit, this is Marion. Marion . . . meet Kit.'

Marion's eyes fastened onto Kit's features like a pair of eagles' talons.

'Yes, I'm Marion, from Chelsea . . . in London, you know.'

'I haven't been to London yet, I've been waiting for one of you English girls to take me,' Kit said, looking at Marion and then trying to include Lily in the conversation.

'Well, we'll have to see about that. You simply must go to Harrods, it's the only place to shop and the tea there is divine.'

Lily stood up and with a finality said, 'Well, I'll leave you two to it. I need to go to the bog.'

Kit stood up and started to say something, but Lily put out her hand to stop him. 'It's been nice meeting you. Good night.'

Kit watched her disappear into the crowd, his interest more intense than it had been since he had arrived in England. This young WAAF was just the challenge he needed.

Chapter 31

Lily was still shocked by Ted's death and was certainly not in the mood for romance but there was another reason why she appeared distracted and unimpressed by Kit's charms. A couple of days earlier she had been going off duty and making her way across the airfield when she looked up to see a Spitfire coming in to land. Lily was fascinated by these wonderful planes that were giving the RAF such an edge and she loved watching them fly. She stood, shielding her eyes and watched the pilot skilfully bring the plane to a complete standstill as if it were a graceful swan gliding to land on a pond. She peered at the pilot who was climbing out and then uttered an exclamation of complete shock – it was a woman. Lily was stunned. Was this one of those mythical creatures from the Air Transport Auxiliary who delivered planes around the country? She had heard about them but never thought to meet one. The girl hurried off, leaving Lily wandering around all day in a daze, looking everywhere to see if she could spot the female pilot.

The following morning, Lily was on her way to the control tower to sign on shift. For once she was early as she hadn't slept well, tossing and turning, imagining herself piloting a Spitfire. There was a figure in front of her – it was her! Lily stopped in her tracks and took a huge gasp. Like a schoolgirl with a crush, she surreptitiously followed the girl as she made her way to the guard-room. Lily mumbled something to the desk officer that there may be a message for her before sitting down so she could watch the girl in front of her.

Oblivious that every move was being scrutinised, the girl took off her helmet to release a glorious mane of deep, auburn hair She confidently put her delivery chit on the counter and announced she was waiting for her transport back to base in Hamble. The man behind the desk looked as surprised as Lily at the confident young woman standing at the desk and eventually just nodded. The pilot turned around and sat on the wooden bench next to Lily, who smiled shyly at the girl but could not help staring at the insignia on her tunic. The golden wings shone out like a lucky charm and Lily was completely overwhelmed. She could not take her eyes off them.

'I am in the ATA, my name's Roberta,' the girl told her, to break the embarrassed silence. 'That's the Air Transport Auxiliary. I deliver planes.'

In that second, Lily fell in love – with the idea of a woman who could fly, with the glamour of the uniform, with the thought of being able to be on an equal footing with the men. It was if the clouds suddenly parted and she could see miles and miles of blue sky and a chance for women like her to soar.

'My name's Lily,' she stammered, and then came out with a torrent of questions, each merging into the next. How did she get to be an ATA pilot, what did she fear most, how did she deal with all the male prejudice, which aircraft was the best to fly? She could not stop.

'Woah,' the girl laughed. 'One question at a time.'

Roberta explained to Lily that she was brought up on a farm in Norfolk. She paused and then went on to explain that her only brother had died at birth, leaving her to take on a huge range of tasks on the farm from mending and driving tractors, to organising the farmworkers.

'You see, there was no one else,' she patiently explained. 'I was never treated like a girl.'

When the farm was extended, she added, her father agreed to pay for flying lessons so they could spray the crops from the air. It sounded the most natural thing on earth to have flying lessons, Lily thought, remembering her own father struggling to pay for piano lessons for her as a child. The girl had no idea what effect her matter-of-fact revelations were having on her captivated audience.

'My name may be Roberta, but I prefer Bobby,' she said, leaning over to whisper.

Lily ran the name over her tongue; even her name sounded glamorous. Bobby smiled at Lily's blatant admiration and then tried to reply to the succession of breathless questions that were fired at her.

'Once I heard about the ATA, I couldn't resist the chance to fly to help the war effort. It beats knitting socks,' Bobby laughed. Lily cringed at the memory of her disastrous attempts at knitting in the morning room at home. She felt completely inadequate. She had never felt the need to compete with men as to her they obviously had a very defined role in society that was different from hers, but here was a woman, a girl even, taking on the men at their own level.

Lily concentrated again, wanting to drink in every single word. Bobby was telling her how her flying experience had meant she was snapped up and had been fulfilling the unofficial motto of 'Anything to Anywhere' ever since. She leaned over to Lily and whispered, 'We girls say the ATA stands for "Always Terrified Airwomen" but we don't tell the men that.'

'So what . . . I mean . . . how . . . I mean, it's so unusual for a woman to fly. Is it difficult?'

Bobby was used to being scorned by men who hated seeing a woman taking the controls of a Spitfire or a Wellington, so to see the naked admiration in the young woman's face was a welcome change.

'No, not really,' she replied, thinking about it. 'I think learning to fly one plane is quite easy really, which is what

RAF pilots generally do. We've got to learn to fly over a hundred,' she said proudly. 'The problems come when the weather changes. We're not allowed to fly above the clouds, which is quite difficult sometimes and we have no radios, which makes it hard if we get into difficulties, and of course we don't get to hear if barrage balloons are suddenly put up or if the enemy's been spotted nearby. Maybe that's a good thing though,' she laughed.

'What's it like, up there?' Lily almost whispered in reverence.

Bobby was about to give the usual spiel about it being fine, nothing out of the ordinary really for a girl who had been flying since she was sixteen, when she glimpsed the world that she took for granted from this young woman's perspective. She closed her eyes and Lily followed suit. Bobby whisked her mentally away from the ground at Upper Heyford and up into the sky above them.

'It's . . . it's incredible. I feel the controls in my hands, the throb of the engine under my feet and I look towards the runway knowing I can whizz over it in a matter of seconds and then that moment when I lift the wheels up . . . there is nothing like it in the whole world. It's as if I was an angel, taking my wings and flying off into the unknown. I feel as if nothing can touch me – although, to be honest, we're at risk from the enemy just like any other pilot, but for some reason, I never worry about that. I am in control and nothing can hurt me.'

'Is this what you were waiting for?' The desk officer burst their reverie. He was looking at them both as if they were unhinged. He handed a sheet of paper to Bobby.

'Oh, thank you,' Bobby stood up. Lily was staring at the man as if she was surprised to see another human being standing there, in this, her dream world.

'Goodbye, Lily, it's been nice to meet you,' said Bobby, and as an afterthought, she added, 'Go for your dreams, Lily. No one can deny you the chance to try. You know, you could apply to join the ATA. They've introduced what's called the *Ab Initio* programme and are looking for people who've never flown but are interested in learning.' With that she swept out of the guard-room.

Lily got hurriedly to her feet. She muttered something to the desk officer about having got it wrong about any message, but he stopped her leaving and gave her a second piece of paper. 'Well, as long as you're here, you can take this over to the control tower.' She grabbed it and ran out to catch Bobby up.

'Where do I find out about this programme?' she asked breathlessly.

'Just talk to the powers that be, they'll sort you out,' Bobby replied.

'I will, I will, thank you so much . . . and, Bobby, we may never meet again but I want to say you are the most amazing woman I have ever met and you may have changed my life. I will never, ever forget you.'

With that Lily fled across the camp. In a daze, she delivered the message to the control tower, staring blankly at the hand that reached out to take it and then signed on automatically.

'In love,' the flight lieutenant mouthed to the telephone operator as Lily walked into the door on her way to her Morse station.

Chapter 32

1st November 1943

Dear Lily,

Thanks for your letter, I was so sorry to hear about your friend. It is really hard to lose people. I know you couldn't tell me what happened or much about it but I felt how upset you were and I hope you are coping better, especially now you are in your new post. In a strange way, moving on might be a good thing because you have so much to concentrate on that you just don't have time to think about the past. I am fine but it's really cold and wet. It's been a bit of a mission recently and we too have lost some good men, one of them, I am afraid to say, was Frank, so we are down to 2Js now, which is hard. I am finding it increasingly difficult to remember a time before this war. I wonder how long it will last. I heard from Mum and Dad last week and it was so nice to have news from home. I am looking forward to some leave shortly, just a few days and we can't go very far, but it will be a welcome break to get away for a bit. I wish I could come home. Manchester seems a long way away.

I received your mum's cake, do thank her for me. It was really nice of her to send it and I shared it out to the lads, who were very grateful.

I heard that the Citizen was lost off Accra in July. That must have been terrible for Liners. I wonder how they are all doing in the office. Most of the youngsters will be away at war now so I presume Mr Spencer is having to make his own tea.

The girls seem fine, they write regularly, although as we are moving on, it is hard to catch up with post and sometimes it takes ages to reach us so I feel I'm way behind with all your news by the time I get it. They are both still home-based and I think Pam is getting frustrated, but she is better off there.

I hope you settle in to your new station. I know it's hard to move on, but you will hold on to the friends that matter.

Must go now, but do take care of yourself. We have our whole lives to enjoy when this is all over.

Love,

Danny x

Danny put more feeling into that little cross at the end of his letter than she would ever know. He was almost at the end of his tether. The death of Frank had devastated him. It had happened so suddenly and was a prime example of the waste of war. Frank had been in a truck further up the convoy and they had struck a mine. The explosion ricocheted down the narrow valley that they were in and Danny had ground his vehicle to its slow, heavy halt, holding his breath. The Germans had blown everything up in their path, knowing that the allies had little choice but to travel up the narrow gorges. The troops had been constructing Bailey bridges to cross rivers, hurriedly fitting together the pieces of light steel to let the convoys of artillery make their way north. There had been five casualties and he had watched the medics taking the bodies away with the detachment that had etched itself into all their hardened hearts but later, when he went to find Frank, he was told that he had been one of those hit. It was a moment when the hopelessness of war threatened to completely overwhelm him, and Danny had to go for a long walk round the perimeter of the camp. He desperately wanted to go further away from anything with khaki on it to see some normal foliage but the rules were strict. Looking over the letter, Danny realised he had not been able to litter it with his usual off-hand exclamation marks or quips. He felt a deep connection with Lily and her loss and despite a slight quiver of fear wondering whether Lily's dead 'friend' had been male, he sent her a hug across the continents.

Chapter 33

Lily folded Danny's letter. It had taken so long to reach her and there was no sign of the ebullience that had dominated his early letters. It was dull in tone and there were none of the jokes she had become accustomed to. She had been hearing stories about the army moving through Sicily and suspected that was where he was. She knew there had been fierce fighting there. The detached way he described Frank's death did not fool her for a moment. For just a brief moment, she felt her stomach lurch as she thought of the dangers Danny was facing and it brought her up sharply. She had started to think of Danny as a fixed point in her life, always there, a solid memory she could lean on, but the newsreels had shown a very different story. It had never occurred to her that anything would happen to Danny, but now she was beginning to fear for him. For a moment, she sat on her bunk and thought back to how off-hand she had been with him before he left. Her experiences of the last year had made her realise that not all men were as honest and reliable as Danny.

He's fun too, she thought, as she had a flashback to him clowning about on a walk with Patch. It made her sad so she dismissed the disturbing vision and went back to her overriding obsession . . . flying.

She had managed to get the address to write to about joining the ATA from a senior officer and immediately sent off for an application form. Then she begged and borrowed as many books as she could lay her hands on to find out as much as she could about the controls and ways of flying but it only served to make her feel as if she were clasping at a cloud because she knew in her heart that the girls who were chosen for the ATA were highly qualified and much more technically capable than she was. But Lily did not like being thwarted and she wrote to her mother to express her frustration.

The reply was sympathetic but reminded her of when she informed her family she was going to be a famous ballet dancer. Her mother's response at that time was, 'Yes, very nice dear, but first, can you help me pod these peas.' This time, she replied that she thought Lily would look very nice in an ATA uniform but didn't she get travel sickness?

Lily had to find a way to achieve more than everyone seemed to expect from her.

Kit searched the bars in Upper Heyford every time he was off duty to try to track Lily down and although he found her friends, he failed to find Lily herself. The more she eluded him, the more determined he became and the Don Juan of the American group decided to give this intriguing girl his full attention and tried to distance himself from the willing crowd of girls who surrounded him. At the front of this crowd was Marion, who had set her sights on the attractive Yank. She used all her wiles to get his attention and was getting increasingly cross that he was ignoring her. After the first thwarted attempts she realised why he was so disinterested. He brought Lily's name into every conversation and scanned the room regularly to check if she was there. Marion was not used to being ignored and she decided it was time for revenge. She just needed to bide her time until an opportunity arose.

A new batch of WAAFs had arrived at Upper Heyford and watching them march towards the huts, Marion was looking out of the window when she spotted a small, pert sergeant at the front of them, arms swinging, feet determinedly pointing forwards and two hair grips holding her hair in place under her cap.

Sergeant Horrocks! Marion smiled slyly. Her day was complete.

Lily was on duty that afternoon, but new pilots had been stood down because of bad weather and only the more experienced trainees were flying. She was making peppermint creams to pass the time when she glanced down at the pathway next to the runway. Surely not . . .? She peered in horror. It couldn't be.

She groaned. Hilda, who was helping to form little round shapes with the peppermint mixture, while keeping her ears out for crackling sounds from her machine, turned towards her.

'What's up?'

'I can't believe it. This is a huge war, there are Bomber Command posts all over the country and the two people who can make my life a misery end up here, in Upper Heyford.'

'Who are you talking about?'

'Marion for one. She's enough to send anyone to wave a white flag at the Germans, but now there's Sergeant Horrocks. She was at Blackpool with us and for some reason absolutely hated me. I never found out what I had done to deserve it, but she loathed me and she made sure I suffered for it.'

Hilda passed her over an oval shape.

'Here, have this, it sounds like you need a sugar rush.'

Lily chomped despondently at the peppermint cream and then reached for two more. It was going to be a long shift.

Sergeant Horrocks took the parade the next morning and her mouth curled into a sneer as she recognised the tall, blonde WAAF at the back of the line.

'Well, if it isn't Lily Mulllins. How lovely to see you. I felt sure our paths would cross again.'

Lily carried on looking straight ahead and over Sergeant Horrocks's shoulder into the distance. She was determined not to give the sergeant any opportunity to catch her out.

Horrocks moved to within an inch of Lily's face and then peered down to inspect her buttons.

'Hmm. I see your housekeeping hasn't improved much. My office tonight at 1700 hours.'

Lily felt her shoulders droop. She knew her buttons were clean and shiny but she also knew that no matter how much she abided by the endless list of rules and regulations, her behaviour would never be enough to satisfy Sergeant Horrocks.

At 1700 hours, Lily knocked on the sergeant's door. A sharp 'Enter' came from the other side.

Lily marched into the room, holding herself as straight as she could. If this woman wanted a war, Lily was ready for her.

For a moment, Sergeant Horrocks said nothing. She just walked round Lily, inspecting her from head to toe.

'I believe you want to join the ATA,' she said finally.

Lily took a sharp breath. How did Sergeant Horrocks know about her dream? She must have gone through the mail. She said nothing, deciding that discretion was the greater part of valour.

'What makes you think a frivolous girl like you could ever amount to anything?'

The tone was vitriolic and the sergeant practically spat the words out.

'You're nothing but a low-born girl from the back streets of Manchester. On a charge.'

Lily was taken aback. Even she hadn't suspected that an officer could be so unfair.

'May I ask on what charge, Sergeant?'

'The insolence! The charge is that your hair is touching your collar.'

Lily felt up with her right hand and discovered one stray strand of hair that had unfurled onto her collar.

She knew there was no chance of defending herself.

'Yes, Sergeant,' she said.

'Dismissed,' the sergeant said, looking down at her paperwork. Lily turned on her heels and walked out of the door.

'Kit will be disappointed,' Hilda said, when Lily told her she would be scrubbing pans the following night instead of going for a drink.

'Oh, he'll live, and anyway, Marion will be there to take up his full attention.'

Scrubbing six large saucepans with a very dilapidated Brillo pad, Lily sadly pondered how she was going to deal with her time at Upper Heyford. It had all started so promisingly and now, with Marion and the arrival of Sergeant Horrocks, her life was being thrown into turmoil and all her recent good record was in jeopardy. She decided she was going to have to be ingenious if she was going to survive unscathed. She scrubbed the pans with more enthusiasm than the slightly burned bottoms warranted and envisaged Horrocks's and Marion's faces in them as she smeared the dirty Brillo pad across the base. When she saw the pans gleaming at the end of her endeavours, she nodded with satisfaction. All traces of her foes completely eradicated. Very satisfactory. Now for real life.

Chapter 34

Lily walked slowly back to the hut, thinking. She was still trying to work out what she had done to alienate the two women. She thought back to Blackpool. Marion was easy, she knew that Lily was far from impressed by her high and mighty ways, and Lily had never been backward in taking the mickey out of the London girl's pretentions. She suspected her version of a sense of humour was lost on Marion, who liked to lead the pack and be looked up to and admired. Alice had escaped Marion's venom because any sort of subtlety was wasted on her down-to-earth nature, but Lily had been an easier target. She had been popular with everyone because she made them laugh and sometimes that laughter had, she had to admit, been at Marion's expense. So that was Marion's reason for disliking her so much. Sergeant Horrocks was another matter.

She thought back to the night she had seen her outside the Medical Centre. She then tried to think further back to when she first met her. From that moment, when Sergeant Horrocks had taken the roll call and stopped to look at each WAAF to register the face against the name, her eyes had narrowed as if she recognised Lily. She went on to stumble over the other names and at the end of the list, turned slowly on her heel and started to walk away, staggering as she went.

'Surely I can't have done anything to upset her.' Lily said out loud as she rounded the corner near her hut. She was no further on and in any case, she was exhausted, her hands were rubbed raw and she had an early shift the next morning. Sergeant Horrocks's hate campaign was going to have to wait, she was going to bed.

At that moment, at the other side of the camp, Sergeant Horrocks was going through all the admin and mail that had come in for the WAAFs. She saw an announcement that Aircraftwoman second class Lily Mullins was to be promoted to Leading Aircraftwoman and she seethed with fury. Then she saw a typed letter thanking ACW Lily Mullins from the Air Transport Auxiliary for her application and enclosing a form for her to fill in. The sergeant was entitled to check all mail for any infringement of secrecy but she was not entitled to pick up a box of matches, put her tin waste paper bin on the desk and set light to the letter from the ATA, gleefully consigning the charred remains to the bottom of the bin.

The next night was domestic night, when all the WAAFs had to clean their huts. The evening was one when a

WAAF officer would inspect kit laid out on the bed, when shoes were to be polished and when the floor area around each bed was to be cleaned until it shone. Anyone who failed the inspection would have their name and bed number posted on the mess wall with a note in capital letters saying 'DIRTY'. It was a public shaming they all studiously avoided. There was always a great deal of moaning and groaning about domestic night but it was also a good chance for a gossip and a giggle.

'Just what my poor hands need,' Lily told Hilda, looking down at her already chapped hands.

'Here, try some Vaseline. I've got a new tub of it,' Hilda replied. Hilda's background of helping out on the touchline at Tranmere Rovers had led her to a life of inventive cures for everything from acne to warts.

But the Vaseline meant that Lily kept dropping things and, eventually, the girls forbade her from touching anything breakable and gave her the sanitary towels to clean the floor with. This was a tradition that had started at the beginning of the war when the girls realised the free towels were eminently suitable for a long list of uses including cleaning shoes, padding out shoulders and buffing up buttons and floors, as well as face masks.

Trixie was from Newcastle and her accent was almost impenetrable, but while she polished, she sang some of the old fishing ditties from her childhood and the girls all started to sway and clean in time. Hilda glanced at Lily and grinned.

'There are moments when I just love this war,' she said. 'At home, it's always so quiet you can hear the clocks ticking. Mum and Dad are quite old and Dad likes his newspaper while Mum knits. I was so bored at home, this war has given me the chance to live with a group of girls and, do you know what, Lily, I love it.'

Lily looked around and nodded in agreement. She had almost forgotten what it was like to live at home and she knew it was going to be hard to go back there permanently when the war was over, but due for some leave, she realised she was going have a chance to practise very soon. It had been weeks since she had sent off her inquiry about the ATA and she had heard nothing, despite checking the post room three times a day. Her bitter disappointment was somewhat alleviated by the fact that she had been promoted to LACW, which meant she was a Leading Aircraftwoman. She had proudly sewn the badge of a propeller onto her sleeve, rubbing it so much that it looked a bit old and worn and as if she had been a LACW for years. She could not wait to show her parents.

A full week's pass was on offer and Lily began to be excited. It had been a long time since she had been back to Manchester and she knew that her mother had been saving coupons in readiness for a feast. Her dad had written that he had swapped his day off work so he could spend it with her.

The train was packed with servicemen and women all over the carriage. Some showed signs of injury and Lily was pulled up sharply when she saw a young soldier with bandages over his eyes being helped along the carriage by a nurse. She suddenly felt a need to write to Danny.

When they stopped at Crewe, which strangely always smelt of fish, they all piled into the cafeteria but had to scrabble round to find their mugs. There ensued good natured bartering as one serviceman, with a suspicious number of mugs available, managed to bag a variety of food items, clothing and cigarettes in exchange for his prized tea containers. Lily finally found her mug, which she had left at the bottom of her kit bag this time, but the rest of the queue was amused when five hair rollers fell out as she delved into the muddle that was her usual style of packing. They rolled across the platform, disappearing under legs and bags, leaving her no option but to set off in hot pursuit, unceremoniously upturning sleeping soldiers to find them. She had to deal with a good deal of ribaldry before she found all five and by the time she got back on the train, they were like a group of friends who had known each other for years. Lily was finally one of them. The chatter did not cease until the train pulled in to Oxford Road.

Lily craned her head out of the window and waved furiously as she spotted her mum and dad looking anxiously along the train. Her mum broke into a run when she finally spotted her daughter, clutching her platform ticket like a trophy.

'Oh Mum, it's so good to see you, it's been ages.' She hugged them both, jumping up and down on the spot.

'I know, I know,' said Ginny, dabbing her eyes. 'You look so grown up and look at those tapes on your uniform, a proper qualified WAAF. Oh, you're so smart, Lily.'

They linked arms, talking non-stop while her dad carried her bag, and headed off to catch the bus home.

Lily was shocked by the state of Manchester when she saw that there were even more bombed out buildings. Everywhere there was rubble where houses used to be. Familiar sights were obliterated and for a sickening moment, Lily thought of her beloved family being bombarded from the skies.

'Have you been sleeping any better, Mum? Manchester looks a mess.' she said, fearfully, squeezing her mum's arm. 'She looked sideways at her. Ginny was definitely thinner and a little more lined but she was reassuringly still her mum.

'I don't want to talk about the war, I've had enough of it,' she replied with that determined pursing of the lips that Lily knew so well. A sweet, gentle woman, but when Ginny Mullins's family was threatened by anyone or anything, she became a formidable force.

Lily wondered whether Hitler realised what he had taken on.

It took less than five minutes for Lily to check out the house: her bedroom, the garden and the Anderson Shelter which she patted to give it renewed strength. She raced around at breakneck speed, dropping her jacket at the front door, leaving her mum to pick it up. Finally, she plonked down in the morning room armchair with a sigh of relief.

'I'll get us a cup of tea, and I've baked some of that cake you like,' Ginny said.

Lily closed her eyes and then sprang them open again to check everything was still there. Yes, the range was lit, the damask tablecloth still had the burn on it from the candles that Don knocked over three Christmases ago and the wireless was in pride of place in the corner of the room. Her letters were stacked behind the photograph of her at school and as she looked closely at it, its glass reflection showed her older, hopefully wiser, face superimposed on the naïve young girl.

For a second, Lily allowed herself to think about sitting in the morning room with no war going on outside, being able to wear civvies and to be planning a night out with Hannah and Ros in Manchester. She heaved a huge sigh. It all seemed like another world. She realised how tired she was, fell back in the chair and closed her eyes once more.

It was going dark when she opened them again and the cup of tea next to her on the table had gone cold. Her mum was sitting in the armchair opposite doing some darning and her dad was poking the fire to try to make the most of the meagre bits of coal they were trying to make last through the evening. Lily knew they had gone without a fire all week so that the coal would last for their daughter coming home, and she smiled sleepily at them both and then glanced at the clock on the mantelpiece. It was five o'clock. Don had gone to a friend's house after school but was due in any minute and they would all sit down for tea together before her dad left for work. It was all so normal.

Five minutes later, the back door flew open and her brother raced in, chucking down his satchel and flinging himself at Lily, taking the wind out of her.

'You've grown!' she said, laughing as she caught her breath.

'Yep, nearly as big as Dad now,' he said, drawing himself up to his full height, and sizing himself up next to his father. His dad grinned down at his son, who was almost up to his shoulder.

'I'll make a good RAF pilot, won't I?'

A little bit of sibling rivalry from years gone by prompted a tiny twang of envy. Lily knew Don's marks at school would probably allow him to apply at pilot level. She had spent nights dreaming of flying Spitfires, Wellingtons and Hurricanes, wearing that wonderful uniform emblazoned with gold wings but without a reply from the ATA, she had almost come to terms with the fact that girls like her just did not get the chance to rise to such dizzy heights. A pang of regret hit her as she thought of her school years when she had been more interested in having fun than getting good grades. She groaned, remembering the wonderful chorus of 'It Had To Be You' on the back row in science that got her detention while others got top marks. This war was opening up new opportunities for women – and she so wanted to be part of the revolution.

Still, she had managed to rise in the ranks of the RAF and she fingered the tapes to remind herself.

It took very little time for Lily to relax back into being at home with her mum fussing about her. She murmured in ecstasy at the homemade creations Ginny somehow magically conjured up from limited rations and luxuriated in having some warm water to wash in.

Lily was particularly excited that her two schoolfriends, Hannah and Ros, had been able to co-ordinate some time off and were coming over to see her before she went back. It was strange to see them again. They immediately fell into the old chatter and laughter around the morning room table, but Lily knew they had all changed.

Mrs Mullins was revelling in serving them tea and freshly made oaty biscuits and imagining the last four years hadn't happened. The diminutive Ros was working in the munitions factory close to home so she could help her widowed mother with her two younger brothers. She had been making Lily and Hannah laugh with stories of the antics the girls got up to relieve the boredom of packing bullets but while she tried to make her life seem exciting with the importance of the war efforts at the factory, she could not compete with her two friends. Ros looked enviously at their uniforms and felt out of place in the skirt and blouse she had changed into specially for the reunion. Her work overalls were so drab.

Hannah stood up, unfurling her tall back. She wore the green jumper and brown corduroy trousers of the Land Army. She claimed she had been lured by the glamorous posters into wanting a rural life, but as she described the hardships of life in the depths of Norfolk, without running water or any form of heating, her two friends soon realised why she grabbed every chance to come back to the city. Her life seemed one long round of planting potatoes and leeks followed by digging up last season's, but she did seem stronger and certainly had a healthy glow to her cheeks.

The more Lily looked at Hannah, she started to suspect there was more to her shining eyes and wondered whether she had met someone, but Hannah was giving nothing away, changing the subject rapidly when Lily started to probe. Lily shrugged, war romances came and went, and she was sure Hannah would reveal all when she was ready.

Hannah and Ros's war seemed much more mundane and Lily tried hard not to feel superior. She found herself underplaying the dramatic existence of a WAAF wireless operator. Lily told them briefly about Ted and Ros nodded in sympathy. Her cousin, Alan, had been killed on the Prince of Wales during its battle with the Bismarck off the Danish coast. Sitting curled up on the bed, they all talked about how their lives had been altered by the war. Lily told them about meeting the ATA pilot. She did not mention that she had had the temerity to apply to join and become a pilot herself. Now she was back at home, she felt it had all been a feeble attempt to raise herself above her station in life.

'Now I come to think of it, Han,' Lily said suddenly, 'that pilot came from Norwich. Her name was Roberta, Bobby for short.' She felt as if she were claiming an acquaintance with royalty and said the name with reverence.

'That's the name of the daughter of the farm I'm at. It must be her, she's in the ATA,' Hannah exclaimed delightedly. 'Well, fancy that! She's a bit terrifying. I've only met her once. Apparently, she was a strange child, something about her twin brother dying at birth. If you ask me, the whole family's a bit batty.'

Lily refused to have a word said against her heroine and pushed Hannah playfully off the bed. During a midday meal of potato pie and peas in the cosy morning room she plied Hannah with questions, but Hannah was billeted half a mile from the farm and had little to do with the family. Lily was disappointed she could not find out more but was thrilled that she had a small connection with the pilot who had made such an impression on her. One day, she would love to meet her again and tell her she was doing something meaningful, quite what, though, now the ATA did not seem to want her, she had no idea.

After their meal, they all raced upstairs again to talk in private, revelling in the gossip and banter that they had all missed so much. The familiar noise of them giggling and arguing over who had had the most teenage spots sent a reminder downstairs to her mum of the innocent days before the war. She listened in from the bottom of the stairs and breathed deeply in satisfaction.

'Ginny, come here,' she heard her husband's voice from the front room. 'Ginny,' he sounded more urgent. She ran down the corridor to find him staring out of the bay window onto Slade Lane.

'There's three Yanks coming up the road. You don't suppose they're coming to see our Lily do you?'

She had no time to wonder before the front door bell went. The two born and bred Mancunians took a moment to stare at each other in horror before Ginny started to clutch frantically at her pinny to tear it off and stuff it behind the settee.

'You get the door, John, I'll get Lily.'

Chapter 35

John Mullins could see his neighbours' curtains being fingered to one side as the smart figures of three American airmen stood nonchalantly on the doorstep in the cold December air.

He could barely manage a polite 'Yes?' as he took in their olive-green uniforms and 'Ike' short jackets. *No wonder our Tommies are worrying about these Lotharios being over here*, he thought as he waited for the visions to speak.

'Hi sir, I'm sorry to bother you. We wondered, is Lily in?'

Behind him, there was the familiar sound of footsteps racing down the stairs.

'Kit! What the hell are you doing here?'

U.S. guests notwithstanding, John Mullins uttered a very sharp 'Lily!' to his daughter. She had never sworn in front of her parents before.

'Sorry, Dad,' Lily blushed at her outburst.

'Please come in', Ginny said from behind them both, her hair freshly combed.

'Yes, of course, please come in,' Lily said quickly, standing to one side to let the men in through the door. They all swept off their caps, put them under their arms and stood to attention in the hall. She started down the corridor towards the nice, informal morning room but was steered to the left into the front room by her mother, who had already rashly put the gas fire on.

'Would you like some tea?'

'Yes, please, ma'am.' The Americans had been schooled in visiting English homes and knew that the hot, brown liquid that tasted of tar was a pre-requisite to international relations.

Her parents stood waiting patiently as Lily stared at the three men.

'Sorry, Mum, Dad, this is Kit and Wally and . . .' She tailed off.

'Chuck,' the small blonde one supplied, creasing the dimple on his cheek with a grin.

'Yes, of course you are,' Lily said, smiling, taking in this piece of Hollywood that had walked into her terraced house in Manchester.

She turned to Kit accusingly. 'So how did you find me?'

'Wally's going out with one of the admin staff and she forgot to hide the file with your address on it.'

Lily couldn't decide whether to admire his nerve or condemn his cheek. Her mother had disappeared into the kitchen to rustle up some cake but her dad sat determinedly down in the armchair next to the window to watch the most amazing scene he had ever witnessed. Lily gave up trying to subtly signal to him to leave them all to it and sat down, waiting for Kit to speak. She could hear Hannah and Ros creeping halfway down the stairs, whispering excitedly.

'We had some leave so we got a train to come and see what Manchester was like. We'd heard so much about it, sir,' he added, turning to Lily's dad. John Mullins nodded approvingly.

'Aye, well, it's the second capital of the country and it does have beautiful buildings and heritage. That's if the Germans would leave it be.'

Lily could see that her dad was warming to a theme about his beloved city so interjected. 'I have two friends here; we were thinking of going out for a walk in a bit. How long have you got?'

No sooner had she said that than two faces appeared around the door. She noticed they had both borrowed her hair slides and had brushed their hair. She put a hand up to her own hair, which had not been brushed since that morning and suddenly felt very shy.

John took over and introduced Hannah and Ros, who were blushing with excitement.

Lily regained her composure and turned to Kit. 'Honestly, Kit, how could you? You didn't even know if I'd be here.'

'It was a calculated risk but one worth taking,' he said. Lily felt her own blush careering up from her neck to the top of her scalp.

'Here's the tea,' Ginny announced, bustling in to put the best tray with a doily on the sideboard. 'And I've found some fruit cake I thought you might like.'

Knowing the cake had been made in readiness for Christmas using up valuable rations Lily smiled warmly at her mum but Ginny Mullins was too busy serving the three young men to notice. Her mother's hands were shaking, Lily noticed, and she stepped forward to help.

'Kit's in Oxfordshire with me,' she explained, passing out the side plates. 'We are in the same crowd.'

Ros glanced at Hannah. Was this really the sort of company that their school friend was keeping? She immediately elevated her dizzy friend to the status of goddess and sat in awe as Lily kept up an incredibly natural banter with the three Americans. As Lily was the only person in the room to have met a real-life American, the others sat in silence. Ros took mental snapshots of the scene to recount at the munitions factory on Monday. It would be an impressive tale.

Watching Lily chatting to the three boys, John glanced at his wife. He knew what she was thinking ... *what about Danny*? They had been so sure Danny was the one for their daughter but looking at the handsome Kit, with his tuft of hair tumbling onto his forehead, they suddenly had doubts.

'So how do you boys like England?' Ginny gushed. 'Where do you come from in America? How are your families coping without you? Would you like another piece of cake?'

The rush of questions made them laugh and they tried to answer each one in turn, but Ginny was only listening to Kit.

'I come from New York,' he said. 'So it's cold there too in winter but England is beautiful. Everything's so small and cute.'

John Mullins winced at the word 'cute'. He was not ready to be father-in-law to a movie star.

'Our lads have just got to Italy,' he said with a meaningful look at Lily, 'although I don't think they're getting much time to enjoy it.'

Lily butted in, knowing that the resentment against the Americans for their late arrival into the war had been thoroughly dissected and augmented over a pint at her dad's bowls club since 1941. 'Kit's a navigator,' she said hurriedly, feeling she had entered a private battle between who, out of Danny and Kit, was making the most impact on the war.

'Uh, huh,' her dad replied, cutting a piece of cake for himself.

'That sounds very exciting,' her mother said brushing meaningfully past her husband's arm as she went to pour more tea. 'It must be very dangerous though.'

'Aw, we just try 'n' give Hitler a bit of his own medicine,' said Kit, blissfully unaware of the British torpedoes that were heading his way.

He hadn't taken his eyes off Lily, who was by now trying to introduce Wally to Ros.

'Did you say you were going for a walk, Lily?' he said. 'Maybe we could come with you when we've finished this delicious cake?'

'Um, yes, I suppose so,' Lily said, looking round for approval from her friends, who were nodding far too enthusiastically.

This was going to be a problem, Lily decided. She had managed to fend Kit off on her own patch at camp but here in her front room, he did look devastatingly handsome, and for a girl who had previously been just one of the crowd at the Boys' Brigade dances, she suddenly gained new heights of glamour and that was all due to a United States airforce-man who had landed in Manchester's suburbs like an alien from another planet.

Chapter 36

Danny had discovered that the Opera Houses in Italy served beer and he was now on his second. The taste seemed alien and certainly not like a pint in The Albion, but the alcoholic hit was welcome. He had been given two days' leave and was desperately trying to enjoy them, but it was impossible when he knew he had a letter to write to Frank's family when he got back to his billet. It was nearly Christmas but none of the 8th Army felt like celebrating. They had heard a rumour that Monty, the General they all believed was the one top brass they could rely on, was going to be moved on. Over the past few months, he had provided a cohesion and purpose that had kept them all going. Danny looked around him at the faded grandeur of the building with the torn posters on the walls for *Tosca*. He closed his eyes to picture the scene before the war when the red velvet seats would have been filled not with soldiers, but with people in evening dress, sipping Campari and soda. He wondered at the irony that the poster was of Puccini's tale of the Kingdom of Naples's control of Rome being threatened by Napoleon's invasion. *How history repeats itself*, he thought.

As the army made its painful and relentless trek up the Gustav Line, the soldiers had two enemies – the Germans and the weather. Winter had arrived with a vengeance in Italy. The rain fell constantly and it was bitterly cold. Danny's company had all been given time off, unable to move on until the troops in front of them had blown up every house to prevent more explosions. Word had reached them that the 5th Army were making desperate attempts to unlock the key to the Liri Valley – Cassino – so that the allies could then get on the road north to Rome. It was a tortuous, and costly, progress.

The picture books of Italy that Danny had seen as a schoolboy bore no resemblance to the devastated villages and landscape the army was passing through. The trek to the mountainous town of Orsogna had been a hard slog with rivers in spate and the surrounding countryside a swamp – a nightmare for the heavy transporters. The memory of piles of dead bodies in the deep mud along the route suddenly threatened to overwhelm his few precious hours relaxation so Danny concentrated on the strains of *Tosca* that had started to play in his brain. The former chorister at Manchester Cathedral School recalled a black-gowned teacher waving his arms to the music to try to inspire a classroom of angelic looking choristers who were just gagging to get out onto the cricket field.

He was playing with his glass, drumming out the tempo of one of the arias when he heard a noise behind him. It was Eddie, also on leave, who had come in with a girl on each arm. He, too, had been badly affected by Frank's death but in one way, it had made this shy geography teacher more anxious to live every moment.

One girl was small with brown hair and the other had luscious jet black locks. They both had that Italian swagger that made them so irresistible to so many of the troops. Danny stood up. '*Ciao signora come stai*?,' he said, in his improving Italian. The girl with the raven coloured hair looked impressed. She sat down on the stool next to Danny and gave him her full attention. Danny dropped his shoulders and gave in.

As the sun rose, Danny moved his arm to relieve the pins and needles travelling down towards his hand. The girl stirred but did not wake. Looking round the basic room above the café where he and Eddie had drunk too much wine the night before, he quickly realised that oblivion had not been such a good idea and searched his memory to find out how far he had gone. They both still had their clothes on, Danny was glad to see, unlike Eddie, whose bare leg was sticking out from a brown blanket on the other side of the room.

'*Buongiorno*,' the girl whispered, her eyes still closed. She was not quite as beautiful as she had appeared last night and her skin was pitted with marks, but she had been good fun and a welcome relief from the squalour and mud that had dogged their journey north. Her name was Carla and her friend was Gina. Since the Italians had surrendered, local girls had fraternised shamelessly with the troops, knowing they would no longer be called collaborators. The soldiers with their constantly replenished rations were desperate for some company and the local girls were desperate for food. The two girls had spotted the slightly inebriated soldier and had made a beeline for Eddie. The English were more relaxed than the Germans with their tightly done up collars and they were certainly more generous at buying drinks. Gina and Carla had giggled at the boys' attempt to speak Italian but Danny had been really pleased at how his language was progressing. He thought he might take a class in it when he got back so he could bring Lily back on holiday. At that thought, he sat up sharply, causing Carla's head to fall onto the pillow.

'Dammit, how could I have been so stupid? After all my promises to myself.' He looked down at Carla. 'Did we . . .?' he ventured, not really wanting the answer.

'My leetle English soldier,' she murmured at him from her sleepy position.

He held his breath.

Carla sat up languidly on the crumpled bed and smiled at him, holding up a bent little finger. 'You have to come back when you are not so drunk, I tink.'

Danny thanked the strong beer and cheap red wine and nodded with relief.

Eddie sat up looking blurry eyed. Gina was still asleep.

'Time to go,' Danny said, straightening his uniform. 'We're on duty this morning.'

Eddie hurriedly got dressed, gave Gina a quick kiss on the cheek and they both left, leaving the girls to sleep it off. They knew there would be a new company through town that evening and that they would soon be forgotten for a few rations from another army pack.

Danny was furious with himself but Eddie seemed more pragmatic.

'Nice night,' he said with a smile, 'what I can remember of it.'

'You'll have to get tested,' Danny reminded him.

'Worth it,' was the casual reply.

Most of their company had moved on, leaving just a small cohort of tank transporter drivers to follow on when the roads had been made safe. The two men had to re-join their unit by 1200 hours and they rushed to the other side of town where their colleagues were bivouacked. Danny did not feel like talking. He kept seeing Lily's face, his father's disapproval and his mother's shock. He knew that Frank's death had affected him badly but that was no excuse. The cases of VD were increasing and more than one husband was going to have to be treated before going home to confess to his wife. They rounded a corner and Danny was so intent on giving himself a severe telling off that he didn't see the German patrol until they were almost on them.

Chapter 37

Kit linked his arm casually with Lily's as they walked towards the park. She glanced sideways at him. He was keeping up a stream of chatter and jokes about life in Oxfordshire and the other service people there. Ros and Hannah were enjoying every moment, knowing that passers-by were looking on in awe as they strolled along the pavement. This moment would be discussed in detail in every pub in the area.

Hannah began teaching them the Land Army girls' song and before long they were all chanting the words in time with their steps.

'Back to the land, we must all lend a hand.
To the farms and the fields we must go,
There's a job to be done, though we can't fire a gun,
We can still do our bit with the hoe.'

It was a freezing cold day but the sun was out and they ran races in the park, with Kit always managing to catch Lily in his arms as she reached the pretend finishing line. She blushed as he pulled her towards him, puffed from her last exertion.

'I knew you'd have to give in,' he challenged her.

'I've given in to nothing. I'm not that much of a pushover,' she retorted, but by the time they all got back for yet more cups of tea with condensed milk, she had softened towards him a little.

'Mrs Mullins, I'm trying to get this gal of yours to go out with me, will you help me in my cause?' Kit suddenly said, casually pushing his cup to one side.

Lily took a sharp intake of breath.

Ginny, by this time, had become quite giddy with the American's attention and Lily could see she wasn't going to able to rely on her for help. She looked earnestly at her father who was sat in the armchair in the corner, fiddling with his cup.

'I'm sure Lily will make up her own mind,' John said, responding to her meaningful stare. 'She always has done. And I do think it's dangerous to start wartime relationships with people from across the sea,' he added quietly.

'Yessir, I'm sure you're right, but your daughter is coping with a great deal of stress and it would be good for her to let someone else take the responsibility occasionally. I know I'm an American, but we're not all bad, sir.' He gave a nervous laugh. He seemed to see through him.

John Mullins nodded slowly towards Kit. He remembered another young man sitting in this front room, about to take his daughter out for the afternoon in his Morgan three-wheeler – his pride and joy – and promising to take care of her. Life could have been so simple, he thought. His daughter settled with a nice young man from Stretford, with a promising career, someone they knew and trusted. This American was another matter.

Lily could not bear it any longer and stood up. She felt dizzy with the excitement of the day – the collision of her two worlds – and she felt she was losing control.

'Anyway, Kit, I'm sure you have to get back to Oxford now. The buses don't run that regularly to the station so you'd probably better be going.'

'Yeah, of course. We did say we'd get the five o'clock and we're hoping to get a lift from downtown.'

He looked at the others who stood up, ready to take their leave. Lily ushered them out of the front door amidst calls of 'Do come again,' from her mother.

Kit turned on the doorstep and leaned forward. Before Lily could realise what was happening he had slowly kissed her on the lips. She found herself relaxing and responding.

'Have a good leave, Lily, and I'll see you when you get back. Goodbye, sir, ma'am, girls. Thank you so much for your hospitality.'

Lily watched the three young men saunter down the road and touched her lips. She turned to see four questioning faces looking at her.

'What? What?!' she exclaimed, exasperated. She pushed past them and went to turn the gas fire off in the front room, closing the blackout curtains against the fading light.

The others went back into the morning room to dissect the events of the day giving Lily a moment to lean against the wall with her eyes closed. This war was a giddy experience. She could hardly remember the pre-war Lily who had been able to react sensibly to normal, Mancunian men like Danny, who certainly did not look like film stars.

By the time Lily got back to Upper Heyford she had been bombarded with comments about Kit from all angles – her mother, Hannah and Ros – and even Mrs Cross down the road had made insinuations about Lily and 'her American'. She may as well have been going out with him, she thought, so when Kit cornered her at the first dance of the New Year celebrations, she allowed herself to be jitterbugged around the dance floor. They danced all night, melting together as an impressive duo. Kit's dancing was perfectly co-ordinated and Lily found him very easy to follow. She also discovered she was getting quite good at the American style of dancing and could not help being thrilled when the people around them parted to watch. But, she had to acknowledge, the best moment was seeing

Marion standing alone, sipping a drink, seething with fury. They all had to be back at base by midnight, so as the lights went down early to celebrate the New Year, Kit leaned forward to kiss Lily.

'At last, you've given in,' he joked as he released his grip on her. She was embarrassed to find her face was tilted upwards and her eyes were still closed. He certainly knew how to kiss.

'I've given in to nothing,' she retorted, letting out a little cough and looking away to the side.

'Yeah, you have. I knew you couldn't resist me forever. Nineteen forty four is a new year, and you are exceptionally lovely.'

She glanced sideways at his smart uniform, his dark eyes and her stomach gave a little leap. Lily had not been expecting this electricity between them.

Kit and Lily soon became a couple. She was never sure how it had happened but it seemed easier than fighting. Over the next few weeks, it became accepted that they spent their off-duty days together and danced together at the weekly dances. His easy manner made her relax and she laughed with him and their embraces became more intense but she always kept herself detached from him. This, of course, drove Kit mad and made him even more determined to win her over.

Work was relentless and the wireless operators saw a constant flow of young airforcemen come through Upper

Heyford, struggling with the Lancasters, and then moving on to join the operational stations. Lily's belief that a training station would be without tragedy was misplaced, as some never made it. More than one pilot got a landing or take off wrong and the fire crews were unable to save them. The terrible waste of young lives who had not even entered the war weighed heavily on the ground staff and Lily made a point of saying prayers in church for the young faces that were distant memories so soon.

'Do you want to fly, Lily?' Marion was passing her in the corridor and casually asked the question. Lily stopped in her tracks.

'What do you mean?' she asked sharply.

'They're looking for WAAFs to go on Spitfires.'

Lily could not believe it and grabbed Marion's arm. 'Do I want to fly? You have to be kidding. Of course I do – but how?'

'Report at 1400 hours to hangar three,' Marion said over her shoulder as she stalked off.

Lily felt excitement rising in her stomach. To fly! Surely they would never allow it? But at five to two she found herself racing to the hangar with her heart pounding.

'Here's one,' a ground crewman shouted, seeing Lily rushing towards them.

'Good, let's get her up then.'

Lily did not have time to ask any questions before she was physically manhandled onto the back of a Spitfire.

'Right, just sit there and weigh it down. Good job you had sponge and custard for dinner,' the ground crewman laughed.

Lily looked down, she was sitting astride the tail of a Spitfire in the open air, her skirt wrapped up around her bloomers.

'What . . .?' She shouted down.

'Just sit there until he takes off, then don't forget to jump,' he shouted back as the engine started up.

Lily just had time to curse Marion to kingdom come before the Spitfire started off down the runway. She had heard that the Spits were having problems with their noses dipping, leading them to nosedive, but she had never heard of anyone sitting on the tail before. She saw the pilot frantically waving at her to jump and quickly launched herself onto the grass at the side of the runway.

She lay still trying to catch her breath as the ground crew ran up to her.

'That's my girl, well done' one said. She quickly rearranged her skirt and checked that nothing was broken but could not speak for fright. The Spitfire was already up into the low cloud.

'I . . . I . . . only . . . came to see what was going on. Don't ever . . . do that to me again.'

'Oh, sorry, thought you had volunteered,' he replied. 'Girls are queuing up for the chance. It's the nearest they get to flying.'

'When I fly, I intend to go *inside* the aircraft,' she replied haughtily, standing up and brushing herself down. Her retreat towards the NAAFI was followed by hoots of laughter but Lily was furious with herself. Her desperation to fly had nearly got her killed. She really thought that by now she should be more savvy than to believe anything Marion said.

Chapter 38

The Germans were so close, Danny and Eddie could smell them. The familiar odour of mud, blood and sweat was one that they recognised from each other but there was also a smell of soot. Danny and Eddie had to press themselves into a doorway so as not to be seen, both suddenly alert with a soldier's training.

'*So, jetzt haben wir's ihnen aber gezeigt*" a tall German was laughing as they climbed into their truck. They were brushing their uniforms down and were still laughing when they reached the corner of the square.

'What did they say, Danny?' whispered Eddie, making the usual presumption that Danny had become accustomed to – that, having an ear for languages, he could obviously understand them all.

'I think it was something about showing someone something,' he replied.

They edged their way slowly from doorway to doorway through the town, their guns at the ready, but the Germans had gone. They were now late for the rendezvous. By the time they arrived at the meeting place, they were on full alert and a horrendous sight greeted them.

There were four bodies strewn across the muddy track in front of them. The three transporters had been blown up and the embers of fires were still burning. Danny and Eddie stood for a moment, stunned as the implications of what had happened infiltrated their shock.

While they had been drinking and cavorting, their fellow soldiers, ones they had been fighting alongside for weeks, had been shot. Danny moved across to check their pulses. They were all dead. Behind him, as he crouched by Walter's body, he heard some footsteps. He swung round, his gun at the ready, his face contorted with grief. It was a man and a woman, both in their sixties, their hands stretched out in sympathy. He lowered his gun. Slowly, other townspeople came out and stood in silence. They had seen it all before, first the Italians, sometimes the Germans, sometimes their own neighbours. One woman wiped her eyes with a filthy pinny. Four more young men who would not be going home to their mothers and fathers, their wives or girlfriends.

A man in a priest's collar moved forward. He took charge and signalled to some of the other men to come forward and help carry the dead men to the church. Danny stood up and saluted in respect as his brothers in arms were carried past him. Eddie did the same. They were both pale and their faces grim.

Danny glanced at his transporter. Right to the end it had protected him. He felt it had sacrificed itself along with his fellow soldiers, for him, taking the hit while he was away. He went to put his hand on its charred remains but withdrew it quickly as the heat seared his fingers. The pain was almost welcome and took his mind off the slow walk towards the ancient church that was pock-marked with bullet holes.

The priest conducted an impromptu service that was quick but dignified. Eddie collected the dead men's tags and emptied their pockets, knowing that their families would treasure these last memories of their beloved sons. As the light faded, Danny and Eddie stood outside the church wondering what they should do next. They had lost their unit, lost their transportation and their company had moved north, oblivious to the fact that a rogue German patrol had wiped out the follow-up team.

The priest came out. 'We bury them, here in our village,' he assured them. 'They will have peace.' Then he pointed towards the mountains. 'You must go.'

Danny peered in the vanishing light, he could just about make out a small path that led through the forest. He looked at Eddie. They had no choice.

Chapter 39

Lily took another swig of the sweet liquid in the glass in her hand. She was leaning against the bar in the mess, watching Kit swagger off to get another drink. She supposed she was having fun. Her promotion gave her a new status but she hardly had time to enjoy it, the shifts were so punishing. Kit was a good companion when she did get a night off and he made her laugh After that cold January day in Manchester, they had fallen into a relaxed relationship, but nearly two months later, Lily still felt as though she was watching from a distance. He kept pushing his luck with her as they kissed goodnight at the end of an evening together, but she had kept his hands very firmly above her waist.

Hilda was definitely having fun. She was with Chuck and threw her head back, laughing at yet another of his strange pronunciations.

'It's tomato with an ah sound,' she told him, 'not tomato with an A in the middle.'

'Nonsense,' replied Chuck, 'and there's more of us Americans than you Brits. We outnumber you now.'

'Not over here you don't – well not yet.'

'Well, we'll just have to move around more so it looks like there are more of us,' Chuck replied as he swung Hilda onto the dance floor.

Taking her shoes off that night, Lily reflected that there was one good thing about the awful flatties she had to wear, she was not getting blisters from dancing. Her early efforts to soak her shoes with her feet in them had worked, and the leather was quite soft now. She grabbed her tin hat with her wash things in and made quickly to the ablutions to do her teeth, whilst humming to herself. She looked up sharply to see Sergeant Horrocks striding in, holding an envelope.

'LACW Mullins, I suppose I must now call you. You have a letter.'

She thrust it at Lily and strode out leaving her shocked at the unusual invasion of the WAAFs' private facilities. Sergeant Horrocks smirked, pleased with the fact that she had been the one to deliver bad news to Lily. She was enjoying being the person in charge of checking all letters, it meant she was privy to all the secrets of the camp and could store up the information until it was useful to her.

Lily looked at the letter. It was in strange writing. She leaned back against the washbasin in terror, her toothbrush hanging loosely out of her mouth and opened the letter. It was from Danny's mum. It said Danny was missing in action.

She froze and realised her teeth were chattering. She slowly took the toothbrush out of her mouth and rinsed it in the tiny cupful of water she was allowed. On autopilot, she picked up her penny from the plughole, took her tin hat and walked slowly back to her bunk. Climbing in, she felt the shivers starting and once she started she couldn't stop. Not Danny.

There was no sleep for Lily that night and the morning dawned with her in a daze. She reported for duty and went through the day in a fog. Her mood matched the weather, which had closed in and was causing endless problems for the crews. Lily had to concentrate hard to get them back to the runway safely in a dank November mist. They were all being pushed really hard and some of them were almost cracking under the strain. There had been several pancake crashes on landing, some planes missing the runway or landing too fast, and some young pilots had been seriously injured. A number of aircraft had been damaged or destroyed. Lily felt there was a desperation in the war now and as the desperation grew, so did the cost.

After a run of hectic shifts with no time to think, Lily and Hilda finally had a night off. But when Kit came to pick her up to go the pub that night, she sent a message with

Hilda to say she had a dreadful headache and could not go. Hilda went off, arm-in-arm with Chuck, leaving Kit disappointed and looking through the gates toward Lily's hut.

Kit stood outside for a while and lit a cigarette. He was completely perplexed by this young woman and yet, he wanted her – oh so badly. Her embraces promised so much but never quite delivered. He believed she was a conquest waiting to be taken. Kit had had a charmed upbringing. The younger son of a wealthy motor car dealer, he had been training to take over the family business when the war had beckoned him. He had been lured by the speed and the chance to fly and he knew he looked good in the uniform. He had done one tour of thirty ops and had survived and was now teaching other young navigators. He knew he would probably volunteer for ops again in a couple of months, it was too strange to be on the edge of the action and he was constantly wracked with guilt as he watched other crews taking off. He was in danger of thinking he was immortal but that was an easier option than the alternative and Kit liked living for the moment.

As he stood by the gate, he spied Lily coming out of the hut in her greatcoat. He could see the mist from her breath. He peered into the empty darkness around him and took his chance.

'Kit, what are you doing? You gave me a heart attack. Do you know how much trouble you will be in if you are found . . . or if I'm found for that matter.'

He stopped her talking with his mouth and pressed against her. She felt herself melting in the need for oblivion. She had no more fight left in her. He was very attractive and through the numbness, she felt an unfamiliar excitement building up in her. Lily responded to his kisses and felt her body moving towards him. He felt between her legs with his right hand. She started to speak.

'Hush, be quiet, we'll be caught,' he told her.

'I . . . don't . . . want . . .'

'I know, but just be quiet. You poor love, you are so beautiful, let me love you.'

Kit opened his fly and pushed against her again. Lily felt him moving against her as he fumbled to take her bloomers down. He moved in rhythm with her for a minute and she experienced a sudden rush of excitement, but as she clung to him, he suddenly pulled away from her, before finally leaning heavily with a sigh on her quivering body. Lily, in a rush of panic, pushed him off and ran inside, leaving him to hurriedly re-arrange himself and sprint back towards the gate.

Lily did not know what had happened but she suspected this was the act that Glad had described and she fell into her bunk in shock. Had she just . . .? Had he just . . .? Was that it?

And then it occurred to her, could she be pregnant?

She went cold and felt between her legs. They were wet and her bloomers were wet too. She got up and quickly went to the ablutions where she looked round to check there was no one there before scrubbing herself raw with cold water. She ran into the toilet and splashed the limited water from the bowl into herself, over and over again.

Lily, Hilda and the others were working constant shift patterns and the young pilots were being drilled, tested and moved on at an alarming rate. Lily ate the porridge without milk every morning, chomped on the watery stew at dinnertime and would pick at tea-time's sandwiches of raw cabbage and Marmite. She went through all the chopped-up cigarettes that, like everyone else, she kept in a special tin, her hands shaking. The letter about Danny had affected her far more than anything in her life, but she scolded herself that even so, it was no reason to allow Kit to take advantage of her. A week went by before she heard that Kit had been posted to somewhere in Lincolnshire.

Chapter 40

The mountain road was gruelling. Danny and Eddie climbed early morning and late at night to avoid detection, knowing also that in the pitch black, their next step could send them careering over the edge of the ridge of the mountains. They kept to the side of the track, dodging in and out of the trees to avoid being seen. They did not dare light a fire, even though they were freezing cold, and when they did manage to take a break, they huddled together surrounding themselves with bracken. Their rations had been eked out from day one and it was now the end of day three.

Danny had never been more pleased that his dad had made him join the scouts, sending him on survival trips in the Trough of Bowland and the Lake District. The training had stood him in good stead and he quickly adapted to living out in the open, but the problem was the time of year. He looked at Eddie's pale face. Eddie's early life in the gentle hills of Bideford had not prepared him for winter in a mountainous region of Italy. He had always said that he preferred to look at the geography of the land from the warmth of a nice café. Danny knew that they could not survive another night and it was time to take a risk and walk to the top of a mound to look for signs of life in the surrounding countryside.

I'm not losing another one, Danny thought angrily as he looked round to see his friend leaning exhausted against a pine tree.

He scanned the darkening horizon. At least there was no sign of the Germans. Apart from the one truckload that had done so much damage, the rest were fleeing north. Just down the track, about 500 yards away, there was a barn. That would give them much needed shelter for the night, he decided, and bounded back down the mound to alert Eddie.

By this time Eddie could hardly walk, his toes were getting frostbite and his hands were shaking. Danny took hold of him under his arm and steadied him to his feet.

'Come on, old chap, we're going to make it. I've found a lovely hotel just round the corner.'

Eddie grimaced at him.

They struggled on, Danny helping Eddie to half walk, half stumble down the track. When they got near the barn, Danny propped Eddie behind a tree and took out his gun. He edged around the barn and put his ear to it to listen. Silence.

He moved around the front and gently eased open the door. It creaked and Danny braced himself, but there was nothing. He breathed again and tiptoed around the door. Adjusting to the dark against the weak sunset outside he could see piles of hay, propped up ready for early spring fodder. He heaved a sigh of relief. Quickly returning to get Eddie, he helped his friend into the barn, doled out half a biscuit each and a teaspoon of water and they settled down into the comfiest bed they had had in months.

Danny woke to find a gun nozzle pushed into his temple. He sat up quickly, nudging Eddie, who tried to stumble to his feet only to be knocked back down again. There were four men all with guns staring down at them. They were dressed in rough clothing, two of them with string holding up their trousers, and speaking angrily in Italian. They were suddenly pushed out the way by a scruffy boy, who came through the middle of them.

'*Sono loro*!' he said. '*i soldati di cui ti ho parlato*'

'Georgio?' Eddie whispered in disbelief.

'*Si, sono io*,' said the boy with a broad grin.

Danny stretched his hands out to take the boy by the shoulders. He looked keenly at him.

'*Tu* . . . OK?'

'*Si, questo è mio zio*,' he said, pointing to the man with the gun.

The man put down his gun and started to shake Danny's hand. The others patted him on the shoulders and laughed.

Eddie started to tremble and his knees threatened to buckle. Two of the men caught him and they all started to talk in a torrent of Italian. The two Englishmen found themselves being propelled, half carried, out of the barn and down the path. After a while, they came to a farmhouse where they were taken in next to a warm fire and hot drinks were put in their freezing hands. Danny looked up to the crucifix on the wall, thanked God, Allah, the fates and a small boy who had lost everything.

Chapter 41

Lily did not know what signs to look for in a pregnant body but she kept feeling her tummy under the rough blanket at night, imagining a small human being growing inside her. She veered between not believing for a minute that such a hurried act could result in a baby and seeing her disappointed parents' faces as she told them she was a disgrace. At three o'clock in the morning, she went through the whole of Slade Lane imagining what Mrs Cross, Eric at the sweet shop and the members of the bowls club would say. She was furious with herself for being so stupid, but by four o'clock she blamed Danny.

'It's his fault,' she railed. 'If he hadn't been so idiotic as to get himself killed, captured or lost then I would have had my wits about me and would never have let it happen.'

She immediately retracted all that and started to worry about Danny being dead in an Italian ditch, tortured in a prisoner of war camp or dying of starvation somewhere. She could not believe how those few words, 'Missing in action,' had affected her. It was as if, amidst all the madness of the war, Danny's letters had been her one constant, despite the little attention she had paid to them. He understood her, she knew that now, right from the time that he had gently taken the cigarette she was trying to stub out in the sugar bowl and put it in the ashtray, ignoring her pretence at sophistication. Maybe he loved her? That was something that had not occurred to her before and it made her sit upright in bed.

Could Danny really love her? And could she possibly love him? She hadn't realised before, but now the thought struck her like a thunderbolt. It had been so long since she had seen him, but the idea of never seeing or hearing from him again left an ache inside her.

She flopped back onto the pillow in despair and groaned, screwing her eyes up tightly to block out the world that had become such a confused place, but Danny's face kept appearing in front of her. She groaned again, prompting a series of 'Shut ups' from the girls around her. *Now it was too late*, she thought. *He's probably dead and we'll never have the chance to be together*. As she drifted off into a disturbed sleep, she dreamed of a child with one blue eye like Kit's and one brown like Danny's. Then it turned into a monster.

Lily did not have time to analyse her feelings for Danny as she was too busy working herself up with worry. After a couple of weeks, she had a familiar stomach ache and reached for the free sanitary towels, but her period seemed much lighter than usual and she was left with a lingering doubt. Then she received a letter from Alice. She had some leave owing and wanted to know whether Lily had any as well and could meet her in London on her way to visit an aunt in Croydon.

'Alice!' thought Lily, 'She's a country girl. She deals with the birds and the bees all the time. She'll know. Perfect.'

Lily was due a seventy-two-hour pass so wrote back to Alice to say she could meet her on Friday afternoon in Trafalgar Square.

Lily knew as soon as she saw Alice that her friend had changed. Her eyes were sparkling and her familiar solid walk had turned into a bounce.

They hugged each other, Lily holding on for a few seconds longer than Alice, who was obviously bursting to tell her something.

'Lily Mullins . . . I am in love!' she pronounced, twirling on the spot and throwing her head back in delight. For a moment, Lily wondered whether to tell Alice about her feelings for Danny or the mess that her relationship with a GI had got her into, but Alice was already in full flow with her news and Lily could not bear to stop her. She looked so happy.

'That's fantastic. Who is he? Where did you meet him? When am I going to meet him?'

Alice chuckled.

'All of those things, I will tell, but first let's get a drink. I'm parched.' Alice looked around the devastation of Trafalgar Square as if searching for something. Her eyes fastened on a tea shop on the corner.

'That's the place,' she pronounced triumphantly and linking Lily's arm, she propelled her through the crowds.

Lily looked quizzically at her. 'Are we going somewhere special?' she asked.

'Well the place isn't but if you're a very good girl and behave yourself, I will introduce you to the new man in my life. I only met him a couple of weeks ago but oh, Lily, I just can't breathe. He's so wonderful.'

Lily raised her eyebrows. 'He's here?'

'Yes, coming in half an hour or so. I told him he had to meet my best friend and he couldn't wait. I haven't had time to tell him much about you, but he knows you are a special person in my life and that he has to love you.'

'Well, that's quite straightforward then,' Lily smiled. She couldn't get over the change in Alice. Her usual pragmatic and calm approach to life had gone and, in its place, there was a bubbly young woman who had blossomed. Lily could not have been more pleased and put her own worries to the back of her mind.

They ordered their tea and sat down to have a natter, but then Alice decided she wanted a scone so went up to the counter to choose. There was a long queue and she looked around apologetically at Lily who just waved her arm and settled down, preparing what she was going to say to her friend.

The door opened and a gust of cold March wind made Lily look up. It was Kit! She froze and glanced towards Alice, who was oblivious and sizing up which scone she wanted.

Kit saw Lily and his expression changed from casual cheerfulness to intrigued interest. He came towards her and at that moment, Alice turned around. She frantically gesticulated over to Lily that the man with his back to her was him. The one.

Lily was completely perplexed. This could not be the new love of Alice's life, surely? It was all too quick. Fate couldn't be that unkind. She was trying to remember which station in Lincolnshire they had said Kit had been sent to and whether Metheringham had been mentioned.

Lily glanced over at Alice, who was hardly containing her excitement and was grinning from Kit to Lily and back to Kit. Lily smiled as convincingly as she could at Alice and turned towards Kit, saying through clenched teeth, 'We have met, but don't really know each other, got that?'

'OK,' he just had chance to say before Alice joined them, triumphantly carrying a large scone.

'So, isn't he gorgeous?'

'Mmm,' Lily replied, seeing horns appear on the attractive young man in front of her. 'You're not going to believe this, Al, but we know each other. We met in Oxfordshire.'

'I don't believe it. I'd forgotten you were both at Upper Heyford,' replied Alice, 'but that's perfect. Now you can see why I have fallen for this American idol.' She put her hand affectionately on his arm.

The conversation was led by Alice who was in ignorance of the meaningful glances that were passing between Lily and Kit. Alice took everything Lily said about their previous meetings at face value, never thinking to delve deeper. She took it as a positive that two of the people she loved most in the world had had a head start on getting to know each other and because she loved them both, she just assumed they would get on like a house on fire.

Meanwhile, Lily was in turmoil. Her mind kept returning to that fateful night outside the hut. She put her hand on her stomach, which was churning like a milk machine. Kit, however, was completely at ease. He seemed to think it was funny that his two conquests were friends and he smiled, seemingly quite proud of himself.

'Let's go to the National,' Alice said jumping up as she finished off the last crumb. 'They might have a new picture of the month or a concert on. Myra Hess might be playing.'

Kit turned to the waitress to pay and Alice looked quickly at Lily.

'What do you think?' she mouthed at her.

Lily managed to nod enthusiastically while sitting on her hands to hide the shaking.

Alice pushed herself between Kit and Lily, linking both their arms in excitement and Lily felt as if she was in a bad dream as the little trio made their way through London. Lily dropped back to breathe deeply as they queued at the bottom of the stone steps to the gallery. She looked up at it. It had been bombed, targeted and damaged, but it stood, defiantly behind its lions. It had been a bad few months after a long period without bombers threatening the London skies and the previous week in particular had seen renewed bombing in the capital. Everyone was talking about 'Hitler's revenge' and how the Germans were getting their own back for the relentless bombing of their towns and cities. Lily looked around at the damage and for a moment felt a wave of empathy for the ordinary German people who had been bombarded so effectively by the RAF. Feeling like a traitor, she scanned the cloudy skies above and hoped that the rumours that the 'mini blitz' was over were true. She had deliberately not told her parents that she was going to London. She knew they would be worried. She looked back at the National. Since the Battle of Britain, its art treasures were slowly being returned one by one from the depths of the countryside and in solidarity, its visitors flocked to hear piano recitals, see exhibitions and the pieces of art that had been lovingly protected. She made her racing mind concentrate on the people around her. They were thin and pale but determined and she took strength from their relentlessly cheerful expressions.

'Tough British, tough Mancunians, that's what we are,' she tried to tell herself, remembering Danny's words, clutching her chest as a stab of pain hit her heart at the memory.

She tried to cheer up. *'One little moustached dictator. One little baby isn't going to change that. Oh, who am I trying to kid?'*

They slowly made their way up the steps, Kit smiling benignly at what he obviously considered to be 'his two girls'. Lily was aghast at his nerve.

The gallery was a sad place with empty spaces on the walls and barriers in place in front of open sky where the roof had been damaged, but the people made up for it. Thirsty for a break from a war-torn London, they drank in the beauty and tenderness of the great artists, pointing enthusiastically at a serene face here, a telling brush-stroke there.

'There's a concert starting in ten minutes' Kit said, reading a poster. 'Let's go.'

The gentle music was just what Lily needed. It seemed to soothe her beating heart and allowed her to float out of herself, up to the ceiling where she felt she was looking down on a play that was being acted out below her. A crescendo brought her back down to earth and she glanced sideways at Kit, who was thoroughly enjoying himself, unaware of her trauma. Alice's face was shining; Lily had never seen her so happy. It broke her heart to think that

Alice could have been taken in by Kit's shallow charm. No matter what, she justified to herself, her heart had remained untouched by him.

Although, that makes this worse, she thought. *It might have been excusable if I had loved him.*

As the concert ended, the little trio pulled their coats around themselves against the early spring chill.

'I'm off to auntie,' Alice said, heading to the toilets.

Kit turned to face Lily. 'Never thought I'd see you again. How's this for a coincidence?'

'I cannot believe your nerve,' Lily said, hissing at him with venom.

'Oh, come on, we had fun, didn't we?'

'You call what we did outside the hut that night fun? *Fun*?'

'Aw, you were gagging for it,' Kit said with a laugh.

Lily's voice went quiet. 'I think I may be pregnant,' she whispered, 'and it's your fault.'

Lily heard a gasp behind them. Alice had come back to borrow a penny for the toilet.

Chapter 42

The journey north was a difficult and dangerous one for Danny and Eddie. The terrain was impossibly tortuous, and the mountain roads were washed away by mud and rain, but the Italian partisans passed them from one guide to the next, taking them to safe houses where they fed them with scraps of bread and milk from goats. The two soldiers knew these supplies were scarce and tried to eat as little as possible, but the women stood over them until they had finished every crumb, proud of their limited hospitality. They passed through village after village where ten Italians had been shot for every German soldier killed by the Resistance. Small white crosses denoted the children's graves and Danny and Eddie paused by each of them to say a silent prayer. The cost of rebelling against their own government and the Germans had taken its toll and the grim faces of the Italian people bore witness to their struggle. The beautiful mountains were scarred with muddied tracks, burnt out vehicles and demolished buildings. The Germans' retreat had left a savage mark on the landscape.

Wary of rogue patrols, the partisans kept the two men out of sight, making them walk in the dark without any lights. Danny and Eddie kept very close behind their guides, aware that one slip could send them over a precipice.

Arriving late at night at various safe houses, barns or sheep shelters, the men watched as the skies lit up with the red glow of air strikes. The mountains were magically lit up by strafing fire and ack ack. It was strangely beautiful but the accompanying loud booms stripped the sight of any pleasure. They glanced at each other, aware that they were probably missing some fierce fighting.

'I don't know what I'm feeling,' Eddie finally admitted as they watched a particularly bright red glow spread across the sky through the skylight of their housetop refuge. 'Part of me is so grateful to be here, in the quiet of these mountains, and part of me feels so strongly that we should be there, alongside everyone else.'

His knuckles were white as he grasped the end of the small table that separated their worn mattresses on the floor and he struggled with the moral dilemma that faces every soldier.

Danny too had realised that his body had relaxed somewhat on the trek over the mountains. He was of course alert for noises as they walked, but he was no longer looking death in the face all day every day. Danny found the mountains therapeutic, but he always had. A city boy, he had escaped to the countryside every moment he could. He loved fishing, walking, climbing and cycling and was never happier than when he was standing on top of a mountain, looking skyward and breathing a deeper breath than any Mancunian air could offer him. He so longed to bring Lily to these mountains, although he was not sure that she would enjoy the trek that he'd just done. That thought brought a sudden realisation.

'You do know we will have been posted as "missing presumed dead", don't you, Eddie?'

Eddie looked at him in surprise. 'Oh God, I hadn't thought of that. Our families will be frantic.'

'Either that or they'll think we've gone AWOL, although I'm pretty confident my father knows I would never do that,' Danny replied, with a slight frown.' Danny's father had instilled in him a feeling of duty all his life. Even as the youngest in the family, there was no doubt that he had certain responsibilities, both for his ageing mother and his older sisters. His father would not think for a moment that Danny would run away from his duty, but he also knew the terror they would be facing believing he had been killed.

The next morning, as dawn rose, they walked at twice the speed, making their guides stumble over tree roots. By now, Danny was becoming quite good at Italian and was able to have reasonable conversations with the partisans. He explained that they were worried their families would think they were dead or that their company would think they had gone absent without leave. The partisans seemed to understand and pushed on into the next valley near to Cassino.

Eddie nudged Danny. 'Cassino has a town, a mountain and monastery,' he told him. A geography teacher, Eddie's knowledge of the countries they had passed through had been a mixed blessing. He always knew when the terrain was about to get worse, something Danny often preferred to be left in ignorance about.

'It is a natural defensive position and as far as I remember, the rocky hillsides are full of crevices.'

'Sometimes, Eddie, I wish I was travelling with a maths teacher,' Danny replied.

As they got nearer, the snow-covered trees and the undergrowth had been cleared to make fields so that mines could be laid, every gully had been laced with wire and on the distant hillside, the two men could make out a medieval fort. One of their guides, Antonio, tried to explain to them how the monks were still going about their devotions, whilst in the middle of a battleground.

At that moment, aircraft could be heard approaching. To the little band of men dodging between the trees, it would not make any difference whether they were friend or foe and they all dropped to their bellies, crawling towards the undergrowth. Danny and Eddie kept their eyes focused on the ground in front for any tell-tale bits of wire that would blow up under their weight. To be off the icy stone path could be lethal and there was little to choose between being blown up by a mine or shot by an aircraft overhead.

What saved the men was the rain, however, as its relentless pounding created a mist and the aircraft passed harmlessly overhead. They got to their feet, brushed off their filthy uniforms and trudged on only to be stopped in their tracks by Antonio, who was leading the way. He held up his hand to warn the men behind him. They strained their ears and heard voices.

Then Eddie smiled. He recognised a New Zealand accent and motioned for them all to move forward. The voices came from just behind a prickly pear tree ahead of them. Eddie called out, 'Hello Kiwis, we are from the 8th Army and have been separated from our unit. We are approaching from the south and have two Italians with us.'

The voices stopped and so did the band of travellers. No one moved for a minute, then a voice called out, 'OK Brits, what's the next line of this nursery rhyme? Humpty Dumpty sat on the wall . . .?'

'Humpty Dumpty had a great fall,' Danny replied laughing. 'And all the bloody king's horses and all the king's men, couldn't put that flaming stupid Humpty together again!'

Loud laughter came from the tree as three New Zealand soldiers emerged holding tin mugs.

They took one look at the thin soldiers and the state of their uniforms and their expressions hardened.

'Christ, what happened to you two?'

One of them called backwards for medics and two men in white coats with the recognisable red cross on came hurrying through the undergrowth.

As soon as Eddie and Danny were surrounded by their own men, Antonio signalled to Paulo that they should go. Shaking their rescuers firmly by the hands, Eddie and Danny could hardly speak. The risk to these men of the mountains had been huge and they had delivered them safely.

'*Grazie mille, grazie mille*' said Danny pumping Antonio's arm up and down. '*Un giorno tornerò*' he promised, imagining bringing his children to this beautiful country.

They vanished into the undergrowth with waves of their hands.

Danny and Eddie breathed a sigh of relief and gave themselves up to the medics, who quickly helped both exhausted men back to the field hospital. Danny was being checked over by a doctor when he heard a commanding voice from behind the screen.

'Where is he?'

Danny automatically stood up and sprang to attention in readiness at the sound of the Captain Fuller's voice.

'Not yet, my lad,' the doctor said, pushing him back down.

Danny sank back onto the mattress, too exhausted to argue.

'Entering,' announced the Captain, not troubled by field hospital protocol. He pushed the screen to one side and looked Danny up and down.

Embarrassed by his state of undress – he was only in his underpants – Danny struggled to sit up and this time the doctor let him. The doctor tutted, but briefly told the Captain he was signing the young private off with nothing but exhaustion and left to attend to the crowded ward behind them.

'So, Jackson?'

The question hung in the air as Danny searched for the right words.

But when he could not find them, he just shook his head, dropped his chin onto his chest and started to shake. How was he to explain that he was still alive when his friends were dead?

Captain Fuller softened his expression.

'It's all right, lad, we've talked to Jenkins and he's told us what happened. We knew the unit had been annihilated but we thought you two were goners too.'

'We should have been,' Danny muttered. 'We should have been with them.'

'Then we'd have had two more dead soldiers. You were just bloody lucky. But we need to have a proper debrief. Get your uniform on and report to my office in one hour.'

'Get some food and a warm drink first,' he added kindly as he turned to go. 'You've been through the mill. Don't worry, I'll get letters off to your families to let them know they haven't got rid of you just yet, although heaven knows how long it will take to reach them, mail's impossible from here.'

Danny wobbled out of the hospital, passing through a ward of wounded soldiers. The stench of blood and sweat was unbearable but the tall, commanding figure of the doctor in a white coat somehow seemed to inject a feeling of cool, mountain water into the Brueghel painting in front of them. Danny had a sudden twinge of envy. That was the profession he would have loved to have followed had he not been the youngest of three children. One soldier reached out his arms to him as he went slowly past.

'Doctor, help me,' the man said, weakly. Danny took his hands and held them tightly for a minute before he realised that the soldier could not see him. He was staring blankly into space, with no recognition.

'I'm not a doctor,' he told him. 'Just a Tommy like you.'

The man dropped his arms and turned despondently onto one side. Danny sat for a minute on his bed and watched as the young man took his last breath.

He had never felt more useless in his life.

Chapter 43

Alice's face had turned the colour of the stone wall next to her. A girl who believed in no shades between black and white saw her previously unshaken beliefs crumbling alongside the bombed-out dust that was all over the National.

Lily could not speak. She just held out her arms with a guilt-ridden face but there was no response. Alice looked from Kit to Lily and then turned on her heels and walked briskly out of the room.

Lily glared at Kit with the hatred, shame and despair that engulfed her and then she fled after her friend.

Kit called out to her.

'You can't be, you ninny. I withdr . . . Oh Gawd, don't you English girls know anything?' But it was too late, Lily was already half way down the stone steps.

Lily tried to catch up with Alice but had to weave her way through the crowds and only just managed to keep the tall, striding figure in view ahead of her. She followed her to a bus stop where she saw her get on the platform at the back of the red bus. She just heard her asking whether it went to Paddington when it pulled away taking Alice with it.

It seemed an age before Lily could get the next one and by the time she reached Paddington, there was no sign of Alice. She ran into the station, checking the hordes of service people for Alice's tall frame but it was impossible to distinguish one RAF uniformed woman from another.

She was almost on the point of tears when she spotted her. She was getting a cup of tea from the café on the corner. Lily noticed that Alice's hands were shaking.

'Alice!'

Alice swung round. She narrowed her eyes and turned to walk the other way, her cup and saucer in hand.

'Alice, please!' Lily called.

She caught up with her and took her arm, nearly upsetting the tea as she did so.

'Alice, I—'

'I don't know who I am more furious with, you or him.'

'I don't know what to say, we met and had a sort of thing, but he . . . he . . .' Lily trailed off.

'Yes?' her friend asked pointedly.

Lily stood with her head hanging down. The tears had started to flow and once she had started they turned into sobs.

Before either of them could speak, the sirens went off.

'Oh no,' Alice said furiously. 'I thought they had finished with London after last weekend.'

She grabbed Lily's arm and propelled her towards the underground with the rest of the crowds, still with the cup of tea in her hand.

They queued patiently with everyone to get down the steps but then they heard the planes and everyone started to push. The cup of tea went flying down the steps and the two girls were being manhandled from behind as the first bomb fell. The ground shook and so did Lily and Alice. They had not been this close to a bomb since the Blitz and it made Lily shiver with fear as she remembered cowering in the Anderson shelter with her parents, waiting to see if their road, their house or themselves were going to be obliterated. In those days, the raids had been so regular that it became commonplace but she had almost forgotten what it was like to be bombed from the skies. Now it came back to her with a vengeance.

They pinned themselves against the wall halfway down the stairs, hoping it would protect them.

In the next few minutes, there was an eerie silence as everyone listened intently to the sound of the planes above. Lily grabbed Alice's arm. It was now or never.

'Alice, you are my best friend and I love you', she whispered. 'I don't love Kit but I think I might be pregnant with his child. There was one night when I had heard that Danny was missing when I didn't care what happened and he . . . I think I might love Dan . . . oh, I just don't know anything anymore. Can you be pregnant if you've had a period?'

Alice looked at her, stunned, and then started to laugh, slowly at first and then she threw back her head and let out a loud chortle.

'Oh, Lily Mullins, what am I going to do with you?'

At that moment, a bomb fell out of the sky and everything went black.

Chapter 44

The first few days back with their company were strange for Danny and Eddie. They felt they belonged but they saw the spectres of Walter and the other three at every corner. The fighting was intense and the road to Cassino was gruelling and bloody. Danny knew that while a letter to say he was alive was wending its way to his parents, at any moment he could be wiped out and another letter would have to be sent. The cruel irony made him more determined than ever to survive and to make sure Eddie did too.

The 8th Army was detailed to break into the Liri valley while the Polish Corps finally took Cassino on 16th May. Once in the Liri valley Danny's company would push north on Route 6. After that it would be Rome. Danny tried to keep this in mind as he fired his gun, hid in ditches and got covered in mud. He had never been to Rome and he had told Eddie they would see the Colosseum. The Germans were close but no one seemed to know exactly where. One corporal from the Welsh Guards had told Danny that they had sent messages out in Welsh to confuse the enemy and the following day, they had been showered with German propaganda in Urdu. That had given the lads a short-lived moment of triumph at the Huns' confusion. On every front, as the late spring progressed, more tanks, more shells and more aircraft gradually wore down the German opposition, but the cost was high. Danny and Eddie were ordered to launch their assault boats into the rushing waters of the Rapido. They had to paddle frantically across to the other side with Danny suddenly grateful for the Sunday afternoons spent rowing at Heaton Park. As they got there, there was a storm of machine-gun and mortar fire. It was the early hours of the morning and the pitch black was lit up by flashes and bangs. The Cassino front was lit up for twenty miles. By the time the Bailey bridges were constructed, the soldiers knew the Gustav line was caving in. Those who had survived could taste victory.

A few days later, Danny, in his new tank transporter, was being moved on north to Piedimonte from the ruins of Cassino and he tried to concentrate on the pitted road ahead, ignoring the many bodies that littered his route. He would never forget the sickening bumps as the tyres moved forward. The advance up the Liri valley was a huge movement of troops and vehicles with mile after mile of them slowly snaking their way through thick, wooded terrain. As usual, minefields and wire had been laid all the way along the route so progress was slow. The men had to run to the field kitchen one at a time, eat their meals when they could be sent back from the shooting for a few minutes and wash and shave when they could. In between times, they had to unload ammunition when the truck came along, clean their guns, dig gun pits and sleep. There was no time for reflection or banter.

On 4th June, 1944, the 8th Army entered Rome behind the Americans . The streets were lined with people cheering and crying. Danny's transporter was boarded by two beautiful girls who leaned through his window to kiss him. He laughed for the first time in weeks and gave them a cigarette to share.

The unit was being given more time off than they had had in months and it was a welcome relief. Danny had taken to wandering the ancient streets, breathing in centuries of shadowy figures in togas, then medieval hoods and onto jack boots. He stood before St Peter's, staring up at the watchful figures of the saints on the Cupola. How had they escaped damage? He twirled around very slowly, feeling like a pencil on a compass in the vast piazza. He was completely awestruck by the scale of Rome's buildings and the depth of its history. He wished he had concentrated more when his history teacher, a bespectacled Mr Harvey, had tried to explain the classics to him. He had never been sure where history ended and legend began and he frantically tried to recall which characters were from Roman mythology and which were real. He experienced a desperate urge to learn again and made a mental promise that he would study when he got home and better himself, even if he was trying to be the perfect salesman as well. He smiled at himself, the salesman, the doctor, the historian, the soldier. He was not sure whether one life would be enough.

He so wanted to teach his children about the fascinating history of the countries he was passing through and had a brief vision of himself with a child on each knee, reading a book about Caesar. He peered into his mind's eye and let the vision wander until he found Lily, with a fetching little pinny on, bustling in the kitchen. But then she seemed to fade, like a mirage. He found he was struggling to remember what she looked like. He felt a shiver up his back and was taken by surprise in the bright sunlight. He was becoming a superstitious idiot, he decided, and shook himself.

The eerie feeling stayed with Danny all day and despite the sun, he felt cold. He wondered if he was coming down with something. A cold in the midst of all this death and destruction seemed like an ailment from another world but in actual fact, it was more a feeling of unease that had come with his thoughts of Lily that he could not shake off.

The feeling was overtaken a few days later by a huge celebration when word reached the soldiers that the allies had landed on the Normandy beaches. Apparently, the Germans had been taken by surprise and the combined forces were gradually working their way into Europe. For the first time, the men allowed themselves to feel optimistic. Maybe this war would end after all. Maybe the allies would win. Maybe Hitler could be defeated. Maybe they would one day be allowed to go home.

The troops were given the opportunity to celebrate and there was dancing and merriment in St Peter's Square. Danny and Eddie were in the throng when they were approached by a middle-aged Italian with a bottle of Chianti in his hand. He handed over the bottle for them to swig from and then pressed a wine-soaked kiss firmly on each of their cheeks. They all laughed and the sound seemed to resonate towards the heavens in the early evening light. Eddie was swung away by a very attractive Italian girl with dark skin to join the dancing in the middle of the piazza and Danny signalled to him that he would see him back at the camp. Eddie grinned and gave him the thumbs up. Danny walked away, smiling to himself. He felt the need for solitude amidst all the noise and he wandered down along the River Tiber, letting the crowds lessen and the noise become a distant hum. He reflected on how much better the distant sound of laughter and music was than that of guns.

He walked for a couple of hours, watching the sun gradually disappear behind the tenement flats of the residential area he had wandered into. He had no idea where he was but was confident enough of his Italian to know he could ask someone the way back. He peered in through open doors, where loud Italian families were arguing, cooking meagre meals and laughing. The buildings had been bombed in places and amidst the rubble there were chilling reminders of the recent history: a child's blue shoe, a shopping basket, a book dropped in haste.

On one pavement, two children sat. A girl in a tatty red dress and a boy in torn shorts. She was playing with a doll. It was a rag doll with a yellow spotted dress on and she certainly looked as if she had seen as much action as Danny, but the girl was muttering in rapid Italian to it, seeming to scold it in an affectionate way. The boy was playing with a stick, making patterns in the dust at his bare feet. They both looked thin and pale and eyed his uniform suspiciously. Danny smiled reassuringly, then reached in his pack to offer them some crackers. They sprang to their feet, their eyes suddenly wide with excitement. They grabbed the dried biscuits and rammed them in their mouths, but the little girl held her hand out and signalled to her doll. Danny nodded in understanding and delved back into his pack to find a few crumbs at the bottom that he ceremoniously handed over to the girl. Her face became wreathed in smiles as she carefully fed the crumbs to her 'baby.' For Danny, it was one of the most precious moments of the war.

By now, the sun was disappearing and Danny realised he was going to have to find his way through the maze of streets back to the camp. He talked in halting Italian to the children who responded with wild gesticulations and lengthy explanations.

'*Lentamente, lentamente*,' he said with a laugh and the boy spoke slowly and deliberately, explaining a tortuous route that it took all Danny's concentration to absorb.

He thanked them and as he started to walk away, the little girl ran after him, holding up her dolly to his face for him to kiss. She then reached up and kissed him in return. He walked off between the houses, touching his cheek. The softness of her kiss made him realise how long it had been since he had had any affection.

Five streets later, Danny desperately tried to remember what the boy had said. The road was deserted and he knew he was on the edge of the city. This was becoming a risky journey. There were parts of Rome that were rough and in times of war, a soldier with a backpack was a tempting target. He cursed himself for not thinking. Concentrating on war had made him forget that it was not only the Germans who could be his enemy. He sped up his walking, trying not to look concerned, rather just purposeful.

His soldier's training made every muscle in his body tighten in anticipation and he felt for the trigger of his gun, but all weapons had been left outside the city gates. He cursed and automatically started to glance over his shoulder at regular intervals, keeping to the centre of the road.

He turned a corner and pulled up sharply. A gang of about ten youths had gathered on the opposite corner. They had been celebrating and their eyes were wide with a desperation he had seen in soldiers on the front line. They were looking for trouble and when they spotted Danny, their faces lit up.

He made a quick assessment of the possible escape routes but knew that if he started to run in the opposite direction, they would overtake him. He tried to smile and walk past them but they circled him. They started to push and shove him like a skittle doll. He turned on the one he thought was the ringleader and shouted every obscenity he had learned over the past few years. The boy started to laugh and put his hands up in mock surrender while two behind him tried to take Danny's backpack. They were starving and one soldier's life was a small price to pay for some food.

Danny tried to speak Italian to them, using the coarse language he had learned in the mountains. They took no notice but taunted him in a guttural accent that Danny could not decipher and tightened the circle around him.

The next moment, Danny fell to the ground, a knife in his back.

Chapter 45

Lily gradually regained consciousness. She shook the dust out of her eyes and winced at the pain as the grit moved under her eyelids. She felt down to her legs. They were both still there. She wiggled her toes and felt a surge of relief as they moved in her flat brogues. She looked at her arms and turned her hands over. They were covered in scratches and dirt but her fingers seemed to be moving. Bit by bit, she tried to sit up but every part of her body hurt. She let out a cry and realised she couldn't hear anything. There was an eerie, dust-laden muffled noise but she could not distinguish any sounds. As panic welled up in her, she tried to think rationally. There had been a huge explosion and her ears were readjusting. She nodded to try and reassure herself.

'Alice!' She let out a cry as she straightened her back to peer around her. Just to her left was a huge piece of masonry. If that had been three inches towards her . . . but never mind her own body, she looked around her to the spot where Alice had stood with her head back, laughing heartily. All she could see now was rubble.

Her own injuries forgotten, Lily started scrabbling in the pile of stones next to her. She spotted a Lisle stocking with a shoe at the end of it. She shouted for help, not knowing whether anyone else could hear her. She still couldn't hear a thing. From above her, she saw the shadows of two orderlies appear against the light. They were mouthing something. She signalled to them that she couldn't hear anything but pointed to the leg next to her. They scrambled down nodding purposefully. They seemed to yell to someone behind them and two more figures appeared holding pickaxes and shovels. Lily sat back on her bottom, ignoring the pain in her side and let them pass. Her hands were shaking and she felt like she was going to be sick.

While the digging was going on next to Lily, another orderly came and took her by the hands, pulling her to her feet. A young man firmly pushed her up the rubble-covered steps. Lily arched her back towards the digging, desperate not to leave and to help find Alice, but the orderly mouthed something at her and pushed her gently but determinedly out of the Tube. Lily was crying and the salty tears were welcome moisture on her lips. Her last sight of her friend was a skirt being painstakingly unearthed from a pile of stones.

Lily was taken to an ambulance where a doctor pulled up her jumper to reveal a gaping wound in her side. Lily looked down with mild surprise at the blood that was pouring from the wound. At that point, she slowly slipped into the doctor's supporting arms and lost consciousness.

Chapter 46

The white curtains blocked Lily's view of the ward. It hurt to move and she let out a groan as she tried to stretch her back. A nurse came through the curtains.

'No, no, my dear, you stay exactly where you are. Now, let's see how you are doing.'

Bustling with importance, the red-headed woman in her thirties was firm yet imperious. Lily did not have the strength to disobey and obediently opened her mouth for the thermometer to be thrust under her tongue while her wrist was held with two determined fingers.

'My friend—' she started, trying to sit up.

The nurse shook her head.

'No, no my dear. You stay exactly where you are.'

The nurse's repetitious phrase did not brook any argument but Lily was fretting about Alice and could not let it drop.

'I have to know about my friend. Alice Colville,' she said, her mouth set like her mother's. 'Please.'

The nurse shook the thermometer and marked the clipboard at the base of her bed. Paddington Hospital was packed with patients and there was no time for chit chat, so she brushed the curtains aside, along with Lily's plea.

Lily had a temperature and kept drifting in and out of consciousness. One minute it was bright sunlight and the next it was dark. She lost track of the days, only vaguely registering that she had another stomach ache that was reassuringly similar to all her other monthly period pains. She heard murmurings of doctors sounding concerned about her temperature next to her bed but nothing was connected in her fevered mind.

After what felt like months, but must have only been a couple of weeks, Lily was able to face a little soup. As she finished it, the curtains were pushed to one side and a nurse said, 'You have a visitor.'

Lily tried to sit up straight, still very weak, confused as to who her visitor might be.

The curtain moved and she saw her father.

'Dad, oh Dad,' was all she could say.

'Ee, lass, what have you done to yourself?'

She burst into tears as he tentatively sat himself down on the edge of her bed. He very slowly and carefully enveloped her in his arms and she let out a sob, then another, and then sobbed uncontrollably, ignoring the pain but thirstily absorbing every fibre of support and love coming from her father. His strong arms seemed to block out the world: a place where the man she might love was missing, where bombs were dropped, where Kit had taken advantage of her and where her best friend might be hurt or even dead.

'I'm that glad to see you,' John said, brushing away a tear from his cheek. 'I managed to hitch a lift with the early editions and I've got to go back with the returns on the train. Your mum's frantic with worry. We just had to see if you were all right.'

'Alice—' Lily started, too frightened to go on.

'Your friend? She's in the next ward.'

Lily stared at him in disbelief.

'She's . . . all . . . right?' she said haltingly.

'Well, I wouldn't say all right as such, at least not yet, but it seems they're looking after her.'

Lily sank back on her pillow and said a rapid Hail Mary to the heavens above.

'And Danny? Have you heard anything about Danny?'

He shook his head.

Trying to convince herself that no news was good news, Lily went on.

'I'm sorry, Dad, sorry for not telling you I was coming to London. I didn't want to worry you.'

'Yes, we'd certainly hate to be worried,' he gave a wry smile. 'Anyway, I've spoken to the doctor and they say you're going to be transferred to Manchester Royal soon so your mum can see you and I should think, most of Slade

Lane. You're on the mend, love, but it's going to take time and they need to get this infection under control before they can move you.'

'That's enough now, Mr Mullins,' a voice from the edge of the curtains signalled the arrival of the stern sister. 'She needs to get her rest now.'

John Mullins stood up, looking with concern at his daughter's face as she'd gone a sickly pale colour with the excitement.

'Aye, I've got to meet the distribution lot at Fleet Street at five.'

'Oh, Dad, do you have to go? I've got so much to ask you.'

'Yes, I was told I'd only be allowed a minute or two and your mum will be hopping up and down wanting to hear every detail from me. We can catch up properly when you're transferred. And as you know, I'm not used to London. I've never been and believe me, if that chaos out there is anything to go by, I'll not be coming again.' He frowned, thinking of the devastation outside.

'Oh, do give Mum my love and tell her I'm sorry but I am all right.'

'Yes, I'll do that. You're looking fine,' he lied.

He clasped her hand and gave it a reassuring squeeze.

'Now you do everything you're told, young lady, for once in your life. We want you up and about in no time, but you need to take care of those stitches.'

Lily nodded, too exhausted to speak.

'I love you,' she mouthed as he moved backwards from the bed.

'Aye, and we love you too,' he said in a broken voice.

Lily lay back and sighed in relief. She knew what it had cost her dad to get to London both in organisation and in effort. The capital was another world to her parents and it must have been a huge adventure for him, but she also knew it had helped her turn a corner and that with the strength of his hug and the news that Alice was alive, she could fight any infection. If only she could find out whether or not Danny was alive.

Chapter 47

Looking down at the floor through the hastily made hole in Danny's mattress had become a monotonous experience. He had no memory of being brought to hospital but the orderly had told him that he had been found bleeding on the ground, without his backpack. Two Italians had bundled him into a wheelbarrow and pushed him to the hospital where he had been treated initially before being transferred to the military one. Danny had been told that he could not move, or he risked the wound opening again and becoming infected. He was furious with himself for having been so stupid and did not want to cause his unit any more problems so was determined to get better as soon as he could.

He had already had a very uncomfortable visit from his commanding officer, who minced no words about what he thought of soldiers who put themselves in unnecessary danger and had hinted at negative comments being put on his record. Danny's heart had sunk at that. He had tried so hard to toe the line and be a good soldier and he needed a blemish-free record for his job after the war. He also wanted his parents to be proud of him. It had been humiliating to hear the officer's stern voice remonstrating above him while he was unable to stand to attention or even face his accuser.

His company had moved on, up towards the west to join the oncoming allies but Danny was stuck in Rome, unlikely to move for several months and he was, for the moment, out of the war. Eddie had come to see him before they moved on and made jokes about him thinking he was an army all on his own, taking on the ruffians of Italy. Danny had smiled but it was forced. Once again he was letting his comrades down.

Danny was improving but the recovery was painfully slow and he had a blood infection. He had been in the hospital for days and the doctors were still unable to tell him how long it would be before he would be able to return to his unit. The worst thing was that he felt his injuries were self-imposed whereas the moans and groans from the other soldiers demonstrated that they, at least, had been injured in battle. He shook his head at the floor below him, almost embracing the boredom and pain as punishment for his stupidity. The indignity of being washed and toileted whilst prone were a small price to pay he felt.

'You're being shipped home for specialist treatment to that back of yours, Jackson,' a voice said from the bottom of the bed.

Danny strained his neck sideways to see the legs of the padre. 'Home, Padre?'

'Yes, next week, you're on a hospital ship home. You need specialist treatment. They're giving you sick leave.'

Danny sighed. This was the last betrayal of his military responsibilities. How could he go home when the job was not completed?

'Don't worry,' the padre said, reading his mind, 'they only want you to get better and then they'll get you back out to join your unit. They haven't finished with you yet.'

That was small comfort but it helped Danny to feel a rise of weak hope in his stomach.

'You've had a lucky escape, Jackson. Captain Fuller intervened on your behalf. I'm following the company tomorrow after the latest batch of burials but he told me to tell you that as you were on leave at the time, you will not be punished for this. But,' his voice hardened, 'he said to remind you that a soldier is part of a unit. If you want to be an individual, free to wander off on your own, you will have to wait until the end of the war.'

A huge weight was lifted off Danny's shoulders. He knew the Captain to be a fair man who had been understanding after Walter and the others were killed. A man who had climbed the mountains of Italy before the war, he had been impressed at Danny and Eddie's fortitude in making their way back to the company at Cassino, but Danny also knew that to get into a street brawl was a serious offence and he was lucky to get away with it. Although, he did think that on that same night many soldiers had been drunk and had behaved badly whereas his only crime had been to wander off alone, and he hoped that had been a factor in the leniency he was being offered. The usual sparse fare of spaghetti and tomatoes that he was fed by an orderly crouched at the end of his mattress somehow did not taste as bitter that night.

The following week, Danny was still flat on his front but able to lift his head from time to time. The pain was still there but its intensity had diminished. He felt his body being manhandled and put onto a stretcher and then being marched briskly towards an ambulance. He briefly felt the day's searing heat pierce his bandages before being bustled into the baking hot army ambulance. The journey to the port was excruciatingly painful and there was considerable tutting from nurses who were checking the wounded onto the ship.

'This one's bleeding,' a lilting Scottish voice said.

'Get him on board and we'll change the dressings there,' another voice said.

Being dependent on disembodied voices was becoming a way of life for Danny and he was desperate to be in charge of his own destiny again.

The journey home was long, hot and dangerous. Even a hospital ship could be targeted and there was an air of tension throughout the journey, but Danny hardly noticed it. The first few days were so painful he just wanted to die. Then, gradually, he began to feel a bit better in himself, although his back was still agony, and he began to find comfort in the quiet conversations of his fellow passengers. The fact that he was on his front meant he could hardly see anyone and it made it easier to talk. He found he was able to speak to the friendly voices that emerged from the dark above him about his experiences, blaming himself for his injuries and even about Lily. He discovered it was liberating that he would never have to face the other patients to whom he had been so honest once they were all carried off at the other end, and talking so openly somehow had a therapeutic effect on his agonised guilt.

Portsmouth was a shock, even to Danny, prone on a stretcher. All he could see was a mass of rubble and bombed-out buildings and for the first time, Danny caught a glimpse of how much England had gone through. He was so relieved his two sisters had been moved to the north coast and were away from the action. The hospital staff were efficient but rushed off their feet. They had little time for chit chat but Danny did glean information about what life had been like since he left England's shores all those years ago and it frightened him.

He was transferred to Haslar, a specialist military hospital unit, with new facilities in blood transfusion to help him fight infection and the next few weeks were a relentless round of treatments, injections and temperature checks. He managed to write from his upside-down position to his parents telling them he was safe and about the injuries he had suffered. He openly told them how foolish he had been and got a quick reply from his father who censured his naïveté but sounded relieved that he was back on British soil.

Danny's letter to Lily went unanswered and he knew that worrying was delaying his recovery. He tried writing to his parents again to see if they knew anything about Lily, but they had never met Mr and Mrs Mullins. He wanted to write to the last camp she had been at but knew they would ignore his letter as he was not a relative. Having time to think was a luxury Danny could have done without. He was tortured by the thought Lily would despise him for his foolishness and, staring at the ground beneath him for hours, he had never loved her more. There was nothing he could do but wait and he found he was learning a patience he had never had before. The days dragged on and he spent the time writing letters – to his family, to Eddie, to Frank's parents and, finally, to Lily's parents with a note enclosed for Lily he hoped they would pass on.

Chapter 48

Lily was starting to plan her escape route. If she hung onto the bed, then each of the beds down the ward, she worked out she could make it to the door, especially if she timed it to coincide with the nurses' changeover. Then she knew the intensive care ward was to the left and she could just spot a rail along the corridor she could grab. It was all a matter of timing. She felt excitement bubbling in her stomach as the hour of the changeover came nearer. As soon as the door closed on the sister's room, she edged her way gingerly out of bed. The girl next to her, Anne, from Bedford, who had also been injured at Paddington, looked up with interest. Lily put her fingers to her lips. She would explain later. Very carefully, she made her way along the ward, trying to suppress the gasps as the pain caught her side. She made it past the sister's room, grateful that the nurses were all too busy making notes to notice her and headed out into the corridor. The sign on the door was unequivocal: 'Intensive Care – DO NOT ENTER'. Lily did not intend to go in, she just wanted to peer through the little window in the door.

If she craned her neck, she could just see the beds. She counted along, checking each one, then . . . she saw her! Lying down, bandages everywhere and her leg stuck up in stirrups, but it was unmistakably Alice. For the first time, Lily believed her friend really was alive and it overwhelmed her. She sank to the ground, weak with exhaustion.

'What do you think you're doing?' a nurse said, leaning down towards her collapsed frame. They looked at each other and both gasped. It was like looking in a mirror. Lily was paler and in the unattractive patients' gown, whereas this woman was in a nurse's uniform, but otherwise they were almost identical. The nurse became professional again.

'Let's get you back to bed. You shouldn't be out here.'

Lily muttered that she had wanted to see her friend, Alice, who was in intensive care. Then she looked into familiar hazel eyes and said, 'Please, I need to know if she is going to be all right.'

For once, the cool exterior of the nurse faltered. She had never seen anyone who looked so much like her and through that physical link, she could almost feel the anguish that this girl was experiencing.

'I'll see what I can find out, but we must get you back to bed.'

Lily accepted the help and gratefully sank back onto her own bed. The nurse was about to walk away when Lily grabbed her hand.

'What's your name? I'm Lily. Can't you see how alike we look?'

The nurse nodded, aware that the whole ward was now staring at them. At that moment, the sister bustled in with a look of fury on her face. She frogmarched the nurse out of the ward, obviously with a great deal to say to her once she was out of the patients' hearing, but as the nurse turned on her heels, she turned and mouthed to Lily, 'Betty' and smiled.

The following evening, Lily was told she had a visitor. She sat up more easily this time to see an off-duty Betty in a smart gabardine grinning at her and then pulling up a chair to sit next to her.

'I think we need to talk about the fact that we look like two peas in a pod,' the girl said.

'Yes, I can't believe it. I've never seen myself in the flesh before,' Lily answered, 'but first, please tell me about my friend, Alice Colville, is she going to be all right?'

Betty checked over her shoulder and whispered: 'I'm not supposed to tell you anything because you're not a relation, but yes, she'll be OK. It will just take time. She was badly injured.'

Lily's eyes filled with tears. If only they hadn't been in London, if only they hadn't fallen out over Kit, she would never have been at Paddington Station. But wars were full of ifs and buts, it was too late to think about that.

Betty would not, or could not, tell her any more but they spent a very pleasant hour exchanging family histories, just to check they were not related. But Betty's home was in Hackney and there was seemingly no possible connection. It was just an odd coincidence.

It was a few days later, when Lily was beginning to feel much better, that she heard she was being transferred to Manchester Royal Infirmary. She was excited to be moving nearer to home and being able to see her family and maybe find out some news about Danny. Stuck in her hospital bed, she told herself he was alive and to prove it to herself conducted imaginary conversations with him where she told him she loved him and where he forgave her everything. The daydreams always faded when she got to the part where he was supposed to hold out his arms to her and, today, it left her feeling chilled. Her shivering was interrupted, however, by a sound of the click click of heels heading down the ward. She looked up and her heart sank as she recognised Sergeant Horrocks's shrew-like features moving inexorably towards her bed.

'So Mullins, still making a mess of things I see?'

Lily decided she was not strong enough to take on Sergeant Horrocks and made a feeble attempt to sit up straight while keeping her lips firmly pressed together.

The sergeant had a clipboard with her containing papers which she thrust under Lily's nose.

'I've been diverted from very important business to deliver these to you. Your orders. You are to be given six weeks' sick leave and then you report back to camp.'

Lily nodded, her delight at having six whole weeks to see her family tainted by the feeling that she needed to get back to work. She also desperately wanted to be able to see Alice before she left.

The sergeant's visit was mercifully brief and only consisted of the bare essentials that Lily needed to know before she was transferred.

It was as Sergeant Horrocks was gathering her papers together to snap back into her clipboard that Betty sidled into the ward, checking to see if Sister was around before making a quick dash towards Lily's bed. She obviously had some news for her and Lily looked up expectantly at the same time as Sergeant Horrocks.

'You!' said Horrocks through gritted teeth. 'You . . .'

Betty was completely lost for words and Lily looked in amazement at the two women who were staring aghast at each other.

'I might have known you would be in cahoots,' the sergeant spat out at them both.

She fumbled to pull her uniform straight, grabbed her clipboard and headed unsteadily to the door while her legs seemed to crumble beneath her.

Lily looked up at Betty for an explanation but she, too, was pale and was staring in anguish after the departing sergeant.

At that moment, Sister Mulhaney came charging down the ward.

'Nurse, if I have to tell you one more time, you will be disciplined. You are not assigned to my ward now get out and don't come back unless you are off duty.'

Betty scuttled out of the ward leaving Lily speechless, thoughts whirring around her head.

How did the two women know each other? What had happened to make Sergeant Horrocks hate Betty so much and was this, finally, the clue as to why Horrocks seemed to have a vendetta against Lily?

It was only after a few minutes that Lily remembered that Betty had come in to tell her something. She called out to another nurse, Sally Hughes, who was a small blonde with a cheerful smile.

'Nurse, could you help me?'

Sally came over, glancing back to check where Sister Mulhaney was.

'I think that nurse from Intensive Care was coming to tell me something about my friend, Alice Colville. Do you think you could find out what it was? Pleeeaaase . . .'

Her pleading got through to the little nurse, who had always tried to stop to chat with Lily.

'I'll see what I can do but don't expect miracles. Sister's watching us all like hawks.'

Two hours later, Nurse Hughes sidled back to Lily's bed pretending to straighten the covers. 'Your friend is sitting up and looks to be on the mend,' she whispered. 'I'll take her a note if you like.'

Lily couldn't wait to put pen to paper but when it came to it, her hand hesitated over the pad. What could she say? How could she tell Alice how sorry she was? In the end, she wrote a brief note saying she hoped she was feeling better and that she hoped she could forgive her. Then she paused. Could she tell her about Sergeant Horrocks? She decided not to. It was something that the two of them needed to chat about when they were back to being friends again. For a moment, she envisaged their heads bowed together while they speculated and giggled like they used to. She breathed a heavy sigh. There was a great deal of work to be done first.

Chapter 49

Lily's transfer to Manchester was delayed by two more bouts of infection. Every time she seemed to be improving, her temperature went up again and the doctors would not let her move. She got regular bulletins from Nurse Hughes about Alice but no reply to her letter came, which distressed her. Betty had apparently been called home after her brother was injured in a bombing raid over Cherbourg, taking her secret with her. In addition, Lily was beginning to seriously panic about Danny. It seemed as if all her experiences with Doug, Ted and Kit were just distant memories and as she lay, tossing and turning with her head spinning, all she could think of was Danny lying dead in a ditch covered in blood. She had nightmares and would wake up yelling, disturbing the rest of the ward and resulting in nurses dashing to her side to calm her.

The slow but successful progress into northern Europe following the D-Day landings vaguely registered with Lily but, in pain and still with no word from Alice or Danny, she only nodded distractedly at the excitement in the ward around her. Her war had become far too personal for her to take real delight in world events.

She finally started to improve and once her temperature was low enough, she was ushered into a waiting ambulance and taken to a train heading north. She had no time to let Alice know and her attempts to track down where Betty lived so she could send her a letter had failed dismally, leaving her with nightmares presenting various scenarios that always failed to explain the sergeant's enmity towards them both. With the help of painkillers and a rush of adrenalin, the train journey passed in a blur for Lily from her position on a stretcher in the guard's van and it seemed no time at all until the train pulled into Piccadilly. Too tired to notice the journey to the hospital, Lily smelt the air, telling herself she knew she was home.

The first few days in Manchester were a mix of pure pleasure and pain. The journey had taken it out of Lily and her exhaustion could cope with little more than five-minute visits from her anxious mother and father but, gradually, Lily could manage some congealed porridge and soup, and with an improved diet, even of hospital war ration food, started to feel more like herself and was allowed home.

To be in her own little bedroom with her mother fussing around her felt like being enclosed in a warm, safe blanket. Lily luxuriated in it and played endless games of Ludo with her brother, who would come in to see her every afternoon after school.

She wrote to everyone she knew to see if they had had any news of Danny but even Mr Spencer at Liners had heard nothing. Lily started to imagine the life they might have had, the little house in the suburbs, the tidy kitchen and little garden and maybe children . . . She stopped her dreaming suddenly. Would Danny still want her? Was she still a virgin? She was still a bit vague on the mechanics of sex and longed to talk to Alice.

She wrote regularly to Alice but received no reply. She had failed her friend and Danny and this was her punishment, she felt. She deserved to be abandoned, unloved. It was a good thing her parents still cared for her, she thought, and started planning a life as a spinster looking after them into their old age.

On the day she was allowed downstairs for the first time, she heard her parents talking quietly in the kitchen. The post had just come and her father had picked up the letters off the mat on his way in from the night shift. They came into the morning room like two wary animals.

'What is it, Dad, Mum? You're scaring me. Please. Is it Danny? Alice?'

Her mum sat down next to the armchair where Lily was cuddled up and took her hand.

'No, it's good news, love, we just don't want you to get excited.' She plucked at the blanket and tucked it unnecessarily around her daughter's legs.

Lily looked from one to the other. 'Please tell me, I promise I'll keep calm.' She was glad they could not hear her thumping heart.

'It's Danny, he's alive,' her dad said.

The rush of blood went straight from Lily's stomach to her heart, then to her head and back to her heart again. She felt as if she was going to faint.

'You see, I was right,' her mum said to her dad accusingly. 'She isn't strong enough.'

'No, I'm fine, please tell me,' Lily said quickly.

'He's been injured, not a war injury but he was attacked in Rome. He's in hospital near Portsmouth.'

Lily's mind raced through the streets of Rome, imagining some faceless assailants attacking a lone soldier. She then paused, puzzled as to why they had not sent him to the Military Hospital in Malta. He must be desperately ill, she concluded.

'Is he all right?' she whispered.

'Apparently, yes, he sent us a note and enclosed this letter for you.'

Lily grabbed it from her dad's proffered hand and greedily read it. The fact that it was written by Danny made her heave a sigh of relief. If he was well enough to write then surely . . .? She carried on reading. It was all about her and whether she was all right. He said little about the injury but talked about having had specialist treatment on his back. Lily's thoughts went to Dickie Ashcroft, down Slade Lane, who had returned from the war in a wheelchair. She gulped back a short, panicked breath and made herself concentrate on the fact that he was alive.

She sat back in the chair and felt her life had just been restored to her. Lily could not wait to write back but, like in her letters to Alice, she was unsure what to say. Yes, he had been constant with his letters, all of them had hinted at a future together, but this was a very different man from the one who had gone off to war four years earlier. She did not know how he felt about her and certainly she was a very different girl from the one who had tossed her head uncaringly at him as he walked out of the office.

28th June, 1944

Dear Danny,

I can't tell you how relieved I was to find out you were alive. I had been watching the post every day to see if there was any news of you but when my parents brought me your letter today, I could finally breathe a sigh of relief. I am all right but I was hurt in a raid on London and have come back home to recuperate. Mum, as you can imagine, is loving fussing over me and is, I know, giving me all the best titbits of food while she goes without but as she's banned me from the kitchen, I can't check. I am feeling much better and I think I'll be heading back to camp soon. It's been good to be in Manchester but you may not recognise it, it's been pretty badly damaged. The Mancunian spirit is still alive and kicking though, you'll be glad to know.

She sat back and paused. Had she said too much? Not enough?

Oh blow it, she thought, he could have been dead. She could have been dead. She took up the pen again.

Danny, I don't how you feel about me. I have been so offhand with you for so long but when I thought you were dead, I felt as if my heart was going to burst. It was as if my life no longer had any meaning. I know I was young when you left but I have grown up a lot and I do hope you still like me. I would love us to start again. Can we?

With my love,

Lily

She slowly sealed the envelope and ran her fingers over it, stroking it. The longer this war went on, the more there was to say and the less she had been saying it, she thought. First Danny, then Alice. Everything moved too fast, there was no time for deep discussions, no time for developing emotions at a reasonable rate.

She felt her forehead and hoped all these tumbled emotions were not because she was coming down with another infection.

The following day there was another letter for her.

29th June, 1944

Dear Lily,

You will have to forgive the terrible writing but this is the first time I have been able to hold a pen. My right hand was badly hurt and I haven't felt like writing to anyone, even my ninny of a friend.

Lily, just before that bomb dropped, as I looked at your horror stricken, naïve face, all the anger I had felt about Kit fell away. It was just like you to get the facts of life wrong and all muddled up. Kit was a fantasy, a really good fun one, but once I realised what you'd been through, my straightforward Lancashire upbringing came to the fore and he became a glam story I will relate to my grandchildren – or maybe not. Anyway, the only thing that matters to me is my best friend. We've been through so much, Lily, and one randy American isn't going to change that. So, let's put him down to experience and enjoy all those stomach pains . . . you deserve them!'

I am going home for a bit to recover but I can at least write now. I can imagine all the guilt you've put yourself through and all the Mullins drama you've been creating but, my daft Lily, we are and will always be the best of friends.

Love,

Alice.

PS. I did meet a rather nice doctor but you'll have to wait for the gory details about that one. My hand hurts now!

Lily would have skipped back to Upper Heyford if it had not hurt so much. She felt as if a huge weight had been lifted off her on all fronts. Firstly, whatever the outcome, Danny would know how she felt about him. Secondly, Alice did not hate her and had even met a new man and thirdly, Hilda had written to her telling her that Sergeant Horrocks had been seconded to another camp for a few weeks. Lily found she could smile again. She was surprised how quickly she got back into the routine at camp. At first, the liberation of Paris and Brussels encouraged a feeling that the end of war was in sight, but then the wanton destruction by the buzz bombers meant the RAF were kept incredibly busy. To add to everyone's consternation there were rumours that an even more destructive weapon was being developed. It was a bomb that made no noise until it exploded. No one knew much about it but it became known as the V-2 and represented Germany's vindictive revenge for the bombing by the allies.

The shifts during the winter months of 1944 into '45 were relentless and everyone was exhausted as the operational stations tried to retaliate. Lily was still struggling with her health and, weakened by the infections, she had lost weight and looked pale. One night in late February, when she was making her way wearily back to the barracks, she bumped into Sergeant Horrocks, clutching her kit bag close to her chest. It was the first time the two women had met since the hospital and both reared up in surprise in the dark.

'So, Mullins, so, you're still here, causing problems no doubt. Well, I'm back now so you had better watch out."

Lily's training should have kept her in check but it was one o'clock in the morning after a harrowing shift.

'Sergeant, I know you hate me. I am not quite sure why but I suspect it has something to do with Betty. I am not related to her. I only met her in hospital and I have done nothing to hurt you.'

Sergeant Horrocks spat out her reply.

'You're all the same, you girls. You have no morals, no pride and certainly no idea of how to behave. You're just a slut like the rest of them.'

Lily stepped back as the sergeant's spit hit her in the face. The venom in the woman's words was like a snake's poison and Lily reached up to wipe the spittle from her cheek.

She took a pace forward, red with fury and opened her mouth to speak. At that moment, a plane started to weave its way overhead, lurching from side to side as if drunk. They both looked up and their argument hung in the balance as the pilot struggled to re-gain control.

Lily took a sharp breath and reined in her anger. This woman was her superior. She could never win.

She turned on her heels, listening to the sirens at the end of the airfield and reminded herself that nothing was important in this war except surviving it.

Sergeant Horrocks stared after her and then, muttering to herself, marched off on her heels and disappeared into the darkness.

The following morning, the base was buzzing with the news that a body had been found.

Chapter 50

Rumours abounded the next day, but nobody knew the truth. There were police officers all over the camp, taking photographs and notes. Lily, like the others, was checking all the faces and beds to find out who was missing but there was no clue as to who the body was. Hilda said a girl from two huts down had seen a stretcher with a sheet covering a body on it, another girl said she had seen the Company Commander striding through the camp with two MPs and a policeman looking very serious.

Two hours later, they were all occupied with the latest batch of rookies and Lily was kept busy frantically pressing the Morse pad trying to keep her crew on course and safe. There were some very dodgy landings and everyone in the control tower held their breath as the two inexperienced pilots followed each other onto the landing strip, bouncing from side to side in the wind.

At the end of her shift in the early evening, Lily was called in to see the warrant officer. She straightened her hair and her tie as she stood nervously outside the door, waiting to be called in.

'Enter.'

The officer was sitting behind a big wooden desk with sheaves of paper on it in neat piles. He picked up the one on the top as he acknowledged her salute.

'At ease, LACW Mullins.'

Lily stared straight ahead, her head held high, but her stomach was turning over.

He glared at her.

'This is most irregular, Mullins, but you have a visitor. Report to the guard-room. You have thirty minutes. Be back in your barracks ready for tea.'

Lily clicked her heels together and saluted. He immediately forgot she was there and picked up the second piece of paper off the pile.

When Lily left the office, she stood for a moment perplexed and then broke into a fast walk. The panic was welling up inside her. Her mum? Dad? What disaster could have prompted a personal visit?

She hesitated as she reached the guard-room but then took a deep breath and pushed open the door. There was a small group of WAAF telephone operators waiting for pass outs, two ambulance crew delivering their report sheets and standing to the side, shifting nervously from foot to foot, there was a Tommy.

As she walked in, the man turned around. For a moment, they both looked at each other, and then Lily stepped forwards.

'Danny,' she whispered.

He held out his arms to her but then dropped them as she hesitated.

'What are you doing here?' Lily winced. She had imagined this moment so many times in recent weeks but never had she realised how awkward she would feel.

'Hello, Lily.' The words of delight that he had rehearsed all the way from Portsmouth fell like broken slivers of glass between them.

She scanned Danny's face, looking for the familiar smile, the recognisable, cocky confidence of a boy she once knew. Instead she found a man behind an unfamiliar mask.

'I told them I was your cousin, on compassionate leave, due back in Europe in forty-eight hours. Is there somewhere we can get a cuppa?' He turned towards the door, looking for the NAAFI. He could not stand her stare. He was sure she could see through him.

'I only have half an hour,' she replied, putting her hand on his arm to make him turn towards her again.

Danny reared up as if her hand was a hot poker. The proximity of her body was making him shiver uncomfortably. He searched her face as if committing a map to memory and coughed in embarrassment, catching her inquiring look.

'How are you?' he blurted out. 'Have you recovered? Your parents told me how badly you'd been hurt in the Paddington bomb.'

'Yes, I'm fine, just a few twinges now and again. What about you?'

'Yes, I'm OK, I'm actually being shipped back out next week.'

Lily let a moment's fear cross her face. 'Oh, Danny, haven't you done enough?'

He turned away and started to march purposefully towards the door. 'Let's get out of here.'

She followed him out and he strode towards a low wall near the entrance to the camp. He sat down gingerly and looked back at her. He beckoned her to sit next to him.

'I—' he started but he did not know what to say. He had waited five years to see her again and now he was messing it up. He did not want to talk about his injuries or the shame of how he had got them. He suddenly felt he was not worthy of this young woman and he was sure she was regretting her letter to him. He glanced sideways at her, hardly recognising the young girl who used to stride around the office, trying to look important. Now, she really was important. She looked so smart in her uniform and her waved hair under the cap made her look so commanding and in control. He noticed her tapes – she was a higher rank than he was. A leading aircraftwoman was the equivalent of an army corporal. She had done so well while he had been stupidly putting his military record in jeopardy. She looked pale but very beautiful. How could he ever have thought she would still feel anything for him? He felt his shoulders slump.

Lily waited for him to speak. Was this the same Danny who had written all those confident letters, who had joked with her but always made her feel secure in his feelings for her? He seemed so distant and she immediately felt he was disappointed in her after all this time. She looked such a mess and touched her hair to try to wind it on her finger back under her cap.

She had to disturb the silence.

'It's been a long time, Danny.'

'Yes, Liners seems like another life.'

They glanced at each other and for a second their eyes recalled the past that they shared.

'I wonder what Mr Spencer would say if he saw us now,' Lily attempted a smile. 'I wonder if we'll be able to go back there, when . . . when this is all over.'

'I wonder if we'll want to.'

Lily felt a rising panic. This was not the romantic reunion she had imagined. Danny felt like a stranger and now he was regretting coming to find her. He had not mentioned her letter.

Danny was beginning to feel beads of sweat appearing on his forehead. He had so wanted to return a war hero, standing proud knowing he had done his bit but all he had done was be a naïve fool and end up abandoning his comrades, leaving them to fight while he sat on a wall in Oxfordshire talking to a stranger. This was not the little girl who needed his protection, his advice or his help. His mind was racing but no words came out of his mouth. He could have kicked himself. He had been up at dawn, hitched all the way to London, through the devastated capital and out to Oxfordshire in such excitement. His back was killing him. After her letter, he had been so excited, envisaging meeting her again, practising what he would say, how he would fold her into his arms as she sobbed with relief at seeing him.

'Danny,' she finally ventured, unable to bear the tension, 'it is so lovely to see you.' Her voice started to break but Danny did not look up, he was too busy examining his boots.

'Yes, well, I happened to be in the area so I thought I would call in.' He stood up quickly, looking towards the road for a passing truck that might offer a potential lift and an escape route before he broke down and destroyed the last vestige of pride he had left.

She felt her heart plummet and looked up at him in horror. Surely this couldn't be it? It was as if her life of the past three years was passing before her eyes. Doug, Ted, Kit. What had seemed like growing up experiences now made her feel like a harlot. It suddenly occurred to her that he knew all about her lurid past, that, somehow, he could see the guilt on her. She wanted to reach out and hug him, feel his arms around her, his voice telling her he loved her and that when the war was over, they would be together. Instead, he straightened his uniform and coughed again.

'I had better be on my way. I need to be back in Portsmouth by midnight. Remember me to your parents.'

Lily found it hard to speak, opened her mouth and then closed it again.

'Take care of yourself, Lily.' For one, brief moment, his eyes seemed to envelop her in affection but then the mask came down again.

'And you, Danny. Write to me, won't you?'

'Yes, if you want me to.'

'Of course,' she blurted out in desperation.

'OK. Well, so long, Lily, it's been good to see you.'

'And you, Danny.'

He walked away. It was the longest walk of his life.

Chapter 51

The baked beans were awful, dry and congealed but Lily could not taste them anyway. She felt utterly desperate. She thought back to all the times she had been offhand with Danny and bile rose in her throat. She thought she was going to throw up.

Hilda tried to talk to her about the drama taking place in the camp but there was no response. She just sat playing with her fork, prodding the beans as if they were her enemy.

For so long, Danny had been like a lighthouse for her: solid, dependable and always there. She had felt so secure, basking in his obvious admiration and had had no doubts that, now they were older, that admiration would turn to love. The soldier who had visited her earlier had been a stranger, untouched by her and even by life, she thought, remembering his cold expression and short sentences. He had lost all his fun and excitement but worse than that, he was obviously disappointed in the girl Lily had become.

She looked up and caught sight of herself in the window. No wonder he didn't want any more to do with her.

Her eyes looked haunted and were surrounded by dark shadows. The long shifts and her injuries had taken their toll. She looked terrible. She suddenly pushed her chair back, scratching the floor and making the whole room stare. With wild, desperate sobs, she fled from the table, forgetting her irons and mug. Hilda automatically picked them up and thoughtfully looked after her friend as she stumbled out of the room.

Word went around the camp like wildfire. The dead body was Sergeant Horrocks. She had been found with some pills she had apparently stolen from the medical centre. When Lily heard she felt a shockwave ripping through her body for a moment but very soon guiltily realised there was also a certain relief that the woman could no longer make her life a misery. Amidst so much death, 'Horrible Horrocks's' apparent suicide seemed a disgraceful waste of life and apart from a vague disquiet about what had made her so desperate, Lily did not feel able to mourn too deeply and she very quickly went back to analysing the dreadful reunion with Danny. In a state of numbness on domestic night, she polished the floor around her bed as normal almost oblivious to the high-pitched excited chattering that was going on around her as the rest of the hut mulled over the news. A door opened and the noise was immediately quelled.

'LACW Mulllins, report to the Company Commander immediately.'

The Duty Officer stood over her and Lily looked down to notice the woman had a scuff on her left shoe. She almost reached out and polished it but then vaguely remembered she was supposed to spring to attention and salute.

She followed the officer, watched with interest by the rest of the hut.

Under normal circumstances, Lily would have been shaking as the Commander told her to enter but, enveloped in a blanket of misery, she was only a mildly surprised to see Marion standing to attention facing the large walnut desk.

'Dismissed, LACW Hill.'

Marion saluted, turned on her heels and with a knowing look at Lily, swept past her and out of the door.

Lily stood to attention and tried to concentrate.

'Mullins, this is Inspector Bailey. He is here to question you about the death of Sergeant Horrocks.'

At this, Lily jerked her head back. His words pierced her apathy and brought her up sharply.

'Me, sir?'

'Yes, we believe you were the last person to see her alive.'

Marion's smug face suddenly made sense. She must have seen the sergeant with Lily and reported it to the Commander.

All thoughts and worries about Danny vanished from Lily's mind. This was serious. A woman she had hated and one who had hated her had died and as she looked from the inspector to the commander and back again, it suddenly dawned on her that she was suspected of having something to do with her death.

'I bumped into Sergeant Horrocks on my way back from my shift, sir.'

'Did she speak to you?' The inspector's eyes narrowed.

The memory of that last exchange came back to Lily like a Pathé News clip, the anger, the venom and the near physical attack.

'Yes, sir.'

'What did she say?'

Lily looked in desperation at the two men. Lying was something she had never been able to do and she had no choice but to tell them the truth – and all of it.

It took Lily an hour to go through the story of Sergeant Horrocks and her relationship and by the time she had finished, for the first time, she realised how bizarre it must have sounded. She also knew she was criticising a senior rank but she had no option as there was really no cause that she was aware of that could have prompted the hatred she unwittingly engendered in the dead woman.

As she described the final scene, she swayed on her feet and the Inspector reached forward to take her arm.

'Sit down here,' he said, more kindly than he had spoken before.

She glanced at the commanding officer and he nodded his permission, passing her a glass of water from the sideboard.

She sipped it and looked up at him.

'What will happen now, sir?' she asked fearfully.

'We have several other people to question and then we will get back to you.'

Lily's heart sank. Sergeant Horrocks was dead, she was not going to be able to corroborate Lily's story. If they spoke to Marion, she would take any opportunity to land her in trouble and would make it look as if Lily was lying and that she was somehow complicit in a woman's death.

'You may go, but you are confined to camp until this matter is concluded,' the Commander said.

Lily nodded and stumbled out of the room.

Back in the hut, she was greeted with silence. Marion had been standing in the middle of the floor and Lily knew she had been regaling them with speculation and rumours about her. It occurred to her that rushing out of the mess in tears had added fuel to the fire but she had not wanted to discuss Danny with any of them. She got ready for bed in silence and climbed under the blanket. It was almost time for lights out and Lily couldn't wait for the lamps to be extinguished so she could vanish into her own thoughts without anyone watching her. She closed her eyes and longed for Danny, for Alice's common sense and for a hug from her mum. The tears fell hot and fast and it was all she could do to not cry out loud but the rough blanket heaved in jerks as she caught the sobs in the back of her throat.

The next morning, she was on duty early so crept out of the hut before the others were awake, grateful that she did not have to talk to anyone. She felt like a criminal, a murderess and yet she knew she had not done anything wrong.

The crew she had that morning were ones who were nearing the end of their training and had been on a night sortie, but it was a foggy morning and she had to help them as they struggled to navigate their way back. Lily furrowed her brow as she pressed the Morse key hard and concentrated to send the correct coordinates until they finally appeared through the clouds above the camp. More than one crew had been lost in fog only to crash into the sea and never be seen again so survival was a team effort and Lily was determined she was not going to lose any more young men.

At breakfast after the debrief, the crew joked and laughed with her, hiding their relief at having landed safely and Lily enjoyed being away from suspicion and actually managed to eat some egg and toast. She sipped at her tea and looked over the rim at the seven young boys in front of her. They would soon be going out on raids to retaliate for the new bombs that were exploding over England. She shook her head in despair. *Would it ever end?* she thought.

The rest of the day was so busy with the next crew that Lily had little time to think of anything, but later that evening, when she returned to the hut, the girls all went silent and started to frantically re-organise their kits ready for inspection. Lily tried to get on with sorting her own pile but finally the silence and meaningful looks across the room got the better of her and she swirled round in anger.

'You can all stop talking about me. I know you're doing it. I've done nothing wrong and that will be proved. You're hypocrites anyway. You all hated Sergeant Horrocks so don't pretend you didn't.'

There was silence and then Hilda came across to Lily and put her arms around her.

Tense and surprised, Lily stood stock still for a moment and then buckled. Hilda caught her as she burst into tears.

'There, there, lovey. Calm yourself. No one's blaming you. We just know she hated you for some reason and everyone's making the most of gossiping about something that isn't war-related.'

Hilda looked crossly at the rest of the girls in the hut who had started to shuffle around guiltily.

It was true the 'Horrocks Affair', as it was becoming known, had excited the exhausted WAAFs and was a welcome relief from the daily grind of a long war and while none of them felt any real sadness at her death, the opportunity to speculate and gossip had been too tempting for them to resist.

A voice came from behind the stove in the middle. It was Marion.

'All I can say is that I always liked Sergeant Horrocks. I found her to be a welcome change from the usual type of person you get in a place like this.'

At this, pillows, shoes and hairbrushes shot across the room and Marion had to duck to escape the volley of missiles that were being hurled her way.

Lily started to giggle through her tears and as the tension was released, the rest of the girls started to laugh too. Marion raised her chin and took up her book, sitting down with a thud on her bed in disgust.

The next day Lily received a letter from Alice.

23rd February, 1945

Dear Lily,

I do hope you're all right. I had a visit from the police last night. They told me about Sergeant Horrocks. What a dreadful thing to happen. They asked me lots of questions about you and her and I told them how she had hated you from the beginning for no reason. They seemed to suggest they'd questioned you too. I hope they don't think you had anything to do with it. I gave them Amy's name but they already had it, and of course, you have the Princess with you your end but I bet she hasn't been much help.

Things are busy here. I should think you're having the same problems with the latest little vengeance packages from Germany, but I'm dying to see you – I have so much to tell you. My doctor, whose name is Arthur, has asked me to marry him and I have said yes! Oh Lily, I know you have a lot on your mind at the moment, but I'm so happy I had to share it with you. I want you to be my bridesmaid, will you? We are going to wait until the war is over – surely it can't be long now – and then I am going to take him to meet my parents. I hope he doesn't go off me when he sees how much mud we have on the farm; he seems to think I am very glam! He must be in love with me! Anyway, let me know what happens over this dreadful Horrocks business.

Love,

Alice

Lily hugged herself as she sat in the mess reading the letter. She felt such a thrill of excitement for her friend and not a little regret that while Alice had found such happiness, she had not heard from Danny since their disastrous meeting. She was off-duty for the afternoon but confined to camp so could only go for short walks around the perimeter. She decided some exercise would be good for her and she needed time to put her thoughts in order.

She strode alongside the fence with purpose, swinging her arms forward and back in time with her step. It did her good to have a steady rhythm and for the first time in several days, her beating heart started to quieten down.

'LACW Mullins, report to the CO.' A small WAAF from the admin office was calling to her from the control tower.

This is it, Lily thought, *I will either be arrested for murder or this nightmare will be at an end.*

Chapter 52

The traffic jam went back miles. They had been promised a triumphal entry into Berlin and now they were sitting waiting for the Russians to take the glory. As the long columns of Soviet armies had passed him, Danny had been surprised by the mix of modern tanks and Cossack cavalrymen who looked like remnants from medieval times. He had realised very quickly that although the West and the Russians were allies, they could have been from a different planet. The reality of how Hitler's dream had turned into a nightmare for his own people was being slowly but relentlessly revealed. Gaunt, thin and suspicious of the liberators, the defeated Germans looked like a shrunken race and seemed to have no fight left in them. But then the Russians moved in and Danny watched in horror as some soldiers rampaged through the streets looking for alcohol and women. He watched them drag women out from the crowds and rape them on the fronts of their tanks. He was unable to interfere, unable to help. It seemed any woman was easy prey, be she a grandmother or a child and the drunken Russians did not fail to take the victors' spoils. The perpetrators were like animals, he thought, then corrected himself, because no animal raped, beat up or abused its victim like the troops he was forced to watch. Danny and his fellow soldiers were powerless. They were supposed to be on the same side.

As they approached Berlin, the tank transporter approached a small copse. At the point where they turned a corner, two girls ran out from the scant cover of the trees and in front of Danny's vehicle. He screeched to a halt, knowing there were only a few yards between him and the vehicle behind. The girls were so thin, he could see their ribs through their grubby dresses and he knew they were German.

His heart started to thump. The convoy was close to the designated Western barriers but there were still two Russian checkpoints to get through. It looked like the girls had been sleeping rough, trying to stay out of sight of the revenge-thirsty Russians. They were lucky to have got away without being attacked or even hanged by the roadside. He had already seen the mangled bodies of girls in once-pretty dresses hanging from trees, discarded like abandoned dolls at the side of the road, their legs bloodied and smeared. He leaned out of the window.

'Please, you 'ave to 'elp us. Zey vill kill us.'

Danny had a split second to decide. He could leave them to their fate and let them join the piles of rags that were gradually being eaten by crows, or he could help them.

He opened the door, yanked at the rubber mat under the pedals to reveal a cavernous space beneath and motioned for them to climb in. Looking in his mirror he saw John and Bill approaching from behind and he immediately started to move forward, even before the girls had managed to prostrate themselves under the cabin floor. One of them, who might have been pretty without the dirt and the haunted expression, leaned up and held out her hand to him, her bony fingers strained with gratitude. He ignored it, covered up their cramped bodies with his foot and pressed the accelerator.

It was a two-hour journey of slow stopping and starting and Danny could hear one of the girls quietly sobbing. He revved his engine to blot out the noise. The reality of what he had done only occurred to him when he approached the first Russian checkpoint. He whispered to the girls to keep quiet, saying one word he hoped they understood: 'Ruskie'. The truth was he was as dependent for his life on them as they were on him for theirs. A toothy corporal poked his huge hand through the window signalling Danny to hand over his documents. He grinned and Danny tried very hard to smile back. He wondered whether the soldier could see him sweating. He looked as casually as he could at the Moisin rifle hanging from the Russian's left shoulder and a searing panic swelled up from his stomach. He pressed his foot hard on the floor of his cab, trying to keep the rubber in place and not reveal the heaving chests of the terrified girls.

He handed over his documents with a shaking hand that he hoped the guard thought was the result of last night's alcohol. The guard gave him a knowing smile as Danny signalled a bottle being swigged and with one last look round the cab, the Russian waved him on his way.

The second checkpoint was just a mile down the road. He could hear strangled sobs from beneath his heel and hissed 'Shhhhh . . . for God's sake, you'll get us all killed,' as they approached.

He imagined the girls stuffing bits of their filthy dresses into their mouths as he strained to listen again. This time there was no sound but he was sure he could hear them breathing. He hoped the two Russian soldiers, who were throwing their heads back at some raucous joke as they approached his cab, were too preoccupied to look for problems.

'*Docimenty*,' the one on Danny's side demanded but as Danny reached onto the dashboard to hand the papers over, he was suddenly aware that the second one was examining the floor under his feet very carefully. Danny looked down and spotted a tiny bit of mat that had furled back. From his driver's seat, he couldn't see anything but he could not be sure that the Russian was not able to glimpse a tiny bit of red dress.

Danny had to do something – and fast.

He delved into his top pocket and found the St Christopher medal that his mother had given him. He had laughed at her – a good Church of England parishioner – but she said she wanted to make sure he had all the help he could get. He handed it to the soldier on the far side of the cab. The soldier looked suspiciously at it, then bit on it, realised it was silver and broke into a broad grin. The other soldier quickly went round the front of the cab, arguing. Danny looked in his wing mirror and saw them almost coming to blows as he drew slowly away from them, waiting in sick anticipation to see whether they were going to stop him. A senior officer approached the men, who were now getting into an angry tussle. He shouted at them and Danny took the opportunity to speed up slightly. He whispered to the girls they were through. There was no sound.

'Don't tell me they're dead,' he thought. 'Not after all that.' The rest of the journey left Danny straining with every sinew listening for noises from below, but none came.

'That would be just my luck,' he thought, 'now I'll have two bodies to explain.'

Finally, he approached the British Safe Zone, but the penalty here for helping the enemy would be severe, even if they were dead. He signalled to Bill that he needed a leak and pulled over by a large oak tree. He gingerly pulled back the rubber mat and saw the girls, each with their tattered cardigans stuffed in their mouths. They were almost blue with lack of oxygen but they staggered out as he told them to run into the woods. He hoped his German was up to scratch and that they would understand him. He did not have time to say it twice.

He jumped out of his truck and tried not to look over his shoulder. Pretending to unzip his fly with a trembling hand, he heard the girls behind him. The same one who had tried to take his hand touched him on the arm as she stumbled round the side of the truck. There was so much meaning in that touch that Danny almost recoiled with the heat from it. He looked around and saw tears pouring down her ashen cheeks. *'Lord, she's younger than Maureen,'* he thought.

Shaken, he turned to go back towards the wagon. The last he saw of them was a flash of faded red cherries on the hem of one of their dresses disappearing into the woods. The former chorister at Manchester Anglican Cathedral School said a heartfelt thank you to the Catholic St Christopher.

That night, they bivouacked outside Berlin. Danny bent into the cab and replaced the mat properly. He felt beneath the rubber and his fingers touched something. Bending further in, he stretched his index finger and thumb to try and grasp whatever it was. Finally, he reached it and pulled it out. It was a child's dummy. Danny sat down suddenly on the ground, clutching the plastic object, and closed his eyes.

All sorts of scenarios flashed before him. A dead child, a child to be re-found, a pregnancy from a rape? He decided to go with the child to be re-found and spent a moment imagining a scene where the girl tracked down her baby and they were reunited in the west to live a life together, playing games, talking about the English soldier who risked his life to save the mother.

For a moment, Danny felt the whole war had been leading up to this moment. An instant decision that would make a difference, something that would leave an imprint, a good imprint, forever. He imagined children, grandchildren, great grandchildren who would talk about how their ancestor had hidden in a British army truck to escape from marauding Russians and ruthless authorities. For the first time in months, he felt good about himself.

Chapter 53

The commanding officer fingered the papers in front of him. Lily's teeth were chattering and she was sure he could see her knees knocking. She looked down at them to will them to stop trembling but they ignored her, she noticed with a frown.

'LACW Mullins, we have considered your statement carefully and we have talked to your colleagues, but I am afraid we are left with no alternative than to assume some sort of collusion between you and Sergeant Horrocks. We only have your word against hers and despite testimony from Hill and Colville, I am afraid this case must go to a military court.'

Lily's knees finally buckled and she started to sway.

'ATTENTION!' the commanding officer, a man in his forties barked. His stern face brooked no excuses and Lily forced herself to stand tall and look straight ahead.

'You were seen near the medical centre on the night the sergeant took her life and we believe she may have coerced you into obtaining medical supplies to end her life.'

Lily's mouth opened but no words came out. Her mind was racing and she re-traced the night when Sergeant Horrocks verbally attacked her. She had not even registered that she was standing next to the Med Centre.

'You will have your chance to have your say at the hearing but obtaining medical supplies is a serious offence and if we find that you had anything to do with helping Sergeant Horrocks kill herself then the consequences will be severe.

'You will be assigned legal representation but for now, all leave is cancelled and you must stay on base. You will continue with your duties. Dismissed.'

Lily swirled on her heels and walked out of the door. When she reached the corridor, she slumped against the wall outside the office.

'What's up with yous, Sassenach?'

Lily looked up to see Glad striding down the corridor, holding an armful of files.

'Oh Glad, I am sooo very glad to see you!' Lily started to cry hysterically and then Glad scooped her up in her arms, dropping the files into a scattered mess on the floor.

It took all Gladys's Scottish pragmatism to calm Lily down and get her out of the hearing of the commanding officer. She stopped only to gather up her files and then hustled the weeping girl out of the building.

'What . . . are you . . . doing here?' Lily gasped between sobs.

'Been transferred, upgraded too,' Glad added proudly, lifting her head high. 'All office work but that suits me fine. I've found I actually like being clean and tidy and not smelling of those kitchen cabbages for a change. I might take up a new career in a nice office when this party's over. So, what's been happening to yous?'

They were both going off-duty so they made their way to the NAAFI. Two cups of tea later, Lily had filled Gladys in on the Sergeant Horrocks affair. Gladys frowned.

'Seems to me, you need a few friends in high places,' she said mysteriously. 'Leave it to me.'

Lily was too tired to ask any more and it suddenly seemed perfectly feasible that this Scottish prostitute could save her from being court martialled. She decided to do exactly as she asked.

The shifts were as busy as ever and while Lily was dealing with more and more inexperienced sprogs finding their way across the skies, she actually had little time to fret about the impending case. The other girls were beginning to go out more as better and better news started to filter through about the end of the war being near, but Lily hardly noticed. She was receiving letters from Danny but they were perfunctory, sparse and very short and, she recognised with a sinking heart, lacking in any warmth. The ones from Alice were enthusiastic and excited as she prepared for her wedding. Lily's mum's letters moaned about the worsening shortages but she was as resourceful as ever. Lily determinedly wrote back lively replies, saying as little as possible in as many words as she could.

One evening, as Lily was coming out of the control tower after a gruelling shift, Glad was waiting for her. She looked very important.

'I just wanted to warn yous, you'll be called in to the gaffer any minute now. Just keep yourself calm. Can't say any more – must go.' And like a spy, she scurried off towards the office block, winking at Lily as she turned to go.

Lily shook her head. She had given up questioning anything.

A shout came across the yard.

'Mullins, report to the CO, NOW!'

Lily acknowledged the Corporal's demand and went at a brisk trot to the CO's. She knocked hesitantly at the door.

'Enter.'

The CO was sitting at his desk, his fingers rifling through a pile of papers. Standing at the side of the desk was a Wing Commander.

'LACW, this is Wing Commander Hill, he has very kindly intervened on your behalf and found out some information from one of the office clerks that means you are no longer under suspicion.'

Lily stopped mid-salute and looked inquiringly at the tall, imposing man in front of her, completely bemused.

'The revelations were corroborated by my niece, with whom I believe you are acquainted and she confirmed details of Sergeant Horrocks's unfair treatment of you so I decided to take it on myself to investigate,' the man said.

Lily's brain took a moment to function. His niece? She realised he was talking about Marion and reeled. It was like spilling a hot coffee on her chest. She panicked for a moment, wondering what Marion had in store for her now.

He continued, completely unaware of her but obviously impressed with his own efforts.

'We took some time to discover the cause of her enmity but then tracked down a nurse who bears an uncanny resemblance to you—' at this, he stopped and for the first time, looked at her properly, peering down at her from his great height.

'Well, yes, I can see that. This nurse apparently had some dealings with Sergeant Horrocks's fiancé three years ago which caused the relationship between the young man and the sergeant to founder and, in fact, Nurse Betty Holmes has now married him. The similarity between you and the nurse meant Sergeant Horrocks mounted a hate campaign against you, made worse by your skills in mimicking her, I believe.'

Lily thought back to the scene at the lamp-post in Blackpool. She narrowed her eyes trying to remember whether the sergeant could have witnessed it. She shook her head. She had no idea but it was all starting to make sense.

'My own niece,' he went on with some pride, 'has reassured me of your integrity and the difficult time you had with the unfortunate sergeant. We've since discovered Sergeant Horrocks even went so far as to destroy a letter asking for your application to the Air Transport Auxiliary.'

Lily, who had been staring straight in front of her to attention, reeled at this information. She had actually been considered for the ATA? And Sergeant Horrocks had ruined her chances?

The wing commander was continuing.

'It seems obvious to me, and to your estimable officer here, that you were innocent of any involvement in her suicide, but that she had suffered a mental breakdown, exacerbated by an increasing intake of alcohol and pills that she managed to obtain by having a separate key made to the Medical Centre. This state of mind has been corroborated by the medical officer at her last posting and by a stocktaking of pills from the centre both there and here. I suspect the Coroner will come to the same conclusion.'

He ended triumphantly just as Lily's unreliable knees finally gave way and she grabbed for the corner of a chair.

He looked down at her as she stumbled and added with disdain, 'I think you had better leave now and regain some composure.'

Her CO nodded and said, more kindly, 'Yes, dismissed LACW Mullins, there will be no blemish on your record. You are now free to leave camp whenever you are off-duty.

We have just heard that Hitler has committed suicide so we are hopeful that this war will soon be at an end. Go and enjoy yourself.'

Lily closed the door behind her and tried to breathe. She practised putting one foot in front of the other as she made her way down the corridor and back to her hut. So much was going through her mind, firstly the relief that she was exonerated of any crime and secondly, that, even though it was now too late, she had been considered as a potential pilot. The thought sent a shiver down her spine. She could never forgive the sergeant for ruining that chance for her but never again would she be Silly Lily, the class clown, she would be someone who could have been a pilot. She almost cursed the end of the war but then with a pragmatic shrug, she opened the door to the hut.

She was greeted by a huge cheer and caps being thrown in the air and looked up to see a crowd of girls jumping up and down on their bunks.

At the front was Glad who was holding court regally.

'Y'see, people who know people who know about filing cabinets can do wonders.'

Lily moved forward slowly to hug her and then glimpsed the white, fluffy dressing gown of Marion who was pretending to read a magazine propped up on her white lace pillowcase. She went over to her and put her arms around her.

'Thank you, Marion, thank you.'

Marion shrugged her off.

'I most certainly was not going to be known as someone who was acquainted with a criminal,' she said huffily. Lily just caught a glimpse of the corner of her mouth tilting into a smile.

'So which pub are we going to?' Lily said to them all, clasping her hands together in delight. 'I believe we have a tyrant's death to celebrate.'

Chapter 54

It was a very different group who caught the train up to London in time for the VE celebrations. Lily had attended an early thanksgiving mass to be able to get one of the first trains and rushed to join Hilda, Marion and Glad, who were waiting excitedly to cycle to the railway station to be part of the crowds waiting on the platform. A slight relaxing of rules meant there were strands of hair escaping from caps, buttons were ever so slightly dull and there was not much sign of the strict deportment that had been imposed on them since they joined up. There was singing on the train and some servicemen even tried to lead Glad and Hilda in a waltz down the corridor. Spirits were high and when they piled off the train in London, Lily led the way to Trafalgar Square, laughing loudly.

'There's no need to be hysterical, Lily,' Marion said. 'There are still people being killed in the Far East.'

'I know, but it's been such a long haul to get to this,' Lily replied, determinedly linking arms with her.

Marion gave her haughty sniff and unhooked her arm, brushing off her uniform where Lily's arm had lain.

Lily shrugged and went over to Glad who immediately started to sing 'Roll Out the Barrel', swaying from side to side.

They got the bus to Trafalgar Square and shared a moment of pride when the bus conductor refused to take fares from anyone in uniform. It was as if they were the heroes of the hour and the whole country had come to London to share in the joy of VE Day. Everywhere there were people, sitting on walls, perched on pavements, or seated on steps. Looking round at the excited scene, Lily thought lovingly of her country. It had been saved from invasion, it was going to stay British and even the blue skies above her had lost their dark clouds after the thunderstorm that morning that had, for a fleeting moment, made the familiar pounding return in every Londoner's breast. She loved everyone and it seemed, everyone loved her.

By the time they got to the square, there was hardly a spare inch to be had. People were climbing on lamp-posts, others clambered on the lions, patting them as if these noble creatures had personally defended their country. The pubs were closed but there seemed to be an endless bottle that was passed around and, in every direction, groups of people were singing and dancing. Amidst all the dull uniforms that had lost their lustre over the years, there were office girls in bright prints and Hilda darted off to buy them all red, white and blue favours to wave as enthusiastically as everyone else. The morning papers had suggested that only the young would be resilient enough to stand the crowds and the wait for Churchill's speech to be relayed over loudspeakers at three o'clock but there were babes in arms, elderly couples beaming beatifically and dogs in Union Jack bows. Rosettes fluttered in the breeze and every static structure was strewn with colour. The whole scene was like a village fete, awash with red, white and blue, with sashes, hair ribbons and even flags tied around ankles and wrists. The crowd were behaving like close friends at a drunken party, and they all swore eternal love for each other. Some faces were dazed and gaunt but even they were carried along by the crowd. Many looked nervously up at the skies but they were reassuringly empty. The church bells rang out a glorious sound, after so many years of silence. Cars, using up valuable petrol coupons with gay abandon, tooted their horns as they crawled around the packed crowds, boats on the Thames could be heard hooting too. It was an orchestra of joyful sound suddenly overridden by the imperious call, 'We want the king.'

The little group of girls decided to make their way towards Parliament in the hope of catching a glimpse of Winston Churchill, but it was slow progress as they got roped into conga dances and were offered drinks and embraces. It was as the fourth serviceman grabbed Lily to kiss her very firmly on the mouth that she spotted Betty. Out of nursing uniform, she looked even more like the reflection that stared back at Lily from her bedroom mirror at home.

'Betty, Betty,' she yelled above the noise, pushing the serviceman away. He shrugged and moved on to the next pretty girl. Betty turned around with a quizzical look on her face then she saw Lily.

She was arm-in-arm with a small man in an RAF uniform. He was bespectacled and already had a receding hairline.

'Lily, I can't believe it's you! Fred, this is the girl I told you about. The one who . . .' she trailed off, unable to stop the grin spreading across her face.

The man looked disbelievingly from one to the other and stroked his chin.

'It's uncanny, I've never seen anything like it.'

He stood back as the two girls hugged. Lily looked sideways at him and felt a moment's astonishment as she examined this very ordinary man who had prompted so much rivalry between two women and so much enmity from Sergeant Horrocks.

'Betty, you vanished from the hospital. I couldn't track you down. I was trying to find out more about . . . Did you hear . . .' Lily trailed off.

'About Agatha Horrocks? Yes, I did. I would like to say I'm sorry but I can't.' Betty shook her head and then leaned in to whisper so her husband could not hear.

'That woman was like poison. Everything she touched went sour. So many people have died in this war, that was one death I couldn't mourn.'

Lily nodded and gave her a hug.

At that moment, two old Cockneys who had spent the morning in the pub, shouted 'That's 'im. That's 'is lovely bald head.'

The two girls strained their necks to glimpse Winston Churchill walking at the head of a procession of Members of Parliament back to the Commons after a service at St Margaret's. Betty cheered loudly but Lily just drank in the scene to make sure she would remember it in detail when she got back to Slade Lane. She got a thrill of excitement that she was witnessing this scene and would be able to tell it to her grandchildren – if she ever had any, she thought with a turn of her stomach.

'Oh Danny,' she beseeched the skies, 'will we ever make it?'

She turned back to the crowd behind her but Betty had disappeared in the throng.

The rest of the day was almost an anti-climax and a general listlessness fell over the city as the crowds melted away. Once the excitement abated, it was as if everyone needed to go home to lick their wounds, remembering that they were exhausted and emotionally drained.

Lily's little band of girls also turned for home, or at least the base they had come to think of as home for so long.

They were all subdued until Marion voiced what they were all thinking.

'So, that's it then, we all go back to our normal lives, do we?'

Normality was a distant memory but little by little, it had been seeping through their uniforms like drizzle. Lily realised all the little mental boxes she had kept closed-up throughout the past four years were slowly opening up. She had been allowing herself to think of home, Liners and living with her parents and she was not sure how she felt about it all.

'I'd forgotten how quiet my mam and dad's place is,' Hilda said. 'I've been wanting to go back for so long, but now it's really going to happen.'

They all nodded in agreement and quietly got on the train back to Upper Heyford, deep in their own thoughts.

The day job took over and became a blur of unnecessary paperwork, with endless demands that Lily should deliver this chitty and that chitty here and there. She walked miles up and down corridors, but the click had gone out of her heels. There was no urgency anymore and she felt exhausted and strangely flat. The shift patterns were the same but without the tense waits for crews and the threat of raids, the atmosphere was very subdued.

When the news about the atomic bombing of Hiroshima and Nagasaki came through, there was an almost guilty silence in the camp. It had been so easy to forget that this had been a world war and that terrifyingly huge numbers of people were still losing their lives. Lily could hardly admit to herself that she was torn between being grateful for the nuclear bomb and being completely horrified by its power and effect.

Once VJ Day was declared, the boredom increased and all the service people were desperate to get home and back to normal, but demob seemed to last forever, with married people given priority. There was more time off and the conversations in the pubs, NAAFI and mess were all about what people were going to do when they got home. The bubble they had all created of a separate world for themselves had burst.

At last, Lily got her demob papers and she packed her bag for the last time, patting her rough blanket into a neat pile on the top of her bunk. She could not believe she was crying but looked round to find Hilda doing the same. They hugged each other with the intensity of two sisters being parted forever. She took one last walk down between the beds, a flood of memories overwhelming her and turned to wave at Hilda who had tears streaming down her face.

The trip from the station was a quiet affair with wan smiles across the train carriage to her fellow passengers. Everyone was uncharacteristically subdued and the headlines on the newspaper of the man opposite her reminded Lily that she would be going back to a very different Manchester from the one she had left. Lily craned her neck to read the front page. The country was almost bankrupt, stocks and supplies had to be built up again. The columnists were starting to talk about how the returning men were already feeling threatened by the womenfolk who had been doing their jobs with skill and aptitude. Lily absentmindedly noticed the cows in fields that would never now be trampled over by German soldiers. Gazing out of the train window, she saw a reflection of herself and had a glimpse of the girl she had been four years earlier with that ridiculous red lipstick.

Chapter 55

'Lily, where's my school cap, you said you'd put it away.' Don's voice was muffled from under all the coats in the hallway.

Settling in at home was a strange process. It was familiar but it was Lily who was different. She found herself biting her lip on many occasions, especially at moments like this one when her brother tried to treat her as his personal slave or when her mother fussed over her. She reluctantly unearthed the cap from under the cushion next to her, resignedly holding it out. Her brother raced in, his tie to one side and one arm out of his blazer and snatched it from her. He glared at the clock.

'I'm so late, and it's your fault,' he grumbled at Lily. She pulled a face at him and reached out to ruffle his hair, which he hated.

'Stop it,' his new deep voice said. I'm a prefect now, you can't treat me like that.'

She went to get out of the chair to dive at him but he dodged out of the way.

'When you're big enough, you'll be too old,' he threw back over his shoulder as he grabbed a piece of toast off the table and flew out of the door.

Lily closed her eyes for a moment and counted to ten. She had looked forward to the end of the war and coming home so much but it was a strange transition. She was back at Liners and, initially, had been given more responsibility, but once the men started to come back, she had to move desks regularly, ending up in the corner of the room. She found herself being expected to make the tea again. The initial excitement had been replaced by a routine that she found nothing short of tedious. But today was different.

Lily had just enough time for a second cup of tea before leaving for the bus. She had taken a day off work to meet Alice, who was making a special trip to Manchester to see her. Her father had already gone up to bed and Ginny Mullins was in the other armchair, indulging in the peace and quiet of the gently ticking clock and the normality that for so long had seemed like a dream never to be repeated. She yawned slowly and stretched her arms above her head, then seeming to realise how unladylike that was, brought them down, saying, 'You'd better get off, Lily, you don't want to be late. I've left your coat by the back door.'

Lily forced herself to smile. Her mother still treated her like the nineteen-year-old who had left so many years before . . . a lifetime ago, really, but to her mother, she was still that same young girl. She slowly got up out of the chair, automatically filled up her mother's teacup and went to get her coat.

Lily scanned the Kardomah café for her friend and gave a whimper of joy as she spotted the solid frame of Alice sitting with her hands clasped around a cup of tea.

Alice jumped up and the tea went flying all over the floor, prompting a disdainful look from the waitress who was serving the next table. The two girls bumped heads as they tried to mop up the mess with their cotton hankies and then they both burst out laughing and reached out to each other.

'Alice, we made it!'

'We certainly did you northern ninny. Time to celebrate with another cuppa, I think.'

Alice took control as usual and signalled to the waitress who pursed her lips but nodded.

Lily collapsed into the red plastic bench seat feeling as if she had climbed a huge mountain. Then she leaned forward suddenly.

'Oh Alice, it's beautiful!'

She reached out to take hold of Alice's third finger on her left hand, which she had placed strategically on the table in front of her.

Alice sat up proudly.

'Oh Lily, he's gorgeous, and who'd have thought that awful bomb in Paddington would lead me into the arms of my lovely doctor. I am so happy. We're getting married in October in the village, you will be there, won't you?'

'You try keeping me away!' Lily exclaimed. 'I'm chief bridesmaid, aren't I?'

The next two hours were spent in detailed discussion of how to make coupons stretch to a wedding breakfast and new dresses. As they finally agreed they had addressed every possible issue, they sat back and ordered sandwiches and third cups of tea.

Alice looked closely at Lily.

'You look peaky. Are you OK?'

'Yes, fine, just a bit flat, that's all. It's been such a rollercoaster over the past few years and life just seems, well, a bit dull. I'm back at Liners and home and it's as if I never left.'

'Do you know, Alice,' she went on, 'the war was the best thing that ever happened to me. I've never felt so alive. I know it's awful to say when so many people died and were badly injured, but it was so exciting.'

Alice knew what she meant. Her wedding plans were keeping her busy but the everyday trials of helping out on a hill farm when supplies were so short were a sharp reminder that the effects of war were not going fade quickly and dealing with them was not going to be glamorous.

'Do you remember we said we would change the world at the end of the war?' Alice said suddenly. 'We had such dreams.'

'I know, but now I'm home, it seems so easy to just slot back in where I left off and to be honest, they need my wage from Liners. It's quite tough at the moment, as you know all too well.

Alice thought about the sparse supplies of feed for the animals and the long queues at the shops in Chorley. Glorious post-war Britain was feeling a little ragged around the edges.

'You can't give in that easily,' she said, sitting up in her chair. 'You were an excellent wireless operator – eventually,' she added, 'and look what you could have achieved – being an ATA pilot would've been one in the eye for Marion, wouldn't it?'

Lily had told Alice about Sergeant Horrocks blocking her application to the ATA but apart from sharing it with her best friend, Lily had decided it was just going to be a secret she would hug to herself. To know she could have been a pilot was enough.

'No point thinking about that,' she said, 'anyway Mum and Dad would laugh if I told them I was nearly a pilot. To them, I'm just their Lily. I don't think I'll ever be anything else in their eyes.'

'I have noticed some changes in the country – mostly for the good,' Alice was saying. 'We've all got so much more confidence and I, for one, won't be pushed back into the kitchen any more. I'm taking over more and more of the paperwork on the farm because Dad's eyesight isn't so good now and do you know what, Lily, even my brothers are beginning to treat me with more respect. Come on, Lily, pick yourself up and find that 'nearly ATA pilot' spirit. It's in there somewhere.'

Lily's shoulders drooped, unable to summon up any enthusiasm for the brave new world everyone was talking about.

'What about Danny?' Alice asked abruptly.

'Oh, an odd letter, nothing too deep, just about his impending demob. He's coming back early because of his back injury. They want to give him more treatment. I think he's given up on me.'

Chapter 56

Lily peered through the curtains onto the Pennines. The blackouts had all been triumphantly removed and lay unloved in a corner of Alice's bedroom. The room was a faded blue with floral curtains, a wicker chair and a dressing table with a picture in a silver frame of Alice as a little girl, sporting muddy knees, wellington boots and holding a small lamb. A borrowed mattress had been placed under the window for her bridesmaid to sleep on. The hills looked spectacular on this autumn morning with burnished colours and a faint hint of mist over the barn in the yard. Lily could hear the bleating of the sheep in the field behind and it felt deliciously rural. A shiver of excitement went through her and she looked round at the sleeping figure of Alice, with her rollers pressed against her cheek. Lily grinned and leaned over to shake her.

'Come on, Mrs Simpkins . . . up you get. You can't be late for your own wedding.'

Alice stirred and opened one eye.

'What's the weather like?'

'Glorious, but the day will be over and Arthur will have given up and gone home if you don't get up and get dressed.'

Hair carefully curled, dress ironed, a small autumnal posy placed in Alice's shaking hands and two hours later, the girls were ready.

Lily walked behind Alice in her dusky pink dress, made by Mrs Colville's sewing circle in the village, with their pooled coupons. The church was packed and on the end of each pew was a tiny bunch of flowers from the hedgerows that Alice and her mother had spent the previous day collecting. They had struggled to find colours but the berries of blackthorn and hawthorn provided a lovely contrast to the autumnal coloured leaves. The organ started up, being pounded by Mr Macdonald, who liked to claim his playing could be heard across the Pennines. The vicar stood at the end of the church, next to the baptismal font where Alice had been christened. He beamed with pride as if she was his own daughter. Next to him was Arthur, looking backwards to spot his bride. He suddenly wobbled and Allan, his brother and best man, reached his hand out to steady him. Arthur took a huge breath. The whole village had turned out, keen to see this young woman, who had rarely been spotted without wellies, in a bridal gown. They packed the back of the church, craning their necks to see the bridal party process down to the front. Lily glanced down at Alice's feet. She was determinedly taking small steps so that her feet did not race her down the aisle.

Grinning Lily looked along the pew to the side and saw a smiling Amy, in a pretty, floral dress next to a rounded man with a kindly expression and big red cheeks. Marion, resplendent in a fox fur, stood erect and was unsuccessfully trying to look bored. Viv stood next to Marion with a rosy-faced little girl clinging onto her mother's dress – but there was no Doug.

They reached the front and Lily glanced at the bridegroom. He was tall and quite distinguished-looking. No wonder Alice was in love with him, Lily thought. He looked like a man who could reduce capable Alice to a quivering jelly. She was delighted to see Arthur had eyes for only one person. He was staring at Alice with so much pride and love, Lily felt tears stinging her eyelids.

Would that someone would look at me like that, she thought.

The ceremony passed beautifully and the vicar, who had known Alice since birth, finished the official part with reminiscences of how Alice's loud voice dominated the school choir and how her experience with livestock had helped her to keep her brothers in order. Lily thought Alice was going to burst out of her dress with pride when Mr. Colville made his speech at the village hall afterwards, nervously fingering his collar and unfamiliar tie. His voice was shaking with emotion as he talked of handing over his only daughter to Arthur and gave his new son-in-law such a sharp warning look that the wedding party all started to laugh. Lily had to delve into her pouch bag to pass her neatly ironed handkerchief to Alice's mum and she smiled, watching the three brothers who were keeping an eagle eye on the food that was passing up and down the table. Lily sat back in satisfaction, feeling part of this lovely Lancashire family and hoping that her wedding, if she were ever to have one, would be as relaxed and welcoming as this one.

As the Babycham was passed around, Amy sidled up to Lily. She touched her gently on the arm and Lily turned to face her, unable to keep the sheer delight out of her face.

'Amy, you look wonderful,' she waved her hand in a circular motion to take in the whole vision that was in front of her. Amy's straight hair was cut into a bob, topped by a pretty pink hat with a net front. Her matching suit was pale pink and she was clutching a black patent handbag. She looked calm and content.

'How are you?' Lily's eyes scanned her face and then relaxed as she found nothing to worry about.

'I'm fine. Really I am.' Amy glanced over at the man she had clung onto in the church.

'Who is he?' Lily motioned over towards the man.

'His name is William. He's . . . lovely.' She stretched out her ring finger to show Lily. 'I met him after . . . my illness. He was the butcher and started saving the best cuts for me. We eat lots of meat,' she finished with pride.

'And are you . . . well? Did you tell him—' Lily could not finish.

'Enough, but not all,' Amy confided.

'That's great, Amy, I'm so pleased for you.'

'So Mullins, you made it through unscathed.' A familiar, imperious voice interrupted.

'Marion, how are you?' Lily was not sure whether to lean forward and hug this tall figure, looking like the chairwoman of the WVS but Marion kept her arms tightly folded.

'I'm very well and I can see that you are too. Although I have to say, you look a bit pale, you really shouldn't wear such bright lipstick. It makes you look very brash.'

She swung round to catch hold of the vicar, accusing him in a loud voice of obviously being acquainted with her uncle, the Bishop. Lily and Amy started to giggle as Alice, wearing a very smart navy blue going away hat came down the stairs. Her mother was following behind her, fussing and fretting while her father stood shyly at the bottom, waiting to lead her to her husband who was peering round the front door, looking at his watch.

The normally muddy Land Rover had been spruced up and polished to take the couple to the train for Scarborough, but before it roared into life, Alice threw her bouquet over her shoulder. Marion, Amy and Lily all pretended not to try to catch it, but at the last moment, Marion edged the other girls out of the way and triumphantly grasped at the small bouquet, holding it above her head. Alice raised her eyebrows at Lily and then yelled a cheerful goodbye to the whole group before the car sped off, leaving a cloud of dust in the vehicle's wake.

'God help him, whoever he may be,' Viv whispered from behind Lily.

Lily swirled round.

'Viv, I haven't had a chance to talk to you. Are you OK? Your daughter is beautiful.'

'Yes, she is, isn't she?' replied the proud mum, looking over to where her little girl was playing on the stone step with the little pot figures off the top of the cake. 'Her name is Abigail.'

'Doug . . . ?' Lily faltered.

'Killed two years ago in the Atlantic.'

Lily took a sharp intake of breath but Viv seemed unperturbed.

'I was a war bride. I think you, of all people, know I should never have married him.'

She looked sharply at Lily and Lily blushed.

'I'm sorry, Viv. I should have warned you.'

'No, I walked into it and anyway, I wouldn't have had Abigail if I hadn't met him, and she's all that matters now. My parents have taken us back in and, of course, I get a war widow's pension, so we manage.'

As she walked away to wipe Abigail's sticky hands, Lily thought about how the war had changed lives.

Maybe it was time to change her own.

Chapter 57

'Lily, come on you'll be late.'

Lily adjusted her hat in the mirror. She could picture her mum standing at the bottom of the stairs and her dad hovering in the background. It had taken every bit of self-discipline not to push them away when they fussed around her but most of the time, it was a waste of effort and she had a feeling that was one war she would never win.

Lily automatically straightened the white lace cloth on her dressing table, pausing for a moment with her hand on the application form for a traineeship at Ringway Airport with the air traffic control department. She proudly rearranged it neatly for the umpteenth time and then stood up straight with a satisfied smile.

'Coming.' She raced down the stairs and put a finger on her mum's lips as she was about to make her usual comment about broken ankles.

'I'm ready. I'll get the two o'clock. It'll get me in at half past, which will be fine.'

'I thought you were meeting him at half past?' her dad said from round the banister.

'Dad, it won't kill him to wait another five minutes for me.'

The telegram had arrived the day before. She could not believe that her future rested on those few words. She had dissected them, read them in different voices, touched them with her finger and wet them with tears.

> Demobbed STOP arriving Manchester tomorrow STOP meet me at the Midland at two thirty if you want to STOP love always Danny

She determinedly did not turn around as she walked down the road but she knew her parents had raced into the front room to peer from behind the curtains. Her stomach turned over. She hoped she was not about to disappoint them.

Danny hesitated when the waiter at the Midland Hotel came to take his order. He desperately needed a beer but worried how that would look. Also, he needed his wits about him.

'Tea, I think, but I'll wait thank you. I'm expecting someone.'

He felt awkward and strange in civvies and the rough tweed chafed his thighs. His back was still sore from the pummelling the physiotherapist had subjected him to that morning.

He had never been more nervous in his life.

Then he saw her.

She looked as out of place as he felt in the faded grandeur of the lobby and he suddenly panicked that he should have arranged to meet her somewhere less forbidding. He watched her touch her velvet collar and then reach up to straighten her hair. Danny smiled, realising she was as nervous as he was.

He stood up and walked towards her. He knew he was in the right place.

'Lily,' Danny breathed deeply, his whole being immersed in that one word.

She seemed to take a moment to register him and then she said softly and without question, 'I'm here.'

At that moment, nothing had ever seemed so right and Danny took Lily in his arms and gently held her. The waiter, who had come to see if they needed anything, shuffled backwards silently.

The scene was exactly as they had both imagined, but as they reluctantly drew apart, each of them faltered. Lily pulled back to look at Danny properly, as if seeing him for the first time. He was so familiar, but there were lines at the side of his eyes and he looked thin and a bit older.

Danny's eyes studied her.

'We've come a long way, Lily,' he said. 'I wasn't sure if you'd be here.'

'I'm here,' she repeated, 'but I'm not the same girl I was. I've seen . . . done things—'

She looked so lovely but so grown-up. This was not the gawky girl he had teased; she was now a mature and capable woman.

'I know,' his brow furrowed as glimpses of a dark room in Sicily and a back street in Rome came back to him.

'What do you say we start again?'

'Yes,' Lily looked relieved. His arms felt like home, but it was not going to be simple.

The waiter hovered in the background.

'Would sir and madam like a table for afternoon tea?'

'Yes,' Danny told him, and, smiling, he reached down and slowly laced Lily's hand in his.

'Let's start with sharing an afternoon tea table and we can take it from there.'

Acknowledgements

I have taken so many long-suffering people on this journey with me and there are many who have listened with forbearance to my insecurities, doubts and frustrations but there are some I would like to single out.

Former World War 2 WAAF Vera Morgan read *'Lily*'s *War'* for me and finally made me believe I had successfully made the transition from journalistic fact to fiction and I must also remember Delma Matkin, wireless operator, for her wonderful story of the bicycle race and water fight. Thanks too to Flt Lt Stuart Skilling and Hazel Crozier, who showed me round Cranwell and de-mystified the RAF for me, Lynn Hamill of the WAAF Association, Andrew Panton and Louise Bush of the Lincolnshire Aviation Heritage Centre, East Kirkby and Robert Fleming of the National Army Museum as well as Adam Sutch of the RAF Museum.

The first people to give me the confidence to tackle a novel were the inspiring Owen Sheers and Sarah Hall, tutors on an Arvon Foundation course, which is where it all began as a gift for my 60th birthday from my lovely family. I also had encouragement from the Wirksworth Writers' group, fellow-novelists Tricia Durdey, Alex Davis, Sian Towers, Moira Knowles, Stef Hill and Kate Seymour and my first readers, Sarah Price, Sue Jones, Pam McInally and Kate Roberts.

Kate Barker is my wonderful agent who led me to the equally wonderful Claire Johnson-Creek at Zaffre. They have both helped me enormously. I look forward to continuing to work with them and I can't tell you how proud I am to be part of Zaffre's Memory Lane list.

I must, finally, thank my family, or The Unit as our WhatsApp group is called, especially my husband, Kevin, our two daughters, Sarah (a fellow journalist and first port of call for all angst-ridden moments) and Jayne (praise from her made me believe I had actually cracked it) as well as my sister, Hilary. You never failed to believe that I could actually write this novel and have encouraged and helped me every step of the way. I couldn't have done it without you all.

Welcome to the world of *Shirley Mann*!

Keep reading for more from Shirley Mann, to discover a recipe that features in this novel and to find out more about what Shirley is doing next . . .

We'd also like to introduce you to Memory Lane, our special community for the very best of saga writing from authors you know and love, and new ones we simply can't wait for you to meet. Read on and join our club!

www.MemoryLane.club

MEMORY LANE

Hello Reader,

I'm so thrilled to meet you! I do hope you enjoy my first novel *Lily's War,* a story loosely based on my parents' wartime romance.

'Every journalist has a novel in them' they say, but it took me until I was in my 60s to prise mine out of me. It then took a further six years of research, self-doubt and frustration at the mammoth task I had taken on to finally clip together a complete manuscript.

My mother was a WAAF in Bomber Command and my father was a soldier in the 8th Army but as a 1950s' baby, the war was something that the previous generation had been through; we were too busy inventing the 'teenager' to care very much about what the 'oldies' had actually done for us. It was only as my mother got older and those dramatic years kept coming back into the conversation that I started to take notes. My father had also given me snapshots of such a dramatic time as an 8th Army soldier that I finally decided I would see if I could recreate the ordinary, everyday life in extraordinary times as a novel about them both. I wanted to rediscover my parents as young people, knowing that their romance was a special story that had the same ups and downs of any modern couple with the added stress of being hundreds of miles apart – oh, and with a world war going on.

Of course, by then I had left it all too late to ask them enough questions so I decided to use their story as the inspiration for a novel rather than make it a biographical tale. I travelled the country to interview former WAAFs in their 90s who were so kind to me and surprisingly pleased to share their own experiences with me to fictionalise. I will never forget sharing a day with some of those wonderful women striding into the WAAF Association conference with their heads held high and shoulders back. The war years had given them chances that they were not expecting. They all talked of being liberated from their mothers' sides and being thrust into a world where they could really make a difference and it shaped the rest of their lives and ultimately, ours too. For many of them, as with my mum, the war was an exciting adventure and they lapped it up.

My next book will be '*Bobby's War*', a story of an ATA pilot, one of the women who delivered more than 100 different types of planes all over the country and as part of my research, I was delighted to be able to talk to female pilot, Mary Ellis, just before she died at 101 in 2018. She was so inspiring and even to a woman of my generation, a beacon of achievement few of us could ever hope to emulate.

I hope you enjoy *Lily's War.* I want to write 'curl up and enjoy' books but I also want readers to actually feel what it was like to live through the war years. I have been incredibly privileged to have met the women who laid the foundations for what my generation was allowed to achieve and if I can take their stories to an appreciative audience then I will be doing justice to their legacy and maybe that of my own mother and father too.

Best wishes,

Shirley

MEMORY LANE

Wartime recipe

If you want to make John Mullins's favourite cookies, then this is the recipe for you. The government knew that carrots were plentiful so tried everything to encourage people to eat them, even going so far as to try to persuade children to eat carrots on sticks, telling them they were just as good as ice creams. They also invented 'Dr Carrot', who would make you feel better, and of course the wonderful orange vegetable was promoted as a food that would help you to see in the dark – a vital skill during the black outs that was already helping pilots successfully navigate to their targets. At least that's what the Ministry of Food said – trying to disguise the fact that actually the new technology of radar was of more use to pilots than any carrot!

Carrots were also useful as a sweetener because each person was only allowed 8 oz or 225g of sugar a week so, luckily for Lily's dad, Ginny would have been able to re-fill that biscuit tin with a sweet treat on a regular basis.

Carrot Cookies (makes 12 small or 6 larger)

- 2 tablespoons of sugar
- 1 tablespoon margarine

MEMORY LANE

- 1 teaspoon of vanilla essence
- 6 tablespoons of self-raising flour (if you're using plain flour add 1/2 teaspoon of baking powder)
- 4 tablespoons of grated raw carrot
- 1 tablespoon of water

Method

1. Cream the fat and the sugar together and add the vanilla essence
2. Mix in the grated carrot
3. Fold in the flour – add a bit of water as it gets dry
4. Drop spoonfuls onto a greased tray and press down a little
5. Pre-heat oven to 200 °C
6. Sprinkle tops of cookies with extra sugar if you have it
7. Place in oven for 10–15 minutes

I hope you enjoy them! And do share your baking with us on our Memory Lane Facebook page MemoryLaneClub.

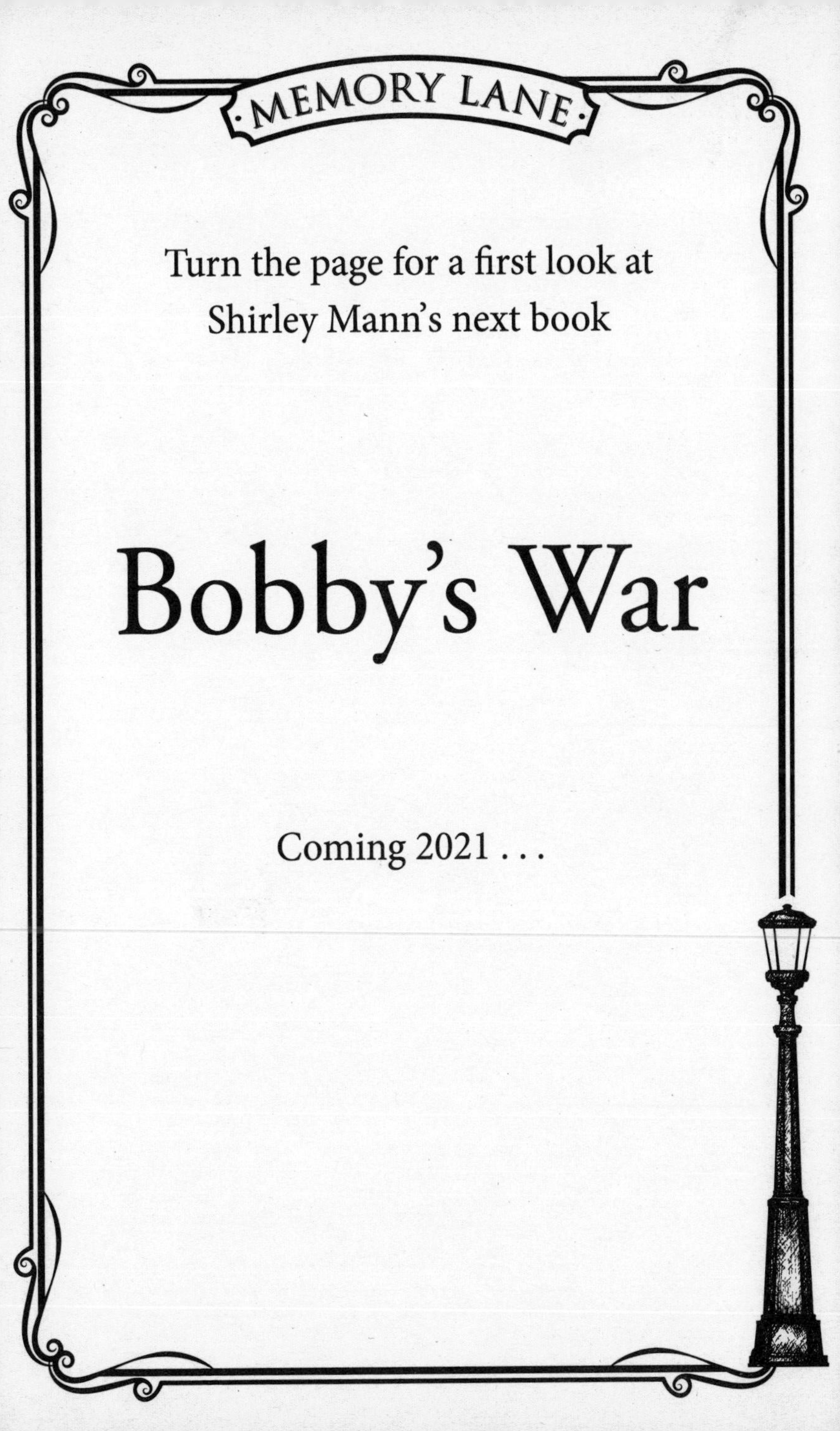

Turn the page for a first look at
Shirley Mann's next book

Bobby's War

Coming 2021 . . .

Prologue

1942

The cow's huge, black eyes stared impassively from its position at the front propeller of the Tiger Moth aircraft. Roberta, Bobby for short, pulled her tongue out at it, but it carried on chewing its mouth. The plane was being rocked by the skittish movements of the twenty or so Friesian cows that had raced across the field to examine this enormous bird that had seemingly fallen out of the sky.

'Hah, fallen, my foot,' Bobby told her sceptical audience, 'it was skilfully landed despite cross winds and the fact that this plane's nose is high on landing.'

She pushed her thighs together and winced. She needed to reach the hedge – and quickly – but she scanned the herd and they showed no sign of moving.

'Shoo,' she yelled at the crowd around her, but they did not react. A farmer's daughter, she had no fear of cows, but she gave them enormous respect. She breathed in sharply and tensed her stomach. She should never have had that last cup of tea.

Bobby glanced at her watch. Time was marching on and she was only in Lancashire. She had to get to Oxford before nightfall.

She waved her arms frantically at the crowd of four-legged admirers and then froze mid-wave as a human face appeared in the middle of the herd. A brown-haired, freckled man in RAF uniform was gently pushing the cows out of the way. Once other uniforms appeared, the cows backed off, sensing defeat. The coast was finally clear and Roberta was able to unstrap herself to jump down to the ground.

'Blimey, it's a girl!' the freckled young man exclaimed. 'You're surely not on your own, darlin'?'

Roberta gave a very curt nod and said, 'Excuse me one moment,' and walked with great haste towards the far side of the hedge. She crouched down and heard guffaws of laughter from the other side of the field.

Roberta Hollis never blushed, but there was a rosy tinge to her cheeks when she emerged from the hedge, rearranging her uniform.

'Now gentlemen, I thank you for your assistance, but could I ask you to move out of the way while I take off.'

'Not so fast,' a blond-haired lad said, standing with his arms folded in front of the wing. 'We abandoned perfectly good pints in the King's Arms and came to check you were ok. We want an explanation.'

'Have you never seen a female pilot before?' Bobby looked in exasperation at her watch. She did not have time for this.

'It's the ATA,' a Scottish voice said from the back of the group.

'What's that when it's at home?' the freckled one demanded.

'Air Transport Auxiliary – the 'glamour girls'. They deliver planes,' the Scot patiently explained.

'Interesting as this aviation history lesson is,' Roberta butted in, 'I've got a delivery to make and I need to get to Oxford by nightfall.

She looked up at the fading sun and pushed past the sentry posts to her plane.

'Does that mean . . . you . . . fly . . . these things on your own?'

'Yes, now you have to let me leave. As you're here, you can get me started. You can wing walk me over this rough ground.'

'Good job we've been specially trained in this war by the RAF or we'd never have known how to do that,' one tall man muttered as he moved to hold the wing tip, ready to walk it forward to keep it steady.

'And you,' Bobby added, pointing to another one with dark hair, 'you can be my Starter. Watch for my thumbs up.'

Bobby mounted the wing and climbed into the aircraft, hurriedly buckled the four straps around her and started the automatic procedure and checks. 'Contact' she shouted to the dark RAF man at the front. He turned the prop several times and then stepped away, shaking his head. She was too furious with herself to even notice the stroking of chins and amazed expressions she was leaving behind as she taxied down the field, scattering the cows once again.

Tutting to herself, she swore never to drink more than one cup of anything again before she set off. That was another lesson she had learned.

On the ground, the crowd of men stood with their mouths agape, watching the wings soar into the air, the tail kept impressively steady and the small plane with a woman at the controls disappearing into the 1942 May sunshine.

Chapter 1

It was almost dark when Bobby reached Bicester airfield near Oxford. She knew the route, but had only just made it in daylight. She walked from the airfield to the WAAF quarters, her heavy parachute on her shoulder. A tall girl with deep auburn hair, she cut a striking figure as she strode across the airfield but, at the age of twenty-seven, Roberta Hollis was not concerned about the looks she got or the nudges that followed her in her distinctive blue uniform. Her complete concentration was on the job in hand.

Roberta did not have time to think about the strange path that had led her to the Air Transport Auxiliary – the distant father, the ethereal mother or the cold atmosphere of the brick farmhouse in Norfolk. There were so many problems at home she had learned to ignore over the years, knowing that one day she would have to deal with her fractured family, but today was not the day. She had a tight schedule to tackle and, once again, she needed to ignore the haunted thoughts that engulfed her every time she had a spare minute. Fortunately, the relentless timetables left her with few enough of those, and that suited Roberta Hollis just fine.

'Flying Officer Hollis, signing in,' she told the WAAF on the front desk.

'No beds, I'm afraid. You'll have to make do with a mattress on the floor,' the WAAF said, and pointed her in the direction of a wooden hut to the right of the office.

Bobby sighed. She had been up since six a.m. and had delivered four planes around the country. All she wanted was a quick supper and a warm bed.

An hour later, after a very lumpy cauliflower cheese in the NAAFI, she had her wish.

'You can use mine,' said a sleepy WAAF, climbing out of her bunk. 'I'm on duty tonight.'

Bobby delightedly pushed the three 'biscuit' mattresses together and smoothed back the rough blanket to climb in. She was so tired she could have slept on a tailfin, and within ten minutes she was asleep, unaware of the constant stream of WAAFs who came in and out of the hut, either going to or returning from a shift. They ignored the lump in the bed until one of them noticed the dark blue uniform with its distinctive gold braid hanging up next to the bunk.

'She's one of those ATA pilots.' She nudged her friend who turned around to look.

'Personally, I don't care if she's the Queen of Sheba, I'm so tired. I've been on duty for more than ten hours and I didn't even get a break.'

Another girl handed them both cups of cocoa that had been warming on the black stove in the middle of the room for latecomers, according to custom.

They sipped gratefully.

'That's better,' one of them said. 'So that's one of the 'glamour girls' is it?' She put her head on one side assessing the curled up, snoring figure in the bed. 'She doesn't look very glam.'

'I heard they get invited to all the parties and are treated like goddesses,' another chipped in. 'It must be exciting, though, being up there in the sky.'

'Bloody dangerous if you ask me. No radar, no radio and no gun to shoot back,' her friend commented, shaking her head in awe.

They finished their cocoa, got their washbags out of their gas mask holders and went to the ablutions block to get ready for bed. They could not wait to tell the crowd of girls in the washrooms that they had a real-life ATA girl in their hut, which led to a constant stream of WAAFs peering round the door to examine the snoring figure of Bobby, tucked up in bed, and pointing in amazement at her uniform hung up behind her bed.

Oblivious to all the attention, Bobby slept like a log, waking only when the morning tannoy went off. She stretched luxuriously like her family's farm cat, Perry, but her mind immediately switched into gear and she bounded out of bed, ready for another day of heaven knows what.

She was into her second year as an ATA pilot and it had been a whirlwind of training, classroom lessons, trial flights and nights spent with a torch under the blanket with her instruction manuals. Each level left her breathless and exhilarated, and had endorsed her belief that flying was the only thing she wanted to do. She had raced through her training at White Waltham, gaining her class one and class two qualifications. She knew she was good, but she also knew that it would only take one unexpected storm, a barrage balloon or a mistake to add her name to the list of names of dead ATA pilots that was posted far too regularly.

She also knew that to fail would not only put her life in jeopardy, but also the reputation of women pilots, which was already fragile to say the least.

Bobby brushed her teeth furiously, using the dregs of a tin of baking powder. There was a tiny cup of water per girl and she measured out three drips into her mouth to rinse with. Nobody dawdled in the freezing cold ablutions block, so she dressed quickly, unearthed her bowl, knife, fork and spoon and metal mug from her bag and ran over to the NAAFI to grab some porridge, hesitating over the tea urn to work out her chances of finding a toilet en route. She made do with half a mug, without milk or sugar, and sat down to look at her notes, trying to second-guess her aircraft for the day. She hardly noticed the stares of the long tables of men and women in the room, concentrating on getting the piping hot porridge down her as quickly as possible. She peered out at the airfield. Bicester was an Operations Training Unit and although it was under Bomber Command, no fighters flew from there. She had heard rumours of collapsing field drains that would sometimes cause pitted holes, and she decided she would like to walk the runway, scanning the surface before she took a plane off the ground from there.

Bobby glanced at her watch. She had to hurry and swished her porridge-smeared bowl and cutlery in the soapy water by the door, like the WAAFs around her did, before racing back to the locker room to pick up her overnight bag, her parachute and the precious bar of chocolate that kept her going on long flights. She then raced across towards the Operations Room to receive her 'chitties' – the list of deliveries for the day – clutching her blue Ferry Pilots Notes, the 'Bible' of every ATA pilot, with its comprehensive instructions on how to fly a dazzling array of planes. Bobby mentally ran through the list of possible aircraft she might face that day. She had flown nineteen different types so far. She looked up at the sky, where the clouds were moving fast. ATA pilots were not supposed to fly above the clouds, which always caused problems in a country like Britain where the weather was so variable. She hoped she would not be assigned to a Walrus. They were so lumbering and a pain in strong wind with a mind of their own.

Outside the office, on the side of the runway, were a line of Spitfires and Mosquitoes, used for training. The ground crews, or Erks as they were known, were all working fast to get them ready for flight.

She recognised a blonde girl holding two small blocks of wood on a piece of string around her neck coming out towards her. The girl raised her hand in greeting.

'Bobby, I didn't know you were here.'

'Daphne! You been here all night?'

'Yes, arrived by transport late last night. Had to sleep on mattresses on the floor. I can tell you, my neck really hurts. Those 'biscuits' parted company at three this morning and left my backside on the floor.'

Daphne was a petite girl from Lancashire whose feet sometimes failed to reach the pedals. She carried around small blocks of wood with her to attach to the pedals so she could reach them, but was an excellent pilot.

'Get any sleep?' she asked Bobby.

'Yes, some kind WAAF left me her bed and it was still warm, so I was nice and toasty.'

'Lucky you,' replied Daphne. 'I was frozen. But I suppose I was lucky to get a mattress, and staying at the Waafery does mean we save the quid for overnight accommodation, which always helps, doesn't it? Are you back at Hamble tonight?'

'Well, who knows. I suppose it'll depend on what those darned clouds decide to do,' Bobby replied, looking up dubiously.

Hamble was the headquarters where many of the Air Transport Auxiliary girls were based. It had a good camaraderie on the days when there was a group of them grounded by bad weather, known as a 'wash-out' days, but more often than not, the pilots got held up somewhere round the country, staying in hostels, Waafery huts, inns and sometimes in train stations. It was not always a comfortable life and their timetables were relentless, so they frequently felt like ships that passed in the night.

'You Roberta Hollis? Here are your chitties,' an Operations Manager called through the open door. 'You'd better get going. You have four today.'

The ATA pilots took turns to be Operations Managers, which was a nightmare job involving ridiculous logistics getting pilots and planes where they were supposed to be, and although she did not recognise the tall, dark girl behind the desk, Bobby gave her a sympathetic smile as she took the top sheet from the huge pile of chits the girl was holding.

MEMORY LANE

Bobby scanned her list – a Swordfish to White Waltham, a Barracuda to Kemble and an Albacore to Woolsington, then a Hurricane back to Hamble. But no Spitfire.

'Damn,' she muttered. She was yet to fly a Spit, but she had gone through the instructions so many times in her head, she believed she could have flown one blindfold. She was just longing for the chance to pilot one. It was the aircraft all ATA pilots loved above all others.

'Well, the plan is to get back to base tonight and my own bed,' she called over her shoulder to Daphne as they struggled out onto the airfield, with their parachutes and tiny overnight bags. 'But we'll see how that works out. Remember what they told us in training – England doesn't have a climate, it has . . .'

'WEATHER!' they both shouted together, laughing.

'See you in the restroom if we get back in time, then,' Daphne said, but Bobby was already checking through her notes to see how the Swordfish behaved in high winds.

Bobby stared up at the sky, threatening the clouds with fury if they got too thick or started to run too fast. She did not want to get stuck again tonight and pleaded with them to behave and then ran over to the Met Office to check the forecast.

'I haven't been back to base for three nights,' she told the good-looking Met officer behind the desk. He had nice eyes, she thought. 'Please tell me it's going to be fine in Newcastle this afternoon.'

He glanced down at his charts, shifted a few papers and then his face cleared.

'Yep, you should be ok. Just don't go anywhere near the west coast.'

Bobby looked scornfully at him. He was not that good-looking, she decided. 'I do know my east from west, you know.'

She strode quickly along the edge of the runway, narrowing her eyes to check the surface and then, satisfied that no new holes had appeared, went over to the Swordfish and walked round it, appraising it. An engineer was making final checks.

'Ah, got a girl, have we? Well, I've just fixed this aircraft, don't you go breaking it.'

'You're only saying that because I'm a girl!'

He paused for a moment before he walked clear of the wings. 'Actually, do you know what? I'm not. It's usually the men who get them damaged in the first place.'

Bobby laughed and mounted the aircraft, settling herself into the pilot's seat. She took her helmet off, shook out her hair and prepared to concentrate fully.

She got her maps out, her compass, protractor, ruler and pencil. She had ten minutes to prepare, but she had done the route from Bicester to White Waltham before, and the one from there to Kemble, so it was just the third one up to RAF Woolsington on the north east coast that she was unfamiliar with. She drew straight black lines to give her the most direct routes she would need to follow with the four different aircraft, noting the landmarks en route, then she checked the handling notes. It was the fourth Swordfish she had flown that week, so she was quite familiar with its foibles and she settled into the seat happily and put her helmet back on.

Bobby carried out her pre-flight checks going through the HTTMPFGG – hydraulics, trim, tension, mixture, pitch, petrol, flaps, gills, gauges, otherwise remembered as 'Hot Tempered MP Fancies Girls' and gently eased the throttle to start taxiing. Her shoulders relaxed. It was just her and the aircraft and that was exactly how she liked it.

* * *

Mathilda Hollis shaded her eyes against the sun as she followed the path of a plane that was flying above Salhouse Farm on the outskirts of Norwich. It vaguely occurred to her that it could be her daughter at the controls, but she shrugged her shoulders and carried on wandering with her scissors amongst the early summer roses. She kept looking fearfully back at the red-bricked farmhouse she supposed was her home, nervous as always that she was doing something wrong.

There was little sign of the dimple-cheeked, dark-haired beauty who had pierced the sang-froid of the reserved Andrew Hollis just before the Great War broke out. This was a deflated woman whose clothes hung off her once nicely-rounded figure. In the privacy of the warm farmhouse kitchen, the cook, Mrs Hill, explained to any new staff that Mrs Hollis was 'not well', a term the family used to explain Mathilda Hollis's distant stare, but everyone in the village knew that she had been like this since she had struggled to give birth to twins in 1915.

One, the longed-for son, managed to take only enough breaths to be christened with the name John before he died in his mother's arms, while the other, a lusty girl, had gone on to thrive, making enough noise for two. Mathilda's elder sister, Agnes, had always thought that Roberta's loud and relentless screams were simply to remind the family she was still there.

Dressed as always in a pale grey, threadbare dress, with a buttoned-up collar, Agnes stood by the latticed drawing room window, watching the diminutive figure of her younger sister in the garden. She felt the usual mix of gloom and concern, and frowned at the sight of her sister meandering amongst the roses, clipping an odd one randomly. Agnes bit her lip, hoping her fragile sibling would remember not to cut herself.

It was a bright June day and, seeing a couple of men walking slowly past the stone gate at the end of the drive, Agnes thought back to a similar day in 1919 when the village men came home from the Great War. So much had changed she thought, and yet not nearly enough.